Margaret Dickson

Maddy's Song

Houghton Mifflin Company   BOSTON   1985

Library of Congress Cataloging in Publication Data

Dickson, Margaret.
Maddy's song.

I. Title.
PS3554.I329M3   1985   813'.54   84-10920
ISBN 0-395-36077-3

Printed in the United States of America

S   10   9   8   7   6   5   4   3   2   1

Maddy's Song

BOOKS BY

MARGARET DICKSON

Octavia's Hill
Maddy's Song

1989

For Howard Morhaim,
Maddy's champion from the first

ACKNOWLEDGMENTS

With grateful thanks to my husband, Peter Dickson,
who introduced me to Bach and Landowska,
and to my editor, Gerard Van der Leun

They shall build houses and inhabit them;
    they shall plant vineyards and eat
        their fruit.
They shall not build and another
        inhabit;
    they shall not plant and another
        eat;
for like the days of a tree shall the days of
        my people be,
    and my chosen shall long enjoy
        the work of their hands.
They shall not labor in vain,
    or bear children for calamity;
for they shall be the offspring of the
        blessed of the Lord,
    and their children with them.

                — ISAIAH 65:21–23

Maddy's Song

CHAPTER ONE

FROM A CORNER Maddy Dow watched her father. She was his oldest daughter, a small dark girl of sixteen, as quiet as the walls she stood by. Her black eyes were carefully blank as she watched; she seemed not to look at him but to wait.

He was a short powerful man. His arms were long, so that his hands swung not far from his knees; those arms could reach anywhere. His skin was darkly tanned — he had only to walk through the sun to take on color, summer or winter — and dark hair grew on his arms and neck like fur. His hair was short on the top of his head and the skin around his ears and neck gleamed between razor-shaved hairs. His face was as thin as Maddy's, but square, his eyes as dark as hers, his nose sharp and pinched-looking. He had on his best dark summer suit: it was Sunday.

Now he moved from the stove to the living room hallway. He knew where she was, of course, but he would not acknowledge her presence except at his own whim, certainly not while she waited for him to do it.

Maddy's slim body made her seem much younger than she was; in rare, unguarded moments her eyes might reveal childhood or age, but not youth. Two dark tails of curly hair flowed over her thin shoulders. The dress she wore was shapeless, plain, belted with a bow in the back like a child's, but she didn't care, couldn't care how she looked. Hands in the pockets of this dress, she stood straight as an arrow, still and taut, estimating the distance between her and her father. Twenty feet? Twenty-five? No arms were as long as that. Swiftly she opened the front door and slipped outside.

There was music in her head. The notes she heard flooded out other sound, pulled her along from sarabande to musette, washed over her, receded, left behind an echo of notes that rose like the ghost of a wave, crested, was gone. She stared down the road. The dust called her, it had notes of its own; you picked up two rocks and hit them together and a tone was made like the ring of struck crystal, a sound worth saving forever.

Stepping from the house to the doorstep was like moving from a cold tunnel into some warm, bright place. She allowed herself to shiver a little, as she would not have dared to do in the cold dark. The trees were just beginning to turn from spring to summer green — there must be a sound somewhere with a change as subtle as that. She wondered: a darkening sound? Buttercup, blue flag, somewhere ferns fully uncurled beside the dried-up shaded roadbed. She felt alone, looking at them, listening. She touched the little notebook in her pocket. She knew better than to take it out.

"For God's sake, Madeline, get to the car. Haven't got all day." Jack Dow's face appeared in the screen; in its shadow the face looked unearthly to Maddy, a skull.

His hand banged the door into her so that her chin snapped back and she stumbled a little down the steps toward the car. She turned, half dazed, as if to ask where the blow had come from and why, but already he was gone, hollering into the dark. "Vinnie! Vinnie! Where is that woman?"

He didn't mean it, Maddy thought automatically, although she knew he did. From the little stone walk that lay between doorstep and car she debated. Should she go back in? Slip past him somehow?

Was everyone ready? Jessica and Allison certainly were, and Phillip's clothes had been laid out. That left only little Stephen. Had he lost his shoes again? Should she go back?

Jessica, Maddy's next oldest sister, had sent her out. Tall and stocky, with short blond hair like their mother's, Jessica was the watchman of the family; of all the children, she worked the hardest to make things go well. Jessica's habitual silence was expected in the family, and the quiet looks she gave, the quiet way she helped out, taken for granted. Maddy thought Jessie mulled over their family life as another child might study a puzzle of wooden pieces, searching for a pattern.

"Music in your head," she'd whispered a few moments ago as she nodded at the door. "You're no good here, Maddy. Go on."

Maddy knew if she went to the house now her father would holler at her: "I told you to get out there!"

But if she went to the car he might forget he'd sent her and come and haul her from it: "Get in there, for God's sake, and help your mother."

At that moment there came the sound of footsteps. "Well," she heard him say. "What in hell took you so long?"

The Dow children had noble names: Jessica Elizabeth, Allison Janice, Phillip Everett, Stephen Alexander. Maddy's was Madeline Lavinia. Sometimes she thought their names were all they had. Phillip came out of the house first, eight years old, round-faced, worried. He was as dark as his father, his hair cut short and plastered back severely with water, giving his child's forehead a naked, knobby look. Then Jessica and Allison, both blond, Jessica, at thirteen, moving in her quiet, careful way. Allison, age ten, her hair in braids, was thin and lightweight and drifted like a feather.

Stephen came last, a six-year-old with black curly hair, curling eyelashes, and dark eyes. He was pale with fear. A big hand on his thin arm twisted him out through the doorway and shoved so that he stumbled down the steps as Maddy had, but he lost his balance and fell. Jessica, her face as immobile as a plate of granite, turned to help him. She picked him up, dusted him off. All the children came to the car.

As they got in, Maddy's mother emerged from the house. Vinnie Dow's face was still and sad. Thin, small, pale-haired, dressed like her children in serviceable church clothes, she moved toward the car with Jack Dow beside and a little behind her. Maddy saw her mother glance back at him, her head lowered, eyes slanted.

Waiting, Maddy thought.

Instantly alert, she turned and glanced once at Jessica to warn her, but the children in the back seat sat very still. They had seen it, too, then. Jessica's lips tightened. Somehow, perhaps from the way their father moved or their mother looked at him, the children knew that there was more punishment in store today. With her eyes Jessica warned Maddy: Turn around, don't look at me. Nobody notice me. There was the faintest rustle as bodies slipped backward in their seats so as not to be seen.

Jack Dow brushed past his wife; he glanced through the car windows at his children. They didn't move.

"My God, Vinnie," he said after a moment. "I'm going to whale the daylights out of that kid. His shoes are still filthy."

Maddy's hands clenched. In the car not a soul breathed. Her father reached in and hauled little Stephen out and threw him onto the grass; then he pulled Phillip out of the back seat and down beside him.

"Don't you ever watch out for your brother?" he cried at Phillip.

"Vinnie!" He turned to his wife. "What is it, do I ask too much of you? To get them into the car clean on a Sunday?"

"I'm sorry, Jack," Vinnie said faintly. "The shoes seemed clean. Please, let's go."

Her distress infuriated him still more. Maddy, stiff as a board on the front seat, reached for the car door, wanting, somehow, to help or to rescue.

Two bulges stood out, one on either side of her father's face. She could almost feel them move as he shook his head. "Jesus, woman," he said to his trembling wife, "even a cripple could do better than this." He looked upward, as if heaven itself must answer.

Maddy didn't dare to move, or to stay still. Her throat closed. For an instant she waited, they all did, half-expecting heaven to intervene for him. And she knew they were all hoping that if they were quiet enough — how much quiet would it take to move her father's hunched body away from the boys, soothe his rage? — this beating could, perhaps, be avoided. At this moment they were all frozen, testing the quiet and listening for heaven, to see if there were, or not, power enough in it — but no.

"I'll show you," he said abruptly. He pulled Stephen up by the arm and drew back and slammed him hard on the buttocks. From Stephen came a shocked hiccup, horrified silence, and then, as another blow followed and another, the open-mouthed, thin-lipped scream of a child who is truly hurt.

"No, Jack!" Vinnie Dow cried from an unexpected reserve of strength. "Please. We'll be late."

Late. A magic word. Jack Dow and his family could never be late for anything. The beating ceased; a blow, a cry, it was done. Stephen collapsed on the ground beside the trembling, frightened Phillip.

"Good for him," Jack Dow said to his wife. "Toughen him up a little." Stephen was crying, but not aloud. He knew better than that. For Phillip, the fright was the beating. He, too, wept.

Maddy's father backed off. His hands went to his hair, his belt. He tucked in his shirt, straightened his Sunday jacket. Shaken, Maddy glanced into the back seat. Allison had hidden her face in her hands, but Jessica's was stony white and her eyes flashed.

"Vinnie," their father said, "get those kids in, and if I have any more trouble, there'll be hell to pay." He stalked to the car and got in himself.

Vinnie Dow bent over her sons. "Come on now, Phillip, come on now, Stephen." Her voice was low and desperate and sorry. It begged them to recover for her sake.

Gently she helped Phillip into the car first, then turned to Stephen, who clung to her skirt in silent collapse. She bent over him, ostensibly to tuck in his shirt and straighten his Sunday tie, but Maddy knew her mother was murmuring over him — they all knew the murmur — "I'm sorry, I'm sorry." Maddy knew, as they all did, how the universe looked to Stephen at that moment: a monster, ready to choke children. The murmurs of their mother would only strengthen that impression.

She saw her mother struggle to help Stephen into the car, but he would not let go of her. It was Allison who reached out for him and pulled him onto her lap. Maddy knew that motion, too. It said, I'll take care of him, he's my responsibility. Go sit in the front seat, Mother, quickly, before the sky falls in.

Of course Vinnie Dow would have to sit in front beside her husband. She was required to be there when they arrived at church, part of the public face of the Dow family. She got into the car, sitting in her prescribed place beside Maddy. Neither she nor Maddy looked at each other. The car started, moved down the dirt road.

Daisies, buttercup, vetch and lupin along the road. Bouquets so rich beside the roadbed that they seemed to laugh at the little civilizing efforts at flowerbeds Maddy saw here and there on neat lawns by houses. Ahead of her down the long hill before they reached the church lay the finest houses in Freedom. Well-kept white clapboards, shining shutters, foundation plantings, big old trees and ornamental shrubs. But the flowers that grew wild, she thought, could grow anywhere, could defeat any effort at neatness, could take over where they wished.

At the foot of the hill the road, which was now tarred, rose sharply again, and at the crest of this rise was the church, a one-story white building with a little square steeple on top. That steeple was visible for miles among the green hills. Jack Dow was in charge of seeing that the bell in it rang every Sunday.

It was far too early for the bell to ring this morning, but he needed to be early, they all knew. "Early" was "on time" to him. In the parking lot were the cars of other early arrivals, including the car of the new minister, a young man fresh out of Bangor Theological Seminary and recently called by this and two other churches widely scattered in this west-central part of Maine. The three churches would share the minister's expenses and salary. The Reverend Mr. Howarth was a good man, Jack Dow had told the other deacons of the little Freedom church. "Somebody willing to learn. We can afford him, which is good, too."

Everyone listened to Jack Dow and took his advice. In public he was quiet and dependable, always ready to help.

Stephen had stopped crying. Maddy could just see his little arms in their dress shirtsleeves wrapped around Allison. The ten-year-old girl sat him up, straightened him, brushed his hair with her hand. Maddy turned away quickly so as not to be caught looking.

She stared at the car's dashboard of molded aqua plastic, then down at the turquoise seats. As they pulled into the churchyard sounds again occurred to her, wild strong notes so real that it was as if she had two pairs of ears, one for the noises of the world at large, one for notes that drowned the first world out, took her over, shook her. She needed to write them down, felt it as she might have felt hunger, but this was not the time.

Jack Dow was staring at the other cars in the parking lot. He knew each one, its driver, the family who owned it. Maddy saw him glance at his hands: the nails were clean and cut straight across. She saw him examine his shoes, which were immaculate. He looked his family over to see that they were well dressed, clean, and quiet.

"Jesus Christ," he muttered. "Your relatives are here in force today, Vinnie."

More cars were arriving. A shiny blue Cadillac for the Arthur Heberts, a yellow station wagon, the David Heberts. The Hebert women were sisters, once known as the Packard girls. They had married brothers, Arthur and David. Vinnie Packard Dow was their distant relative.

David Hebert got out of his car and raised a hand to wave at Maddy's father, who without a backward glance got out and went to speak to the man who paid his salary. One of the many Hebert concerns was a sawmill located not far from the church, on the Mettagawasett River; Jack Dow had risen from truck driver to manager of this mill.

"All right," said Vinnie Dow. "Now we'll go in."

It was a matter of staging. They must all be neat and quiet as they filed past their father. Arthur Hebert had joined him, too. Short, balding, outwardly affable, the toughness in their eyes carefully concealed by a Sunday friendliness in the same way that their Sunday shirt collars at once concealed and irritated their sun-browned, work-thickened necks, the two Hebert men looked solid. They were what they were, they seemed to say as you passed them. You could take it or leave it.

Her father, Maddy thought, was different. He was always changing, reaching, never quite arriving but always on the way. Eyes down, the children moved past the group of men. They knew their father watched; they felt some pride at making a good showing. They filed through the vestry, a boxlike gray room that served for church suppers and meetings, and into the sanctuary, where they moved to their accustomed pew and sat. In the winter there was Sunday school for the children; in the summer they sat through the whole service without a murmur. The Dow children were always quiet.

Maddy stared at the church walls. They were painted a light blue, so that if you looked at them long enough they seemed to rise and float like the sky. Behind the pulpit up on a platform was the minister's carved chair with its dark blue velvet seat. The wall behind this chair was arched and cream-colored. If you sat still long enough, it, too, would seem suddenly more like a curtain than a wall, about to rise, to reveal — what?

In her life, Maddy had had a lot of time to watch that wall and wonder.

On one side of the pulpit was a painted arch on which was written

"God Is Love," on the other, "God Our Father." The letters and the arches themselves had been painted to look three-dimensional, constructed out of wood, but Maddy knew if you went and laid your hand against them, you discovered it was only a clever paint job. "God Is Love" and "God Our Father" — a child could go crazy from a distance, trying to figure out if the woodwork were real.

Up near the ceiling of the sanctuary was a dark blue line that matched the cushion on the minister's chair. Without that line, the walls of the church would have floated right away, Maddy sometimes thought, and never come back. Everyone would float away. Sometimes she wanted to creep inside those walls, dissolve, and be gone forever.

Little Stephen relaxed against the back of the pew. The other children were very still.

Let's all dream, Maddy thought. There was music, nowhere, everywhere.

She saw her father standing to the side. He nodded and smiled as people began to move through the vestry into the sanctuary. His counter, a gadget he held in one hand, clicked busily. Counting people and keeping records were part of his job as deacon of the church. The church was really the only social gathering spot in Freedom, Maine, a town with a population of twenty-five hundred people. Of these, one hundred came here, but not regularly; a count of seventy-five was considered large. Today, however, even though it was early in July, there would be more since it was a baptism Sunday. Maddy saw her father study the faces, counting, his own expression as smooth and familiar as milk. When there were this many people he always relaxed, gave himself up to pretending. He reached a hand to every comer, welcoming, nodding, smiling. "How are you today?" he asked again and again, and his joy in this action increased. "How are you? Nice to see you in church."

In the Dow pew, Maddy twisted so as not to look at him. All the other children were still except for little Stephen, who now nodded sleepily against her arm. She moved slightly to make him more comfortable. Her father probably couldn't see him anyway, she thought, since the backs of the pews were high, and perhaps the little boy would sleep, feel better. She would have to manage it in such a way that her father would never know. She shifted in the pew, half hiding Stephen behind her. Jessica did the same.

People had begun to come in in groups. Old ladies sat near the back in pews they had had by custom for fifty years or more. A few families, nodding at the Dows, took places closer to the front. There was a stir and in came Eleanor Packard Hebert, Arthur's wife. Her blond hair was combed high on her head in a fascinating series of loops and curls, her dress was perfect, her stockings shed the light.

It was like watching a creature from another planet. Maddy stared. A planet where everything was easy and comfortable, she thought.

The David Heberts came in. David was short and stocky. He was dressed in a plaid sport coat and white pants and shoes. His wife, June Packard Hebert, was also short and wide. Her clothes were dark and practical, her hair done in high coils like her sister's.

Maddy wondered: Could these people live and not be punished? How blessed, how lucky.

Jack Dow strode down the aisle to his family and leaned toward his wife. "Gonna baptize the Cummings baby," he whispered.

Not an eyelash flickered among his children.

"You kids sit still," he whispered hoarsely. "You are not to move a little finger."

No one had seemed to, but Maddy and Jessica were moving in ways they hoped wouldn't be detected to rouse the sleeping Stephen. Maddy could feel his head sag against the back of her arm. She sat twisted and Jessica sat forward to hide him. Behind Maddy, Jessica's arm moved painfully inch by inch until she supported him. Maddy felt Jessica's warning fingers close around Stephen's inner arm. A moment later he was awake.

"You children sit up there, sit around." Jack Dow frowned at them until they were properly aligned in the pew. He stared at his wife.

"Vinnie, I expect you to see to this."

With a nod he strode off to the little room to the side of the chancel where he would put on his robe and return, with the new minister, as lector of the church, to read the lessons in the service.

Maddy was conscious that her mother's pale face had lowered itself and that her good hand now covered the crippled one in her lap. On the other side Stephen sat bolt upright. Ahead of her, the white wall in the center arch swam before her eyes. "God Our Father," she read. "God Is Love." She blinked, glanced down once at Stephen.

His eyelashes were wet and his hair curled damply around his face.
A handsome little boy. People said so, often.

Maddy knew there was irony in this, that in the one place in the
world where they should have felt the safest, the most protected, the
freest among friends, they were cut off. It wasn't safe to trust anyone. How could you?

Vinnie Dow rarely did more than smile and nod at people in
church because once, when Maddy was much younger, Eleanor Hebert
had stopped her mother to discuss the church fair and Jack Dow had
come out of the minister's office and seen them talking. That noon at
home Maddy's mother had been forced to recount every word and
punctuation mark of her conversation.

"Tryin' to buddy up with the Heberts?" Jack Dow had accused her.
"Talk about how we live, talk about me behind my back?"

"I had no such intention." Vinnie Dow flared unexpectedly. "I was
just talking."

"Talking, yes! What else did you say?" His fist slammed into the
table. His wife jumped, then turned tiredly to the kitchen, to begin
to dish up the waiting meal.

"No sir," Maddy's father said. "Nobody's gonna eat around here,
Vinnie, 'til you tell me."

No one did eat. Jack Dow had spent the afternoon alternating his
catechizing with accusatory silences and small abuses of his children — a slap here, a punch or pinch there — more to punish his
wife than to hurt anyone specifically, enough to keep his children
huddled in corners, too scared to talk to each other and too miserable
to cry.

When finally at the end of the day he'd left the house, Vinnie
Dow had called the children together and quickly fed them dinner
and supper together. They'd finished fast and then gone upstairs to
get ready for bed, all but Maddy, who could not bear the sight of
her mother's face as she gazed out the window, down the road.

"What is it?" Maddy had whispered, as if "it" could be put into
words.

That once — that once only, was that why Maddy remembered it?
— Vinnie Dow had stared at her daughter without her usual careful
guard. The glance she gave was young and full of confusion. "If
only I weren't so alone," she'd muttered, and she made a helpless
little gesture with one hand.

"There must be some way out," Maddy said. Hope burgeoned inside her so suddenly that she could hardly breathe, certainly say no more.

Vinnie Dow gazed into some darkness she saw in an imaginary distance; she seemed to measure it. "No," she said, "I can't."

"Why? We have to!" Maddy cried.

"No. It's all right, everything is fine," Vinnie Dow said. "Go to bed, Maddy. You don't understand."

Shouts and weeping in the bedroom below Maddy's that night. Maddy lay stiffly in bed, hating her father for how he hurt her mother, all of them. Over and over she tried to make some sort of escape plan, but she knew her mother was right. There was no escape. No one in the family could drive a car except Jack Dow. No one had so much as one friend to call upon. Most people believed that Jack Dow was a fine man and that his family revolved lovingly around him.

Lying in the dark, a child could do very little except wait while one by one muscles quivered and gave in to sleep. During the day there was nothing to do except keep to yourself. At church you sat still. You were polite and you did nothing, nothing at all, to draw attention.

Maddy stared down at Stephen. She felt fiercely protective toward him. If only she could shield him somehow.

To the right of the church sanctuary was the choir loft. Now Mrs. Chamberlain took her place at the organ to begin a prelude. The organ was a fine old instrument, well preserved, its few pipes still in good working order. Maddy had a soft spot in her heart for the old hymns Mrs. Chamberlain played. Surely they offered, out of the darkness and dignity of time passing, some comfort.

Today it was "Sweet Hour of Prayer." Maddy saw her mother's good hand close painfully on the hymnal in her lap. She saw as well Mrs. Chamberlain's comfortably rounded back, her gray frizz of hair, glasses perched just so on her nose. The loose flesh of her upper arms swung with her effort to extricate herself from the difficulties of the arrangement. Mrs. Chamberlain's job had traditionally been a volunteer one in the church and she did it out of pure love. In the last few years she had received a kind of honorary stipend of ten dollars per Sunday, but she had been heard to declare that if the church would only find a real organist, she'd step down in a minute.

Her musical difficulties took on emergency status, and Maddy heard her mother sigh very softly. In the generation before hers, Vinnie Dow's family had included well-educated musicians, and Maddy knew that her mother found in Mrs. Chamberlain's organ playing one more evidence of life's purgatory from which she, Vinnie Packard Dow, would never escape. Maddy liked Mrs. Chamberlain. If she'd known her better, she might even have loved her, a woman from whom kindness radiated, a woman not afraid to be sentimental, to love the familiar.

Two more people entered: old Beatrice Packard, accompanied by Miss Ann Packard, her cousin and companion. It was a rare occasion when Aunt Bea Packard felt well enough to come to church. She was a thin, aristocratic old lady, bent over slightly, with frail-looking shoulders, dressed in cream-colored lightweight wool. Dressed in light, Maddy thought. She moved down the aisle slowly on Aunt Ann's arm. Aunt Ann was huge. When she moved, Maddy saw two big flowered circles rolling independently, one on the top and one on the bottom. Aunt Ann hovered over Aunt Bea, carrying an extra shawl, settling her comfortably, then tucking the shawl around the old woman's shoulders.

Last to come into the church was the baby, on her mother's arm. Elaine Hebert Cummings, Eleanor and Arthur Hebert's daughter, was in her twenties and lovely to look at, with curly blond hair and large eyes. Slender, well dressed, she looked to Maddy like a picture on the cover of a magazine. Beside Elaine moved her tall, good-looking husband, Cyril Cummings. All Maddy could see of the baby was a yard or more of pink and white flowing lace. She thought wistfully, It must always be so easy, so nice.

Mrs. Chamberlain began to bring in the sheaves. While she lingered over the notes of the old hymn, the Reverend Mr. Howarth, in a dark robe, came out of his office. This was the first Sunday after his acceptance in the church and the first time he had held the worship service on his own. He was a young man, small and plump. He blinked a little behind his black-framed glasses and looked out at the congregation as if pleasantly startled to find them there, then climbed the steps to the platform and sat in the ornate chair. When he was seated Jack Dow, also in a robe, entered and moved to the left of the platform, to the lector's chair. In the Dow pew no one moved, no one dared. Mrs. Chamberlain finished the hymn.

Mr. Howarth stood and raised his hands, and the congregation stood for the Call to Worship. He began to read. Maddy looked from his face to that of her father. " 'This is the day the Lord has made,' " the minister said. " 'Let us rejoice and be glad in it.' We'll sing hymn number one."

Mrs. Chamberlain swung in to "Holy, Holy, Holy."

Many members of the church could sing, and the words of the hymn rang out gladly. Here and there a stronger voice picked it up. Over all the voices sounded that of Judy Hebert Russell, another member of the Hebert family. Her fine soprano was unmistakable; Maddy loved to hear it. She wished she could tell Judy someday.

In the front of the church, Mr. Howarth seemed at first surprised at the volume of sound in this congregation, then pleased. He sang for all he was worth in a well-placed tenor.

A river of sound, Maddy was thinking. She heard notes below and above what were played and sung. She felt she was not in church at all but in some great place where the human voice flowed into an ocean of voices.

"Maddy, time to sit." Jessica's hand was on her arm. Maddy sat, glanced at her father to make sure he hadn't seen, and smiled a little at Jessica, whose lips tightened humorously before they both faced front again. Mr. Howarth led the prayer.

Jack Dow stood to read the announcements. "Anyone who is interested in joining a Freedom chorus is invited to stay after today's service for more information. We have learned that television station WGME, Channel Thirteen, is running some competitions among small-town choruses over the next nine months. The winning chorus will appear on television as part of next year's Fourth of July celebration. I don't need to tell you that a television appearance could be an excellent opportunity for promoting our church and our town as well. We are fortunate in the number of good voices we have in this church, and we're hoping that many will stay for this meeting following the service." He sat down and looked at his fingernails.

Another hymn, and then Mr. Howarth began the long prayer. Maddy was listening to his words, setting them to the music of that last hymn. One of her arms was locked against the dress pocket her notebook was in.

"Oh, Father, we ask your blessing on the President of the United States and all who labor with him," Mr. Howarth prayed. His voice had a rhythm Maddy liked. "Watch over those who are suffering or in pain this day," he continued. "Make us all effective servants of the release from pain."

Maddy could feel her notebook, like a treasure, hidden. Later she would find the time to scratch in a staff, choose a time signature.

"In Jesus' name we pray," said Mr. Howarth. "Amen."

Mrs. Chamberlain played a few chords in organ response to the prayer.

These were Jack Dow's cue. He stood up, moved to the big Bible atop the carved pulpit, opened it to a marked place as he did every Sunday, and began to read. Maddy thought he was two people, one crafty and watchful, the other proclaiming his safety like a little boy newly arrived at a goal in a game. "Today when you hear his voice, / do not harden your hearts," he read.

Maddy heard the words, but she couldn't look up. She thought her father was like an actor who wanted to believe his part so much that he did believe it. Scripture always took on a sinister quality for her. She found no peace or joy in it, only endless demands and punishments; a folding up of the self, hiding it away where it could not be found and threatened.

" 'For the word of God is living and active,' " her father read, " 'sharper than any two-edged sword, piercing to the division of soul and spirit, of joints and marrow.' "

Maddy stared at the walls as his voice went on and on. She stared until the blue became white in her imagination, the voice faded, and something else echoed and vibrated blessedly in her head. She saw notes, lines, a staff. She was in a place where, with endless attention to detail, she could construct music of a kind different from anything she had heard, a music that haunted and healed. She was far away.

"Maddy," Jessica hissed. "Stand up." She tugged at Maddy's hand. Around them the congregation was standing — why? Maddy stood up.

Elaine and Cyril Cummings waited at the front of the church, Cyril holding the baby. Mr. Howarth was smiling. Jack Dow had removed the cover of the baptismal font and was standing to one side.

"Elana Lee," said Mr. Howarth, "I baptize thee in the name of the Father, Son, and Holy Ghost."

The baby whimpered a little but didn't cry. Among the congregation a murmur of approval ran, a ripple of a fond laugh. On request, they raised their hands and promised to help to bring the child up in the "nurture and admonition of the Lord." In a moment everyone had bowed their heads to pray. Then Mr. Howarth took the child in all its wonderful pink and white lace gown into his own arms. One small hand reached toward his face, its five tiny fingers flexing and curling. Mr. Howarth beamed at the parents, who turned back to their seats. For an instant he stood smiling at the baby in an abstracted, charmed way that sent another murmur of affectionate approval through the congregation.

"Today," he said, "we have done something very important. We have welcomed a new soul into our congregation. We have become the parents of a child. We have promised to nurture that child, give her a good place to grow and the love she needs to realize her full potential. We have blessed this child with holy water.

"The parents have agreed that this is a good time to let you get a closer look at their baby, your church baby. So that you may get to know little Elana better, I am going to give her into the arms of our deacon, Jack Dow. The parents aren't a bit anxious about this, I assure you. They know Jack has had plenty of experience."

The baby was transferred from Mr. Howarth's arms to those of Jack Dow. Almost at once the little hand turned bright red, the one visible fist clenched, and the baby began to squall.

Maddy felt a clutch of fear.

Mr. Howarth chuckled, the congregation tittered; Jack Dow managed a smile. Maddy thought, No! She tensed to stand, even to rescue the baby, but she felt Jessica's hand on her arm. They glanced at each other. The baby snuffled, wailed. That sound was the death knell of the Dow family afternoon.

"This is our child." Mr. Howarth spoke above the baby's crying. "Jack here will go up and down the aisles and stop at each pew so that each of you can see her, your child, our newest church baby."

Mrs. Chamberlain began to play. Jack Dow made his way through the church, stopping at every pew. Everywhere men, women and children smiled and nodded, spoke to the baby, who continued to squall. There were mothers and fathers of all ages in the congregation; they nodded at Elana, light playing on their faces as she cried. Women clucked and smiled. It was plain they knew what to do for an unhappy baby and would do it if allowed.

What Maddy saw was pink and white against that dark arm. The baby cried, people smiled. Maddy stared straight ahead. "God Our Father," she read. "God Is Love." Jack Dow walked toward the front.

"Great service, Pastor," Jack said. "Good sermon. Sorry about the baby."

"You mean that she cried?" Blaine Howarth shrugged. "Not your fault."

"No, I guess not."

The young minister sat at his desk. "It looks as if the chorus will go off well. I must say I'm surprised at how you've brought it all together. So many people signed up today, you must have been doing a lot of work."

Jack Dow crossed one foot in front of the other, looking, as he very well knew, both humble and sincere. "A little witness to the faith, Pastor," he said. "That's all. I'd better go, my family's waiting in the car. Vinnie's put a roast in, and she hates to be kept waiting."

It was not true; it might have been true.

The young minister believed him. "You go right along, then, don't wait another minute. I'm going to finish up a little reading here." He looked up through the thick-rimmed glasses, a glance that saw Jack abstractedly and yet might, at any instant, see right through him.

"All right then." Jack turned. "Tuesday night's another meeting. We'll make this real big. Put the church on the map a little."

Again the abstracted, almost puzzled, look. "See you Tuesday, Jack. Thanks."

Out of that room with its dark desk and green rug, the white woodwork and the pegs in the corner from which robes hung, and into the blue sanctuary. Jack Dow thought, This chorus comes just when I need it.

Why he needed it he would not whisper even to himself.

Eleanor Hebert had said, "I don't know, Jack. It would take a lot of organization."

Her husband, Arthur, had said, "Is it a moneymaker, Jack?"

All Jack had to do, and he knew it, was look at them. "It's what you put in, course," he'd said. "But it would do an awful lot of good." That's all he wanted, really. An awful lot of good. They would believe that, right?

They did believe it. Eleanor Hebert, whose organizational skills were famous in the town, took right over, with Jack's support and skillful direction. Now the thing was safely under way. Money would begin to flow.

He passed into the vestry, pausing for a moment to check the faucets in both bathrooms and in the kitchen sink. Once someone had left the water running by accident and it had pumped the well dry. A fire hazard. Couldn't have that. Everything was shut off; everything was clean. A clean church. The heat he felt, so that he mopped his forehead, was due to the mugginess of the day. He was a good man. He read from the Book, didn't he? He headed for the sunlight.

Hot July sun. He stared about the churchyard, almost deserted, and then out into the distance. To the south in front of him was the town cemetery and, beyond, the hills of Freedom. Near Sebago Lake on the Mettagawasett River, the land of Freedom rolled gently, its picturesque hills shimmering and green in the sun of noonday. Near at hand was the road that passed between church and cemetery. Up and down the road were the historic homes of the town. Fine old white farmhouses, a few saltboxes. Chief among them all was the Arthur Hebert farm, its large barns and many-storied white farmhouse gleaming with fresh paint. Farther down the road was where the David Heberts lived. David's holdings lay at a distance from his house; he had corn knee high for over a mile of bottomland along the Mettagawasett. There were also smaller farms here and there on the road. At the far southern outskirts of the town, not visible from the church, was a small settlement of bungalows and new split-levels belonging to the people who worked at S. D. Warren, a paper mill in Westbrook. To the north behind the church was where the Dow family lived.

Jack turned. You couldn't see his house from the church. The northern part of the town was densely wooded, miles of ruffled green and the pointed tops of spruces. At one time there had been many settlements along Jack's dirt road, but now there were none; a few old cellar holes were mute witness to the agonies of the Great Depression, which had never quite left this back area of rural Maine. Hidden in the woods at the far northern outskirts of the town were many of the poor, the food stamp people, welfare mothers scraping by as best they could. Well hidden, out of sight of the big farms, the indigent turned up in the town office when they needed a loan, a load of wood, some heating oil in the winter, or at the minister's office to borrow from the church for a child's glasses or a doctor's appointment.

At a distance from all the woods was a slice of blue, Crescent Lake, a large body of water whose beach was divided into three sections: one for estates, most open only two summer months a year, a long section of town beach, and an area of smaller shanties, cottages up on posts, some neat with whimsical names, others with rusty screens and peeling trim, dark among the pines. From the church in the blazing sun the woods to the north and the blue slice of lake seemed cool and elegant.

Jack turned back to his car. This was a good town, he thought. Right in front of him was proof of that: fields edged with stone, all those cool-looking stands of trees, all that dark green shade. He glanced into his car, soothed by the stillness of those who waited for him inside it. He climbed in. "A little too hot for a roast today, Vinnie," he said. "It's good we'll be eating something cool."

Vinnie Dow nodded silently.

Jack looked into the rearview mirror. No one moved. How clean they were. With any luck, Jack Dow was going to be all right. He turned the car out of the churchyard and headed north.

CHAPTER TWO

I T WAS A BRIGHT Tuesday in July, Aunt Ann Packard's morning to clean the kitchen. She got up early and slipped into an old dress, not bothering with her usual corset-type girdle. Feel good to jiggle for a change, she thought. She didn't put on shoes or stockings, either. It was summer, and the bare linoleum was cool under her feet.

She had some breakfast — just a bit, really — toast and coffee and a piece of last night's rhubarb pie. For extra energy — she'd decided she deserved it on floorwashing days — she stuck a dollop of ice cream in her coffee, and then she had to have a few cookies to go with that. Of course she ate standing up at the back door screen. She hadn't been able to sit to a meal in years.

It was a pretty morning. The grass stretched away from the back steps into a field of glittering wet gray-green. A few hundred yards away beside the lake was a stand of virgin pine, the shadows among their high cloudy needles almost blue. The sun made dappled places on the pine floor beneath those shadows. Here and there a fern grew or a thick-leaved wildflower. From the back door screen Aunt Ann was able to smell the pine, at this time of day a cool, cutting fragrance. She thought this was just how life should be: still and clean, open to the weather, waiting for the light. Standing in the doorway, she drank a toast to the morning with her coffee. Then she filled a bucket with hot suds and got to work washing down cupboards and counters, not stopping until the kitchen floor was shining and slick. She did love a clean kitchen floor, no matter how pooped she was after.

Aunt Ann had come to stay with old Aunt Bea Packard in what she herself thought of as kind of an odd way.

Aunt Ann was a distant cousin of Aunt Bea's, born up above Caribou, in northern Maine, to scratch-poor potato farmers. For all that, Aunt Ann felt she hadn't done so badly. She'd left home as a young girl without a cent to her name and hired herself out as a cook for a wealthy Bar Harbor family, working for these people steadily for a number of years until the man she thought of as "my Roger" had left her.

After that, it was time for a change. In her late thirties, Aunt Ann had found with her employers' help another good job, this time in the western mountains of the state, "away from the ocean, away from the memories." Aunt Ann would have said this while staring straight ahead of her. She did not like to think of her Roger.

Her new family was a large one: "four boys and fourteen hockey sticks," she told people. It was a big, comfortable house, and as time went on, the kitchen became a focal point. Aunt Ann loved having people underfoot, and with four sons the house was always full — doors slamming, running footsteps, shouts, tussles, laughter. Aunt Ann thought of these as her golden years, always sunny then, or it was in her memory. She worked in that household for almost twenty-five years.

By the end of it, however, "her" family had grown up. "Her" boys went off to college, married, moved away. Their mother died, their father went to live with one grown son, and Aunt Ann had had to take her courage in both hands and go with a comfortable annuity to live by herself in a nice set of rooms on State Street in Portland.

They were nice rooms. She had everything she needed; she certainly would never starve. "No, no danger of that whatsoever," she would say, surveying herself in her apartment's one mistake, a full-length mirror. "I certainly won't starve to death," she muttered, shifting her wide girth in one direction, then in another. "Not for a good long while anyways."

She kept busy. She tore into the apartment — three rooms and a bath — and cleaned it from its old-fashioned ceiling moldings to its solid oak floors. "Other people's dirt," she had always said, "looks so much worse than your own."

Aunt Ann read her Bible regularly, sitting alone in her apartment with her breakfast coffee perking and the Book open on the kitchen table in front of her. A day came when she read: "They shall not build and another inhabit / they shall not plant and another eat. . . . and my chosen shall long enjoy the work of their hands / They shall not labor in vain."

For some reason the words, intended for comfort, hurt. Aunt Ann put her head in her plump hands and wept.

It was not in her to be discouraged or lonely for long, however. One day when the cleaning was done, she took up some newspapers she hadn't had time to read. She was glad to read them even if they were old; sitting in a strange, clean apartment was unfamiliar to her. To sustain herself she ate while she read, at last coming upon a bit of hospital news that interested her. Aunt Beatrice Packard, a distant cousin, was now critically ill at the Maine Medical Center in Portland.

Aunt Ann remembered Aunt Beatrice Packard. Back in the twenties she had attended Aunt Bea's wedding: in yards of tulle, Beatrice Armand had married the young, handsome August Packard. Money to money, it was whispered in the back of the church where Aunt Ann sat, plump even then and fresh from Caribou, proud of her new job. Aunt Ann remembered Aunt Bea Packard, as sweet, gentle and understanding a girl as anyone could wish, with a kind and welcoming smile, a pressure of the hand, even for a young cook from Caribou who was not very pretty and certainly not very well dressed.

Reading the paper, it occurred to Aunt Ann that she would like to visit Aunt Bea Packard in the hospital.

She won't remember me. She'll be too sick to see me, she thought. And then she thought, But what else have I to do? Then, I could pack a basket of food. A little change of diet couldn't hurt Aunt Bea Packard.

In the end, basket packed, she went.

When Aunt Ann arrived at the hospital she found that Aunt Bea was ill with a viral infection of the kidneys and was connected to tubes of various kinds. She could hardly open her eyes, certainly not speak or eat. Aunt Ann, staring at the form in the hospital bed, was shocked at what she saw — a frail wisp with an old face, aged hands, and a head of silver-white hair.

Why, Aunt Bea Packard is old, she thought.

Aunt Ann set down her basket and caught sight of herself in a mirror at the far end of the room. Her dress had hiked up somehow along one hip so that three solid inches of white slip showed below one hemline. Her gray hair, always unruly, now seemed to stand on end.

"Oh, Jesus, God," she said softly, giving the dress a tug. "There's two old women in here."

And this was the old people's floor. It smelled sour and sweet and frightening, and Aunt Ann wanted to get out of there and take Aunt Bea with her. "How depressing," she muttered. "How damned depressing."

The old woman on the bed didn't move. After a moment Aunt Ann shrugged and set about making herself comfortable.

It was a private room with a tall plate glass window, white walls, and the usual hospital paraphernalia. Two bouquets stood in a window that gave sunless but clear northern light. Nurses looked in from time to time. They smiled at Aunt Ann, made small talk. When no one came in, Aunt Ann nibbled from her basket. She thought, Somebody's got to.

Toward the middle of the afternoon the Arthur Heberts and the David Heberts came for a visit. They were gracious enough when they realized that Aunt Ann was a distant relative.

"She's not very well," Eleanor said as they stood in the corridor to talk. "It was kind of you to come, Miss Packard."

"Aunt Ann, please. Listen, could I come back tomorrow?"

"But she doesn't know you're here." Tall, blond and competent, Eleanor Hebert frowned.

Women like her bothered Aunt Ann — always so afraid. "You don't know me very well," Aunt Ann said, "but I'm a relative. I haven't got much to do these days, and" — she turned to Eleanor's sister, dark-haired June, who seemed a bit less rigid — "it couldn't hurt. I might help in some way. At least I could watch."

"Oh, why not?" said June. "Eleanor, if she wants to. It might be nice for Aunt Bea to have someone here."

"Aunt Bea doesn't know." Eleanor paused, touching carefully one waved wing of her hair. "Well," she said with a sigh to Aunt Ann, "I suppose it doesn't matter if you have the time."

"I got nothing but time." Aunt Ann tried to laugh.

After a while they left. Aunt Ann walked back into the room. Aunt Bea hadn't moved; she was breathing noisily.

Aunt Ann settled herself. She opened her basket again.

Every day she went back to the hospital. She took a basket of food with her and sat and watched. Aunt Bea couldn't eat, but Aunt Ann shared with the nurses so that her basket always went home empty.

Over the long hours of studying Aunt Bea's face, doing small things for her, sponging her forehead or rubbing her hands with lotion, Aunt Ann began to think that somehow Aunt Bea Packard was happy to have her there. Sitting beside that bed, hour after hour, Aunt Ann began to feel a communication between them. The body on the bed, the pale face, wrinkled skin, white hair, the tubes, would all somehow speak to her.

"Am I dead, Ann?" frail Aunt Bea seemed to ask. "Am I dying?"

"Am I dead?" In fact, that question would seem to skitter back and forth between the two old women like a whisper of ghosts, not a sound in the room.

"Hell, no," Aunt Ann would say silently. "We've got to buck up, Bea."

Sometimes in the midst of that silent whispering, Eleanor Hebert would come into the room with her husband. It was clear that she didn't know what to say to the mountain of a woman who had set up squatter's rights in her Aunt Bea's hospital room. "Aunt Ann," Eleanor would manage. "Still here? Any change?"

"Doesn't seem to be," Aunt Ann would mutter uncomfortably.

Days passed. One day June Hebert would come in, the next day Eleanor. Sometimes they came together with their husbands. Neither sister stayed to visit. They read the doctor's reports, talked to the nurses, patted Aunt Bea's hand, and sighed.

"It may not be long," they told each other in the hallway.

Aunt Ann began to feel that old Aunt Bea Packard's spirit was like a little butterfly fluttering at a tall fence. It would fly delicately forward out of some dark cold place and then one or both of the nieces would appear. The butterfly would retreat, to cling somewhere out of sight, wings dormant, exhausted.

Aunt Ann, feeling this happen day after day and continually

undergoing the piercing glance of one niece or the other and the
question "No change?" began to think that her own customary
answer, "Doesn't seem to be," was part of the problem. In the world
of the spirit, wasn't that answer a lie? After all, dead women didn't
ask questions. Every time she said, "Doesn't seem to be," wasn't she
making matters worse, even for good in the universe — in which,
God help her, she did believe?

So that that daily question "No change?" became a test as the days
passed, not of the sick woman's state of health so much, but of Aunt
Ann's own honesty.

One day Eleanor and June both appeared, husbands in tow. Aunt
Ann, sitting in her usual lump beside Aunt Bea's bed, felt that the
family was afraid: afraid if Aunt Bea died, afraid if she didn't. Suddenly Aunt Ann felt their attempt at control of this situation as if
it were a tangible presence in the room, like a piece of cold deadly
metal, clammy to the touch.

Eleanor Hebert said, "Well, Aunt Ann, still here, I see. It's good
of you to come, but it must be tiring for a woman of your age."

"Well, I'm not dead yet," said Aunt Ann, glancing quickly at Aunt
Bea, still and white on her bed, an oxygen tent over her now because
she was finding it difficult to breathe. What Aunt Ann saw was a
butterfly clinging to a stick in a dark place while a high fence cast a
million slatted shadows. Aunt Ann put away a half-eaten sticky
bun and wiped her fingers.

Eleanor Hebert said, "No change?"

Aunt Ann felt for the usual reply, but it wouldn't come.

"There, Aunt Ann." June Hebert shook her head. "Maybe Eleanor's right. Stay home tomorrow, why don't you? It's the will of
God, maybe." She shrugged sadly.

But that, for good and all, did it.

"She's fighting!" Aunt Ann burst out. "My God, she's not gone
over!"

Shocked, Eleanor Hebert frowned at her sister; they gave each
other a telling look.

That didn't matter; Aunt Ann felt better. A bit more room, she
thought, toward Aunt Bea's butterfly spirit. A bit more air for you,
my dear.

The old lady on the bed didn't move. Aunt Ann looked from her
to the two surprised nieces, then settled herself more firmly in the

hospital chair. If they wanted to get her out, she decided, they were going to need more muscle than she saw before her.

"I guess I'll stay," she said. "I have an idea Aunt Bea might pull out of this."

Later the sisters and their husbands withdrew and huddled together in the hallway outside Aunt Bea's room. From time to time as they whispered they glanced in at Aunt Ann — as if she were some kind of a freak, she thought. Or maybe they were a little afraid of her. Or maybe they hoped she was right about their aunt Bea. After a while they left. Aunt Ann sat with Aunt Bea, and she watched.

Aunt Bea still didn't move. The sound of her breathing filled the room. But Aunt Ann felt something was stronger.

Each day a sister came in with her husband. To their inevitable question Aunt Ann now always put the same reply: "I think she might be all right." More air, more space.

"Am I alive?" Now the form on the bed seemed to ask this, a new question.

In a few days the lips of the sick old woman moved fretfully, but the sounds she made were nonsensical.

"Don't worry," Aunt Ann whispered to her. "We know."

Slowly Aunt Bea Packard began to recover. She began to awaken, smile, after a time even to taste what Aunt Ann brought, in tiny bits with the doctor's permission. It was many days until she could, feebly, relish a mouthful, but she did eventually, particularly Aunt Ann's baking, again with the doctor's permission. The dreadful tubes went. It became a matter of building up her strength. Aunt Ann knew all about that. She would leave a small box of treats and be sure that by the next day Aunt Bea would have eaten them all. Aunt Ann took to bringing two baskets for the daytime, one for Aunt Bea, one for her and the nurses.

At last one day, frail and trembling, Aunt Bea Packard sat up in bed and said faintly, "Ann, I look like a wreck."

She and Aunt Ann smiled at each other and giggled like children. Each knew the other had never looked worse, or better. Pretty soon it was one wide lady and one narrow lady holding on to each other and moving with solemn concentration down the hospital hallway.

It was worth it all, Aunt Ann thought.

"Ann, you are the elixir of life," Aunt Bea told her one day. Aunt Ann blinked back tears.

For Aunt Ann, life was now frail Aunt Bea Packard sitting up in bed with a peach satin bedjacket on, books and letters piled about her, the faintest rose flush of returning health coming to her cheeks. For Aunt Ann, that flush was proof that hope was possible, that there were a million good things left to do in the world.

The Hebert sisters came and went, vying with each other to make Aunt Bea comfortable. They both seemed genuinely happy to see her recover.

"They're good girls, Ann," Aunt Bea would say when they left. "They're coming along fine."

At any other time it might have seemed strange to hear an eighty-year-old speak of two matrons that way, but Aunt Ann knew what Aunt Bea meant. They still had things to learn, those two.

"Thank God," Aunt Ann muttered again and again.

One day Aunt Bea said with some shyness, "You know, Ann, they'll be sending me home from the hospital soon." At the word "home," her eyes darkened, and Aunt Ann knew she was frightened. "It's a big old place," Aunt Bea said. "A handful when you're by yourself. I was by myself and I used to get so tired, I used to forget to eat or sleep. I imagine they'll find someone to take care of me at home."

Aunt Ann burst out, "Oh, let me come, I'd like to come, Bea! I'll cook you such food as you've never tasted! I have a little income, I could pay my own way."

"Oh, Ann." Lips trembling, Aunt Bea managed to look both frail and stern. "Taking care of me is hard work. I can still barely get around and I can't accept anyone without pay."

"I have my pay. This is my pay." Aunt Ann was desperate enough to remember her knees and to try to figure out how to get to them. "I'm used to work. I've worked all my life. Please, I need it, Bea." Once again, she looked at the old woman through tears.

Aunt Bea's face reddened and two wet drops ran down the wrinkled cheeks, touching the tips of a gentle smile. "Ann, only if you want to."

"I want to. Please."

Aunt Bea Packard's health improved greatly. She spent her mornings in her room at home, reading, sewing, writing letters. In the afternoons she napped and at two o'clock came downstairs on Aunt Ann's arm, to move from room to room in her house and exclaim over the work Aunt Ann had done to clean it up.

Named "The Cottage" in the 1890s, the Packard property in Freedom was an estate, and the house large enough, Aunt Ann thought, to house two cottages, or three. The main portion was three stories high, with a widow's walk at the top that looked down through pine to a sandy beach and on to Crescent Lake. On either side of the big white frame was a two-story wing, one of which featured a music room, the other an unused plant conservatory made of domed glass, with a rounded section toward the back of leaded, three-inch glass squares.

It was a showpiece of a house, built in the last century and renovated in the nineteen twenties, just before Aunt Bea and Uncle August Packard moved in. They had planned to fill it with children, and when they were unable to do that, they invited members of the Packard and Armand families instead, including Eleanor and June, whose own parents had died during the Depression, and even, for a very short time, Vinnie Packard Dow.

For thirty years or more, the Cottage had been a focal point for the town and Uncle August Packard had been the town benefactor, supplying as necessary items for the school, town offices, and church. His lovely wife, Aunt Bea, had graced all of Uncle August's activity, tempering his vigor and ambition with her gentleness and understanding.

When Uncle August Packard died, Aunt Bea mourned him deeply. The big house was empty by this time — Vinnie Dow mysteriously estranged, the Hebert sisters busily engaged in their own lives and in the many public functions of town and church. Suddenly it had seemed to Aunt Bea that she simply didn't have the energy to go on.

"I climbed into a dark place," she explained to Aunt Ann, "and pulled the cover over my head."

The unused corners of the big house were dank — "dirty, I call it," Aunt Ann would mutter, now flopping to her knees with grim determination. "Damn sinks are full of germs, catch your death just lookin' at 'em," she told Aunt Bea sternly, and that gentle old woman lifted her hands to her face and said, "Oh, Ann, how awful for you. I am sorry."

"It's not me I'm worryin' about. Now don't you go near there 'til I can clean it out."

Aunt Ann saw to it that the house got clean and stayed that way — it was not so much work that she couldn't manage it, with just the two of them to cook for. She was happy. When Aunt Bea was happy, she was very happy.

Today, when at last she put her scrub brush aside, Aunt Ann was feeling good. Today, she thought, has to be one of the finer works of creation.

Then she saw it, through the sink window — a familiar blue Cadillac.

"Oh, God," Aunt Ann muttered and stared down at her plump bare feet and the old housedress she had on, now slopped with suds. Too late to change. "Oh, damn."

On inspiration, she fished around under the sink. By the time the doorbell rang and Eleanor's voice called out, "Hello? Aunt Ann?" Aunt Ann was as presentable as possible in a pair of knee-high stockings she'd thrown out the day before and crocheted bedroom slippers she'd found in a ball in an apron pocket. She had not yet pinned her hair down, the front of her was damp, and as she hustled to the front door, her whole huge form moved a little more freely than she would have liked.

"Figures," she muttered. "Lord, God, good morning, Eleanor!"

"Good morning, Aunt Ann." Eleanor saw everything about Aunt Ann, and her look was enough. "Is Aunt Bea up?"

Aunt Ann clasped her hands in front of her, more or less to stop the jiggle. "Yes, Eleanor, by this time I shouldn't think."

Eleanor Hebert frowned. Once again she looked Aunt Ann over from top to toe. She herself was beautifully dressed in a pink suit with shoes to match. "Aunt Ann, you should always look in on her. You know she's a sick old woman."

"Not that sick." Aunt Ann forgot herself. "Not strong, maybe, but she knows what she wants." She pounded one damp hand against the other.

"Ann? Is someone there?" Aunt Bea Packard herself appeared anxiously at the head of the stairs.

"If you'll excuse me, Aunt Ann." Avoiding Aunt Ann's wet wide girth, Eleanor slipped past her and up the stairs. "Why, look at you, Aunt Bea," she said brightly. "Up and dressed, all by yourself."

Aunt Bea regarded her niece. "Oh, yes," said the frail old woman in cultured tones. "Wasn't I clever?"

Below them Aunt Ann snorted, but Eleanor Hebert never even paused. "Aunt Bea," she murmured, "let me help you back to your room and you can sit down. We'll have some breakfast and a nice talk."

At the foot of the stairs Aunt Ann heaved a sigh upward. Aunt Bea Packard turned. Utterly thin, frail as a dry leaf, and moving as if she were balancing her head carefully on her delicate old neck, she glanced down at Aunt Ann and one eyelid drooped in a handsome, old-fashioned wink. "I'll have the usual, Ann," the old woman said.

"Right," said Aunt Ann. Snickering a little, she went back to the kitchen.

"The usual," she'd learned, was a two-minute egg and a pot of English Breakfast tea. Aunt Ann liked to dress it up a little. This morning she added a slice of cantaloupe with a tiny bowl of honey set strategically by it, and a piece of coffee cake she'd made herself, high and delicate with many beaten eggs, laced with swirls of cinnamon, brown and twinkling with sugar on the top. Aunt Ann believed that every meal should be an event and she saw to it that it was.

As she set up the tray, however, she did worry just a little. What if Eleanor Hebert still wanted to get rid of her? When Aunt Bea had gotten out of the hospital Eleanor had wanted to hire a nurse for her, somebody, doubtless, just like Eleanor herself. Efficient. Slim.

But Aunt Bea had had her way. They'd done pretty well since.

Aunt Ann cut herself a piece of coffee cake, ate it, and then cut another, swallowing it down as one might swallow a pill, in one gulp, before she headed up the stairs.

She didn't mean to listen as she headed across the hall to Aunt Bea's room. But she couldn't help hear Eleanor say, "We'll have to tell Aunt Ann, of course. She may not be happy."

"Just so long as you realize, Eleanor, I must have final say," Aunt Ann heard Aunt Bea reply.

"Of course, of course." That was Eleanor's smoothest voice. How smooth it could be when she wanted something!

Out in the hallway Aunt Ann scowled. She grasped the tray tightly and strode into the bedroom, setting it with a noise at the table in front of the window, where Aunt Bea usually took her breakfast.

Aunt Bea lifted the cloth and said, "Oh, Ann, it looks good."

Aunt Ann sniffed, but she felt a little better. "Thank you, Bea."

Eleanor Hebert recrossed her ankles. "Aunt Ann, I'm glad you're here. We've been discussing —"

"I would like to point out," Aunt Ann said firmly, "that eating is more important than stockings, and I'm sorry my dress is wet, and I don't intend to leave this house unless Aunt Bea asks me to."

"Leave?" Aunt Bea Packard set down her spoon. Her old lips trembled. "Oh, Ann," she said. "You're not planning to leave?"

"Well," said Aunt Ann, "I dunno."

"No, no," Eleanor said. "Nobody wants you to leave, Aunt Ann. You're doing a fine job. We all think so."

Aunt Ann's jaw dropped. "You do?"

"Yes. Of course."

"Oh," said Aunt Ann. "Well, that's all right then. Thank you."

"You're welcome," said Eleanor. "Thank *you*. What I was telling Aunt Bea was that I've finally found a man to be the director of our Freedom chorus. He has an excellent reputation in the Portland area. He's really the best we can find. We have to have the best."

"That sounds like you, Eleanor," said Aunt Bea. She smiled faintly and opened her egg.

Aunt Ann watched. The egg was hot, the white solid but tender, the yolk warm and deep yellow and runny. Just as Aunt Bea liked it. Watching Aunt Bea eat, Aunt Ann almost began to feel a little hungry herself.

"You may say so, Aunt Bea," said Eleanor, "but you have to admit it's worked so far."

"The best? Of course, dear. Now tell Aunt Ann what you told me. You'll like this, Ann." Aunt Bea began on the coffee cake. Aunt Ann's mouth watered. She did like to watch someone having a good meal.

"Well," Eleanor said, "his name is Professor Jonah Sears. He's in his early forties, pleasant. I asked him what his price was."

"You didn't," said Aunt Bea. "Eleanor."

"I didn't say it in those words," said Eleanor. "For the Freedom chorus. He understood."

"Ah. But tell Aunt Ann what else."

"He said," Eleanor went on, "that what he really wanted was a quiet place in the country where he could work on his doctoral dissertation."

"Doctoral dissertation, Ann. Think of that," said Aunt Bea in a hushed voice.

"So I thought," Eleanor said, "that the professor might like to stay here this summer."

Aunt Ann had been ready to encourage Aunt Bea to use all the cream in her tea. Now she paused and looked at Eleanor. "Here?"

"Here, Ann. Isn't it perfectly exciting?" Aunt Bea hesitated. "But you must think it over carefully."

"He might sleep in the west wing, we thought," Eleanor said. "Close to the lake. He'd have his own entrance. He could get his own meals if you like. You wouldn't have to cook for him." Her glance flickered up at Aunt Ann and then down, quickly, to hide this masterstroke.

"Cook?" Aunt Ann blinked. "Cook for him? Oh. Well. I could cook for him. Far as that goes. No problem there."

"I didn't think there would be," said Eleanor.

"Course," said Aunt Ann, "we'd have to do out the west wing."

"Too much work, I knew it." Aunt Bea shook her head.

"Hell, no, that'd be easy." Aunt Ann frowned. She clasped her hands at her waist. "But how do we know what sort of person he is, Bea? Does he drink? Go to parties? Eleanor, I won't have a drinker around, not since my Roger." She stared straight ahead of her so as not to remember him.

Eleanor Hebert smoothed the air with one hand. "What Professor Sears wants is quiet," she said. "I thought we might even offer him two summers, this one and the next, in return for his work with the Freedom chorus. But I told him he would have to come out and see the house and meet you, and that you would have to get to know —"

"Blueberry slump," said Aunt Ann. "Haven't made that for years. You know what men like, Bea? A good beef pie. Egg salad with bits of bacon in it. There's plenty to cook, God knows. Crabmeat salad when it's hot, Bea, doesn't that sound good? A nice chocolate cake."

"He is a musician," Aunt Bea said again.

"We'll have to like him, o' course," said Aunt Ann.

Eleanor stood up. As she did, her pink skirt smoothed itself flawlessly. Aunt Ann felt some envy.

"Good, then," Eleanor said. "I'll bring him out, introduce him to the search committee and to you, and see where we go from there. I'll feel safer about you if there's a man on the place, anyway. In case of emergency."

Aunt Ann's head came up. "There aren't going to be any emergencies, Eleanor."

"No, no, of course not, Aunt Ann."

"Eleanor," said Aunt Bea suddenly, "is June on the search committee?"

"You know she is."

"What does she think of Professor Sears?"

"Well, I haven't had a chance to ask her yet."

"You mean," said the old lady, "that you thought of it, you went to him, and you came to me first? I think you'd better tell June before the rest of the committee, don't you?"

"Aunt Bea, it's not my fault if June's sometimes resentful."

The old lady smiled. "You present such an example," she said gently.

"Now, Aunt Bea." Eleanor shrugged. "Aunt Ann, I've got to run." At the door she paused. "I'll tell June ahead of time if you want me to, Aunt Bea. I do hope everything works out and you like Professor Sears."

"Without him, Eleanor," asked the old woman, "what will you have?"

Eleanor stared at her. "Without him? A whole town waiting for me to do something, I guess. Why me? I don't even know." She shook her head and for a moment looked tired. Then she was gone.

The west wing contained a sitting room and a music room on the first floor, a bedroom, bathroom and tiny study on the second. The front rooms, the sitting room down and the bedroom up, had windows on three sides. Aunt Ann washed these. She washed the curtains, too, and cleaned the Oriental rugs, beat the cushions, stripped the bed to the bone, and started over again, washing all the bedding, drying it outdoors, and putting it back on the bed again. It took her a week to do out the whole wing, but she had the time and she was fussy. The last thing she did was to sweep the entry.

Aunt Ann liked to sweep. She liked the feel of the broom; she liked to see the dirt collect. Sometimes, these days, she felt that she worked to no particular effect when she cleaned, chasing phantom dust created by two old women with no messy habits. Now that Aunt Bea had begun to get better, there were large spaces in the house that waited for running feet, Aunt Ann felt, laughing or crying, or maybe just the slamming open of a door and a nice rattle of wind to stir the curtains or lift the corner of a tablecloth a little. Sweeping made some activity, and she swept with energy, gathering the entry's meager dirt near the screened door that opened onto the back lawn and the lake. When she finished, she discovered she'd forgotten the dustpan — vacuum cleaner training, she supposed. For a minute she stood debating; the kitchen was some steps away. Then she smiled, a cute puckery smile in a damp, plump face, and her little round eyes gleamed with mischief.

She opened the screen door, blocked it open, and in one satisfying flurry swept the accumulated pile of dust out over the granite steps and onto the grass. With experienced movements she gathered up all the remainders — what she called the "skrits" of it — into her broom straw and swept that out, too. Then she stepped outside and swept the grass. There, all done. When that man came and started tracking sand in from the beach, it would be a joy just to sweep it right back out again. She guessed he wouldn't care if she used a broom; men never did.

Professor Jonah Sears. He'd met with the music committee and they'd liked him, and today the Hebert sisters would bring him out here. Aunt Ann thought she knew how he would look. She'd seen those college people down to Portland: so young, busy and fast-walking. Hair like haymows, some of them. She and Aunt Bea would probably have some adjusting to do: these intellectual musicians. She hoped he would be thin. If so, that was good; she would fatten him up. She hoped he wasn't finicky about food, she couldn't stand that. And although she'd put up with tobacco and burnt-out matches and ashes, if there was anything she couldn't abide, it was the smell of liquor, not to mention the empty cans and bottles, the dirty glasses.

Aunt Ann remembered her Roger — no. She would not remember him.

Now she went to the piano room just to check, but everything was in order. She had cleaned the piano keys with milk and mild soapsuds, rinsing them carefully, and they shone with a fine old luster. Aunt Bea had watched her do it and smiled happily. "Ann, you are my good angel."

"I guess they come in all sizes," Aunt Ann had replied.

Today, because of the strenuous afternoon to come, they'd agreed that Aunt Bea would rest until lunch. Then she would be ready for the afternoon onslaught. "We're going to need our wits about us to size up this fellow," they had told each other. "We could be getting a bad bargain here. These modern musicians."

They hoped they were wrong. "He is a college professor," they said, as if that would make all the difference.

Aunt Ann went up to check on Aunt Bea, to see if she needed anything or was ready for her lunch. Aunt Bea's room was painted a light shade of peach. Apricot rose, she called it, and unlike many of the other bedrooms, which were filled with big mahogany furniture, here the furniture was on a smaller scale, of simple wood, painted white. At this time of day, shaded from the sun, the room took on a cool delicacy — just where a butterfly might rest, or so Aunt Ann thought. She found Aunt Bea up, dressed in a white slip and stockings, and going through her closet with small, mothlike fluttering gestures.

"Oh, Ann," the old woman sighed when Aunt Ann came in, "I don't have a thing to wear."

Aunt Ann looked from Aunt Bea, all straight small bones and unrelieved angles, to the big closet filled with dresses and suits of every color.

"Then don't wear a thing," she said.

"Ann!" Aunt Bea stopped short. Her eyes were big and blue and anxious — too anxious, Aunt Ann saw, even to smile. "Now you help me!"

Aunt Ann knew how she felt; she herself had been thinking about this matter since very early morning.

"All right, Bea," she said. "Let's look. I'm fond of blue, myself. Nice quiet color. You never know about these college people."

Aunt Ann searched out a dress she knew was one of Aunt Bea's favorites. "Blue says, 'I'm goin' to consider all the angles, and I'm goin' to be calm.' "

Aunt Bea was plainly in no condition to consider anything calmly. She wrung her hands. "Do you think — will he play the piano for us, Ann?"

"Well, if he doesn't I'll break his arm."

"Ann!"

"Bea, we've got to be calm, we have to be careful. I, for one, intend to be mighty stately."

"Stately?" It was a word Aunt Bea seemed to like. "Stately?" She held still to consider it while Aunt Ann helped her with her dress, her thin arms reaching, then falling from the effort.

"Yes, indeed," said Aunt Ann, helping her to sit at a little white vanity table. "You know men, Bea. Nice looking on the outside, but inside they're a bundle of problems."

Aunt Bea considered this. "You may be right, Ann."

But then she clapped both hands onto the top of her head. "Oh, oh, my hair is a mess!"

"Now, your hair is just fine," said Aunt Ann comfortingly. "You sit here and run a brush through it. My Lord, Bea, I don't envy you anything but that hair." It was a fine silver-white and sprang back from Aunt Bea's forehead in soft waves so orderly they might have been drawn.

"Ann, you are too good."

Aunt Ann was staring at herself in the mirror with some dismay. "You know what I've got?" She sighed. "One of those faces in a kid's funny book. Put me upside down, I'd still look like I was smiling."

"Why, that's foolish, Ann," said Aunt Bea. "I won't hear it. You are a handsome woman."

"You think so, Bea?"

"Of course." The two old women looked at each other in the mirror and at once began to smile. "We are a pair, aren't we?" said Aunt Bea at last. "What's for lunch, Ann?"

"Chicken salad," Aunt Ann said promptly. "I put in a bit of basil and some chives. Summer squash Kelly brought me from the garden, some carrot bread."

"I'll have it downstairs, I think."

"Oh, Bea, do you think you should?"

"Now, don't fuss, Ann."

"Wouldn't think of it, my dear."

"Oh, Ann, aren't you just a little nervous about this?"

"Not so you'd notice, Bea. Course the tea's had mint in it since seven o'clock this morning, and I did do a bit of baking — butter cookies —"

"Well, that should be —"

"Cupcakes with chocolate bits in them. Some lemon squares."

"Oh, Ann."

"I couldn't help myself, Bea."

"Well, it's all right."

"Have to be, I guess."

Aunt Bea had her lunch in the small dining room, from a tray. Aunt Ann ate a little of this and a little of that, just to keep Bea company. Food was better, she knew, if people ate together. Then Aunt Bea went to the piano room to check through her sheet music, in case there might be something that a professor at a university might like to play. Aunt Ann went to her own room to get dressed.

Her clothes had been laid out since sunrise: a dress with big pink roses on it and what she called a Merry Widow, a foundation garment that held her in from armpit to thigh. She had new stockings, as well, and her best pair of low-heeled shoes.

But the dress zipped up the back, which was a nuisance, and while she strained to reach the zipper she felt the knee in her left stocking give way.

"Oh, damn." Aunt Ann frowned as she spotted it, a big, ugly white run. "Damn and hell."

Her top bureau drawer was full of stockings. She found one that matched and was whole and slid it on, fastening it fore and aft to the garters on the Merry Widow. Then she ran a brush through her wiry gray hair and pushed bobby pins into it wherever it seemed to stick out.

"There," she muttered, "you're ready."

"Handsome?" she added. "Bea must be dreaming."

Tall, thin, bent, some blond hair about his ears but cut short and combed, dark eyes in sockets etched with fine lines, a lightweight shirt, a pair of slacks — Ann, running to the front door, nearly mowed the man down in an effort to get to the professor. She slammed into him at full speed, then stopped. He bounced on impact and stood looking, if anything, puzzled.

"I'm sorry." Aunt Ann blushed. "I heard the bell and I was looking for the —" Slowly her eyes took him in. Beside him stood Eleanor and June, identically distressed.

"Aunt Ann," Eleanor said quickly, "may I introduce Professor Sears?"

Aunt Ann was flustered. She could think of nothing to say. She held out her plump hand.

"Please, do call me Jonah." Courteously, the man took the hand she offered. There was faint surprise in his voice. He spoke with unexpected precision, a man accustomed to think and act carefully. This flustered Aunt Ann still further.

"Fancy bumping into you," she burbled, huge and shiny-faced. "Please, call me Aunt Ann, when you recover. Everybody does."

"I should be happy to," he replied and smiled at her, enjoying something. He had a nice face. Once again Aunt Ann found herself unable to speak.

"Aunt Ann, do bring everyone into the parlor, please." It was Aunt Bea Packard, speaking gently from the doorway. "We will be able to greet each other in comfort. Professor Sears, how do you do? I'm so very happy to meet you. Please, do come this way, Aunt Ann."

This was an Aunt Bea Packard Aunt Ann had not seen before. Utterly at ease, the old woman led the way into the parlor and seated her guests. Like royalty, Aunt Ann thought.

"And how was your drive from the city, Professor?" Aunt Bea asked, now enthroned like an aged queen in her accustomed corner of the parlor sofa.

"Well, it's a lovely road, Mrs. Packard. The countryside is beautiful, and there are many wonderful farms in this area. I must say, this house took me by surprise. All week long people from Freedom have been referring to it as 'the Cottage,' and I thought it was a small home." He laughed. A good laugh.

Aunt Bea nodded, smiling. "I know what you mean."

So, Aunt Ann thought, this is Bea Packard, too.

Aunt Ann did not sit. Instead, as the talk continued, she escaped to the kitchen, where with awful surmise she realized she'd forgotten to zip up the last four inches of her dress. She struggled, zipped, spoke to the lemon squares set in neat rows on her counter. "I don't know," she muttered. "I just don't know."

She allowed two of the squares to slide down her throat since there were plenty. Taking a deep breath, she went back into the parlor to sit.

Professor Sears was speaking, and after all he did seem like a nice man. Kind of ordinary, quiet. Smart, too.

"I'm not sure that Freedom should base its whole celebration on a competition of singers, Mrs. Hebert," he was saying to Eleanor. "An observance of the Fourth should be a town matter, perhaps?"

"But you understand, Professor Sears, that there is some competition for the tourist trade in Maine, and that Freedom can put its best foot forward if its celebration has its own appeal," Eleanor Hebert said. "Of course, the possibility of television coverage for the town is really invaluable publicity —"

"And can be put to all kinds of uses," June Hebert broke in, regarding her sister somewhat cryptically. "If we could all work together to figure out those uses."

"Of course I do understand," said the professor. He smiled at Aunt Bea. "I'll do my best with the chorus. But you know, an accident — lost music, a bad night, somebody gets sick — and that's that."

"Perhaps," murmured Aunt Bea, "Professor Sears would like to lead a chorus but not feel responsible for a whole town."

"Just so." The man nodded. "Of course, if the singers do turn out to be winners, it will be a happy addition to the festivities."

"You know that some of us don't read music," said June Hebert. "Still, there are a lot of talented people in the town."

The professor nodded. "I grew up in a small town in Pennsylvania. My father led a chorus of thirty voices. None of those people could read a note. But it's amazing what a group can do if it's of one mind about something. Dad's group became good enough eventually to give a concert or two in Philly."

"You do understand then," said June Hebert.

The professor smiled again.

It was a nice smile. Aunt Ann began to like him. His face was thin, the forehead broad, the lips mobile. The eyes in their deep sockets were dark and understanding. Not much gets by him, she thought.

"Perhaps we should show you the west wing," said Aunt Bea. "You can see if you might be comfortable. I imagine it will be a change for you, to live in a small town out in the country, after the city."

"Oh, but the truth is, Mrs. Packard —"

"Aunt Bea, please. The whole town calls me that."

He bowed. "Thank you. The truth is that in the five years I've been in New England, every time I've driven through a town like Freedom I've wished I lived there. There's something magnetic about small towns."

"A fine compliment." Aunt Bea rose and everyone else did, too. The professor politely offered her his arm and she took it. "Thank you. The west wing is this way."

As they all began to move, it occurred to Aunt Ann that there was one subject that had to be explored. She would have to have it straight out. "I don't like liquor bottles on the good furniture," she announced.

"Ann." A shocked whisper from Aunt Bea, close to a reproof, but Aunt Ann could see a tiny demon of mischief in her eyes.

Professor Jonah Sears paused, blinked. "Excuse me?"

"Aunt Ann is taking care of the house for Aunt Bea," Eleanor Hebert hurried to explain. "She is, as you can see, quite . . . fussy."

"It's just that he looks nice and quiet and bright," said Aunt Ann. "I might like him. I think I do. But if he's going to drink —" She stared straight ahead of her.

"Oh, not at all," Jonah Sears said. "I'm not a habitual drinker, Miss Packard. Did you think that?"

Eleanor Hebert was flustered. "But I never said —"

"Well, what about parties, then?" Aunt Ann wanted to say "wild" parties, but she felt even she had to stop somewhere.

The professor seemed to understand. "No, no, Aunt Ann. I am a quiet man. I assure you, all I want is peace and quiet and a chance to work." He looked her in the eye.

After all, he didn't think she was being funny or strange. "Well, that's all right then," Aunt Ann said, relieved. She wondered if he'd eat noodles amandine. "I'm sorry."

"Not at all," he said. "These things are important."

"Well." Aunt Bea smiled. "Shall we?"

He was obviously unprepared for what he found in the west wing. "It just shines," he said softly.

It did. Every bit of furniture had been polished, as Aunt Ann well knew. The fine wool rugs gleamed with a soft clean luster that satisfied her.

The professor said, "When I asked for a quiet place, I never dreamed it would look like this."

They moved from the wing's living room to the room where the baby grand piano stood. Aunt Ann had opened it reverently. To one side was a small sofa and some comfortable chairs. Like the conservatory in the east wing, the piano room was round, its shelves lined with books.

"Oh, my," the professor said. "Oh, my. Here, look at this. Are all these rooms for me?"

"If it will do," said Aunt Bea. The old woman trembled a little. "If you thought you might be comfortable."

"Comfortable." He helped her to the sofa and then moved — on tiptoe, Aunt Ann thought — around the room and back to the piano. His face was alight. "I'm overwhelmed," he said. "The piano. The rooms. It's all just beautiful."

"Please, would you play?" There was a childlike hitch in Aunt Bea Packard's voice.

"Well —" But he couldn't help himself, they saw. He sat down and touched the keys. Piano notes began to fill the room. He played something soft and rippling. Aunt Ann saw Aunt Bea's hands close themselves together in a little cup.

"That was lovely." It was Eleanor Hebert who spoke when he finished.

"Yes," said Aunt Bea. "Yes. In the piano bench is music if you thought you might play something else."

Seeing that this was a way to please her, he stood up at once and opened the bench. "Debussy?" he said.

Aunt Bea flushed. "Do you know, when August and I first knew each other, that was still a new kind of music."

"A wonderful kind," he said. "I don't know, I could try."

If there were mistakes, Aunt Ann couldn't hear them, but old Aunt Bea sat very still, frowning with concentration.

"This is a wonderful instrument," the professor said when he finished. He stared at them as if he still didn't believe it.

"I'm sorry, I think there's one note that is not quite right," said Aunt Bea. "It's been some time since anyone played."

"Yes, the B, I think. It's nothing. A small adjustment." He played the note.

"We shall have to have it tuned," said Aunt Bea. "That is, if —" She shot a quick glance at Aunt Ann, who raised her eyebrows cautiously.

"So you are a pianist, too, Mr. Sears?" Eleanor Hebert said.

"Yes, I teach piano as well as voice and chorus. A little bit of everything."

Aunt Bea sat still as a flower. "You know, Professor, Aunt Ann has made a number of good things to eat, if you will join us."

"Jonah, please," he said. "I would be happy to."

Aunt Ann brought in first one and then another heavily laden tray of food.

Eleanor Hebert stared at the array. "Aunt Ann, so much?"

"It won't go to waste." Abruptly, Aunt Ann began to serve.

It was surprising how much everyone did manage to eat. This Jonah Sears had a good appetite on him for a skinny man, Aunt Ann thought.

"These lemon squares are food for the gods," he said, a touch of helplessness in his voice, and bit into his fourth. Aunt Ann was counting; her old heart was no longer her own and she knew it.

"Well, there," she said. "There, Jonah."

It became like a party. Eleanor and June forgot themselves and ate as if everything tasted good, which it did. Aunt Ann thought she had a glimpse of the sisters as they must have been when they were younger, laughing as they indulged themselves. She even saw Eleanor Hebert lick a bit of lemon filling from her fingers. Everybody talked, the professor asking many questions about the house — how it had been when it was full of people, about the relatives for whom the west wing's private entrance had been built.

"He didn't want the whole family to see his skin, or his bathing suit," Eleanor explained, laughing. "That was Uncle Jamie for you."

It was some time before she remembered to look at her watch. "Good heavens, June, it's after three. We must decide." She looked from the professor to Aunt Bea.

"If you'll excuse us for a moment" — Aunt Bea rose — "Aunt Ann and I will have a word together."

On Aunt Ann's arm she moved out of the room. Just beyond the closed door, the two old women looked at each other for one instant and then began to laugh in a quiet twitter.

"I think he'll do," said Aunt Ann. "He's got a good appetite on him. What do you think?"

"I think he's a lovely man." Aunt Bea's hands trembled. "The piano — Ann, I used to play it. And Vinnie, you should have seen how her fingers flew. Oh, I do miss that! Ann, let's risk it."

"I think we might," said Aunt Ann slowly, "if he's willing."

"You don't think he will be?" A shadow on the older woman's face.

"Course he will," said Aunt Ann hastily. "You can tell. He liked everything. But perhaps it's best not to let everyone know how eager we are."

"Ah, I see. Quite right, Ann. Keep the upper hand?"

"Right."

"Well, then." Solemnly they moved back into the music room and to Jonah Sears, who rose. Aunt Bea held out her hand. "Professor Sears, Jonah, if you would like to visit us and try the west wing," she said with old-fashioned formality, "we shall be most happy to have you."

It was a dignified moment. "You are both very kind." He took Aunt Bea's thin old hand and bowed slightly over it, seeing and acknowledging a ceremony. "Thank you very much, I feel fortunate. I am happy to accept."

Aunt Bea glanced at Aunt Ann, one quick delighted glance.

A week later Jonah Sears moved in, and gradually the aunts got acquainted with him. They learned that his real name was John Sears, but that his students had long ago nicknamed him Jonah, because he spent so much time in agony, they said, teaching them various pieces of music he thought they should learn. One day soon after he got settled, Aunt Bea called a piano tuner, and the professor hung over the man while he worked, watching him carefully as he replaced one of the three wire strings that made up the B note. Jonah questioned the man when he brought out his electronic machine to test the pitch and was only satisfied when the tuning fork came out as well.

"The celestial choir," he told Aunt Bea. "You must hear it, and I think he does."

"The celestial choir?" Aunt Ann said later to Aunt Bea.

"When you play a third, you should hear the fifth note in the harmony," explained Aunt Bea.

"You mean, when it's not being played?"

Aunt Bea smiled. "Yes, you use two fingers to play the third, but if you listen carefully, you'll hear another note implied in the sound of those two. It's not being struck by human hands, but it's there. Crystal clear, if you know what to listen for. That's called the celestial choir."

"Aunt Bea Packard," Aunt Ann demanded, "are you joking?"

"No, not at all. The tuning fork and the celestial choir were ways of tuning the piano long before electronic equipment came into use."

"Well, for heaven's sake. Can you really hear it? Something that's not there?"

"I can, sometimes, if I listen hard. Jonah can probably hear it always, and if a tuner hears it these days, well, so much the better."

Luckily, it was clear from the start that Jonah would not do his own cooking.

"Aunt Ann has a way with vegetables," he would murmur. His favorite, Aunt Ann soon learned, was fresh leaf lettuce, which he ate with her delicate homemade dressing of oil and vinegar and herbs.

But he was amused to find Aunt Ann eating the same lettuce in the kitchen one day without the dressing but with a sprinkling of sugar instead.

"Eat my tomatoes that way, too," she told him by way of apology. "Grew up in the country. We never had much, but when new things came into the garden, they always seemed better than dessert, and we ate them like dessert. You know how I fix new peas?"

He shook his head.

"I get them when they're tiny and shell them just before supper. Then I cook them in a little water until they're tender. I drain them and add cream and butter — the real thing, mind you — and just a little sprinkle of sugar. Jonah, you never tasted anything so good in your life."

"You know," he told her, smiling, "I think I'd forgotten how many good things there are to eat."

"Go ahead." Aunt Ann prodded him. "Try a little tiny bit of sugar on the lettuce."

In the end he couldn't do it.

Finally Aunt Ann gave up. "Course," she said philosophically, "I guess you got to grow up with it."

She gave him supper. "Supper," he said once. "The word has a nice sound."

He would leave his desk piled high with books and papers. "My dissertation." He would laugh, a bit hollowly, then come and eat and feel better, she could tell.

After a day or two, he insisted that she not set a place for him in the dining room. He would take his meals out on the back porch beside the kitchen, just take his plate and go out and "set," as Aunt Ann said it. She couldn't blame him; it was a fine place. From the kitchen would come the good smell of the meal, and across the darkening lawn, the sweet smell of the night.

Aunt Ann ate by fits and starts as always, just a bit at a time so as to be light on her feet. As time went on, the professor seemed to find it easy to talk to her. As for her, she thought he was immensely clever just because he was there and because she knew he would eat.

She thought it was awful hard work he did every day, bent over his desk for hours, a pencil between his fingers or his typewriter going *clickety-clackety*. He didn't seem to have much fun. She was curious about him but tried not to ask too many questions. One thing he liked to talk about, and that was teaching. He would tell her about his students, and about some of the things he told them.

"Some of you will have excellent voices, that's what I say," he told her one night. "Some of you will be good sight readers. You will learn from each other — the singers from the readers, the readers from the singers. And all of you will learn to count time, or heaven help you." He laughed.

Aunt Ann thought this was an excellent lecture and repeated it word for word to Aunt Bea the next morning. Aunt Bea decided to join them for supper after that; she'd been eating, by custom, in her room. So on warm nights it was the three of them taking their meal on the back porch, or on rainy nights in the small dining room off the pantry. There was a larger dining room, but it hadn't been used for years.

Their meals were wonderfully pleasant. The aunts knew how much the professor was struggling every day over his typewriter. They hoped he would win. Meanwhile, as Aunt Ann told Aunt Bea, "just to hear him talk!" It brought a whole new world to both old ladies — the world of young people, the university, music.

"I say something else, too," Jonah admitted to them one night.

Aunt Bea laughed, delighted. "You must tell us what it is right away," she said. "Let us think about it."

"Well," he said slowly, "I tell them we're here to make music and nothing else. I tell them they have to sing together, without jealousy in the parts, without competition among the singers. Without competition." He looked at the aunts, his hair gleaming with silver-blond glints in the light, his eyes in their dark sockets lonely somehow.

There was a short silence. Across the grass came a drift of wind, the smell of pine and of the water beyond it. After a moment Aunt Ann saw Aunt Bea nod, satisfied. Suddenly Aunt Ann herself felt very good.

"Jonah," she said, using his first name comfortably at last, "I know two old ladies who are glad you're here."

CHAPTER THREE

MADDY REMEMBERED SWINGING up the church steps hanging on to his thick fingers. She remembered the rhythm of it — one, two, and up! She would fly into the air and land, laughing, on the top step. People smiled as he swung her.

"Cute," the ladies would say. "Isn't that adorable?"

Back then the two of them, the four-year-old girl and the full-grown man her father, had been a team, two against the world. He had liked her in those moments, and because he had, she'd known in her upright little child's soul, she would participate in any show he wanted to make. "Daddy!" she would cry in a voice full of laughter, like a challenge to the world. "Daddy!"

Smiling at the ladies they would swing inside, then walk quietly into the shadow of the church vestry. It was all a show; he knew it and she knew it. But it was a blessed show, one you wanted to believe in. At a glance from him she would be utterly quiet; he would pretend to remind her lovingly, and she, lovingly, to obey. They would pretend so hard she almost believed it, going up the stairs to the sanctuary. In church she would hear music and think she had come to some new place, some safe place.

"Remember that, remember it," Maddy told herself now.

Because memory could trick you. At once she was lost again, another dark summer day, afternoon. She was again four years old, this time standing on the sofa in the living room wearing nothing at all but a little slip. Her mother, thin and tense, sat beside her. Her father came into the room and lifted her until her head touched the ceiling — how she had crowed! A creature of opportunity then, eager to laugh at any happy time. This was a wonderful joke, to be up so high. Maddy Dow, the tallest person in the world. He laughed, too; so did her mother. They were all laughing.

He swooped her down and laid her across his knees while he sat beside her mother. Maddy's head, with its mop of dark curls, sagged toward the floor. She felt the roughness of the material of his pants against her cheek; she hung on, still laughing, looking at the world from a funny perspective, upside down. Cool air moved against the back of her, her bare legs, bare bottom. Any minute, she thought, he would haul her upright again.

Instead she felt his hand crack against her bottom.

She drew in breath, too surprised to do anything but continue to laugh, and heard him laugh, too. Sure enough, there was even a little laugh from her mother. He would haul her up now.

Instead he held her there. She heard him say, "Did that hurt?"

"No," she cried happily, squirming a little. His hand fell again.

"Did that hurt?" He laughed.

"No," she cried.

"Jack," said Vinnie Dow, "you're making her all red."

More slaps came, each harder. "Did that hurt?" he asked.

"No! No!" Maddy cried stubbornly.

"Jack, that's enough."

"Look at her." Maddy's father's voice boomed like bass notes. "She says it doesn't hurt. She thinks it's a joke."

"Jack, please." She was torn off her father's lap by her mother. Her bottom and legs were sore, but she kept a smile on her face to match his.

"Some joke, eh?" he said. "Some joke?" He lifted her up and tossed her onto the sofa. "You liked that joke, did you?"

Maddy stood on the sofa grinning at him, and all the while she was so very sore.

Remember. Don't remember.

Maddy sat half hidden from the house, out of sight of it, perhaps, but not out of earshot. Inside, her mother was trying with crippled fingers to play a Mozart sonata, the allegro. Maddy knew how her mother would look, her face determined, the fingers of the crippled right hand doing their best to keep up with the fingers of the good left hand. Soon her mother would give it up, and when she did, there would be on her face the tightness of pure despair.

It was too hard to watch, so Maddy hid, but she didn't cover her ears. The peculiar thing was that sometimes, in spite of the crippled fingers, Maddy would hear something in her mother's mismatched notes that was unexpected, a kind of better music than what was actually played. Tiny revelations; she tried to remember them.

From a pocket of her summer dress she took a little notebook and flipped to a page that was not completely covered already with lines of musical notation and quickly drew in a staff and bass clef. As if hurtling them onto the page, she wrote what she had for the last few days been trying to remember and which her mother's playing had now renewed: a kind of hitched-upward bass line — dotted eighths, two measures.

She stared at the notes, then sighed. While the Mozart continued, she flipped through the notebook. It was a tiny booklet and fit into the palm of her hand. Anything larger might have been found, and that was too risky. Each page had a crisp feel and was full of notes written hard into the paper, indented with feeling, so that even if you were blind, Maddy thought, you might be able to read them.

As she flipped through the little pages, it occurred to her that they were full of disconnected phrases, too heavy with beginnings and endings, unrelated bits that she collected for no particular reason. Back in the living room, carefully hidden among a neglected pile of sheet music in a small old maple cabinet next to the piano, were other tiny pages full of similar notations.

It was a convenient place to keep them, next to the piano. And although the children's own rooms underwent daily inspection for a neatness in which nothing could be hidden, this cabinet with its little doors, always in view, seemed to hide nothing useful. Their father thought he knew what was in it, as he knew about every other cranny in house and garage: pieces for four hands, or symphonies for eight hands, four separate copies for each one — useless now to his crippled wife. The cabinet stayed closed; he never bothered to look inside. Its presence was enough.

Only Maddy knew that amid the fifty-year-old crumbling pages in that dark little place was something else. Something new. She spoke of this to no one; it wasn't safe.

I should get them all out, she thought. I should see if I've made any progress. Somewhere in her head, although she did not admit it to herself, was the idea that these little scratchings and scrawlings were worth saving, or could be.

Now, carefully, she tucked the notebook away again, buttoning it into a pocket. She stared off down the road, listening to discords.

Music was her mother's one connection to her own childhood, the one thing that, though crippled, had not entirely atrophied. Even though the notes she played stumbled and fell together in strange combinations, there were sounds in it that you did not expect among discords. Vinnie Dow was a thin woman, eyes quieted to a kind of nonexpectant look. Hair once blond was now the color of faded leaves, eyes once blue were now no color in particular. Vinnie Dow expected the world to be hard, and that showed in her eyes, too. Sometimes she seemed to Maddy like a refugee, her expectations dulled or endlessly denied. On the other hand, there was in her a flicker of light whenever she laid her twisted hand on the piano keys.

It was this light Maddy shared with her mother, surpassed her in, maybe — a gleam of something that had been lost and could only be found again in isolated moments. Something that could not be described, beauty beyond reach. A wonderful light that called to Maddy and that she needed to translate into real sound.

When she was a small child, it had called her so loudly that time after time she had found herself at the piano, trying to play, trying something so much more complicated than her fingers were able to do. She'd known her notes very early from flashcards her mother had made for her. Sometimes she would sit and lay her fingers gently on this note, on that one, trying to find something she had never heard but only felt, flowing like some mountain river, deep, clear, and refreshing.

Remember.

It must have been afternoon, she thought. The living room was dark.

Seven years old, seated at the piano, she had suddenly become conscious of a dark presence on the sofa. She remembered glancing immediately up at the piano rack: no, it was empty, she was safe. With all the canniness of a small, watchful child she had known that to act frightened would be dangerous, and so for a moment or two longer she had laid her hands against the notes gently, not searching for anything but for diversionary tactics: it was imperative to act like a small child, playing for fun at the piano. At last, carefully, she stopped, and seeing that he wasn't really looking at her, she started to slip away.

"Maddy." His voice was tired. Was there something wrong? Was he hurt in some way? Immediately she almost forgot to be frightened. She could barely see him: it was late afternoon. All she could see was a dark silhouette against shaded windows.

"You don't have to stop playing on my account, Maddy," he said.

It was a quiet voice; was this her real father? Again she tried to see him in the dark but could only catch in the dim windowlight one side of his forehead and temple, the dark hair, the setting of an eye, from which no eye was visible. "Come here," he said in that tired voice. "Maddy, come here to me."

When she heard that voice she wanted only to help, not to be afraid. She crossed the room into the dark, and after a moment she climbed onto his lap. He put his arm around her, and there they sat for a long time.

"I guess you like me," he said, holding her against him. "I guess you do."

If a person could remember just that, nothing else.

At the end of a time in which Maddy felt almost safe, he'd picked her up and carried her out to the kitchen. "What we have here," he'd announced to Maddy's mother, setting her down, "is a nice little girl. An awful nice little girl."

Maddy's mother, big with Phillip at the time, had even thought to smile.

The sounds, Maddy thought now, have to involve that, must somehow tell the good things. But the sounds, if you pursued them, took you also into pain, the bad valley of memory.

Awakened in the morning not long after that — early, early morning, still gray light outside — she was suddenly quite sure all she had to do was to take the proper flashcards and lay them in a long row on the piano. You could put those notes in whatever order you pleased and each new order would make a new song, one of which might be what she looked for, almost heard.

It was an incredibly simple-minded idea, a seven-year-old's idea, but at that age it had made sense. Some tune without notes had been tangled up in her dreams the night before, had played over and over

so sweetly. The next morning it lay before her like a beautiful object suspended in the air, just beyond her grasp.

Jessica, four at the time, lay sound asleep beside her in the bed
they shared. Quietly Maddy got up, padded down the stairs, tried the
living room door. It was not locked. Carefully she opened it and let
herself in. The room was cool in the early morning summer chill.
Outside not a tree leaf moved, inside no stick of furniture creaked.
Soundlessly she went to the little maple cabinet beside the sofa, where
her mother kept big old music books, some with lettering two inches
high, in German. When the cabinet was opened, a fragrance came
from it like the smell of roses. Maddy loved that smell. Quietly she
lifted the top books, and there her little slips of paper lay. She listened. No sound anywhere for the real ear; good, everyone was asleep.
She held her flashcards in her hand for a moment, shut the maple
cabinet carefully.

Then she stood at the piano — at that time she could barely reach
the music rack — and laid the slips upon it, one by one. After a while
she took them off and started over. Looking at the notes, she could
hear their sounds. Later her mother would be surprised and call this
"perfect pitch" and tell Maddy she had "a gift." But Maddy would
know it was something she had because she had to have it, something
learned into existence.

The living room faced east and began, slowly, to turn orange with
sun as she worked. Maddy, standing at the piano in her nightgown,
hardly noticed this. She was staring first at her notes and then at the
piano. Its keys lay before her. At last she touched them because she
couldn't help it, playing only one note, so tiny and far off that she
could barely hear it, but yes, it was good.

Now the black piano keys began to take on corners of yellow with
the rising sun. It seemed to her that she was in some new place,
where everyone was glad there was music. Her father and mother
would be glad, too. He would not be angry; she would not be afraid.
One by one Maddy touched the keys: such soft sounds, from such a
distance.

"What in hell is going on here?"

His voice, when it came, fell upon her, the harshest sudden discord.

Caught — she knew it at once. She whirled, and notes came off
the piano rack in a white shower.

There was her father, pulling on his pants. His face bulged in that familiar, frightening way. Behind him her mother blinked sleepily.

"Jack, what is it?" Vinnie saw Maddy and her face changed. She looked from her child to the notes and she was afraid and guilty — a child could see that.

"Vinnie, what in hell is this kid up to?"

He didn't expect an answer. He went toward her, and Maddy saw only his arms, long and hairy. Long before he got to her, his hand was lifted back for a blow.

She put up her own hands to ward it off, but it caught one of them and cracked it against her cheek. Her face began to burn, she saw that his eyes were red.

"Jack, please." Her mother went across the room, her voice small and without emphasis that might draw too much attention.

"Get away from me, Vinnie!" It was the roar rather than the blow that followed it that made Maddy begin to sob. That roar hurt the ears, cut through the heart.

"Look, Vinnie, the kid's hitting herself!" In a blur, Maddy felt him grab her wrists and force her own hands up to slap her face — first one side, then the other, hard and fast — but it was her father's sudden snicker that made tears flow, that low little laugh like the plucking of loose strings.

"No, Jack." Her mother's face was ashen. She reached out to steady herself against a chair.

Maddy's head was ringing with slaps from her own hands; it wobbled on her neck. Her father dragged her to the kitchen wood stove.

"Look here, you." He dumped a handful of her notes into the ashes left from the night before. At once a tiny flame began to lick across an edge. With a *whoosh* of air her notes caught, blazed. He held her over the stove to watch.

"Now you leave the goddamn piano alone," he said. "Vinnie, don't you let her get all caught up in that stuff. She'll do as I say and not go sneaking around."

He tossed Maddy aside, then left the room to get ready for work. Later, dressed immaculately, he had kissed his wife good-bye, waved at Maddy as if she were his real daughter, picked up his lunchbox and left, like a real father, her real father.

After he went, her mother had touched Maddy's stinging face with lotion, wrapped her in an afghan because she was shaking although it was warm, set her on the sofa, and told her fiercely, "From now on, Maddy, you are not to go near the piano. Is that clear? You are not to touch it."

Maddy stared at her as if she were talking in some foreign language. "You do! You play it, too!"

How pale her mother's eyes were. "I know I do," she said. "But it upsets your father and we'll have to stop. No more piano. No more."

Tears slid, stinging, down Maddy's face. Wearily Vinnie Dow left the room.

In the aftermath haze of pain and crying Maddy went to sleep, but when she woke, later, and stared across at the piano, hearing tunes, hearing notes, something calling to her, her mother was in the room with her. Quietly she set the cover down over the piano keys. "Maddy," she said, "have some breakfast, then run outside to play."

There would be no piano, then?

Outside was nothing. Maddy wandered across the grass and at last went to sit on the side of the dirt road, where she drew useless pictures of stupid people in the sandy gravel. Later she went inside and sat in the house, not saying a word.

"Oh, for heaven's sake, Maddy," her mother cried at last. "What ails you?"

But she knew, Maddy could see that. "Go outside and play," Vinnie said.

Maddy went, looking no worse than she really felt, and sat on the side of the road again. Dust sifted through her fingers, a cascade of sand.

At last her mother called her into the house. "There," she said. "There it is, or as much of it as I can remember. Go ahead. Play."

On the piano was a sheet of handwritten music, simpler than the music in the maple stand, meant for a child.

"It's my first piece. I learned it when I was about your age." Her mother's eyes filled with tears. "But oh, Maddy, be careful. Save your playing for the good times. Promise me."

"I promise."

Nine years ago. When Maddy learned one piece, her mother would write out another from memory, frustrated sometimes because she could not recall it properly. They would never have dreamed of going to a store to buy music; it was too obvious. Jack Dow took care of the household finances and knew where every penny went.

The other children, as they came along, recognized this as a tiny conspiracy. Very often one or the other of them would keep watch for Maddy while she practiced, running to warn her if her father was coming. What he couldn't see or hear he couldn't punish: that was the theory. He hated the piano more and more as time went on, keeping it in the house mainly, it seemed, to remind his wife of how crippled she was. Also, it had been a wedding gift from the Heberts and Packards, so how could he throw it out?

Through the years her mother had become Maddy's teacher. She would sit in the living room and do the mending while Maddy practiced, from time to time rapping her thimble on the wooden arm of her chair. "No, Maddy, no. More slowly, don't slur over those sixteenths."

If Maddy played something right there would be no sound, only a look at the mending — not enough to cause Vinnie Dow's face to be comforted, but something.

There were even a few rare times when the mending was scattered and Maddy removed from the piano bench. The music would be laid aside, and Vinnie Dow would play the piece by heart, frustrated always by the mistakes in her crippled hand but crying with a voice unexpectedly young and full of fire, "Can you hear it, Maddy, *can you?*"

There would be something she did hear, above the discords, somewhere in her imagination. "Yes," Maddy would whisper. She heard, always, so much more than was there. Then, of course, it would be a practical matter. The music would be replaced upon the piano, the mending retrieved from the floor. The imagination would have to be translated.

Remember, Maddy thought now, sitting in the grass outside her house.

The Dow children had no grandparents. Maddy had asked about this once. Vinnie's parents had been killed in an auto accident. "The same one that did this to me," she had told Maddy, tapping her crooked wrist. "Three people died."

"Who was the other one?"

"A man I was engaged to." A silence. "He was a musician, too. He played the cello. You would have liked him, Maddy."

"They all died?"

"Yes. Only I pulled through." After a moment she said slowly, "I was driving."

Maddy stared at the crooked wrist, listening to her mother's lost-child tone, which came as though from inside a cave of sadness. Involuntarily her own lips twisted, tightened. If there were anything she could do to retrieve, restore, take her mother back past her children, past Maddy herself, her marriage, accident, past all of that and back to the streets of Cambridge and the midcity hush of Harvard Yard. Past that, even, to some free space and time. Most heartbreaking of all was to look at her mother and know, to see that they both knew, that this could never be done.

It made her think of her father. "Daddy has no parents?"

Vinnie looked away. "I don't know."

"Didn't he ever tell you?"

"He told me he came from the north. He said his parents were dead. He has some foreign blood in him."

"French?" Canada was to the north.

"I don't know."

"But not a French name."

"No. He may have changed it." She said this vaguely, to close the subject, but Maddy was not satisfied.

"Why? Didn't he like his name?"

"Sometimes names are too hard to spell, or to pronounce."

"His own name?"

"Maddy."

"But didn't you ask him?"

"Maddy, he can't talk about it. He wants to forget where he came from and keep on with a new life."

"Sometimes he can't forget?" Even then she had known within her skin the poison-hurt of what you wanted to forget and could not.

Only crooked music, that was what Maddy heard from her mother. Frustrating fire in which the right hand always and heartbreakingly lagged behind the left, the music gone before it arrived. The dissonance made you want to run, or even more, to stay and put right what might never be put right again. Maddy sat gripping the edge of a rock. The hurting notes came, her mother forcing her hand to move, to play, a hand that had driven a car that killed three people and would now, never, play music properly, especially not the Mozart that she loved. Maddy's own fingers loosed, began to play out the allegro correctly in little, half-stifled impulses. She saw it and balled them into two fists so tight they hurt, but real pain was the distance between the right notes and the wrong ones.

Remember. Don't remember.

Jack Dow fudged memories; it was the only way to survive. That morning, for example, he had stopped off at the church and picked up a list of things needed for the auditions in the evening. He made no attempt to remember the things but kept them on a list. Stuck in his pocket, maybe, but no part of him.

As at every church function for years, people depended on him to provide paper cups, plates, a big jar of coffee, paper for the church bulletins, cleansers, staples. Jack's turf: Jack would provide.

He remembered the time Eleanor Hebert came to him, wringing her hands. "Jack, we need all these things. Arthur and I have given enough. What shall we do?" She shoved into his hands a long list.

"You just leave it to me," he said. "Old Jack'll take care of it."

He'd been promoted to manager of the sawmill soon after.

"That Jack Dow, he's a good manager," people said.

They had to say that.

A year or two after he became manager, he was voted in as town treasurer, too, with the Heberts' help. It was, they said, because he was such a good provider.

The poor came to the town for help, or to the church. If there was no money in the one, Jack would send them to the other. Pretty soon he was in charge of both, anyway. So few people willing to help, somebody had to do it. And he needed some money for his own pocket as well.

Now he sat at his desk among stacks of ledgers. On top of one he laid the latest church list. He stared across the columns of figures at that list. Everything was fine. There would be no problem. The Scotts' money would come in, cover any little deficit for the time being. He'd get by. Nobody would even have to look at the books. Juggling paper, no problem.

He stared off into space, thinking of the Scotts deal. He didn't know what kind of operation they had there. Didn't want to know. Just so they got the goddamn money to him.

He had to have money. There were always extra expenses coming up — a new car, a house payment. He hadn't had a raise in four years; it looked better that way. But there was always something to spend money on. It got mixed up after a while. Who could remember what was for what? Certainly he couldn't. He just filled the lists, tossed them away.

He stared into space, at the walls of his empty little office with its gas station calendar, file cabinets and metal chairs.

Kids, he thought.

Not his children. His children were all under control. His children were fine.

But where were those kids he remembered: dusty feet, clothes that didn't fit? Where were they now? The boys with their scabbed legs, ill-nourished potbellies, one pair each of baggy summer shorts. The girls in dresses too loose, revealing too much skin, the cloth of those dresses ragged, of no color.

Where were they now?

Gone, he thought. Gone north to the potato fields or west for blueberries, gone south for beans and peaches, and very far south for cotton, even cane. Working, bending, reaching. A baby on a hip, everybody working, nobody getting anywhere.

They were gone if he could keep them gone. If he could just keep what he had, if he could teach his kids what it meant. What they had. If he could somehow manage to hold it all together.

Outside his office was the whine, the constant noise of the saw and the clatter of boards being laid one upon another in neat stacks. But inside he sometimes heard voices. His old buddies and the girls. They stood at the edge of his mind as at the edge of a long, dusty field.

"Jack," they called to him. "We see you now, loafin' this long day. You ain't gonna make it, friend. Come on back. We here, we waitin' for you."

He pushed them away when he could. He liked to think they weren't there at all. Sometimes in the night, though, he heard them, and sometimes he woke up crying.

"What do you want?" he would ask them. "Leave me alone."

He wasn't a kid anymore. He wasn't living in a shack but in a house with running water, a bathroom, rooms of furniture. He'd made his escape.

"Leave me alone!" He said it now, passing a hand in front of his eyes. The room was empty. He slammed the ledgers away from him.

His neck was hot. When he wiped the sweat from his face, his fingers burnt the skin of his forehead. He locked his office from the outside and started home for lunch.

Past all the "good" houses to the turnoff, up into the woods, another turn onto the Dow road. It was dustier than he liked, more shadowy. As he turned the corner, he saw a bit of field someone had set to squash plants. The deep green leaves lifted their twining fingers at him; the orange blossoms seemed to gulp, swallow. For an instant he saw the squash ripe, the dusty silent figures that would have to move among them, carrying those heavy fruits in vine-split, mangled hands.

A little hot today, he thought. Have lunch, I'll feel better. Woods were cooling to him. He pulled into his yard, got out, spotted a few tall grasses in the petunias he'd set out, went to the garage for shears to cut them. Then he heard it: the labored notes of Vinnie Dow at the piano. That was not allowed.

"Vinnie!" he yelled, outraged, from right where he stood in the garage, "cut out the goddamn racket." He headed for the house.

Maddy, still in the field, heard him yell. She was on her feet and racing to the house before the music stopped.

"Vinnie!" From the interior of the house his voice rose to a scream. The music left off. There were children already at the table; Jessica grim and silent, the large-eyed boys. Allison sat in her place, not looking at him.

Maddy took two steps into the house and her father was behind her.

"Bush tails like that," he said roughly, "we cut them right off."

The sun was by now on the other side of the house, leaving these rooms, dining room and kitchen, dark. He was visible to Maddy only in the light from the door. In his hands was a pair of grass shears, and his face had that shiny, warning bulge.

Her hair was what he meant. It was wiry and curly. Today as usual she had put it in two elastics so that it stuck out in two tails, one on either side of her head. She didn't know whether to move or not, facing him. Either way she was caught.

"A little bush trimming, Vinnie? Is that what we need around here to get people to mind?" "People" in this case was their mother. They would all be punished for her piano playing, and they all knew it.

Shiny blades flashed close to Maddy's ear, the sound making her wince and pull away. In a moment, however, Jack was past Maddy and around the table to Allison, his fist closing around her braid. Allison drew in her breath. Maddy saw her father grin cruelly. He flashed the shears close to the braid.

"Jack, no," Vinnie Dow said.

Their father pulled up the braid until Allison's head tilted painfully. "You better sit down," he said across the table to Maddy. "And it better be quiet in here, so a man can relax." Again the shears flashed, long bright blades. Maddy sat.

As she did, the shears flew past her shoulder and through the doorway to the living room, where they clattered to the floor in a corner.

"Wife," Jack Dow said, having established control once again, "let's have some dinner around here."

The younger children relaxed a little, seeing him sit down.

Maddy watched her mother rush back and forth, filling plates and getting food on the table, but she didn't dare to help her. Also, she knew that in some twisted way, doing the whole job while everyone else watched was part of Vinnie Dow's penance.

"Come on, come on," Jack Dow commanded. "You, Maddy, say the grace."

Maddy didn't dare refuse. Her throat was dry, her lips stiff, her hands clenched in her lap.

"Our Father," she whispered, but she could not go on. "Our Father," she said again, wishing suddenly, desperately, that there might be words for what she really carried inside.

"Maddy."

Something for her to say — what could she say?

"Maddy!"

"Watch over us," she continued aloud, "and bless this food to our use. Amen."

"The older they get, the worse they are," Jack Dow muttered, his face over his plate. "Now. Eat."

Vinnie Dow seated herself. Plates were passed. Things became "normal."

"You will be happy to know," their father announced after a moment, as if nothing at all had happened, "that I am allowing you, Maddy, to audition for the chorus tonight. You may sing with the chorus as our family representative, since I will be too busy with our promotions to sing. Right?"

For the sake of the others Maddy had never argued with him. She nodded.

"There'll be a big crowd there, we've seen to that," Jack Dow continued. "Vinnie, you will be in charge of the nursery, as usual."

Her mother nodded.

"It's a point system," Jessica had told Maddy one night in a rare conversation. Usually no one was more stolidly silent than Jessica. They'd been lying upstairs after a beating that frightened more than hurt and trying not to laugh nervously with relief while tears of pain worked out of their eyes.

"You and the children play," Jessica whispered slowly. "There's a giant scorecard in the sky. You get points by doing things in church, in town. If you teach Sunday school, so many points. If you're a deacon, so many. If all your children go to church every Sunday, so many, and so many if they're well behaved, and so many off if they aren't. It doesn't have anything to do with what you're good at, it's the points. They matter. That's what we are, Maddy," she whispered. "Points."

It was true. When Mrs. Chamberlain announced that she was donating the organ money she'd saved over some six years back to the church so that it could hire a chorusmaster from "away," she was much applauded. It was Jack Dow who had complimented her publicly, making her blush by thanking her profusely at the next church meeting. He had kissed and embraced her "from the town." Everyone had clapped, but as much for Jack as for Mrs. Chamberlain — points!

At home he'd only growled, "Goddamn old lady, about time she did something useful with that money."

Soon after the church meeting, a special town meeting was called. It was Jack Dow the Heberts called upon to explain the idea of the Freedom chorus, the television competition, and the subsequent Fourth of July celebration. He'd stood up in front of the group and spoken so smoothly, then opened his hands to them and asked, "What is the spirit of this meeting?" It was a moment of high emotion for the town. He'd seemed to be the servant of all of them.

At home his children bit the insides of their lips as his monologues went on and on: "Bunch of damned sheep, got to tell them what to do every step of the goddamn way."

Maddy thought that if she were able to describe him, it would be in a peculiar ellipse of harmony in which two things happened at once: one of them low and threatening in the bass, one of them so ordinary and normal-seeming.

Without appetite, Maddy chewed and swallowed. Her father was going over the preparations the church planned for the town's Fourth of July celebration the next year. The big plan, he said, was for the town to become the spot everybody else went away to for the Fourth. Everybody would have to work, but the revenues and the publicity would be worth it. "Got to get diggers for one hell of a big barbecue pit," he was saying.

Maddy allowed his voice to lapse away from her. Then she was off, into the world she kept by her for escape. For whole moments while her father talked she heard only the music her mother had tried to play earlier, especially that point at which the notes looped and rose and touched a high sound that had been singing in her own veins for quite some time. Yes, it was an adjunct to the allegro almost — what was it she kept hearing? — there, again, some strain of melody to add, above what was played. In her mind she went over it again — no, not that; yes, there, maybe. Her fingers itched toward the notebook in her pocket, but she would not take it out.

"Vinnie!" It was a cry.

Her mother jumped. The children jumped.

"Vinnie, are you listening to me?"

Maddy snapped back into the present.

"Yes, Jack," said her mother quickly. "You know I am."

The children didn't look at each other. From a corner of one eye Maddy saw her father grip his knife. Just as quickly she knew that other eyes had seen the dark fingers on the knife handle. How bad would it be?

"Vinnie, I know you. You're no more listening to me than the man in the moon."

At once all around the table children who didn't want to laugh at their mother did so with a kind of foolish quelled snicker, like a sob. Vinnie Dow sat rigidly at the end of the table.

Eyeing her, the children fell into silence.

"Vinnie," their father rapped out, "you come here to me."

For a split second Maddy's mother didn't move. Jack Dow stared, then shifted his gaze pointedly from her to the children. Deciding, Maddy could see, on another victim. Her mother saw this, too, and she rose as one hypnotized and went to him.

"Stand here. Right here." Jack Dow pushed back his chair and set his two feet apart, pointing to a spot between them, his other hand still on the knife.

Around the table eyes lowered. Of all the things the children hated, this was the worst.

Wordlessly, Vinnie stood on the spot to which he pointed. She was motionless. They stared at one another. Suddenly he grinned up at her, laid down the knife, and grabbed her at the hips. His fingers dug into her sides.

"Look at her," he said, giving her a little shake. "Isn't she a fine figure of a woman?"

"Jack, let me go."

"Give us a kiss," he said. "Come on now, Vinnie, bend right over here."

"Jack." This was a painfully small remonstrance. She was in his power.

"Vinnie, if you don't kiss me now, we will have to make it more complicated."

Across the table, Maddy saw, Jessica's face was keen-honed and carefully blank. They looked away from each other. Vinnie Dow bent.

Let her alone. Maddy thought it so hard it was almost audible. Let our mother alone.

The kiss, embarrassingly long, was at last over.

"There," said their father. He stared around the table, his eyes like two shiny pebbles. He released their mother with a shake, a slap to the rump, a laugh. He stood.

He looked normal, even harmless, his short hair combed to one side, straight eyebrows close to the eyes, straight nose, thin straight lips. His face without its angry bulges was a square, with an adequate chin. He looked clean, civilized. Maddy thought his appearance could make her doubt herself. Face to face with this normal, even pleasant-looking person, how could she believe anything cruel had happened? "Forgive" — that was part of it, too. And "Honor your father and mother." Oh, she wanted to do that. She'd give anything to be able to do that.

Her father moved across the dining room and into the living room with his peculiar, catlike lightness. He picked up the lawn shears as if finding them in that far corner were the most ordinary thing in the world. No one dared to watch him as he came back toward the table. He passed it and seemed to be on his way out the door when he paused, and Maddy felt his hand close over the hair on one side of her head.

Had he heard her thinking? For a moment she almost thought he had.

Slash went the shears close to her ear, not really cutting anything: the threat was as good as the cut, she saw that suddenly.

A threat could last longer. A threat could last forever.

With a final pull that made her blink tears, he was gone.

Vinnie Dow had been standing. When the car door slammed and the motor started, she came back to the table and dropped wearily into her place. Slowly she began to help herself to food as if nothing had happened.

A threat, Maddy thought, a tiny wedge of white anger opening suddenly inside her, could go on and on. We might never be free.

Never be free.

She knew: freedom was the one thing she wanted. She wanted it so badly. In her mind suddenly there was a vision of what she should have — what they all should have — something beautiful, mixed up with sound, color and light, the freedom of all these.

Would they never have it? Never?

She stood up. For once she was deeply and cleanly angry. She went into the living room, rooted around in her mother's mending. Then she stood in front of the round mirror in the room. She had never thought of herself as attractive, that would have been too dangerous. How she looked couldn't matter; it was too risky. Better to look and act younger than your age, better to seem unaware, like a much younger child. At this moment, however, she thought only of being free. She lifted her mother's sewing scissors. A few sawing cuts above each elastic; it was done.

Her head felt cool.

One threat gone forever. If there were a song for that, in praise of that?

Instantly Maddy was afraid. Already her hair was beginning to curl in short corkscrews all over her head. She knew nothing about how to control it or style it. She had never had a girlfriend to sit with, to talk with about these things in a silly way, preparing to be a grownup. She had been born too old, too young, and it was safe only to be clean and well behaved. She saw that her hair was going to look pretty funny; sixteen years old going on ten, she didn't know what to do. Her father would also see her hair. He would punish her.

She tried to tell herself it didn't matter. She picked the cuttings up off the floor, put a triumphant look on her face, and went back to the kitchen, where she threw them into the trash before facing her mother.

Vinnie Dow stared at her for a moment in which blankness gave way to puzzlement and then to horror. "Oh, Maddy. Madeline Lavinia, what have you done?"

"I don't care," said Maddy.

"Oh, no."

"Let him punish me, I don't care. It'll be one less thing for him to —"

Her mother was staring. "Maddy, your hair curls. In little ringlets. Why, that's the way it did when you were a baby."

Years fell away. Maddy's face reddened. "Mamma," she wanted to say, "I am thinking of a place where we could be free."

She didn't say that. There was no safe place, no free place. Not anymore. To protect herself, she drew years of punishment around her again, a coat of iron, all she had.

"Don't worry," she said. "He'll have to punish me for this. I'll make sure he punishes only me." Empty words. She was afraid. One slip, a momentary anger, had left her whole family vulnerable. How could she have done that? Somebody would get hurt, they all knew it.

Quietly the children cleaned up. Maddy wanted to tell them, "I did it so we could all be free."

They wouldn't have believed her.

One by one they melted away from her, out of the house.

*

That afternoon she went as if driven to her mother's Mozart, studying its pages carefully. She came to the phrase she'd heard: two dotted eighths, a quarter note, a rest, an eighth, marked with a long arc of a slur. She played this phrase over, taking it slowly at first and then up to tempo. She went through the allegro from the beginning, softly, smoothly. She felt strangely light-headed. She hoped her mother would hear what she played and that freedom would somehow occur to her, but that afternoon Vinnie Dow did not come to the living room.

Maddy finished the allegro but could not go on to the next movement. She turned what she played into the first of Bach's *English Suites*.

This Bach was her favorite music, the only book of its kind among the classical pieces in her mother's old collection. The Bach satisfied Maddy. It was precise. It demanded strength, and Maddy's fingers were strong. She no longer needed to see the sheet music; she had the *Suites* by heart. Bourrée, sarabande, musette — in another century people had called them dances. She tried to imagine people dancing, light, unencumbered.

After a while she stopped and pulled out her little notebook. She knew she was only marking time before her punishment. The other children knew it; so did her mother.

They were their father's weapons against each other, they were all afraid. They would hide from each other, hide what they all knew, and the punishment would come. It was all they could bear to do.

Maddy flipped through the notebook to the back, playing out the few notes she had put on paper that morning. Pitiful notes — what good were they? But even while she thought this she heard more, of such allurement, such promise, that she scribbled, then played and listened, forgetting even the haunted faces of threatened children.

The whine stopped, the clapping sound of board laid on board ceased. There was a revved motor, another; a shout: "Gonna tie one on tonight, are you, Bob?" The laughing return: "Hell, no, you old fool, it's only Tuesday." More motors, the rumble of tire on dirt. Jack Dow sat at his desk. He'd been on the phone to the Scotts outfit.

The guy had said, "All our management and our lawyers take their vacations in July, you know. Don't worry, I'll see what I can do."

He would have to be patient. Still, he couldn't help worrying. The phone rang again, and he jumped. It was David Hebert.

"Look, Jack, I been doin' some thinking. Lately I was over watchin' Arthur, just a few days ago, and what he's got for the farm, see, is one of them computers. 'Magine that."

"A computer?" Jack only laughed. The computer was an outlandish thing.

"Well, you know, I thought I felt the same way," David went on. "You know Art and his newfangled gadgets. But some of them things really help both of us, you know. Can't be behind the times if you want to stay in business farming."

"Ain't it the truth," said Jack.

"Well, it is," said David. "Anyways, Jack, he's got himself a computer with a lot of memories, and now he's puttin' all his farm business, bankin', stocks, everythin', on it. Says once he learns how to operate the goddamn thing, it'll really cut down on the work."

"That so?" said Jack. He felt his neck heat: there was danger here.

"Jack, I was watchin' him. One night he pressed the wrong button and lost half a year's finances, just like that, gone forever." David chuckled.

Jack, relieved, allowed himself a scrawny bit of laughter in return. "Well," he said, "damned if that ain't the way."

"But the next time I was over there," said David, "he'd got this accountant guy out with him, and they were goin' hell bent for leather. Once he'd done his finances, he said, he was goin' to start plottin' genetics for his best milkers, and after that, he was goin' to make a plantin' table so's he could have it right there at his fingertips. Well, sir."

"For God's sake," said Jack.

"Jack," said David, "I was impressed with it."

"You were."

"I was. Right there on that screen, in a second's notice, all the money transactions, dates — the whole business."

"You got to learn how, though." Jack's ears were hot. Danger, all around him.

"Well, they'll send people out to help you," Dave went on. "I'm thinkin' what Arthur says is right. Arthur says it's the language of the future, and you know Arthur, he can usually see these things. Hell, he's the one sellin' three heifers a year off one cow — that taught me. You got to keep up with science if you're goin' to make headway these days. Anyways, I was thinkin', I mean to get one of those things, just like Arthur."

"You do."

"I do. If Arthur can, so c'n I, by God. I'm goin' to put all the books on it, here at the farm, and over there at the sawmill, too. Sawmill books I haven't had a chance to look at in years, had to turn it all over to you, hell of a job. Now we'll be able to do better."

Jack said slowly, "Makes me think, David, you don't like my work."

"Your work?" David laughed into the phone. "You been holdin' down jobs enough for three men, Jack. Without you, that mill would have gone right down the tubes. This is just a little help for everybody, that's all. And I think we can use it, don't you?"

"I see what you mean."

"Well, good. Matter of fact, I'm goin' down tonight, talk to the guy with Arthur. Just thought I'd let you know."

A silence. Jack cleared his throat, his face pulsing with heat. "Dave, I have to ask a little favor."

"Sure, Jack."

"Well, right now, I'm in the midst of the big deal with Scotts. We got contracts comin', we got negotiations. It's just not the greatest time to try somethin' new. Could we maybe put the computer thing off for a while, 'til after that deal? Give us some time? That would be a real help, David."

"I hear you, Jack." He appeared to mull this over. "You never led me wrong so far."

Jack Dow began to relax. "Good then. Thanks, Dave."

"Well, what I'll do" — David Hebert's voice held some little-boy excitement — "I'll just get me the best damn computer I can get, then I'll just learn, 'long with Art. By the time you're ready why, I'll be ready. Fair enough?"

"Fair enough, Dave." He kept his voice cool, but he saw orange light grow, flowing, molten.

"You'll be at the auditions tonight, Jack?"

The auditions. He mopped his brow. "Oh, sure. See you there, Dave."

"You bet. Bye."

He hung up the phone. The auditions. Abruptly, he left his office for the day.

Outside he felt a little better. The air was cool, the shadows longer, welcoming. He took a breath. After all, everything would be fine. Soon as the Scotts deal went through. He looked around the quiet mill — the mounds of sawdust, the smell of dust. Sawdust was deceptive, though, he thought. It could get wet and still catch on fire. It held in heat. Fire hazards: he had to be careful.

He went to his car; he was looking for peace, for rest. But there, as always, he saw his mother's face. And on it, as always, that suspicion. Her features were printed on every car he'd ever owned — this one, and all the others — especially the first, a 1942 Hudson, its upholstery in tatters, its running boards rusted off: her round face was reflected in a side window.

"Where you get this car?" she always asked him. "You steal?"

Always he would reply as he had then: "No, Mamma, no. I bought it."

"You buy this? With what money?"

"My money, Mamma." It had been his money.

Over the years he had worked when he should have been in school; she'd made him: sweating in the beanfields when he could have been studying if she could sneak him in, sneak him by the bossman. Or staying home to watch the younger brothers and sisters — somebody had to. Doing his schoolwork by fits and starts, always with a smaller brother or sister on one hip. Never enough time to study, always dirty, without proper clothes. The money he made in those stolen hours when he picked always went to Mamma. She took it, took every penny. He never had a thing.

At age twelve he'd gotten wise to the adult world. He'd left his brothers and sisters alone and roamed the streets, in and out of storefronts, learning to steal little things. Candy bars at first — oh, he had craved sugar, lived on sugar. Small toys, things he could trade. At last trinkets, small pawnable items. He never kept them long enough to be caught. He was careful about that.

He would go to school or not as he pleased or was able. Sometimes he would stand outside the school building and look inside the windows at all the scrubbed children, their restlessness or somnolence.

He studied when he could. At gas stations, on corners by streetlights, in the mezzanines of old hotels and the dirty hallways of apartment buildings, he'd read and learned, trying madly to keep up with all the well-scrubbed, well-fed kids who moved as the hands of a clock, in appointed time, from one grade to another. When he went to school, no one knew what grade he should be in; they put him where they had room. Now and then someone tried to care. But his family would move, too soon.

Where was he? Who was he? In his heart he carried a huge sore place that said to him, "You don't belong, Jack. You're not good enough, you're not smart enough, not clean enough."

When he stole he kept the money back, carrying it in bills in a pouch around his neck and down inside his underwear. That money was his as nothing was in the endless series of shacks and broken-down motels, crumbled resorts in which the plumbing no longer worked — all the places provided by bossmen for workers to live in while they picked, endlessly, strawberries, blueberries, apples, grapes, trekking up and down the eastern seaboard, owning nothing except, perhaps, a broken-down car.

"Your money! Hoo! You got none!" He could see in the reflected face that already she had guessed what he had done.

"You're not old enough to buy a car," she'd cried that time; technically this was true. He was a minor, a skinny little kid of fourteen. But he had paid in cash.

It was no use. The next day she'd given the car back or sold it somewhere, he never knew. She didn't even need the keys to do it. His property was her property, and would be until he was twenty-one.

"You steal!" she had screamed at him. "You take my money for my babies!" With a wide gesture she had taken in the seven children who followed her wherever she went. "You no good."

Now Jack Dow was busy, maintaining his clean house and good business, seeing that his family did as they were told. And this blue Ford was his, light blue inside and out and beautifully clean. No one would take it away from him.

Tonight he rumbled down the road from the sawmill, down the tarred road past the church and all the big houses, down the dirt road, around the corner that led to his house, and he saw none of it, the longer shadows of afternoon becoming evening. He was hot and uncomfortable, and all he saw was his mother's face. You work and work, he was thinking, and everything can be taken away.

"I didn't steal it, I didn't, Mamma!"

But no. He would not mutter to himself about stealing. This was a different world.

"A different world?" whispered a little voice inside him. "Where bad things don't happen, Jack?" The voice laughed.

He slammed the car door so as not to hear it and went into his house. His family waited for him, five children, two boys and three girls, in this room with smooth walls and even floors. He saw the dining table he'd bought, with the rugged round chairs. They used matching plates and glasses from Ward's, and silverware from the Value House, and everything was clean and good, not a patch or a tear or so much as a smudge of dirt. He saw to it, he made his kids see to it. This was a new world; that other didn't exist. When you worked and bought, it added up to all this that was yours, and that sharp question "You steal?" did not exist.

"Oh, Jack —"

Many voices called him. He put away the sound of them, nodded at his family, said the grace, ate without speaking.

Then he spotted Maddy.

"Holy Jesus." He stared. The girl's hair curled wildly in every direction, no longer neat in the controlled style he expected of his children. "What's been going on here?"

No one spoke.

"I said," he repeated loudly, staring at Maddy's hair, "what the hell has been going on here?"

Again, no one said anything.

Which world was this? He had to decide. He stared. What was this wild hair, what did it mean? Through a fog he recalled the lunchtime incident with the grass shears. What had that been about?

"Jack," said his wife, "it's time to leave."

Caught, he glanced at his watch, at his wife. She was right. He examined the glimmer he saw in her eye. Was she enjoying this?

"Vinnie," he said, and he made his voice control all the options, "we won't be late for the auditions, we are leaving now. We will discuss this later, Vinnie. We will have to. I hold you responsible, Vinnie. You and the child and I will discuss this." He felt the sides of his face begin to swell. "There will be time," he told her slowly, he promised her. "I will handle this, Vinnie."

Without a sound, the children went to the car.

"Maddy, you will find a group to sit with, and there you'll sit. Vinnie, we've put some cribs in the nursery. We don't want kids and babies running around loose." Suddenly his voice was ordinary. "There'll be a couple of women in there to help you. About eight-fifteen you'll go into the kitchen and plug in the big coffeepot. You younger children are to help your mother."

A smooth, quiet voice. Was this their real father?

The Dows were the first to arrive at the church, but soon it was crowded with people. Maddy selected a seat near the end of a bench, as far as possible from her father's eye. The other Dows disappeared.

Beside Maddy, as the bench filled, sat Judy Russell, then came her husband, who was nicknamed Russ although his real name was Thomas Russell, and their baby son, little Russ. The Russells talked hilariously up and down the row, including Russ's parents, who were seated on the other side.

"Oh, my gosh," Maddy heard Judy say as she twisted in her seat to see the people. "Look at the crowd."

"Comin' out of the woodwork," said her husband. "Good advertising, I guess. Maddy, how are you?"

Maddy was surprised to be noticed at all. It took her a moment to find her tongue. "Fine." She swallowed, not knowing what else to say: when had she ever been allowed a conversation with anyone? When had she dared, remembering the children at home? Tongue-tied and feeling outlandish, she sat uncomfortably. Russ only nodded in a friendly way, turned to speak to his father.

Maddy knew what the Russells saw. A small skinny girl in neat clothes and weird hair, a girl too young for her age, with dark eyes and, she supposed, no personality to speak of: no words when she needed them.

Down the row, Russ's mother was picking up her grandchild. "I ain't here to sing," she was saying, "just to cuddle this baby. Come here, precious."

"Well, I wouldn't be here at all" — Russ's father stretched his legs out comfortably — " 'cept she dragged me." He hooked one thumb at his wife.

"Oh, ha," said the older Mrs. Russell, hugging the baby. "I couldn't've kept him away. Just lookin' for an excuse, that's what he was." She made a face at her baby grandson, who crowed his delight.

"Hell of it is," the older Russell snickered, "that's the way she's been talkin' to me for fifty years."

Maddy eyed them all shyly. She liked this talk, the laughing. She tried not to stare too much at the woman seated beside her or to let Judy Russell know how much she, Maddy, admired her. Judy possessed a wonderful singing voice, true and gracious, high and pure, with a rich vibrato. Whenever she sang, Maddy listened with awe to the sound. Special, magical, it gave a whole new meaning to words.

She was careful not to stare. Judy seemed to have many friends in the crowd; her son was being passed happily from hand to hand. Surely there was nothing Maddy could offer her, dared offer. Maddy Dow was only a shadow at the end of a bench.

She looked behind her, spotted her father. He was staring at her hair. "I haven't forgotten you," his look said. "Not at all."

Now the David Heberts, Judy's parents, arrived. There was a great contrast between Russ's parents — work clothes, a house dress — and the Heberts. June was stocky but well dressed in pink golf clothes, and David wore plaid pants and white shoes, his farmer's tan a deep leathery brown. Maddy looked away again. None of this family saw her sitting down at the end. She didn't belong with them.

When the crowd was seated and had begun to quiet down a little, Arthur Hebert, dressed very much like his brother, moved to the front of the long rows of benches.

"We're happy to see so many here," he said to the crowd. "Glad to find so much interest in the Freedom chorus. As a town we have a number of musically talented people and a history of music that goes back to our grandfathers and great-grandfathers. We believe this Freedom chorus will be a great way to get us all together to have some fun, do some music, and also to promote our town and maybe earn a little money, which we can always use." There was a snicker from the group. Arthur Hebert grinned and mopped his forehead. It was a measure of the importance of the occasion that he spoke at all. Usually Jack Dow was delegated to do these jobs.

"Now," he continued, "Jack informs me that his wife and a couple of the other women are in the nursery waiting for the children, so when we get ready to audition, they could move back there. After the auditions are over, those of us who are interested in the promotion end of this project will meet in the sanctuary."

Just then there was a baby's shriek and a howl loud enough to discountenance even Arthur Hebert, who paused to locate the sound.

"Good God," he said after a moment of searching, "my own grandchild, wouldn't you know?" There was a laugh from the crowd. When the baby continued her piercing cry, Arthur called out, "For gosh sake, hunt for a pin, Elaine."

Another murmur of laughter, a weaving of heads: there they were, the beautiful Elaine Hebert Cummings and her husband, Cyril, bent over baby Elana, who was stretched out stiff as a board across Cyril's knees. Cyril blushed and called out frantically, "There aren't any pins! She's held together with tapes!"

The crowd laughed again as Cyril stood and exhibited the baby's paper and plastic diaper. Then he took her, still screaming, to the back, where with obvious relief he handed her to Vinnie Dow, who carried her into the nursery. The crying stopped. Arthur Hebert began to speak.

"Now perhaps the first thing we should —"

Baby Elana's howl revved up again. Madly, to laughter, Cyril stumbled over feet and went back to the nursery to dandle the baby, who would not be comforted. At last he took her outside.

Maddy knew her father would be angry at her mother for not keeping the baby quiet.

Arthur Hebert finished his introduction and everyone clapped for Professor John Sears, the new chorusmaster. Slowly this man walked to the front of the room. His hands were long and narrow, his elbows made hard, triangular points on his arms, his shoulders bent in their lightweight sport shirt. When he climbed to the platform in the front he seemed even excessively tall, his hair in a tangle of gray and blond curls. His nose was large, his eyes deep-set, his lips thin, but as he turned, Maddy's impression was of a man who listened, a man of quietness, even a courtesy of quiet. She was not the only one who felt this. The crowd was hushed before he began to speak, as he did speak, with no increase in volume, until they felt, Maddy thought, that they were each having a private conversation with him.

"I wish to thank you all," he said, "for the great compliment you've paid me in choosing me to be your chorusmaster. I have not been at the university so long that I can ignore the musical history of small towns, and I believe we can do some great things with the Freedom chorus, enjoy ourselves, and perhaps even get before the television cameras in a few months if we're lucky."

His voice was pleasant, with a kind of rhythm to it, and an accent that was cultured, educated. The crowd was quiet. In Freedom there was respect, even awe, for those with so much education.

"I would like to thank Mrs. August Packard and Miss Ann Packard for sharing a wing of the Packard Cottage, which, as you all know, is not a cottage at all. It's a lovely place, and they are lovely ladies. I am enjoying my stay very much. As some of you may know, I have taken a leave of absence from my duties as choral director and assistant professor of music at the university in order to work on my doctoral dissertation this summer. The dissertation has to do with rural music, so you can see that our chorus should be a learning experience from my standpoint, as well as, I hope, from yours."

Maddy watched his hands, the precise gestures he made. Once again she felt alone. Here was a real musician. When he spoke, all the people listened. Her loneliness grew. She would have liked to get to know him.

"Our business," he was saying, "is to weed out any obvious monotones and get our chorus organized. However, if anyone very much wishes to sing and knows he cannot carry a tune, I advise him to make his mouth move and let the others carry him, and all will be well."

The crowd chuckled.

"Now we've chosen some wonderful pieces to sing this year," he went on, "four-part music, not too difficult. Some of it will be familiar to you, I know, so please don't be afraid. Also, don't be afraid to audition. I'll invite you to the piano in groups of seven or eight, and no one will have to sing alone. Even the smallest blending voice is what we want, and the bigger our chorus, the happier we'll be. Our other business will include auditions for an accompanist for our group. So let's not delay another moment but organize ourselves and start right in."

Maddy watched his eyes — friendly, courteous, unafraid. She felt alone.

As the crowd began to stand up by benches and move forward to the piano to begin the laborious auditioning process, she slipped "off." The noise and confusion of the audition circulated somewhere at the base of her hearing, while closer to her were sounds she began to construct in her head — a line of good notes, solid, incorruptible, welcoming to a person by herself.

The group currently at the piano could hit no high notes. Dimly Maddy was aware of that. When Judy Russell's group stood to try, she heard Judy, as always, the ease of that voice as it flowed effortlessly up the scales.

In a vague way Maddy heard Professor Sears say, "I hope you'll discuss some solo work with me."

Judy Russell nodded.

Notes, Maddy thought. Some strong notes. She was "off," making a music on which to hang loneliness and fear.

The next time she thought to look around her the professor was standing on the platform again. "This is an excellent group," he was saying. "It's amazing how many really good singers we have. I thank you all for your patience and your good auditions."

Maddy came back with a snap. The voice auditions were over? Already? Why, how could she have missed them? There was a whistling in her ears born of fright, the velocity of time. Oh, he would be angry!

She saw her father in a corner, talking to someone in low tones. His eyes were on her; it was too late. He would punish her — or worse, someone else — because of this, and her hair, and the Cummings baby. Frantically she counted up the things there would be punishment for. There had never been so many. What would happen? How bad would it be?

"... the singers a break," the professor was saying. He was smiling.

Maddy stared at that smile, wide and gentle. Tonight someone would be hurt, and there the professor stood, smiling at her across a gulf.

He was asking, "Is there anyone here who would like to audition to be our pianist?"

She heard the question. She felt the silence around it.

She was frightened, but something was fierce inside her. Something was singing, calling her. Staring at the professor's smile, she thought suddenly, What do I have to lose?

Maddy saw the professor watching the crowd, looking for volunteers. No one moved. She saw her father counting heads, counting hairs. She saw him with horror. Staring at the professor's smile, she could hardly breathe. She had to get away, she had to get *to* something. Brightness, sound, soft light, comfort — were these real? A person couldn't live without knowing what was real.

She stood up and faced the front. She felt herself swimming in a thick, blurred air past people's heads, shoulders, feet. She kept her eyes on the professor's smile as she moved, conscious that behind her another face saw her, hands clenched, a body moved forward to stop her.

He could hurt her later. This time, this once, she would not be stopped. This once, at least, she would find out what was real. Now she was daring to approach a tall man with education and expertise. She was depending on his courtesy, clinging to it in case it might rescue her from fear, from drowning.

Professor Sears smiled again and nodded at her. "Thank you for coming forward," he said. "Don't be frightened. What is your name?"

"Maddy Dow." She whispered it. Suddenly she realized she was standing before a whole crowd of people, not one of whom she knew if she could trust.

Somehow he heard her. "Miss Dow, whenever you are ready." He gestured toward the piano. Then, seeing the fright on her face, he added, "Or would you like to set up a time for a private audition?"

Maddy couldn't hear him. She was thinking that it was too late to run, too late to do anything but go to the piano, sit on the bench. An old-fashioned upright, a practice piano for the Sunday school; Maddy had heard this instrument played many times but had never dared to touch it. You would have to lay your fingers on it so, and so, to make it speak clearly, without a jingle. She went and sat.

She put her hands on the keys and managed a few chords. She was terrified, but still she heard the notes she played and realized the piano was in tune. She paused. Her hands were cold and damp, and she wiped them on her skirt awkwardly. She glanced at the professor. Beyond him, like an exponent on a cipher or a monkey on his shoulder, was Jack Dow, frowning. Deliberately Maddy shifted her gaze. The professor smiled. There were lines around his eyes that said smiles were natural.

The piano keys were blurred. She had no sheet music. There, in the crowd, she saw Judy Russell.

Bach, the first suite, a dance. She touched the notes before she knew she was playing it, catching at something, anything. The piece began in a ripple, running away, but with a hitch in it like a limp and then a fine arch of notes. After a moment Maddy's fingers began to fly. Here were notes telling you you didn't need to run, you didn't need to limp. This was Bach, strong and precise and free, and these were dances, with no punishment in them, only music. And by heaven there was — had to be! — a world that didn't run and didn't limp, where nothing was necessary — not the written notes nor the fingers to play them, but everything was given and the music played itself. Yes, there was Bach, and there was some other music.

She stopped, filled suddenly with doubt, at the end of the piece, and was startled at a sharp cracking noise that she realized was not retribution but applause.

"That wasn't an audition," Professor Sears told her under the noise of it, "that was a concert. Thank you."

"Are you, are you sure?" Maddy whispered.

He nodded. Would he be, could she ever have, a friend?

He set before her a piece of sheet music. She glanced at it, found it easy, played it through without a hitch. As long as she was playing, she could forget there was anything in the room but the piano and the notes.

"Try this." One after another, she went through the pieces he set before her. She thought they were all wonderful. At the end there was more applause.

"Miss Maddy Dow," he said with a smile, "it looks like you may have a job."

"Thank you." She didn't dare to smile back. One quick glance told her where her seat was, and she went to sit down, her heart pounding. That dark figure, her father, hovered somewhere near the back. She would pretend for now that she didn't see him.

Judy Russell turned toward her. "Well done, Maddy. Why didn't you tell us you could play like that?" Judy's smooth dark hair swung

as she nodded her approval. Her blue eyes were alight. "Shy?" she
continued when Maddy didn't — couldn't — speak. "Well, you certainly don't need to be, with a talent like that." Judy patted her arm,
her face friendly.

Maddy couldn't say a word. Her heart was pounding.

From the back little Elana, who'd been brought in again, now let
out another wail, a long keening note. Her parents hustled out with
her, but it seemed to Maddy that the crying did not stop.

What had she done?

The crowd began to disperse. Looking at no one, Maddy moved
toward the nursery. If people stopped her with compliments, she answered them politely and moved away, always under her father's eye.
Her mother, the children — would they be angry? The trouble she
had caused was enough to make them all angry, all afraid.

Professor Sears stood in the doorway of the nursery, looking for
her.

"Maddy is it?" he said.

"Yes, for Madeline. Madeline Lavinia Dow."

"A lovely name," he smiled. "Maddy, you must call me Jonah, and
we must learn to work together. Have you ever accompanied a group
before? No? Well, I'm sure you will have no trouble with it at all,
but there are a few things to go over. I was wondering if perhaps you
could come over to the Packards' sometime soon. There is a wonderful
piano there. I think you would like it."

Maddy couldn't say a word. To the Packards'?

"Come where?" Here was Jack Dow, speaking as if he were out of
breath, or just a little off his stride. Maddy didn't look at him; his
voice was enough.

"Excuse me?" said the professor.

"I'm Maddy's father, and she goes nowhere without my permission." Jack Dow grinned heavily, demanding that they laugh together.

Professor Sears didn't laugh. "Of course she doesn't, Mr. Dow. By
the way, you are to be congratulated. Your daughter has a fine talent,
as I'm sure you know."

Jack Dow didn't hesitate. "I'm glad to hear you say so, Professor.
We wouldn't have wanted her to get up there and make a fool of
herself." His eyes came to rest on Maddy. She couldn't help but look.

In their depths she saw a red light, as in the eyes of a dog picked out by car headlights.

"Oh, no danger of that," said the professor. "I must admit I was a little worried until she stood up, though. We can't do anything without a pianist, as you know. It's the basis of our whole effort. It took courage, I think, and expertise."

"I understand."

If Jack Dow sounded a shade aggressive, the professor's politeness ignored it. "I've invited Maddy to come to the Packards' sometime soon," he said, "so that we can go over what I'll need her to do. Perhaps her teacher could come with her?"

"Her teacher?" Once again the red eyes looked into Maddy. "Her mother is her teacher."

"Well, then, perhaps her mother could —"

"Her mother is staying to home." Jack Dow's smile slipped. Instantly he righted it. "She has four other children, you know."

Maddy felt her father was speaking directly to her, telling her of victims.

"Well, whatever is the most convenient, of course." Jonah Sears lifted his hands.

"I can come tomorrow," Maddy found herself saying. "If it's all right, I mean."

The professor paused. "Well, tomorrow would be fine." He seemed pleased that she had spoken for herself.

Maddy took courage from this. If there were a tomorrow, she thought, it would mean one had lived through the night.

"Now hold on a minute," Jack Dow said quickly. "Maybe that's cutting it a little too close, young lady."

"Oh, not at all," said the professor. "Tomorrow will be fine." He paid Maddy the compliment of speaking directly to her. "Four o'clock, if you will, Maddy? Aunt Bea Packard will be downstairs by then, and I know she will want to hear you play. But perhaps you will need a ride?"

"No," said Maddy. "It's only across a field or two from our house."

"Oh?" The professor looked surprised.

"Got to be home by five-fifteen, though, Maddy." In his extremity Jack Dow winked at her. "Don't want her to skip her chores with all this fuss, Professor. You know kids, they'll take any excuse."

All the Dow children worked at home.

"Chores?" The new chorusmaster seemed to think them unimportant. Maddy felt an instant's sneaking admiration. "There is one thing," he said. "Mrs. Chamberlain has given me two hundred dollars to pay the new accompanist for this chorus. She says playing in the church is all she can manage this year."

"Well, we can take care of the money, all right," Jack said. They had moved so that Jack Dow stood to one side.

"I don't want money." Maddy spoke directly to the professor. "I'd play for free."

"No need of that." Again the professor spoke as if what she thought was important, or how she felt. "You may want that money. Perhaps I will put it in a little savings account for you until you get used to the idea. Now, we will see you tomorrow afternoon?"

"Yes." Maddy saw her father stand by helplessly. She knew his rage, knew what was coming. She held her head up. "Yes," she said. "Thank you."

"Good then." Jonah Sears nodded and turned away. "Nice to see you again, Jack."

"Yes, Professor, yes." Fake cordiality. Maddy knew it was all her father could manage.

The next moment she felt herself moved bodily into the nursery.

"Vinnie," Jack Dow rapped out, "gather up these kids and let's get out of here."

A sharp, quelled voice meant only for those who heard it. Maddy heard from a great distance. Her eyes were blind with tears.

A long ride home in a dark, crowded car.

"You kids keep quiet!"

They were quieter then than they had ever been. Nothing quite like this had ever happened before. All the windows were open as they rumbled and flew home, too soon. There was dust and a cool breeze, the dark, a lone streetlight, then the dark again. In the back of the car their damp, breathing forms huddled together. No one moved. Jessica helped Stephen into the house, daring to whisper, "Just a little farther now."

"I said I wanted it quiet!" Jack Dow yelled.

Maddy's mother switched on an overhead light, but the house was full of strange, sharp shadows.

Maddy and Jessica walked the boys into their pajamas and up the stairs in silence. Their mother was already tucking Allison in, then Phillip. They, at least, might be safe. Stephen climbed into bed and they settled the unnecessary covers tightly around him. All the children clung to extra covering for safety, as they would cling, sweating, until their fingers loosened, as they hoped, in sleep.

"Vinnie? Ain't those kids to bed yet?"

Vinnie Dow had been sitting on the edge of an upstairs bed. Waiting.

"I'm sorry," Maddy whispered, trembling.

"Vinnie, come down here, now. Bring your oldest daughter with you."

Maddy passed Jessica on her way to the stairs; Jessie reached out and touched her arm. "I'll save the side by the window for you, Maddy." It was the choice side in summer. "You did well tonight." A whisper, it followed Maddy's thudding footsteps down the stairs. Behind her was her mother. Neither spoke.

The light in the living room was so abrupt it made Maddy blink. Where should she stand, where sit? In the light she would be obvious, it would be clear she was trying to hide. She slid into the room, chose a chair, took it quickly. Her mother came into the room and stood, a small, weaving figure. Jack Dow paced, shoulders hunched, head down. He moved lightly on the balls of his feet.

"Just what did you two think you were trying to pull?" His voice was like a heartbeat in the night.

"I am the head of this family," he cried at their silence. "I don't get surprised. What I want to know is" — he turned to his wife — "who gave her the goddamn permission? Who taught her?" His voice climbed.

Sharp shadows, sharp light, corners of it on his face. His eyes were black slits; his cheeks began to bulge, shine. One hand clasped into a fist, he leaned toward his wife. His arm pulled back, far back.

"I just did it!" Maddy cried. "Please! I wanted to, and I did!"

Too late. When he hit her mother it wasn't in the face — that would show — but in the neck, at the collar line. A hollow sound. Vinnie Dow reeled, her hand flew up, she staggered.

"No!" Maddy cried, but now the dark arm had pulled back again. Another hollow sound and a shredding as buttons ripped down, exposing pale skin. Vinnie's head fell back, to the side. She didn't defend herself at all, didn't raise a hand. Jack Dow's hands began to swing, fingers open, first from one side and then the other, making horrible rhythmic sounds, fingers snapping at flesh.

"No!" Maddy cried. She ran to face him, to defend her helpless mother, step between them. "Hit me instead — it wasn't her fault."

His eyes were red. Two dark veins stood out on his forehead and the tendons in his neck were corded, purpling the skin. Having reached back, he swung again. His fist slammed up under Maddy's jaw, twisting her head back and up so hard that she sank to her knees and felt for her face. An ear buzzed; the room swung. There were more sounds, awful thuds, upon her, above her. It was the sound that hurt.

When her vision cleared again, her mother's dress was open to the waist and her father's fingers were jabbing at underwear and pale skin.

Vinnie Dow still stood, stood and didn't make a sound.

Like a stuffed doll, Maddy thought. Her mother was taking all the punishment for what she, Maddy, had done. Vinnie's hands hung at her sides.

Slap! Slap! Vinnie reeled; she stood.

"No!" Maddy cried from the floor. "Don't let him!"

"Show that to your relatives, Vinnie." Her father's voice overpowered everything; it was the howl of a train close by. "You want to tell secrets, you can open your dress right up and show them what you are. What you are, Vinnie."

He grabbed his wife by shreds of cloth and hauled her to Maddy. Vinnie Dow swayed, unable to help herself. Her dress was agape.

"Please," Maddy moaned, burying her face in her hands.

"You don't like the looks of this?" Jack Dow was beside himself. "You don't want to see your mother like this? Then you do as I say, little girl. You do as I say, or I'll show you what she is."

Maddy moaned.

There was a cry of springs, a snapping in the air, then came a sting of lightning and the print of a belt buckle rose on Maddy's arm, a jagged cut oozed blood. She looked up, ducked as the belt fell. Her mother lay against the sofa. How badly was she hurt? Maddy couldn't look up for long; the belt stung again and again.

"Are you all right?" she tried to ask her mother, but the belt fell on Maddy's arms and shoulders. "Please."

She looked up once at the sofa and then away again. What she had seen within shredded cloth was one exposed breast, its nipple twisted upright.

"Get to bed!" Jack Dow shouted.

Maddy couldn't move. "Get!" He shoved at her with his foot. "But just you remember, girlie. You remember your mother here, what you do to her. Get to bed. But if you ever in God's world try to trick me again —"

The belt flew, its speed blinding her. My hands, he mustn't hurt my hands, she thought.

Slash! Swish! "Mamma," she cried.

"Go, Maddy," her mother said in a low voice. "Go now, I'm all right."

A scream from Jack Dow: "Don't talk to her!" Swish.

The belt snapped. Maddy dared to look up. Her father was caught in some ritual of rage. As if it were a sport, he flexed his arms and snapped the belt again. Maddy would not look at her mother, for modesty, but now, stubbornly, she stayed near her. The belt spun. All at once she was hurled, tossed away. She was thrown from the living room to the hall, and as she fell the door slammed, and there it was, the click of death, the click of the lock.

In the dark Maddy held her head in her hands. Everything hurt. She tried to think what to do, tried not to think how her mother had looked, that one bare, brown-nippled breast. Wildly she tried to conjure up a weapon, but there was nothing. If she made any more trouble, he might hurt someone else.

"No man would want you," Maddy heard her father say now, beyond the hall door. "No man in his right mind, Vinnie. Nobody wants you, Vinnie, but me. And right now you sicken my sight."

There was a pause, a silence more troubling in the dark hall than the sound of blows. Maddy gathered in her own hurt, trying to listen.

"You're a mess, Vinnie," her father's dark voice went on. "Why, I should think you're not worth much of anything."

Silence again. Then came a low moan, one awful little moan.

Maddy gripped the edge of the stairs, tears rolling down her face.

"Come to bed, Vinnie." Now it seemed to her that her father's voice was drier, too quiet, too soft. "Why did you stay up so late? You need your beauty sleep, Vinnie. Oh, man, do you."

Nothing from her mother.

Blank this out, Maddy thought in the darkness. This is not happening. Never remember this. She stumbled up the stairs.

Jack Dow was remembering himself, underneath a bare light bulb, a cord strung across the ceiling and the bulb hanging down. He was sitting in a wooden chair, the back of which sagged half off and gave no support. He was eight years old. His knees were skinny, his upper legs were pink from sitting, he was without clothes. He'd been there a long time.

"Don't you move," someone cried. Was it his mother, one of his fathers, who?

"I want you right where I can see you." Someone. There he sat.

He didn't know why. He only knew he'd sat for a very long time. Then some adult came and twisted his chair from the table, parted his knees so that he could feel breeze between his legs, and just looked, looked for a long time, until all his little-boy parts curled away into themselves tightly.

His clothes were thrown at him and he knew it was time to work.

A cracked linoleum, he remembered that. A counter, a sink that didn't work, half full of gray sludge and floating cigarette butts. Corn flakes and clothing and peanut butter and beer all littered together. You helped yourself; no one ever helped you. You ate by the handful and wore what you could find. When he got old enough to know how dirty he was, he would wash his clothes in secret and let them dry and try to iron them for school with an iron he "found" in a shop. The iron made a loud ticking sound when it heated, he remembered that.

It hadn't been any good. He saw that now, although he couldn't see it then. He could never belong in a school. Stretching behind him wherever he went was a long dusty field of something green. He carried with him in school or out of it the straining sounds, the hacking sounds, and always, somewhere, the sounds of sobbing children, of crying. In the field he carried within there was always a baby crying. Mothers toted babies along patiently or, as they grew old enough to walk, smacked them to get out of the way, get out of the field, mind their own business, feed themselves, pee somewhere else. What was in the field? Beans, maybe. You couldn't sit and you couldn't bend over; you had to squat or walk the rows on your knees while the cloth-filtered dirt clung to the hairs on your legs. In the rain, water soaked up through, making streaks in the aged dried dirt on your skin. Sun or rain was equally bad, but the picking went on and on.

The crying; also, as he grew older, the lovemaking. It was all the same.

One day he encountered a girl. He was older then, wiser. No one sat him up or poked at his privates anymore, he saw to that. Fifteen or sixteen, old enough, he saw her. She was in high school, she said. Just up from Jersey on a bus the night before. This was a New Hampshire farm, acres of beans, their damp little purple-white blossoms promising more picking and still more.

She had dark hair pinned back with bobby pins. She looked at him out of the corners of her eyes, from time to time rising, taking out her pins, shaking her hair back and pinning again, her elbows up, her breasts inside their dusty blouse pointing up. She had tissues in little packets in her pocket. They smelled of a sharp lemon perfume. She would wipe her face and her neck and then deep inside the opening of her blouse. Her face was nothing — thick lips, dark eyebrows. But that clean neck, the idea that she was keeping it clean. The lemon scent that must be on that neck, plump and secret in its collar. He wondered, could almost feel the skin of it against his face.

As if they had chosen each other that day, they worked together. She picked one row, he the one beside it. By ten in the morning they sweated, she kneeling just behind him in the dust. After a while he heard a little sound and turned to see her lying back against her splayed heels. "I like the sun on me," she said.

He gaped. Half hidden by her row of bushes, she had unzipped her pants to expose her stomach. He stared at the white skin, at the point of the zipper. Slowly she moved her stomach and he saw the beginnings of darkness, a few tiny hairs. The skin behind his ears prickled. He fought for control, staring. "You'd better be picking," he said. "If they see you, they'll throw you off the field."

They both knew that this was only the wildest of rumors.

Slowly she sat up, the zipper crept. They began to work again.

The sun was so hot it made you think of your body. Somewhere a man hollered; there were children fighting. Bean plants rustled; the

beans snapped — these were wax and pale yellow and broke away at
the stem with a neat half-twist, expertly done. He moved down his
row. He could hear her behind him. The sun made him imagine
something soft, pink, swimming wet. He kept moving. He was beginning to itch. After a few hours of picking, your hands and arms
always itched from the rubbing of the fuzzy stems of the bean plants.
You were damp all over from sweat and dew and itching; the hidden
undersides of leaves rarely dried, even on the hottest days.

By noon he was ready to explode. When the noon call came, he
stood over her.

"We could go to the woods," he said. His voice was strange to
him. He cleared his throat. He'd done much in private, but never this.
He looked at her neck, below the closing of the blouse.

"It'll be crowded," she said.

He looked at her and then stared down at his itching, dirt-streaked
arms. What she meant was that this noon, as on every hot day, the
woods — or in another place it might be a warehouse, some tall grass,
even a deep shadow somewhere — would be full of couples too beside
themselves to care about exposed flesh. They did it, he knew, because
of the sun, or the rain, because all they used, all day every day, were
their bodies. All the rest was useless equipment, good only for counting bags, minutes, the hacks of blade against cabbage or cauliflower
stalk. Counting, rhythm. If he could have he would have fought
against it, but he could not.

"I'll show you something," she said.

He couldn't remember her face now, but he still could remember
how she bent toward him so that he could see two breasts bathed in
the red shadow of her blouse. She twisted and one nipple swung forward, wide, pink, taut.

A few seconds and they were in the woods, stumbling along, looking for a place. Around them others looked, too. For the first time in
his life, Jack really saw combinations of flesh locked together. He'd
always crept away with a book, so as not to see, before. Now he
looked, and what he saw was fascinating, horrible, all he wanted.
He and the girl ran farther and farther until there wasn't any noise
and they'd found a place. She turned to him and slipped out of her
few clothes. She was very young. Only a few hairs on the pouched
place between her legs. Her breasts were high, the nipples still too
big for the heft of them.

"Come here," she whispered wildly. "Undress."

He was about to explode, but he could not. "No," he said hoarsely.

He went to her, laid his hands on her, all over her, sat her on the pine needles, pulled her legs apart so the air could tease them. He touched her, pinched, moved her from side to side. "Sit here," he whispered, full of rage and want. "Do this! That! Move, I said!"

Aroused, confused, blind and begging, she did everything he wanted. She had to, he saw to it. Only then could the explosion come.

"Mamma," he cried out at the instant of it. "Mamma."

A form on the sofa — whose it was didn't matter, was tremendously important. The classy Vinnie Packard. She loves this, he thought.

He stared down at his wife, who lay still, only looking at him.

"God, Vinnie," he said. She lay there.

"Who would want you now?" he muttered, and knew that he did.

He raised a fist to hit her, and her head went back so that one bare breast pointed at him. Instead of hitting her·his fist came down like a claw, and then there were two breasts, each pointing in a different direction. He sat her up.

"Hurt, are you?" he said to her. "I didn't hurt you too bad, did I, Vinnie? Come on now, look at me, now."

He bent over her, raised her face. "Course not." He spoke for her. "Course I didn't. You come here to me, Vinnie, and we'll fix you right up."

She began to sob. She loved to cry.

"There, Vinnie," he said. "You come right in here."

She clung to him as they moved into the bedroom. He felt her breast press against his side. "You lay right down," he said. Vinnie loved to be comforted. "Now, you didn't get hit so hard you couldn't stand it, did you, Vinnie?"

Slowly she shook her head.

"No, course not," Jack said. "You are a picture."

His wife sat on the bed bare to the waist, her hair disheveled, her head hanging down.

"You're not mad at me, are you, Vinnie?" It was an old catechism. Easily, ritually, he fell into it and saw her respond, a tiny quiver.

"No," she whispered.

He watched her breasts. Imperceptibly they rose.

"Course not," he said. "Why don't we take off that old ripped dress, Vinnie? We don't need that anymore, do we? You are a mess, Vinnie." Red bruises on her neck. Now she stood naked in front of him. He knew she would do exactly what he said.

"Good." He surveyed her. "Now you lie down, Vinnie. I'm going to take good care of you."

He watched her lie down. "That's a good girl, Vinnie, yes. Now," he said, "why don't you roll over a little? That's it, lay on your side, Vinnie, and reach down, yes. There. That's a good girl. I should take a picture of that. Your crooked hand, Vinnie. Twisted, is that what it is? If only your relatives could see you now."

For a long time he watched her, until the tears ran down his face. Then he was ready.

Maddy's back burnt, her side ached; here and there her arms were sore and dotted with warm, sticky spots. None of it would show. She slipped on a nightgown and flexed her fingers. Her hands, at least, were safe. She climbed into bed, shivering in the warmth of it.

When she did Jessie spoke in the open-mouthed whisper they had learned long ago, so as not to be caught or overheard.

"Maddy, are you all right?"

"Yes. But he hurt her, Jessie. He's hurting her now."

"Is the hall door locked?"

"Yes."

Jessica reached out and touched one hand as it lay clenched on the pillow. "Did he hurt your hands?"

"No. My arms a little. My back."

"Well, we can fix them. Look, I smuggled up a tube of cream." It cooled her back.

"There, that should do it."

"Maddy? Are you all right?" It was Stephen, in from another bedroom.

"Shh." Jessica's shush was like a wind at the corner of the house.

"Can we come in?" Stephen and Phillip, at the door.

"Shh!" Like ghost children, the two little boys came to stand by the bed silently, pulling blankets around them for protection.

"I'm all right," Maddy whispered. "Quiet, now."

"I wanted to come down and help you," whispered little Stephen. His voice trailed away.

There was a caught-back sob, a little girl, Allison, standing in the doorway, her face in her hands, weeping silently.

The staid Phillip went to her, patted her shoulder. "There, there," he whispered.

"If only Maddy hadn't played." She wept, rocking back and forth with grief.

"I know. It's too late," Phillip whispered.

"Yes," said Jessica. "Come here." The children came, and as they did she spoke again, without volition, a whisper unearthly in the dark:

"Maddy, when you get ready to, you should leave."

"But I'm not going anywhere," said Maddy. How could she leave these children?

Jessie didn't hear her. "When you do go, Maddy," she said fiercely, "you mustn't think of anything but going."

"Where is Maddy going?" whispered little Stephen.

"Nowhere," said Maddy. "Nowhere at all. Give me a hug now. Everything's all right."

"You'll stay with us?" he said in a tiny voice.

"I will," said Maddy. "Give me a hug. Everything's all right."

Allison had stopped crying.

"See?" said Phillip. "Maddy will be good now. She won't do any more bad things."

"You will be good, Maddy?" said Allison fearfully.

"Yes," said Maddy.

"Go back to bed," Jessie whispered. "Careful. All of you." She was as much their mother as anyone, more even than Maddy, who tended to go "off."

The children tiptoed away to bed, their feet on the floor like a sudden draft of skittery air.

"I'm not going anywhere, Jessie," said Maddy.

Jessie was silent.

Carefully Maddy rolled over in the bed. "Jessie? What if every time I play he hurts her, or one of you?"

No answer; that was Jessie.

After a moment Maddy reached across the bed. Then she and her younger sister lay there staring into the dark, hands gripped together, a good strong grip because they were both scared.

The next day Vinnie Dow was terribly pale, with one shoulder held stiffly higher than the other. She wore a dress with a high neck and short sleeves. There were no bruises on her arms or anywhere that could be seen.

"Are you all right?" Maddy asked her tentatively.

In all the years of her childhood and adolescence, Maddy had never heard her mother refer directly to a beating. When they weren't happening, it was as if they did not exist: something you didn't talk about. You covered hurt with a collar or — Maddy stared down at her own arms — with a long-sleeved cotton shirt.

Pale skin hung on the bones of her mother's face as she looked, not at Maddy, but at the piano keys.

"But you didn't do anything!" cried Maddy. "It was my fault."

"Don't think of it, Maddy, please." Painfully, her mother shrugged.

"But what if every time I . . ."

Vinnie Dow looked into Maddy, looked right through her. "You know, when I sit outside a doctor's office and I hear a baby cry," she said slowly, "I try not to imagine bad things. Sometimes a person overhears something that seems bad but actually isn't so awful for the people involved." She paused. "I want you to go to the Packards' today, Maddy. They are expecting you. Your father will get used to the idea and everything will be fine."

"Get used to the idea?" Maddy believed she had not heard this correctly. Her father would not get used to the idea, never. Why, then, did her mother want her to go? Maddy thought of the years of piano practicing. Could it be that her mother was glad of what Maddy had done the night before? Could it be that her mother was willing to suffer so that she, Maddy, could play?

Her mother's face revealed nothing. "Come out, Maddy, and have some breakfast." The subject, then, was closed.

It was a quiet morning. Vinnie Dow held her shoulders stiffly, but she ironed a dress for Maddy to wear to the Packards', and after lunch she took up some blue jeans to patch while Maddy sat at the piano for her usual practicing.

As it grew closer to the time to leave, however, Maddy grew more

and more nervous. "Maybe I shouldn't go?" she found herself saying, tremulously, aloud. "Maybe it was all a fluke, my playing last
night, and if something bad happens to you . . ."

Her mother said nothing, but Jessica was in the living room at
the time. "Of course you're going," she said as she ushered Maddy
up the stairs. "You can't miss this."

"Yes," they heard their mother say to no one in the room below.
"She mustn't miss this."

Maddy was scared, and as she came down the stairs, she saw again
her mother's pallor. It was a tremendous burden, to be suffered for.
"Are you sure?" she asked, almost begged. "Don't you need some
help here?"

"I'll take care of everything," Jessie told her firmly. "You go now,
Maddy."

"Yes," said Vinnie Dow. "You go right along, Maddy. You have
to."

CHAPTER FOUR

A SMALL DOT across a field. While Aunt Ann Packard watched at the kitchen window it became a young girl, fairly small, thin, so narrow that as she turned she seemed about three inches from back to front. Not a pretty child, either, Aunt Ann saw, face pale, hair in a tangled froth of outrageous coal black curls. As the girl came closer what Aunt Ann saw was her hands: long-fingered, blunt-tipped, graceful. She studied the child's face for expression and saw, of all things, fright. In fact, what that girl might have to be scared of became so interesting that Aunt Ann forgot she should answer the front door, and she rushed toward it at the last moment only to have the bell jangle directly above her head.

"Holy God," she said as she skidded to a stop. "Don't I hate you, you damn bell!" She glared up at the chiming box and tugged her skirt down over her hips. Then she opened the door.

She saw two dark eyes, liquid brown and scared to death.

"Well, you come right in," Aunt Ann said more gently than she'd expected to to any young musician with such hair. "You're Maddy Dow."

"Yes." The girl's reply was so quiet, Aunt Ann wasn't sure just what to do.

"Well," the big woman said. "Don't be bashful." She held out a plump hand. "I'm Aunt Ann Packard. I think I've seen you in church sometimes."

The girl had a strong hand, but cold. Aunt Ann saw her eyes falter over the front hall: the white balusters, the mahogany table, the mirrors, the Oriental rugs. She looked as if she were about to run.

"It's a stopper, ain't it?" Aunt Ann heard herself say.

"Wh-what?" But now the girl took a step inside.

"This house, I guess. Me, I grew up on a farm up to Caribou." Aunt Ann came down hard on the last syllable, humorously mimicking accents she hadn't heard for years, a blend of Maine and Canada; Caribou was closer to Québec than to Portland. "Come on in," she said. "We're not so bad as we look."

The girl smiled, almost like weeping.

This was not the time, Aunt Ann saw, to take her into the front parlor to wait for Jonah. That room, so big and beautiful, was also a little overwhelming. And then there was Jonah. Aunt Ann remembered how awed she had been, in the beginning, by the professor himself.

"Come on," she said sociably after a moment, "you come out to the kitchen with me for a few minutes." After all, once a young girl from Caribou, in cheap shoes and a homemade dress, had stepped all alone into a huge house on the ocean, there in Bar Harbor. Aunt Ann remembered that girl now.

"We'll be in the kitchen," she said firmly. "Jonah will just have to come and hunt us up."

Jonah Sears was sitting at his desk in the Cottage and staring at his title, "Rural Music and our Musical Future." He hated this title. In fact, he viewed the whole effort with some distaste.

He had said he would do it.

He had submitted his subject and an exegesis of all its possibilities, and it had been approved. He'd spent hours in dusty archives, pulling out yellow-paged volumes bound in tattered leather. He'd had his own cubicle high up in the cages of metal and glass, the long stacks of the university library, and there he had gone, day after day, whenever he could find the time. His research had been painstaking; it had filled whole file boxes with three-by-five cards, whole folders with sheafs of yellow paper — notes and outlines — the files and folders that lay all around him now.

He had liked doing all that, that part of it. Audrey, his wife, had shared his excitement as his research became more and more demanding. When they'd talked about it, it had been his dissertation with a capital *D*. It touched a subject that fascinated him. "Because," Audrey would laugh, "you are just a rural boy, Professor."

Audrey had a direct way of looking at things that made him uncomfortable sometimes; it was easier to deflect the clear look of those eyes with a joke.

"Long ago and far away," he'd replied lightly.

"Maybe."

From the isolation of the university, small towns had seemed remote to Jonah, a perfectly safe area of study. He had his cubicle at the library, his office, his classrooms — all that was safe. He and Audrey lived in a Western Promenade apartment in Portland, in one of the fine Victorian mansions, with views of the ocean to one side, the city to the other. His subject was New England. No, he hadn't felt too involved in small towns when he chose it. He supposed he would have to admit some germ of personal interest, perhaps. He suspected that had to be present.

Jonah Sears had worked for two years researching his dissertation, digging for information not only in the university library, but also in many areas of Maine, Vermont, New Hampshire, Massachusetts. The data he had accumulated were of such range and depth that the more file cards and yellow sheets he filled, the more excited he became. Sometimes during the early research he would awaken at night in a cold sweat, anxious that somehow he would not get to this important work or that he would not be able to do it justice. It was, he'd hoped, a study that would fill a distinguished volume, maybe two. He'd even thought that surely this project had been meant for him, Jonah Sears, that it would be important not only as a compendium of valuable research but also in real life, as a guide to teachers and parents, for their children.

He would lie in a sweat while details — how important each tiny nuance was — occurred to him: Would he forget? Should he get up and write this down, or that? In the morning he would wake in their sunny apartment, consumed with ideas, and would kiss Audrey and rush out breakfastless, with the impression of white and green and cleanness and new hope all around him, to get to his work. Audrey would sit at the table and smile — she had a career of her own, thank God, and she did understand — when he rushed off. He suspected that she was glad to see him go and take his excess energy with him. She would putter around the apartment she'd painted white and filled with green plants, then get ready for her own work in peace.

He would go to the university before anyone but the janitors was in, to scribble notes quickly before classes began at eight. He was hungry only for his work at that time of the morning, and Audrey knew this. Often when she got to work in the morning she would call a coffee shop, and his breakfast would arrive at his office when he did, at last, in midmorning after his first class. He would look at the covered foam containers and know she loved him.

He'd been happy then, he thought. There'd seemed to be a point to things. All his other work — the teaching, choral direction, lessons — had seemed even more worthwhile.

Some of it was Audrey's influence. "We all have great work to do. We have to find it and do it," she would say.

She had auburn hair, and he remembered now that as she spoke, the waves of it brushed her shoulders and caught the light. He remembered her light eyes, full of prescience, belief.

What had happened between them made him writhe at his desk in this beautiful room in Freedom, made him so uncomfortable with shame that he wanted to cry out.

Jonah was a man for details. Musicians were, he very often found, of a mathematical turn, exacting, able to lose themselves in precision. His old professor at Eastman would say, "Your sense of timing is incorruptible, Jonah. Your playing is athletic in its precision. You, I must teach to sing." It had taken Jonah years to master that in musicianship, to know that within every orchestrated split second of music there was an unpredictable, quite wonderful quality of note that came from some unorchestrated place. In music, Jonah had learned to sing.

In life, he stumbled along. Audrey looked things in the eye and said what she saw. He was far more likely to ignore what he didn't want to see or, Audrey said, to screen it so only the aspects pleasant to him came through.

Audrey would say, of a mutual friend, "She is going too far, she is taking advantage of me."

Jonah would say, "Oh, she's a nice person. No need to upset her."

"But" — Audrey would look first astounded, then dismayed — "don't you see how I feel?"

"Keep it polite," said Jonah.

When they were first married, Audrey had argued about this with him. "Yes," she would say. "If you need a rule."

It made a little space between them.

Two years of research. Mostly joy, as he remembered it. Then came almost a year of outlines and the cataloguing within these of exhaustive detail. Then, as detail demanded, more outlines.

Jonah had ignored at first where the detail pointed. He had expected to draw, as a matter of course, definitive conclusions from his research, full of instructive references, with a constructive criticism or two perhaps, which (he'd flattered himself) would be important, perhaps even vital to the future of musical education. A nice polite little dissertation, full of quiet good value. He had expected to do that, and indeed, the very structure of a dissertation required it. A scholarly document, measured with careful judgments. Instead, he had discovered as soon as he rounded the corner of his second chapter outline and began on the third, the truth he saw was so radical and the detail so unglamorously clear that he'd felt he had to be wrong, that there must be something flawed in his judgment or in the way he was handling this work.

But there it was, lying in front of him, each step implying difficult conclusions. All he had to do was write it.

He had struggled. At last he'd even returned to his file cards, tried retrofitting the outlines he'd done, changing them. So obvious, so desolate. He did write; he threw away what he wrote. Gradually the life began to drain out of the whole project.

Audrey said, "Just write it down."

He had tried, but by the end of his third year of work he'd begun to average about a paragraph a month. Working on it had become sheer drudgery.

He began to make tentative jokes about his "sometime dissertation."

The light in Audrey's eyes turned quizzical. She was disappointed, he knew. Not that she was ambitious for him in the usual sense. "Dr." Sears — all that would have meant to her was that he had done part, at least, of what he was meant to do.

It was frustrating, he found himself thinking as the third year drew to a close, to have such a believer on your side. Hard to look into her eyes and see love there, and in the two dark centers, two tiny openings like questions. After a while he made jokes about his dissertation. She got angry. Then they didn't speak of it anymore. It lay between them like a dead body.

Jonah still rushed off to his office in the morning, Audrey still sent in his breakfast; but over the next months her constancy in disappointment touched the dissatisfaction he was feeling for himself, and that feeling ran wide and deep and began to cover her as well as him, a tide he would do anything to escape.

Curling auburn hair, eyes of light. She wore her watch below the bone of her wrist, and her arms were covered with golden hairs. When they were married she'd said aloud, clearly, so that everyone could hear, "I promise to love you, John Sears." She'd smiled a little over his formal name, but the look in her eyes was determined and shy and loving.

He began to want to escape her, too. He knew he was failing her and couldn't help it, wouldn't admit it. He spent more and more time at his office to escape — not the dissertation so much, he told himself, as his wife: that will of steel, the dedication of a nun.

A bare blank time came next. His office became his refuge, its piles of papers making him look so busy, far too busy to tackle more than day-to-day departmental work. Audrey went to her own work. She wasn't fooled. Indomitably she sent him breakfast, and when he didn't come home for supper, she took to going out with friends. Still, somehow they managed to get along together. Or to think that they did.

A period of months, and then a girl named Laura was hired as a secretary for the music department. Jonah hated to think of this now. Tall and sturdy with tousled hair and a flushed face, she always looked as if she'd just awakened. All day Laura came in and out of his office, bringing him papers, doing errands, making phone calls, consulting about schedules. At first there had been only the usual office banter and gossip. She would tap him on the arm when they joked — remembering that now made his flesh crawl with wretchedness.

But then it hadn't seemed to matter, nothing mattered. His days were a blank. Water hollowed stone, a rock basin in a mountain could become a pocket in the ocean floor, all with the steady, eroding drip of a day upon a day. He became friendlier with Laura. Quite sweetly she seemed to be drawn to him. Sometimes she would rub his neck, her big breasts close to his cheek as he turned to talk to her. It was all a joke. She was comforting and she didn't judge him. After a while Jonah thought in compartments, Audrey in one, Laura in another. The rule was that he was two people and he had two women. Simple.

"I don't do this for just anybody," Laura would say, laughing. "Just for you, you know." Her strong hands, unfamiliar perfume on them, soothed his neck. If he felt the ridges of her fingers move cross-grain on his skin, if he heard the scraping they made, he told himself it was some other man who minded that. The compartments in his mind would work automatically; you shut Audrey's and Laura's — now he couldn't remember her face — would open. With Audrey you were one kind of person, with Laura — Laura, what was her name? — you were another. For a while Laura seemed sweeter, more unexpected, tentative, tantalizing. Certainly she had a crush on him.

"Just for you!" Sometimes she would bend over and whisper this in his ear. She had a way of swinging toward a door that made you feel her hips under your hands.

"Come back soon," Jonah would say and laugh. She would turn and they would glance at each other. It was harmless for Jonah, unreal. Laura didn't know that; he couldn't tell her. Sometimes he wanted to nudge the corners of those pouting lips into a smile.

He'd been working too hard. Audrey wasn't home so often in the evenings, and he wouldn't question her about it, or ask her to be there, for fear of what she would ask in return. Instead, he worked until late at night, got up early, and worked.

One morning he kissed Audrey a suffering good-bye and went to the office and thought, You can't make love to a misery. What he wanted was large forgive-anything breasts, something comforting.

Laura came in as usual that morning; he hardly looked up from his papers. "Shut the door, will you?" he asked.

She shut it without a murmur, not looking at him.

"These are the hour exams," she said. "We ran them off yesterday afternoon. A student called. Amy Morey has the flu and won't be in class today."

He didn't look up. She didn't look at him. But when her hand rested on his desk, empty, he took it and laid it against his neck.

"Bad night last night?" Her hand moved fluidly, catching at his skin, her fingers like reeds.

He was caught, he knew it. He turned to face her, to see in her eyes what he'd brought into existence and did not want to see: need, dedication, tremulous love. She was standing and holding him at arm's length, his face on a level with her breasts. She expected him to look at them and he looked openly, then gallantly, thinking, My God, she's so big.

When she took off her blouse, her fingers were practiced, easy. He preferred coaxing, he suddenly knew. He preferred a delicate spirit sensitive to timing. He preferred narrow shoulders and a tiny waist and a white bowl of a belly, quivering away from his fingers until they enticed more carefully, delicately.

This big girl was experienced. She wanted to stand there while he looked. The need in her eyes was embarrassing. What could he do? He put a hand out and touched that heavy hip. It was a gallant hand, a little shaky, somehow on its honor.

Laura held Jonah's neck with both hands, her fingers scraping, playing with his ears. Viewing her from this angle was like looking up at the figurehead of a ship. The hull of this vessel bent toward him; he felt smothered, airless, there was a roaring in his ears and a clicking sound as the ship ran over him.

The click was the door to his office, opening. Audrey was there, standing in the doorway as in his worst nightmare, her face completely blank.

"Oh, my God," Laura said, and tried inadequately to hide, so that Jonah had an instant's vision of something dirty, a sketch on the wall in a roadside privy. He closed his eyes.

"I just wanted to see you," Audrey whispered. Her face showed horror, fear. "Oh, Jonah." He knew then he was lost. She took one look at him, his face so suddenly pulled back from those huge breasts, and turned and left, closing his door meticulously behind her. He heard her careful footsteps, walking away.

"Oh, God, I'm sorry," said Laura, pulling her clothes on.

"It's all right," Jonah had said evenly. "But this is the end. You have to understand that." Her face crumpled; he couldn't look at her, at what he had done to her. He never saw her again.

He left her there and went after his wife, catching up, jabbering and trying to explain, using any excuse he could think of to hold her, hold on to her. At last she said, "I hear you, Jonah. I'd like to believe you. But this is something I can't do anything about. You know that."

"Audrey."

"Go to the library, go to work, go to hell, Jonah. There's nothing I can do for you."

The pain of a newly emptied bed. "This does not dissolve the marriage," she'd said. "Only gives us a little space."

After the first night of his sleeping in one room and her in another he wouldn't plead, although each successive night was harder than the one before. She was trying to decide what to do, so was he. They left each other alone in a polite universe; they were both helpless. Audrey was courteous because she knew no other way of communicating would work with him. Jonah was courteous because otherwise he would drown. On the fifth day Eleanor Hebert appeared in his office.

Jonah didn't care what happened to him. He agreed to try the Freedom chorus because he had to get away. He and Audrey settled nothing, agreeing only to separate; not wanting to look at the place they'd shared, Audrey took some rooms. Jonah went north. Where didn't matter, it was all subterranean to him. He was a competent professional, the Freedom chorus was a job. The pay: to be away from pain.

Of course, he wasn't away from it. Every day he was in the same hollow, lonely place, pretending to do something he wasn't really doing, pecking away at his typewriter and not working.

He would do anything but this work. In the mornings at the Cottage he took advantage of Uncle Jamie's private entrance and went down to the beach for a long swim. Aunt Ann insisted on making him breakfast and he lingered over it. Sometimes he spent an hour or more back in his wing of the Cottage, just staring out the windows. Often he saw the man Aunt Ann had hired for the gardens, out with his hoe. At times Jonah would have given anything to be that man, to have his work.

Once he even put on his oldest clothes, stuck his hands in his pockets, and went out for a walk. He'd thought he might strike up a conversation with this man — his name was Kelly — and take up a new hobby, give himself a rest from music. But the sun was surprisingly hot, the ground was hot, his shirt burnt on his shoulders and his feet in his shoes, and when he got to the garden it was hell he saw, dirt and heat and the smell of bone meal and death, and a man who smoked and hoed, a dark little bent-over man.

"Nice day," said Jonah.

"Ain't it?" Plainly he waited for Jonah to speak about something specific, or move on. Jonah stared at the dirt, turned, went back to his desk.

"Paean." He had written this beginning to this chapter — how many times?

> Paean was an ancient Greek god of healing. The name became an epithet of Apollo, god of medicine, music, and light. Paean appears in the works of Homer and other early poets as a personal god, a divine physician who was invoked to cure disease and also to avert threatened destruction from other causes. The term eventually became a name for a recognized division of Greek lyric poetry. Paeans were composed by the ancient lyric poets. As a prayer for safety the paean was chanted before battle. It also became a shout of victory and by extension, in modern times, a song of joy or triumph.
>
> Although music and musical awareness seem to be common in rural areas today . . .

But there, as usual, he had to stop. He crossed out the last sentence.

"Music in the home," he began again. But no. Again he made scratch marks. Then he found himself making a note in the middle of his script, over the platen of the typewriter, in a sloping, rebellious handwriting. It read: "Gaps and packages."

He glanced at the clock. Four. Another long day.

He thought of the Freedom chorus and the Heberts. He wasn't fooled by the Heberts. This was a small town, and people like the Heberts, however competent and well turned out, tended to run to its measure. He, Jonah, came from the liberal halls of the university and so he had to view the Heberts with some distaste. They were middle class and typified all that was problematical in the middle class: its emphasis on acquisition and appearance, its emphasis on money. No, he would not get involved with the Heberts. He would make some rules with them: politeness, distance. The Freedom chorus was a job, that was all, and a chance to take a breather, make some simple music.

Four o'clock. Maddy Dow would be coming. With relief Jonah remembered and stood up, putting his papers aside. Finding such a child in such a town was like finding a flower under the sea, he thought. Indeed, in the ribs of some hollowed rock under the water.

Sun, that was what Maddy saw as she followed Aunt Ann to the kitchen. Sun on white paint, then a blur of things, then a huge cupboard with glassed doors, and inside, all the shining dishes. Then they were in the kitchen and she saw a towel rack over a register, with dishtowels on it drying, a long yellow counter, a plate of cookies, a table with a yellow checkered oilcloth. All so light, she was thinking. She shivered a little.

Aunt Ann studied her face. "Would you be hungry?" she said.

"No, no, thank you." "Hungry" seemed suddenly like a word in a foreign language.

"Well, I am, a little," said Aunt Ann. "Have a cookie? Have two?"

Maddy's heart was where her stomach should have been. "Oh, no, no, thank you."

"Aunt Ann, Maddy Dow should be — why, here she is."

Jonah Sears, tall and distinguished-looking, came into the room.

Aunt Ann saw the look on Maddy's face. "We were feeling hungry," she explained. "Least, I was."

Maddy saw Professor Sears nod. "Well, Maddy," he said, "I'm pleased you're here. When you're ready, we'll go to the music room and meet Aunt Bea."

"She's all down?" said Aunt Ann.

"Oh, yes," said Jonah. "I helped her." He smiled at Maddy again as if he were glad to see her. Maddy tried to smile a little — could you trust any person from one day to the next? She wondered. He opened a door, and she went toward it.

Aunt Ann delayed her, trying to help. "Can't give you a cookie?" she said.

"No, no, thank you." Maddy's lips were dry.

"Later, then."

Maddy nodded.

"Aunt Ann is the cookie maker of all times," said Jonah. "Wait 'til you taste them. Come along, we'll meet Aunt Bea and you'll see the piano."

Jonah could feel her fright. "Now, you mustn't be at all nervous." He led her out of the kitchen. "Not at all nervous," he repeated reassuringly as they went into the hall.

"Course not." Back in the kitchen, Aunt Ann spoke to the sink. "This is only the other side of the world, that's all," she told it. "And no matter how often you come or how long you stay, you'll always wonder if you belong."

Aunt Ann helped herself to two chocolate chip cookies and put them together in a sandwich with some whipped cream in between. She munched, then swallowed the last of it whole. This was called a Cambodia; Aunt Ann had had the recipe from the television. She made herself another, ate it. "Like a damned refugee," she said to the air, feeling better. "So maybe I'll pack up some of these cookies. Then that child will take them home. Couldn't hurt. Be a shame to have them go to waste. If there's anything I hate, it's wasted food."

The furniture was all dark and shining. Maddy felt her hands go numb. Ahead of her was Professor Sears, so tall, his shoulders bent. He seemed remote to Maddy. She saw the effort he was making to put her at her ease, and that frightened her, too.

"Are you lost yet?" he said now. "I couldn't find my way through the house when I first got here. I still can't find the odd light switch now and then. Come in. Aunt Bea, you know Maddy Dow."

"Indeed I do."

Brightness, and within the light Aunt Bea Packard's white dress of some summer wool, very soft. Maddy saw white hair, deep blue eyes, a silver pin with blue stones in it on one shoulder. She thought this old woman might be the most beautiful person she had ever seen.

Aunt Bea rose with the professor's help and held out two hands. "Maddy," she said, "I'm so glad you're here." Her accent was cultured, a Maine hardness softened to advantage.

Maddy couldn't have spoken for the life of her, but she knew Aunt Bea Packard had seen that. Her two cold hands were now taken into two warm ones. She felt herself helped to the sofa. All the while

Bea Packard talked, continuing along on some train of thought or other which demanded only that Maddy nod at intervals while they seated themselves. It was to give Maddy — she knew this sharply and was grateful — a chance to get her bearings.

"I've seen you now and then in church, my dear," the old woman said. "I feel as if we should be old friends, in fact, although I've never really spoken to you. Strange how that can happen, even in a place like a church, isn't it? When I see you there, I always remember you are as slender as your mother. I'm afraid I haven't really talked to Vinnie in years. How is she?"

"Fine." It was a strange word. Maddy's voice cracked, speaking it.

Aunt Bea smiled. There was even a glint of humor in the fine old eyes, as if she were saying, "Yes, the first moment is always uncomfortable, but it will be over soon, and you and I will be great friends."

"And your brothers and sisters?" she continued aloud. "Now, there are five of you, aren't there? I don't know how Vinnie does it. You tell me their names, and see if I can remember."

The light made her white hair look like clouds with the sun behind them.

Maddy took a breath. "There's Jessica, she's three years younger than I am," she began, finding her voice. As she did speak, she felt something with a hard, hurting grip let go a little of her insides, and she breathed more easily. Aunt Bea Packard seemed, not judgmental, as everyone seemed in church, where everything you said went on the scales, to be weighed and judged, but kind and genuinely glad she was there.

"Aunt Bea," the old woman said now. "You must call me that. Vinnie does, or she used to. We wrote it all out once, I remember. I am second cousin to your mother's uncle Danny Packard. Now try to figure that one out." She laughed.

"And I'm worse," said Aunt Ann, coming in with a tea tray. "I'm your mother's grandmother's third cousin, twice removed, I believe. Maddy, you have a cookie now."

This time Maddy did, and managed to eat it. She was conscious of the professor, sitting in a far chair. He'd said nothing. Was he laughing at her, did he think she wasn't good enough? She couldn't look at him much, for fear. He seemed so polite, remote. But in a while she could look at the piano. And then she forgot to eat or talk. The piano was large and fine, of highly polished ebony, and it was open. Maddy heard the notes a piano like this might play.

"Do you?" said Aunt Bea, laughing.

"Do you like chocolates, she means." From his quiet corner Jonah had been watching Maddy Dow. It hardly seemed possible that this large-eyed, thin creature could be the musician she had seemed the night before.

So many smiles, they took Maddy's breath away. "I'm sorry," she managed. "It was the —"

"The piano," said Aunt Bea. "Please, try it if you wish, Maddy. Go ahead. It would be such an event for me. Two musicians in the house at once, Ann!" For an instant she seemed to look far away, her old face turned up as a child's might be, listening to a favorite story. "Lovely times," she murmured. Then she interrupted herself, patted Maddy's hand. "Do play. I'm sure Jonah thinks it's time you were getting to work."

"On the contrary, Aunt Bea, it's all up to Maddy." He smiled at the girl. "Whenever you're ready."

For an instant Maddy looked at him as if she would reply, but she couldn't trust him, after all. She rose and went to the piano and seated herself.

Jonah Sears admired the economy of that movement, without fuss, from chair to piano. Now she lifted her hands and all three grown-ups saw the strong, narrow fingers, the precise movement they made, and the straightforward descent, however softened, to the keys.

She has the hands for it, Jonah thought, from long practice at watching piano students, without specifying to himself exactly what he meant.

Maddy saw only the piano keys and the reflection of her hands in the dark wood as her fingers touched them. The ivory was smooth to the touch, worn smooth, accustomed to fingers and yet clean. Now she leaned far forward, oblivious to everything but the first sounds that should come. Her fingers touched, and there without a whisper of difficulty it was, a sound so far different from that of the mismatched action of the spinet in the Dow living room, or the jangle of the church piano, that she frowned, surprised, and lifted her fingers.

Was that a sound she could make? If so, could she cope with a sound as clear and deep as that? Was she a musician, or maybe just a dreamer whose ears heard? She frowned.

Aunt Bea saw it and sent an anxious glance to Aunt Ann, who shook her head slightly. They both saw that Jonah was not alarmed but was watching the girl carefully.

Maddy lifted her fingers from the keys. Still bent way over, as if her ears alone should be the first to catch the barest perceptible sound from this instrument, she lowered those narrow, precise fingers and softly, quickly, to become acquainted, she began to play Mozart.

My God, double time, Jonah thought.

Fast and quiet, the intricate notes came perfectly from the piano, loud enough for Maddy to hear them, just loud enough for Aunt Ann, Aunt Bea, and Jonah. They all bent forward trying to hear, their eyes on Maddy's fingers, her face.

It seemed to them that the girl's features had changed. Her face closed in, becoming very pale, sharp-nosed, sharp-chinned. The mouth was now a straight, demanding line. The face was a picture of concentration so complete, even fierce, that they knew she had forgotten them.

The piano was dark and gracious and full of response. Maddy felt alone in the room with it. It made a sound like the call that answers a cry. She played the Mozart to the end, wiped her hands on her skirt and then, as if greeting a friend, touched the keys again. Far away she went, into as good an allegro as Jonah or Aunt Bea had ever heard, now perfectly at tempo. Aunt Ann's jaw dropped to see those narrow fingers become bands of steel as they flew, to see the girl's face so still and full of light.

Jonah found he was sitting on the edge of his chair and made a conscious effort to relax. Maddy Dow played without affectation or large motions. Sometimes her eyes closed, to help her listen. Her hands pleased him. More than Mozart, he thought. She could handle more.

She finished the piece and Aunt Ann shook her head. "Well," she said with a gust of a sigh, "for heaven's sake."

"Oh, that was fine," said Aunt Bea softly. "Ann, wasn't it fine?" She looked about her as if this moment could exist somewhere in the room, golden and precious, to be seen and identified.

Jonah said abruptly, "Maddy, what about Bach?"

The girl stared across the room at him, and he had the feeling he was calling her from some distance. "I don't know," she said in a low voice. "I have only the *English Suites*. My mother has some Mozart, Chopin."

"Ah. Then, Aunt Bea, we shall have to —" At the last second Jonah remembered: this was not the university and this girl was not one of his students. He had made rules about this small town: he couldn't get involved in anything. He looked at the girl seated at the piano. She was silent, staring at the keys. She looked small and lonely. He found himself wondering: could she use a friend?

"Well," he said after a moment, "let me give you the choral music. Of course you'll have no trouble with it."

Carefully she glanced at the sheets he set in front of her. At a nod from him she began to play.

Freedom, Maine? Jonah had done enough research to know the odds, overwhelming, against musicians like Maddy Dow. But when she played he found himself deeply pleased.

"Excellent," he said, unable to restrain himself when she had finished. "Fine. You are something. Now, Maddy, on the bottom of page one, you see this rallentando. Of course the chorus won't hear it at first, but . . ."

Line by line they went through the piece while he indicated the spots he planned to work on at the first rehearsal. He had the uncanny feeling that she understood immediately what he meant, almost before the words were out of his mouth. She played again, and he saw that indeed she had heard him, in depth and detail.

Aunt Bea and Aunt Ann sat very quietly. Bea seemed, Aunt Ann thought, to be seeing something new and something old, all at once.

"Excellent," Jonah was saying. "Now, accompanying is different from solo work, Maddy. I always say that no matter what kind of musician a singer is, an accompanist must be better, to listen, watch, supply notes, support. But you'll have no trouble with that."

Aunt Ann was watching Jonah, too, how his shoulders had straightened, the expressive motions of his hands. Now and then as he moved his face or arm caught the light from the window. He was excited by what the girl played. Aunt Ann thought Jonah must be a very good teacher.

Jonah spoke because he couldn't help it. "Maddy, are you familiar with the recordings of Gerald Moore?" He knew before the words were out that of course she was not and he continued hastily. "Aunt Bea, this child must come back right away. She has a great deal to do." Then he shut his mouth. The ambition he suddenly felt for Maddy Dow, the hope and necessity — he didn't understand them himself, didn't want to.

But Aunt Bea saw it all at once. "There are many in our family with musical gifts, Jonah," the old woman said. "But it seems to me that Maddy has something special."

"Yes." His face caught corners of light.

Aunt Bea nodded. "I see. I wonder . . ."

Maddy heard them talking, but from a distance. In her head were many notes, a progression so irresistible that she wanted to climb into it and never come out. She suddenly wished to manage to stay near this piano forever, sleep in a corner of its shadow, make her home underneath it and never leave.

"Thank you," she said. "This is — you have — a beautiful instrument."

There was a touch of regret, the hint of distance, in that young voice. The adults heard: this girl didn't allow herself to have friends easily.

Pan of fudge? thought Aunt Ann. I could send that along with the cookies. But it was far less than she wanted to do.

Jonah couldn't help it; he found himself thinking, We must lose no time. She has a great deal to do to be ready. For what, he did not specify, but it was more than the accompaniment of the Freedom chorus. Helplessly he watched her stand. He supposed she would disappear into the landscape and appear again only at rehearsals, and months would be lost. Perhaps everything would be lost. Something had to be said, something wrapped up in sheets of paper and endless file cards, something to save them, too.

"Maddy," said Aunt Bea, "August and I went to hear your mother play once in Boston before her accident. I won't ever forget that day. It was a piano competition that began in the morning and lasted all day and I sat through the whole thing. August, I remember, got tired in the afternoon and only made it back just in time to hear your mother. Brahms's *First Concerto*, two others had played it earlier.

Evidently it was the piece for that sort of competition. But I knew from the moment that first note sounded that Vinnie Packard was going to win, and she did, Maddy. It was our family's finest hour — August always said so. She played, how she played! We felt so rich, to know her. She was young, you know, like you, only in her teens."

Aunt Bea shook her head and blinked back sudden tears. Maddy stared at the floor. She couldn't allow herself to feel this as Aunt Bea related it. The old woman went on quietly, "I have missed the music, Ann. Jonah. I'm an old lady, and I didn't know how much I missed it. Maddy, I would like you to do me a great favor. Will you? Do you suppose . . ."

But now she looked straight into eyes over which an unchildlike veil had been drawn. Aunt Bea felt she must plead, and Jonah and Aunt Ann saw that she wasn't too proud to. "Would your mother loan you to us in the afternoons? For a while? Not for very long. Oh, even for an hour or so. Would she? Especially now, this summer, while we have another real musician in the house, tell her. Couldn't you come to play for me, and let it be something I could count on? Oh, Ann, if I could count on it!"

It was more, richer, than Maddy could have imagined, to be invited back. More than anything she wanted to say yes. But of course it could not be for her. "My father —" she managed to say.

Aunt Bea only smiled. "I can arrange it with him. I shall speak to him, he is so nice. You must come often, every afternoon. You could play, and we could have tea. Oh, Ann, I am beginning to feel quite young!" Somehow she did manage to look young and delighted.

Maddy's brown eyes did not grow less guarded. "My — my father," she managed again.

"I shall ring him up right away, and it will be arranged. Surely he won't mind? He is always so willing. I've never seen anyone so obliging as Jack Dow. Every afternoon at four, I think, don't you, Ann? That is, Maddy, if you would like to."

"Oh, I would like to, but —"

Aunt Bea's smile included Jonah. "Don't you think so, Jonah?"

"Why, yes, I do, Aunt Bea," said Jonah, relieved without knowing why.

"Well, good, that's settled." Aunt Ann heaved a sigh of relief.

"And I'll pack a box of treats, Bea. That piano playing is hard work, got to keep up your strength."

"Yes, Ann, and now we must eat. Professor, do the honors." Aunt Bea laughed and clapped like a child.

For a second Jonah was startled, then he saw. He unfolded himself, picked up a small silver dish of chocolates from the tea tray, and with some ceremony offered them to Maddy. "Do you like chocolate?" It was like sealing a bargain.

"Oh, yes, I —" The girl took one. Here? she was thinking. Every afternoon? With this piano?

"Aunt Bea?"

The old lady took two. "One for each hand," she murmured, childlike.

"Aunt Ann?"

As lightly as a feather Aunt Ann trod across the rug. "Stomach has been a bit unsettled lately," she said, placing one hand delicately upon it. "But I might manage one or two." In the end she took four. Two she popped quickly into her mouth, like peanuts. Aunt Bea, watching her, blinked with surprise, then followed suit.

"Maddy?" Two more Aunt Ann ate, and Maddy, remembering the sweet in her hand, tried it. It was good.

In a little while Maddy left, a heavy package from Aunt Ann under her arm. She walked across the field, trembling a little. At that house? she was thinking. Every afternoon? At that piano?

Surely there could be no punishment for something so good.

But there would be, of course, although she couldn't believe it just now. Someone would be hurt. "Let it be me," she prayed, not believing, believing. "I don't mind. It would be worth it."

Jonah Sears watched Maddy leave, her small, thin, sober form, all arms and legs and the music he'd given her. With some curiosity he watched her, thinking of those remarkable hands, all bone and muscle, and that understanding of tempo, almost terrible in its precision.

"I didn't have any idea she could play like that," Aunt Bea said. "I believe better, even, than her mother used to."

Jonah turned away from the window. "But — excuse me — your own relatives? They are, aren't they? And they live close by." Ordinarily he wouldn't have asked such a personal question.

"I know." The old woman looked troubled. "We used to be so close to Vinnie. She came here to visit, after her accident. The Heberts had just hired Jack Dow then. Right away she wanted to marry him. After that awful time — three people died, her parents, her fiancé. She was driving — a car accident, you know. And because of her wrist, her piano career was over, too. It was a trauma, Jonah. I knew she was suffering.

"How she clung to Jack Dow! 'Vinnie,' I told her, 'wait a little, it's too soon.' She married him anyway. I couldn't stop her. She needed him."

Aunt Bea sighed. "I felt to blame, not being able to protect her from that accident. I don't know, after that nothing was said. Jack always has acted nice enough, and Vinnie and I didn't stop knowing each other.

"I see her in church sometimes and I always say hello. When her babies were born we sent gifts. But distance, Jonah. Like being on a boat, pulling away from the shore . . . the shoreline seems there forever and then suddenly you notice it's gone. People go. You live alone." Suddenly her voice was too light, too high.

"Now, Bea," said Aunt Ann. "You remember we're right here."

The older woman sighed. "I know you are, Ann. Thank God. I think I've felt bad about Vinnie for a long time. She never talks, or comes to visit me. I think she doesn't like me. Well, that does sound self-pitying, doesn't it?"

Jonah cleared his throat. "You've invited Maddy back."

"Yes, and I shall see to it. There's something about that girl — she's too sad. Didn't you feel it? Like a thin bird caught in a net."

"Bea's done her supper and sent me down, and said to tell you to eat if you haven't."

Aunt Bea had been tired after her talk about Vinnie Dow. "Is she all right?" Jonah asked.

"Oh, she's fine. Ate well, went to bed. I expect by the time we're finished supper she'll be bored to tears."

"It's all right, Aunt Ann, if you don't feel like cooking just for me," Jonah said politely. "You've already made one meal for Aunt Bea, and I can fend for myself." The truth was he'd felt unsettled since Maddy Dow left, he'd disobeyed his own rules. Now he wished to reconstruct some distance.

But Aunt Ann only stood on one foot. "Oh, for cripe's sake," she said.

"After all, it's not in the agreement," Jonah continued a bit foggily. "Your cooking for me, I mean." This was not a suggestion he had thought to make before.

"Holy hell." Aunt Ann frowned. "What ails you? Come along now." Abruptly she left.

After a moment he followed her into the kitchen.

"You know," she said to him, "all you men are just alike."

"Oh?" Jonah was taken aback. He hadn't seen Aunt Ann scold before.

"That's right." The big woman planted her feet apart on the kitchen floor and put her fists on her wide hips and just looked at him. "Transparent as glass, the whole living bunch of you."

Jonah gaped.

"Slave over a hot stove," Aunt Ann went on, "and then have some man allow as how he's doing you a great favor, just showing up at your meal. Well!"

"Aunt Ann, I didn't mean —"

"When I feed you," she said severely, "I'm not doing you any favors. I'm doing it because I want to, and if I didn't, I wouldn't."

"Of course," said Jonah, fully routed. "It's good of you, Aunt Ann."

Frowning all across her wide face now, she stared him down. "You look like somebody I used to know," she said.

It was an accusation. Confused, Jonah tried to smile.

"And that's another thing," she said, turning to the refrigerator. "A big smile does not solve the world."

"I'm sorry, Aunt Ann. I certainly didn't mean to offend you."

"Like fun," she said.

She poked around inside the refrigerator, then suddenly shut the door with a slam. "Oh, hell, Jonah," she said. "Look, it's not you, it's me. I'm remembering ghosts, I guess. Something about that girl who came today, us being here and her having to go off. I haven't been right with myself since, and I don't know why." Her usually clear shoebutton eyes were cloudy.

He nodded. "I know what you mean, Aunt Ann."

"I guess I chewed you out for it. I'm sorry."

"Oh, please, think nothing of it. I think I was feeling the same way, just didn't want to admit it."

"Can't live like that."

"People keep saying so. But we'll have Maddy back. And if you don't mind, I really would be glad of some supper."

This cheered her, as he had meant it to do. "You would?" She went back to the refrigerator. "Well, I got ham," she said. "And fried potatoes. I got strawberries. That do you?"

"Aunt Ann, anything. I'm starved," Jonah said, for her sake.

She smiled a little. "All right then, sit you down."

She motioned to a chair at the kitchen table. The frying pan was on the stove at once, and there was the butter in it, melting. Aunt Ann sliced potatoes with lightning-fast chops, and the next moment they were in the pan and releasing an astounding fragrance. "I used to make these for my Roger," she said. Huge, gray-haired, and so round-faced her eyes were like two raisins on a big cookie, Aunt Ann sighed a young girl's sigh. Then she shrugged.

"Gone now," she said philosophically. She sliced ham onto a plate and piled some freshly washed strawberries beside it.

"You start right in," she said. "Be a while 'fore the potatoes are done. I like 'em good and crusty, don't you?"

"Oh, yes," said Jonah, suddenly finding his appetite. "Oh, yes. Aunt Ann, won't you join me?" He knew this was an idle inquiry.

"I never sit to a meal." Aunt Ann tapped her stomach. "It's my digestion, Jonah. But you go right ahead."

The ham had been cooked with something tart and something brown-sugary, and it melted away on his tongue.

Aunt Ann turned the potatoes, muttering to them: "You're looking good, you're going to be fine."

She came back to the table with the ham, a knife, and a plate. She eased her bulk down and cut herself a large slice, which she proceeded to take apart with her fingers.

Jonah watched this efficient and somehow dainty operation. She ate the ham with her fingers, too, snacking along. Then she frowned at the meat and cut herself another slice, which disappeared just as fast.

Finally, she sat back, relieved. "Had a minute there," she said, "when I thought I'd used too much pineapple." She was beginning to feel better, Jonah could see. "My doctor said it was glands, all this weight," she confided after a moment. "I told him I never sat to a meal, not ever. Eat like a bird."

Jonah wouldn't smile: the ham so sweet and the mustard so tangy. He was beginning to feel better, too. There was something about Aunt Ann that made his rules seem extraneous.

"When I was young," Aunt Ann continued, "we didn't have anything. I mean, boiled beans and cottage cheese, every meal. We'd eat dandelion greens in the spring, that and fiddleheads."

"Fish?" Jonah said.

Aunt Ann's laugh sailed up. "Bless you, no. Ferns. You pick 'em before they're uncurled, just little, you know. You have to know what you're looking for, be sure to get the ostrich fern, not the cinnamon, nor the royal, which are poisonous. Anyway, you bring 'em home, soak 'em, steam 'em, eat with butter if you have it. In those days we never did, my folks had to sell all they made. I remember I'd go to the garden and cheer on the vegetables. 'Come on, lettuce!' I'd say. 'Ho there, peas!' "

Once again she laughed cheerfully. Then she shrugged. "Never enough to eat. Especially the fruit, the vegetables. We don't know how lucky we are these days. And never any good meat. Plenty of potatoes — my God, the potatoes."

She leapt up to turn them, and the floor quivered as she moved over it. Jonah saw that the potatoes had begun to sizzle and get brown. He felt he was looking at fried potatoes for the first time in his life, the brown crust on each piece, golden and hot, sizzling as she turned them.

"That explains why you cook them so well," he said, his mouth watering.

Calculating, Aunt Ann hardly heard. "A minute more for you, I think," she told the potatoes. She sat back at the table again.

"What we'd do, see," she said, leaning toward him on plump elbows, "is, we'd go out to the garden and wait for that first radish. The first one to find it would pull it and wipe it off with the thumbs, see, standing right there in the garden, and when it was clean, why, he'd eat it. Young radish, not bitter at all. The clean feel of that against your teeth. To this day a radish says to me, 'You made it through another winter and now there'll maybe be a little more to eat.' "

She cut herself a third slice of ham and savored it as if it were the first and best radish of the year.

"This ham is very good," Jonah said. He felt he was once again in his own grandmother's kitchen, being fed. His grandmother was dead, but his long disregarded feeling for her took him back now suddenly, and he felt at home.

"Roger left me, you know," Aunt Ann was saying. "I didn't meet him 'til I'd been cooking for this one family for fifteen years. I was thirty, old enough. Roger and I had good times, I thought, but then he said I was too much of a woman for him. What he meant was I was too big. Didn't he think I wouldn't guess it? I mean I'm big, maybe, but not dumb. But Roger drank, you know." She stared straight ahead of her, then looked at Jonah. Behind the good cheer in her face he saw a memory of suffering.

Jonah nodded. In every way this was not the sort of conversation he was used to having anymore, but he wanted it to continue. He felt bad for Aunt Ann, and perhaps, if he admitted it, for himself.

"Yes. No great loss," said Aunt Ann. "He just went off. But I'll tell you this." She got up and lifted the potatoes off the stove, settling a generous amount, about half of them, onto Jonah's plate. "He didn't need to use me, how I was, as an excuse for his problems, did he? No. There. That do you?" Each small slice of potato was done to a crackling brown.

"It's wonderful," said Jonah.

Aunt Ann nodded and returned the frying pan to the stove, then stood over it with a fork, eating a morsel at a time until the pan was clean. "It wasn't fair," she went on. "Especially since I was ready to marry him — and worse," she added with a sigh, "I'd told him so." She faced Jonah again, the old embarrassment still in her eyes.

Jonah stopped eating. "I'm sorry," he said.

"Not your fault," said Aunt Ann. "But you know, I keep thinking he might come back some time. Course, I been thinking that for years. Like that woman down to New Hampshire, I read about it somewheres. Her husband went out for a walk one night and didn't come back for thirty years. She put a candle in the window for him every night of that time, waiting, you know. Thirty years later he came back, and you know what? She was dead. He was too late." With a philosophical air, Aunt Ann rinsed the frying pan. "There's a lesson in that, Jonah."

"Oh?"

"Yes. I don't know how I'm going to do it, get out of it, I mean. But I'm not going to wait around for Roger forever. Thirty years, maybe. But not forever." She smiled a little tiredly, and Jonah found himself smiling back. "I don't suppose college professors ever get into such predicaments," she said. "They're way too smart for that, I know."

He was at his grandmother's table, all his feelings begging for this sympathetic audience.

"Oh, yes," he said. "They do, Aunt Ann. The predicaments college professors get into —" When he tried, he found he could barely put it into words. "I'm separated from my wife right now." He shrugged to help obscure the tightness of his voice.

"You are?" She frowned sympathetically.

"Yes. It was the dissertation, mostly. Or no. That was part of the problem. Now I don't think she —" Jonah shook his head as all theoretical language suddenly left him. "I don't think she wants me back, Aunt Ann." He laughed, but ruefully. He felt unable to hide himself. His grandmother, he remembered, had always loved him no matter what he did.

"Well, there," said Aunt Ann. "Do you, will you, talk to her?"

"I don't know," said Jonah. "Not until I finish this work, anyway. And I don't know if I'll be able to finish it." The brows above his deep-set eyes drew together.

"She only loves you for your work?" Aunt Ann frowned protectively and Jonah felt better.

"No, it's not that. She loves — the best me, I think you could say. Whatever that is. She knows things about me I don't know myself. What happened between us was my fault," he confessed.

"Ah. She's a good woman, then?"

"The best."

"Well," said Aunt Ann after a moment of deep thought, "you'll be all right."

"You think so?"

"Of course."

"Aunt Ann," he said, "you're tops."

Aunt Ann grinned. "Jonah, the feeling is mutual."

Two mismatched companions — the outsized old woman, the ascetic-looking man — they regarded each other appreciatively.

"You know," she said suddenly, "I got something to fix those strawberries right up."

From the refrigerator she brought out a small bottle of something Jonah hadn't seen since his childhood: fresh heavy cream, so thick you could scoop it with a spoon. "Kelly found it for me," Aunt Ann said. "A dairy not too far from here. The woman sets aside the cream for her house, makes her own butter." She spooned a mound of cream onto Jonah's plate, where it lay in a rich dollop.

"Oh, my God," he said.

"Powdered sugar, too," Aunt Ann insisted. "Then you got a dessert, and not something you can buy at a restaurant, either."

Still standing, Aunt Ann daintily dipped strawberry after strawberry into the cream that clung about the neck of the bottle, then sprinkled sugar, and ate. The strawberries disappeared.

"Oh, my gosh, six-thirty," she said after they'd eaten for a few moments in comfortable silence. "My boyfriend's on."

"Roger?" said Jonah blankly.

"No, no! Well, it used to be Walter. I could just watch him anytime. Now it's that young one — black hair, brown eyes? Except he's a little tense around the mouth. Never noticed it on *Sixty Minutes,* did you? Needs kissing, I don't doubt. Well, I know a nice old lady who wouldn't mind."

By this time she'd rinsed the dishes and was at the door. She paused. "Jonah, did you get enough to eat?"

"Oh, gosh yes," said Jonah. "Thank you, Aunt Ann."

Aunt Ann shook her head at him and said with genuine regret, "Must be nice to sit down and have a good meal, all in one place, like that."

CHAPTER FIVE

M OVING TOO FAST, but the ride home was so routine, the car seemed to drive itself. Except for the orange corner of a house here and there, a flaming window, or a tree picked out by sunset, its wide summer leaves gilded by late sun, the roadside lost color as he drove, a graying backdrop for the replaying of scenes.

First, David Hebert.

"Jack, Art and I are going computer shoppin' tonight. Ain't that somethin'?"

"Guess so," Jack had said.

David moved his sunburnt stocky shoulders against his clean shirt. "You know what Art was sayin' which I thought was good, Jack? He was sayin' he'd like to computerize the town books, and the church books, too, for that matter. Not right away, course. When we learn. Save us all time, Art says."

Jack's expression did not change. "Good idea," he said, leaning back to give the appearance, at least, of control. "Kind of a long job, I shouldn't doubt."

David Hebert was a slow man. He took his time to think this over. Then he said, "Course you're right, Jack. Should've thought. Hell, you have enough to do for three men, been sayin' that for years. No wonder you ain't so keen on this. And what do we know about it?" Dave continued reasonably. "Not an awful lot. Almost seems 's if we all need an expert in here, show us what to do."

"Got to be cautious," said Jack. His neck was heating.

"Me?" Dave Hebert laughed, his sun-dark face complacent, his eyes playful. "Mostly, people's tellin' me just the opposite of that. See you, Jack. Let you know what we do."

"Sure thing, Dave."

Hebert started out the door, then turned. "Say, Jack? Scotts' contract come through yet?"

"Not yet. Soon, though."

"Well, good."

No time for the fire to die: no sooner had he left than the phone rang.

"Jack, so nice to speak to you again, it's Beatrice Packard."

"Mrs. Packard, it's a pleasure. How are you feeling?"

"So much better, Jack, with Ann here, thank you. Jack, your daughter just left us and I want to tell you something."

"Oh?" He tried to laugh. "What did she do?"

"She played for us. She is a treasure, Jack, and I intend to tell everyone so."

"Well, that's kind of you."

"Jack, I would like to ask you a favor."

"Of course," he said smoothly. "Anything."

"I have invited Maddy to come to play for us this summer. Every afternoon, in fact, at four. I am convinced it will do wonders for my health. But Maddy seemed to think you might not like this idea."

"She did?" Heat rose to his ears. "What exactly did she say, Mrs. Packard?"

"Nothing, really. I told her I would talk to you and you would surely not refuse me."

"Couldn't do that."

"Oh, that's so kind of you, Jack. When that girl plays, it takes me back so, to when Vinnie was young. I'm sure you understand."

"Oh, yes. I understand."

He understood. The road was a maze, he would find his way out. Gray, dark gray-green and brown, stabbed with orange fingers of fire.

He thought of fire. He saw a thousand fires dancing. He blinked them back, preferring the dark. Secrets in the dark?

He knew secrets. He knew the still little looks, the eyes seeing escapes, flung upward only for one unguarded second, their color sharper than usual, quickly veiled. He would let Maddy go on to the goddamn Packards' since they asked it, but by the gods, she'd better watch her step. He knew the signs. He'd watched for them in himself. The sign of escape began as a plan, imperfectly clear, but a tiny plan, hatched in the dark at the back of the mind.

You would need money for escape, and clothing, a place to go; but mostly money. Of course there had been none for Jack Dow. After the car incident, his mother had watched him closely. There was no way to get money. When they picked, he picked on her bill, passing for older than he really was. When they did piecework at the factories, she kept his hours and collected his pay. There was no way of escape. But there had to be. In secret, caught, he had watched for it.

Late fall, Lewiston, Maine. They hadn't gone south, and wouldn't now until after Christmas. Jack hated Christmas, he hated this damned windy hole of a city; there must be some way out. The younger children went to school that fall, not Jack. He was not allowed. He was sixteen; he worked.

It was a miserable place to live, the first floor in a four-story frame building with rickety wooden fire escapes and a front hall that smelled of old damp wood, kerosene. In September, when they could live in all five of the rooms and no one was cold, it wasn't quite so bad, but as the weather drew in on them, they drew in on each other, at last confining their activities to two rooms in the center of the apartment, all the doorways blocked with cast-off furniture and heavy plastic sheets to keep out the cold. Which you could not keep out. It crept in around the shaking wooden sashes of the windows, and passed through the walls in an endless curtain of ghostly damp air. They heated the two rooms with a little pot-type kerosene heater.

His mother was good at "understandings." She had one with the owner of the garage across the way. Every night, after the garage was closed for the night, Jack was sent across the street to pump gas into his kerosene can. The garage owner left that pump unlocked, just for them. It was understood that it was a secret.

The heater in their rooms ate up fuel. Sometimes twice a night Jack would have to cross the street for more. The street would be bare and cold in the white streetlight. It would have a swept look, all the dirt and trash in corners of curbing, the paving and tar surfaces clear. There would be no one around.

One night she sent him early and the garage man was there.

"This is for your mother's car, ain't it?" the man had said, wiping his face with a rag.

Jack nodded. His mother didn't have a car, and they both knew it.

"Good," said the garage man. "Because if I thought she was burning this gas in that firetrap of a house, I'd have to tell her it could be dangerous. Clogs up heaters, you know. This is for her car, then, ain't it?" As if, with Jack's say-so, his responsibility ended.

Jack nodded and handed him the money.

"Good, good," the man said. He looked away from Jack. "You tell her what I said, now."

At first if the garage was closed, Jack would leave the money under the door — three gallons, one dollar. Only, when it began to occur to him that that money was, just possibly, his escape, he began sometimes not to leave it. He pumped the gas and brought it to the house, and kept the money for himself.

By December he'd collected fifteen dollars, but the garage man had begun to complain.

"You leave the damn money, you leave every last cent of it," Jack's mother would threaten. They stood eye to eye. She looked so much like him it was like looking into a mirror: dark face, muscled jowls, slits for eyes and black pebbles in them. He would pick up the can and go.

Dead tired, earning money at the shoe shop by running a clamp that pressed fake stitching designs into leather. Hour after hour, day after day, driving his hands to work faster and faster, to prove he was better at least than the machines. At night, eight of them now sleeping in the two rooms, his job to keep the heater running by the light that seeped into the dark room through the dusty window and tattered curtains. Squares of black-ribbed light on the floor. All around him as he tended the stove were the huddled bodies of children who slept forced together, so that in the daytime all they wanted to do was explode, get away, never see each other again.

Pretty soon it would be Christmas, he hated that. The Salvation Army would come with boxes of things. You would get all excited about them, your mother would look thankful. But that was a fake, because soon whatever had come that was salable would disappear.

His family would go south, end up picking oranges. She had a friend of a friend with a truck, and some night, he knew, they'd pack the sleepy, chilled children into the creaking back, tucking them down in quilts against the frostbite. He knew it all. He was a veteran of those rides. When what he wanted was to have clean clothes and to go to school.

He had fifteen dollars; you could get a bus ticket north, as far north as that would take you.

Night after night across the numbed street: the muffled bell of the pump, the cold trigger, the pouring gas, the dollar under the door or not, on impulse, just as he dared. Back into the rooms, the smell of rotting wood, of something damp and half frozen and gaseous in the cellar of the place, the odors of bodies, old blankets, musty feathers and the shining, oily ticking of pillows that were never washed. Under that, the smell of the heater, at times so strong they had to leave a window open, and when one broke, they left loose cardboard in it so they could breathe.

All that cold season escape was growing in him, at first only a tiny whisper in the back of his mind, then a plan beginning to fill out. He kept his eyes down so his mother wouldn't see his thoughts. But when the garage man began to complain, she watched him more carefully.

"Jack, you've got money! You give it to me!" she screamed at him one night.

Would he never grow? He was still small for his age, only just her height. She outweighed him. Her personality in that big body outweighed his.

"No," he insisted reasonably. "No, really."

She didn't believe him, she was furious. She scooped up one of his younger brothers and threw the boy headlong across the room into a wall.

"You stay there!" she cried at the child, whose blood now began to trickle into his upper lip.

Jack kept his eyes down. He had to or he'd be found out. His mother raged, forced him to undress, searched his clothes. She didn't find the money. He'd hidden it outside the house.

The garage man came again and complained. Jack's mother began to make plans to get out of the apartment without paying the rent, persuading her friend-of-a-friend to leave sometime soon in secret.

Jack knew it was almost time. He was dead certain that he would never again be dragged away to a place where the trees were more important than children, the fruit worth more than the tired expert hand and the wrist, often too skinny, sometimes even too young, that must twist and pull and bring no leaves with it, neither pull the stem from the fruit nor the twig from the branch, hour after hour.

"Jack! That baby is crying! You see to that baby!" It was his mother's usual shriek at night.

Always a baby, just as there was, always, a man somewhere, a "friend." Sometimes she made them call him Daddy. The men never were around for long, but his mother, with her plump body and long black hair, her snapping black eyes in a face that didn't seem to age — she could get them and keep them for a while until they grew tired of the crowding, the children, the filth. Then they would leave, and his mother's women friends, whom she got and discarded at about the same rate, seemed always to be around for a birth.

Always money for births, but no money for children.

Jack waited for his chance; he knew, now, it would come to him. It had to. At night his eyes studied the spaces around the street-lights. He waited for the phantom buses to come, to pick up a phantom boy, Jack — Jack Dow. A phantom boy with a nice, plain name. The bus would take him far away.

One night when, as usual, he turned the fire in the little pot-type heater off so as to pour in the new gasoline, the flame did not quite go out, burning on gook left at the openings. He knew the heater was still burning, he saw that. But something inside his eyes snapped off suddenly, the connection between eye and brain no longer functioned. He saw inside the heater a ring of tiny blue beads of flame, so tiny they might exist or might not — and he didn't see it. What he saw didn't matter. Except that as he stared at that little blue necklace, a baby began to cry.

"For Christ's sake, Jack," his mother mumbled out in the dark, "quit fooling with the damn stove and get that kid a bottle."

A blue necklace. He poured the gasoline through the opening in the back. For a second nothing happened. The stove merely filled, with a liquid sound almost as innocent as water. The can emptied. Behind him the youngest child screamed.

"What in the fucking Christ —" His mother half-turned on her pillow.

Jack, with one fling of shaking fingers, turned the stove way up.

There was a whir and a gust of sound that stunned him. The little blue necklace suddenly burst into a dazzling pot of flame that licked out the front and the back of the stove, down the floor, up the wall. Little daggers of fire landed here and there in the room. One caught on the wall behind the stove and began to lick upward. It was almost white, a nice bright white.

The baby screamed. Jack's mother cried out. Here and there in the room a child stirred, someone sat up and rubbed his eyes. Somehow no sparks had fallen on Jack, although the gas can sat on the floor just by his toe.

He looked about him and knew instantly that it was still not very serious. He could cover the stove, maybe, use a blanket on the little bonfires in the room, throw the gasoline can far away, out into the frost.

But the damn baby was crying, it confused him. There was always a baby crying. He was so confused and so tired of hearing those screams. Children began to rout and run for the door. Only Jack's mother didn't move. Half out of bed she watched Jack's escape; he knew it and she knew it.

Now he held the gasoline can and the baby shrieked, and with his hand, a hand separated from the rest of his body, he tipped the can up until it splashed into the middle of a fire at the foot of his mother's bed, and at once he made for the door and began to run, to run and run away from the explosion that followed.

Far away up north he read the little news story, on page 11 of the *Bangor Daily News*: "Fire claims the lives of mother and child."

For a time no baby cried.

But, oh, yes, Jack Dow knew a search for escape when he saw one. Only this time he was the parent. He would be sure that none of his children got away from him.

All you had to do was be careful of secrets.

He pulled into his yard and stepped on the brakes. The car wrenched forward, then back. Vinnie, he thought, dangling the keys. Vinnie.

Vinnie Dow looked into the box Aunt Ann had sent. "What is this for?" she asked. "What does she want?"

"Nothing. She just sent it. She wants me to come back. They all do."

"Oh?"

"Yes, I'm sorry. I should have said no. I —"

Maddy couldn't go on. She couldn't meet her mother's eyes. She went to the table. They were all seated when Jack Dow came home.

There was plenty of light but it was dim, bulbs through a brown curtain. Her mother sat still at the table, her face a blank.

Had Aunt Bea Packard called him?

Jack Dow came up the steps and Maddy strained to listen; they all strained to hear his footsteps, understand his grip on the door-knob and the way it opened, to know his feeling, be prepared to see his face, not to look for his eyes. Round-eyed, Phillip and Stephen listened and Maddy felt sorry for them. They had soaked in the emergency without understanding it. Guiltily she stared at her plate. If they were hurt this time, it would be her fault.

The footsteps were too heavy. The knob turned with an impatient click and he was in the room, ruddy from the heat of the car, spinning his car keys down the kitchen counter before he turned to stare at them all.

His face was a mask. He moved to the sink, washed. The children could tell by the way he shut off the faucet in the kitchen, with a jerk that banged in the pipes, that there would be trouble. Maddy watched him carefully, covertly, as he came back to the table. His eyes were black seeds in slits. Aunt Bea Packard had called him then. He knew: every afternoon at four. This was Maddy's fault.

For a moment there was silence. Vinnie Dow didn't move. Her husband gave her a long look down the table filled with food that steamed in all its dishes. It was an unnecessarily hot meal: roast and gravy, mashed potatoes, beets. A hot night for such a meal. It would make him angrier, since every little annoyance counted. Maddy wondered. Didn't her mother see that?

Silence. One by one the heads turned; they couldn't help it, they were all looking at him. Maddy's eyes had blurred, the air felt thick. Even now, Maddy knew, if his mask were to fall and he were to turn to them and smile, or say anything quiet or gentle, then in their relief it would be as if he had never hurt them in their lives. They would be, depending on his smile, a new family in a new house.

Unwillingly, Maddy found herself remembering how her father had been when Stephen came into the house as a new baby. "Well," he'd said, "look at this nice little fellow."

While Jack Dow spoke to his new son so gently, the other children watched their mother smile, and they hoped that a good life would be possible. How their mother had loved the babies!

"Look," she would say, holding up the newest one. "Look at this baby give me kisses, great big open-mouthed kisses." Her voice was like a symphony as she moved the baby, whichever child it was, rhythmically, back and forth in her arms.

"Stephen!" their father rapped out now. "Say the grace." All the children bowed their heads.

"Dear God." Stephen spoke in a well-trained whisper. "Thank you for this food and bless it to our use. Amen."

"Amen." They all said it. They waited for their father to serve.

He did not. Once again he looked down the table at his wife. "You know, Vinnie," he said, "they want your oldest daughter at the Packards' every afternoon at four."

"I know." Vinnie looked down. "She told me."

"So she knew about it? She agreed?"

"She said there was nothing she could do, Jack."

The mask dropped. He stared at his wife, his face scowling, swelling. "Well, Maddy, I guess you think you've pulled a fast one on me now."

His eyes were still on her mother: he had chosen his victim.

"No," said Maddy. "I'll just play the piano and then I'll come home."

"You haven't got any goddamn business up there. They don't care about you, they just want whatever they can get from you. Look at me."

Maddy met the eyes: so shiny, nothing in them but hot shine. "Yes," she said.

They might have been fine, they might have escaped. Maddy could feel the children hang on to this moment of her submission. Would it appease him? Breathlessly they watched the moment pass. Another second and they might begin to breathe. Another second. Jack Dow's face seemed to relax. He reached for a serving dish.

Maybe it'll be all right, Maddy thought.

But then Vinnie Dow reached out one crooked hand and spilled Stephen's milk.

Jack Dow's tight check gave way: the world collapsed.

"Goddamnit!" he roared. "Goddamnit!" He reached for the first child at hand, Phillip, and slammed him so hard across the chest with his fist that the little boy fell backward, toppling out of his chair and hitting his head on the floor. He took a corner of the tablecloth with him — food careened, spilled. All around the table people jumped to help, mop, get out of the way, and were at once stopped by their father, who picked up a dish of vegetables and threw it so that it smashed in a corner not too far from where his wife stood utterly still.

"Mom-my!" cried Phillip from the floor. "Mom-my!"

Vinnie Dow went and knelt by her son, but at that instant Jack Dow gathered the remains of the tablecloth together and picked up whatever was left in it.

"No," he raged. "No! No!"

The steaming bundle struck his wife's shoulder and covered her with food.

"You'll burn her," Maddy cried.

Jack Dow raved. "She's no good. She doesn't deserve —"

Maddy knelt beside her mother, scraping hot dishes away from her. "I did it, it was my fault." Vinnie Dow's clothing steamed; the woman inside the clothes did not move. Maddy stared, sick with horror.

Allison and Jessica dragged at the tablecloth, leaving a mass of spilled food. Stephen was on his knees, whimpering. Jessica took Phillip; still, Vinnie Dow didn't move. Steam rose from the food on her clothes. If it burnt, she seemed not to feel it. Her eyes were on her husband, no one else. He roared incomprehensibly.

"This is my fault," Maddy mumbled, a sick feeling at her lips.

Phillip wailed. "Mom-my! Mom-my!"

Over that came Jack Dow's voice: "You deserve this, Vinnie. You deserve every mess I make." There were more crashes as he hurled leftover silver and spilled dinner plates onto the floor. "You want a mess?" he cried at his wife. "You got a mess. You are a mess, Vinnie. Now, clean it up. Clean it up."

Sickness, seasickness, the ocean in a storm. Maddy saw how food fell from her mother's clothing.

"Jack," said Vinnie Dow, "please." She watched him, small and still and waiting, her face pale, dark circles under her eyes.

"You think you know more than I do, is that it?" Maddy's parents looked only at each other. "For years you been begging me: Jack, punish me, Jack. Now you think just because you got a daughter that plays the goddamn piano, you can do just what you please?"

Vinnie Dow stayed on her knees; she clasped her hands in front of her in a curious parody of worship.

There was no end to this horror — spilled food, their humiliated mother in the gobbed-up wreckage on the floor, the weeping children.

"This is my fault," Maddy said sobbing. Her father's voice went on and on and still her mother didn't move, watching him while food dropped from her arms and from an enormous clot of it on her chest.

Jack Dow leaned over, dug his fingers into that beet-stained goo, and wiped them on his wife's shoulder. Maddy couldn't look, no one could look. It was the complete subjugation of their mother.

"Now," he said, "you stay right there on the floor with your children and you clean this all up, Vinnie. Right now."

"Jack, let me change."

"No!" he cried. "Don't you dare to! I'm going out. When I come back I expect to see you just as you are, Vinnie. Just as you are. You hear me?"

"Yes," she whispered.

He hovered over her. "Then you better listen," he said. He turned and left the house. In a moment they heard his car leave the yard.

"Mamma," Maddy said, "I'm so sorry." How could she have done anything like this?

"No." Vinnie Dow looked at Phillip, who still whimpered, a tired but protective look which said that at all costs, of course, the little children must be protected. Never had Vinnie Dow seemed more selfless to Maddy.

"Well," Jessica said, her face stony with anger and pain, "at least let us wash you off."

"No," whispered Vinnie Dow. "It doesn't matter. He'll be back soon. When he comes back, he'll bring new dishes." She spoke dully, as if it were all simple.

"We can't just forget this," Maddy said.

"Maddy, please." Vinnie Dow stared at the other children, possible victims. "All it will take," she whispered, "is new dishes."

Averting their eyes from the food clinging and beginning to crust on their mother's clothing, the children turned to the mess. Numbly they began to work, collecting the broken dishes, scraping the food from the floor, the hot paste of potato that dried to beaded ribbons when they washed at it, everything stained pink, reminding them of blood.

Before their father came home the room was clean and they were upstairs in the dark. Below, it was quiet. The children began to drop off to sleep.

A long time later Maddy heard the locks at the foot of the stairs click. She couldn't stay in bed. Horrified, fascinated, she tiptoed down to the downstairs hall and stood there in her nightgown. On one side was the door to the living room, on the other, the door to their parents' bedroom. Both doors were locked.

For long moments Maddy listened, standing between the dim whiteness of the two doors, like two ghosts, one on either side of her. There was nothing until, turning to go up the stairs, she heard an inexplicable sound; she thought, in fact, she might have made it herself: her foot on the step, skin twisting on wood. An odd sound wrenched from a human throat, possibly, but not human. She lifted another foot, stood on the first step.

She heard someone whispering, a dry whisper like a rattling of old leaves.

"Mamma," rattled the leaves in a frenzy. "Mamma. Mamma."

Then silence. Maddy's head rang with the quiet. She waited. Nothing. At last she moved back up the stairs.

Weeping by herself, Maddy tried to imagine what would happen if she went to the church, to the Heberts, or to that new young minister with eight hundred square miles of rural Maine to cover. What would she say? "My father beats me. He beats my mother and my brothers and sisters." Would anyone believe her?

Jack Dow would go to them and say, so smoothly, "Maddy is not herself today. You know children. Maddy is having nervous problems." They would believe him.

So what if all the Dow children, banded together in a group, went to the Heberts or the new minister, and they all said the same thing? Eleanor Hebert would pause for a moment and look surprised, and then Jack Dow would go and say, "Some little trick my children are playing, right?"

Eleanor would laugh and Jack would laugh, and she would walk off busily, and so would he. There would be punishment, later, when no one could see.

Their mother would have to go with them, to corroborate their story, to help them explain. Everything hinged on their mother. And she — why would she never trust anyone enough to tell them what life was really like?

There must be something their mother could do, someplace she could go, for help? The Packards? Jonah Sears? Maddy knew at once her mother would not allow these people to help. Why?

Vinnie Dow's only social functions centered around her husband's, especially in the church, where she smiled in that pleasant, distant way. If the church needed anything — someone to fix the windows, drag out more tables for a supper, or read the lesson — there was good old Jack Dow, ready to step in and do it. Vinnie would always mind the nursery. She loved children. She'd protect her children. Maddy told herself, "My mother must be a saint."

And even if they did get free, then what? Where would they go? What would they do? She, Maddy — could she ever make enough money to support her crippled mother and four other children? When she thought of this, the world seemed cold and blank and hard and she was very frightened.

And maybe she was wrong to be so upset. She'd been told since her childhood: "Love your enemies, do good to those who hurt you." "Honor your father and your mother." Love. Forgive. Perhaps she, Maddy Dow, was a little crazy if she couldn't do these things. Perhaps the whole thing was her fault to begin with, for playing the music, rocking the boat.

Either that, or there was something wrong somewhere else. Something wrong with the church and the Heberts. Could there be something wrong with God himself if the Dow children were meant to forgive, forget, whitewash, love, and help the man who continually hurt them? Love the devil himself?

Once on a layman Sunday Eleanor Hebert had stood up and spoken of God's goodness as it was shown in the holy sanctity of the family. Among the Dow children on that Sunday not an eye wavered. In spite of their troubles, they all felt they were probably proof that Eleanor Hebert was right. What good children they were, how good they were at proving they had a good family!

It was an endless maze.

After that night Maddy continued to go to the Packards'. Her mother made her. "You must, Maddy. Please." Maddy went because she thought her mother was a saint to risk so much pain for her and because, she knew guiltily, she couldn't have stayed away.

Each afternoon she went, and each night at supper in the dim light there were the questions from her father: "What did you tell them, Maddy? What did you say about me?"

"Nothing."

"Well, you better not talk about me, young lady." He would look down the line of his children, selecting for her benefit and for future reference a victim. At last his eyes would come to rest on his wife. Maddy would feel her insides curl up and try to creep away.

A catechism, every night at supper: "What do you do over there, damnit?"

"I — I play the piano."

It was half of the truth: after a few days she was allowed to walk through the Cottage on her own, as if it were her house, and into the piano room like one of the family. In that quiet, lovely room she would find Jonah — as she dared to call him now — and he would smile at her, for no reason that she could see, and listen seriously while she played. By the second week of her playing he had brought her new music, much of it from the seventeenth century, Bach and his contemporaries.

"You might want to try this," he would say in an offhand way that couldn't conceal his hope that she would try it. He taught her, too, when he couldn't restrain himself. "Drop your wrists slightly, Maddy, thus." He paced around the room, pretending not to listen, but of course he heard every note, and then couldn't restrain his comments, which were keen and helpful and supportive.

Also in the room would be Aunt Bea, who sat quietly watching and listening. If Maddy happened to look up, the old woman would smile, in her eyes such a fine and understanding light that Maddy couldn't look at them for long.

"Go ahead, my dear," Aunt Bea would say, and fold her hands. Then all there was in the room was the piano, its keys polished, now familiar: it was nowhere, everywhere, nothing and everything, all beneath her hands.

"Try this," Jonah would say, and perhaps, "Andantino, Maddy, a little lighter, and this in an arpeggio. It's for you to create one."

Sun on many white curtains. She was allowed to play the wind as it rippled them in an arpeggio, and then she would play until she no longer knew what it was she had in her hands.

Sometimes she caught Jonah looking at Aunt Bea as if to tell her something important. Once he said to Maddy, "Have you ever written any music?"

"No." Her notebook was hers, the only thing she owned and not for anyone but her. She couldn't trust anyone with it.

"Perhaps you will try," he said. "Sometime."

No. She would never show anyone.

But sometimes she thought she might like to show these people what she wrote, if she could share with them as they did with her, if they could make any sense of it.

Every night Maddy's father would ask, "What did you talk about, Maddy?"

"Music."

"Only music?"

"Yes." Only a new heaven and a new earth, but she wouldn't tell him that.

"Were they all there?"

"Yes."

Aunt Ann, too. Blueberry squares and iced tea. They all smiled gray-tooth smiles, Aunt Ann and Jonah, and Aunt Bea, too. And Maddy. When Aunt Ann smiled, Maddy wanted to creep into her arms and stay there, protected, forever.

"Did they talk about me?" her father would ask. "Or about your mother? This family?"

"No."

They did, of course. Now Aunt Bea could recite all the names, ages, and birthdays of the children and describe each one.

"It's so amusing to me," she would say. "When I don't drop off to sleep right away I think of those children, I say it all over again.

Stephen, age seven, birthday March eighth, small, dark curly hair, big brown eyes, likes little cars, likes — let me see — to run them across the kitchen floor."

As if, Maddy thought, she were really family and really interested.

"Not that they're interested!" Jack Dow would shout sometimes. "Nothing here would interest them, would it, Vinnie?" Sometimes he would snicker, asking that.

"No," their mother would say, a quiet little movement of pale lips in a pale face.

"What do they say about me, Maddy?" he asked over and over.

"Nothing. Nothing!"

"Damnit, are you sure?"

"Yes." Of course it was nothing. Absolutely nothing. For them he barely existed. "And your mother?" Aunt Bea sometimes asked, "How is she getting along?" A wistfulness would come into the old eyes.

"Aw, they don't give a damn," Jack Dow would cry, at home. "You remember, Maddy. You remember me. You remember your mother. And don't you ever let me catch you lying."

"I'll remember."

Every afternoon she went and sat at the piano and played in that shining room. She talked a little, sometimes she even managed to eat, sometimes to smile. It was a place that became more beautiful to her every day. Sometimes she would be startled and guilty to find herself feeling comfortable in it. Once Jonah made a joke, and without thinking she laughed, hard, a gale of laughter that gathered three other voices with it and flew. Then, hearing herself, she fell silent, leaving the others to stare at her, a peculiar hopefulness on their faces. But in the midst of that laughter she had heard her father's questions, the catechism to come, and known suddenly that she'd better be very, very careful.

"So they don't talk about me," he would say wearily at last. "You play the music, you come home, that's all? Damnit, are you sure?"

Enough to make you wonder, handing your mother a box of cookies — squares, cookie bars, even meringues — why didn't Vinnie Dow like what Aunt Ann sent? In this world of punishment, her mother's face would tell Maddy, There is no tiny hope, nothing like trust, nothing strong enough. Vinnie Dow would hide the boxes away or throw them out, the contents untasted. She was, Maddy told herself, protecting her children.

Again and again, her father: "You play the music, come home, that's all?"

"Yes, that's all." Maddy knew that in part, at least, she was lying. There was so much she didn't say. Jack Dow repeated himself endlessly, she knew he was dangerous. But in the end she began to feel a double guilt: Wasn't this almost like lying to an anxious child?

CHAPTER SIX

It was the evening of the first rehearsal of the Freedom chorus. Judy Hebert Russell found herself watching Maddy Dow. The girl had surprised her so at the auditions. No one had even known Maddy could play the piano, now why was that? Judy herself had been singing solos since she was eight. Musical talent didn't hide itself easily, and usually it surfaced young, she knew.

So why had it been so different for Maddy Dow?

Forty people had gathered for this rehearsal, a big crowd for a town like Freedom. Judy handed her two-year-old son, little Russ, over to Vinnie Dow in the nursery, and found herself speaking more to Vinnie than she had in years. "He's been good today. I hope you won't have any trouble."

Vinnie Dow looked away. "Oh, no," she said. "I like to take care of little ones."

"It seems your daughter has inherited your musical talent, Vinnie," Judy went on. "Did you teach her to play? Why didn't we know about her before this, such a gift?"

"Oh, I don't know." The woman flushed and seemed to search for words, at last only shrugging and smiling as she turned away with little Russ in hand.

As she turned, Judy happened to look up. In the doorway was Jack Dow.

It occurred to Judy that she didn't know Jack that well, either, although she'd seen him all her life. "Well, Jack," she said, "I bet Maddy will really shine tonight."

He smiled. In her memory, Jack Dow always seemed so willing and helpful and self-effacing. Then he said, "What makes you think so?" Behind the sooty warmth in his eyes Judy saw something hard and shiny. He was smiling.

"Oh, I don't know." At a loss, she floundered as she moved past him and out of the nursery. "It's just that she auditioned so well."

"Oh, yes," he said, nodding agreeably. "She did, didn't she?" He moved on.

It was a perfectly good response, but Judy was puzzled. She went to sit down. She guessed she'd never really thought much about the Dows before.

Watching people take their seats, she set aside everything but her pleasant reaction to any musical event, an increasing excitement and happiness. She waved at her husband Russ, seated across the way with the basses, and took her seat in the soprano section, nodding at friends and acquaintances. Also taking a seat was Judy's cousin, Eleanor's daughter, Elaine Cummings, looking beautiful as usual, this time in a new red dress with a wide belt and a full skirt. The dress set off Elaine's blond hair. Judy waved and told her how nice she looked. Elaine sat with the altos.

Professor Jonah Sears stood on the platform in the front of the room. Beside him was the piano, set at an angle so that Maddy could see him while she played. She's so thin, so small, Judy thought, staring at the wreath of black curls that partly hid the girl's face. At a nod from Jonah, Maddy began to play softly through the piece of music he was handing out. Judy found herself watching the girl's hands, the strength in them and in the narrow arms. She thought again, How could the Dows have kept it quiet so long?

At another nod from the professor, Maddy struck two vigorous chords, and the talking died away. Jonah Sears stepped forward.

"Thank you all for the wonderful response tonight. It's great to see you all here. Do you have music? Yes? Fine, we'll get started soon. First, a few organizational notes."

He proceeded to set up the rehearsal times and to explain about the series of competitions the chorus must participate in. There would be three: one at the end of the summer, one in November, and one the following March. If they were successful at all three, their performance would be taped for television, to be aired on WGME-TV,

Channel 13, as part of their Fourth of July observance. There would also be a cash prize of $2000 and a lot of free advertising for Freedom.

"Also, I understand," he concluded, "they will use the whole program of the winning chorus. By itself it will be a regular television program with full advertising, and the chorus will be paid for that. So you see, we have a lot to work for. Now let's all stand and begin some exercises. Maddy, please, a B chord."

She struck it. The singing began.

They practiced first by doing vocal exercises and then by singing chords in four parts, beginning to learn to watch Jonah's hands, to attack at his signal, hold, increase, diminish, extinguish the sound. His hands moved to cup and hold notes, he cut consonants with the meeting of thumb and forefinger — a nice, complete little gesture, Judy thought. Then they began to try the sheet music.

At a nod from Jonah, Maddy played it through first. Judy, who read music well and who had had a few voice lessons in high school, sang as helpfully as she could. She knew from long experience that one sure voice could lend courage to another, and this she wanted to do, not only for the sake of the music, but also now for Jonah's good direction, which gave her joy when she saw its ease and precision, and for Maddy's accompaniment, which was as good as Judy had heard anywhere.

When they finished the first sight-reading Jonah seemed surprised, pleased. "I can't tell you how well you're doing," he said. "This is not easy music."

The singers went on, foundering occasionally, but Jonah kept them going, helping them up and over by his praise. Maddy continually supplied notes; sometimes all Jonah did was look at her and she knew what was needed. By the end of the evening, they pretty much understood the notes in the first piece of music and they had tried several others. Jonah nodded at them.

"You've done a fine job tonight," he said. "Now there's only one problem I can see. All of you may know each other, but I don't know any of you. I have here a list of names and addresses. May we take a moment to get to know each other better? When I call your name, will you please raise your hand?"

He began to call out the names. One by one, as each person responded, he nodded and spoke to him or her for a moment, discussing that person's working, singing experience, children, job. It took a long time, but it was amazing how interesting it was. Judy knew there were people in this chorus she'd seen all her life and never really talked to. Apparently others began to think so, too; seeing themselves through Jonah Sears's eyes was like seeing each other from a different perspective. He nodded at each person as if to say "Thank you for coming here to share with us."

When he came to her name, he found Judy in the soprano section before she could raise her hand. "Mrs. Russell," he said. "Let me see, you are married to a member of the bass section?"

"Yes."

"And that means, let me see if I remember, that you have a son?"

"Yes, very good." She laughed at his effort of memory.

"Mrs. Russell, I hope you will do some solo work with us during these competitions."

"Thank you, Professor."

"Jonah, please."

When he called the next name, Judy looked over to her husband Russ and they grinned at each other.

Then the first rehearsal was over. Some singing had been done, but something else of importance had happened, Judy felt. The people in the chorus had begun to know each other better, and everybody, after a few questions from Jonah Sears, had some small subject with which to begin a conversation with another person.

You wouldn't think that would be necessary in Freedom, Judy thought, but it is. In a small town you might know each other's names, faces, genealogy, and political persuasion. In a small-town church you might know who was more or less willing to take part. But in a small town just as much as in a large city, Judy thought, it was easy not to talk, not to find out how other people were really feeling, or how they really looked at life. Easier, maybe, because of age-old built-in prejudices that cut people off from each other.

"Take your music home if you wish," Jonah was saying. "Sing to each other at home — why not? Life could be worse! Just be sure to bring it back on Thursday, ready to work. That's all for tonight, then."

There were chords in Judy's head from the music they'd been practicing. She hummed to herself happily, smiling and waving as she got ready to leave. She felt this chorus was going to be good, going to be great for her. Oh, it was good to be able to sing! She hummed to herself as Russ came toward her, his carrot-colored hair glinting in the light. When he joined her, he, too, was humming. They linked hands, making harmony. Around them people smiled.

"Jonah is all right, isn't he?" Russ said after a moment.

Judy nodded. "He's super. Sounds like you got rhythm, kid."

"You, too."

"Yeah." Russ struck an extraordinarily low note, giving himself a double chin and a potbelly as he reached for it. Judy stared in mock surprise. There was some laughter around them.

Still holding hands, they made their way to the nursery.

"When a stranger appears, we all get to know each other," Judy said.

"Right you are, lady."

They went to pick up little Russ, finding on their way a number of people to speak to, going in and coming out. There were snatches of humming as well as conversation in the room. Here and there somebody whistled a bit of what they'd been singing. Judy, happening to look the length of the vestry on her way out, saw that Maddy Dow stood alone at the piano, penciling a note on a sheet of music.

Because Judy was happy and felt this was going to be a good group and that no one of Maddy's talent should be alone, she left little Russ with his father and flew to the front of the hall, where, seeing Maddy's thin shoulders, she reached out impulsively and hugged the girl.

"Maddy, I just wanted to say you did a great job tonight. I'm glad you're playing for us."

Startled, the girl turned. She trembled under Judy's hands. "Thank you," she managed, swallowing. Then words came more easily; the afternoons with Aunt Bea were helping her tongue. "I think you sing so well. I've always thought so." Her eyes, large and brown, were shining.

But Judy, with a cordial smile on her own face, saw the clearly eager, shy look on Maddy's replaced suddenly by a guarded opacity. The girl had seen something bad, somewhere in the back of the room? Judy turned, saw only a crowd of people talking. Jack Dow was looking in their direction.

"Well, you're nice to say so," Judy said. "Perhaps sometime we could get together, make some music."

"Oh, I'd like that." Maddy didn't look at Judy at all, but she wanted to speak; she would. "I think," she said, "you have a — a free voice."

"A free voice? What a wonderful compliment," said Judy, touched. Russ beckoned to her. "Well, I've got to go. Keep up the good work. Talk to you later."

"Yes," said Maddy.

It was late when the Russells got home, and little Russ settled down in his crib without a murmur. Judy padded, humming, across the tippy floorboards in their old farmhouse and got into the big old-fashioned bed with Russ, still singing softly to herself. She liked to lie in this comfortable, lumpy place and let her voice rise and hang in the air, or, like tiny clusters of crystal grapes, from the corners of the ceiling. She liked to send her voice up there softly, accurately.

This she did now, having climbed into the protective circle of Russ's arm. He liked her music and expected it at night, when sometimes she sang a blessing, very softly to herself so as not to disturb anyone, before she went to sleep. Now the sounds rose quietly from their bed. When she finished she found she had lullabyed Russ, and he was breathing deeply, easily.

She herself was awake, was thinking, Maddy Dow. I wonder why we didn't know she was musical. "A free voice." What an odd thing to say.

A ringing in her scalp, it went on and on.

"What did Judy Russell say to you, what?"

His hands were in her hair. "Nothing, please," Maddy cried.

He pulled, wrenching her back, holding her to keep her from saying anything about him, about what went on in their house. One question, one little answer, that would be all it took. People would find out who he really was, what he did. He would be found out. That couldn't happen.

"I'm watching you, Maddy," he said. "I'm watching you every minute. Just you remember that."

*

Too hurt to cry, Maddy lay upstairs in the dark, her scalp still ringing, waiting for muscles to twitch themselves out. She was hanging on to Judy's words for dear life: "You did a great job tonight and I'm glad you're playing for us." Judy had hugged her. "Perhaps sometime we could get together, make some music."

"I will make you some music." Maddy was promising Judy this fiercely, silently, as she lay there. "I will make you some music, because you deserve to have music made for you."

Jessie was asleep. Maddy stared into the dark. Far off she heard the beginnings of a sound that was high and sweet, gone when she thought of it, but luring her somewhere, far out into the night.

CHAPTER SEVEN

ELAINE HEBERT CUMMINGS'S NEW little red car pulled into Judy Russell's dooryard the next morning. Judy was out at the clothesline Russ had strung between two big old maples beside their house. About the only convenience there was in the farmhouse was a brand-new washing machine and enough water to use it, and Judy used it daily. Every sunny morning she came to this clothesline and hung a new batch of wet things. The shade of the trees was dark and cool; they grew on a little bluff and behind them was an untilled field that someday might be lawn. Now it had gone to tall blowing grasses, daisies, hawkweed, dandelions, hardhack, and Queen Anne's lace just beginning to bloom. It was nice to hang up laundry with that view. Often Judy hummed as she worked and made little chirping noises and did warm-up vocal exercises that made little Russ, playing in the dirt with his trucks not too far off, laugh to hear her.

So she was singing when Elaine drove up, and she continued to sing as Elaine got out of her car, waved, and approached. Elaine Cummings was a picture in a white dress: slender, blond, big blue Packard eyes. The dress was stylish, the makeup artful. Middle America's dream girl, Judy told herself and sighed.

"Elaine!" she exclaimed aloud, the more cordially. "Hi! What are you up to today?"

Rival and friend since early childhood, Elaine had always been the perfectly dressed one, popular, blessed with a generous allowance that she overspent generously. And Judy — Judy had gone in for

jeans, and had gotten a job while still in high school. After gradua-
tion she had married Russ and moved into this old farmhouse because
she loved it, Russ loved it, and because it was such a refreshing change
from the neat, long, modern ranch Elaine had chosen.

Elaine, on the other hand, had allowed her parents to build her
that house when she and Cyril were married. And, Judy knew, the
Heberts had bought her the red car, her closetful of clothes, the dress
she was wearing, and all the rest of it.

It was a crucial difference of outlook, Judy thought.

"Oh, nothing much," Elaine said now. "Actually, Judy, I came to
ask a favor."

"Oh?"

"Yes, a big one. I was wondering, you're such a homebody these
days . . ."

"Well, I like to be, because of little Russ."

"Yes. I was wondering . . . I've weaned Elana and put her on a
bottle and, well, I'd like to start feeling like a person again, if you
know what I mean. I'd like to do something just for me, if you
understand, and so I was wondering . . ."

Helpless and delicate and beautiful, Elaine stood before her. When
had Judy ever been able to refuse Elaine anything?

"I was wondering," Elaine continued, "if you would take Elana
sometimes for me in the mornings. I want to go see if they remember me at the agency." This was the modeling agency in Portland. "I
was thinking, you could earn a little money and get to know Elana."

Big eyes, long curly lashes, a little pout.

Judy had resolved not to get into any kind of monetary arrangement with family. It was too complicated.

"Well, I don't know," she said. "In some ways I'd be glad to do
it. I mean, we're related and all that."

"Double cousins." Elaine smiled.

"Practically sisters." This was an old family formula. Now they
were both smiling. Judy was fond of Elaine. "The only thing is,
Elaine, that you and I don't see eye to eye on a lot of things, and if
there were ever a problem, we'd be bound to have trouble."

"Oh, we could talk it out," Elaine said. "Don't you think? Judy,
if I could just get out from under, at least for the mornings."

There was such helplessness in Elaine.

"Well, all right." Judy agreed at last. "But just to try, Elaine. To see if it will work out. And I don't know about money."

"Oh, we can figure that out, sure we can. Oh, Judy, thanks. Can I — could I bring her tomorrow, then?"

Judy concealed a smile. Elaine always did work fast. "Where is she today?"

"At my mother's. But Mother is so busy. Well, you know."

Eleanor Hebert was one of the busiest people in town. Another reason to feel sorry for Elaine, her daughter.

"Yes, I know. Bring little Elana tomorrow, and we'll see what works out."

"Oh, Judy, you're the best, a real lifesaver." Elaine hugged her. It was like being hugged by something as light and wispy as spun sugar.

Judy extricated herself. "Well, we can try. We'll have to see."

Elaine was already heading for her car, but she stopped, turned to say, "Great. Oh, by the way, Judy, I heard you singing last night."

"At the rehearsal?" Now that she had given in this far to Elaine, Judy relaxed still further. She loved compliments and felt she'd sung well the night before.

"Yes," Elaine said as she jumped into her car and slammed the door. She spoke through the open window. "Boy, you were singing loud, weren't you?"

Before Judy could reply, she roared away.

Judy stood staring down the empty road. "Now what did she mean by that?" she muttered.

Stung but making allowances for Elaine as always — Elaine had never known much about how other people felt — Judy headed back to the clothesline. There she stood, alternately staring out into the field of flowers and hanging the wet clothes, giving each article a little unnecessary extra snap as she laid it to the line. But after a while the snapping stopped, and when she came to herself she realized she was humming once again.

Elaine Cummings's hand, when Jonah Sears took it, was soft. Her blond hair shimmered about her face.

"It was kind of you to see me," she said, smiling at him. "I know how busy you must be." She seemed light, delicate.

"Not at all," Jonah said, bending toward her more cordially than he meant to.

Aunt Ann said, "Jonah, would you like me to bring coffee?"

"Oh, don't go to any trouble on my account." Elaine made a graceful little gesture with a hand as white as a dainty pocket handkerchief.

"Aunt Ann, I'll come and get some coffee in a little while. I don't mind, and it will save you some steps," Jonah said.

Without comment, Aunt Ann went to the kitchen.

"Right this way." Jonah led Elaine into the music room.

"Oh, how lovely," she said. "It looks as if it's being used. It never was before that I remember."

Pretty cushions, a vase of flowers, music strewn on the piano.

"The Packards are kind enough to make a home for me," Jonah said. "And Maddy Dow comes to practice here in the afternoons."

"You mean the little girl who plays the piano?"

"Yes." Jonah thought that when Elaine entered the room, a scent entered with her, of flowers, of candy, delicate, alluring.

"She's a cute little thing."

"Please, sit down, Mrs. Cummings."

"Elaine." She smiled at him again.

"Elaine." Jonah heard the note of chivalry that had crept, somehow, into his voice. It made him a touch uncomfortable. "I'll get the coffee." He went to the kitchen.

Wordlessly Aunt Ann handed him a tray. When he'd left she muttered to the teakettle, "Just like a kid in a candy store."

Elaine had come, it turned out, to ask Jonah to give her voice lessons, and by the time she had brought out her errand with a kind of halting eagerness, her delicate skin was flushed and the wonderful blue eyes swam with tears.

"It is hard," she said, "since I'm also a mother."

"Of course," said Jonah. "I can understand that."

As she talked on, he examined his days. Were they so busy? No. All that awaited him was that misbegotten dissertation. What harm could there be in taking on a voice pupil? This girl was certainly appealing and might, in fact, deserve to be rescued from the daily humdrum she described. The wrong occupation could be excruciating, he knew that.

"I might help you," he said at last, cautiously. "Perhaps twice a week, in the morning?" To rescue him, as well, from those endless pages, from coming down off breakfast into the usual miasma of what he was called to do and couldn't, wouldn't, do. "We could begin, at any rate, and see how we progress. Have you done any singing, Elaine?"

"Not solo work," she said. "My cousin Judy always had that. But I've thought that I have some talent. I can read music a little, and no one has ever told me I sing badly. I would like to learn to sing very well, perhaps even to try a solo someday."

He found himself thinking of penny candy — why was that? Of course, voice lessons would be a diversion only. There was Audrey. He didn't intend to fall into the Laura trap again; he knew better. But he might be able to help.

Jonah spent some moments outlining the sorts of things they would be doing: exercises, tone formation, consonant placement. After a while they both stood.

"Please," Elaine said, laying a hand on his arm, "I know you have important work to do, and I know this house. Why don't I just take the coffee things and go. Thank you again, so much, and I'll see you in a couple of days."

Gracefully she picked up the tray and left the room. She left an empty space, she left him to his desk; he was sorry to see her go.

Aunt Ann was sorry to see her come. She wasn't sure why. As soon as Elaine got inside the kitchen door, Aunt Ann took the coffee tray away from her.

"Thank you," she said, wanting the girl to leave. Why? There are some people, Aunt Ann decided, that you just don't like.

"Not at all, Aunt Ann, thank you." Elaine seemed in no hurry. "Those little cookies were delicious. Made with butter, I think?"

"Shortbread." Aunt Ann had the definite feeling that this girl perceived how she felt and only lingered to get even somehow.

"And the coffee was so good." Elaine clasped her hands together.

"Well, I'm glad you thought so," said Aunt Ann.

"Oh, yes, indeed." Elaine smiled irresistibly. "I'll have to tell Mother what a good cook you are."

"Well, I would appreciate that."

"Yes, I believe this whole household is getting such good care."

Elaine closed her eyes in a gesture of pleasure. "What a good job you're doing! Tell me, Aunt Ann — you're such a great cook and all — do you taste the food as you make it?"

In spite of herself Aunt Ann softened. This was her favorite subject. "Well," she said, "I do. You have to, really. To correct the seasonings and make sure the consistencies are proper. When I beat an egg white with sugar, for example, I do it in two stages."

Elaine held up a hand. "I thought you did," the girl said. "Of course, it was hard to tell."

She left the kitchen.

Aunt Ann paused, dumbfounded, her eyes on the swinging door. She stared into the air. "That started out to be a compliment," she muttered. "Or it felt like it for a while there."

When Aunt Ann heard that Elaine would be coming back on a regular basis, she made a little clucking noise. "Tch, Jonah," she said. "Tch."

"Now, Aunt Ann."

"Well, there's something a little bit — I don't know — funny about that girl."

"Oh, now."

"No, I mean it, Jonah. She's like a batch of show biscuits. You bite into them and, yes, they're crunchy on the outside and light on the inside, the way they should be, and then you realize that, oh, my God, they don't have any salt in them."

"Aunt Ann."

"Jonah, really! Oh, hell."

"Now I deal with undergraduates all the time." Jonah tried to reason. "I can handle her."

Aunt Ann only clucked.

After that, she got into the habit of letting Jonah answer the door for Elaine. And when she could, she stayed away from that girl altogether.

Jonah enjoyed giving the lessons, he discovered. He was convinced he'd been right, in this case, to be charitable. Elaine was not a great musical talent, not like Maddy, for example. At the university he would have asked Elaine Cummings to audition first, then he would have assigned her to the instructor who might help her the most. If her audition had not been fruitful, he would have said so courteously and perhaps suggested that some other branch of the discipline might make more sense for her.

Jonah suspected that he might not have accepted Elaine, had she come to the university for lessons. But this wasn't Portland, this was Freedom, and he was free. Elaine had what he thought of as "presence," and she was certainly willing to try. If her voice wasn't the truest or most powerful he'd ever heard, it was a nice little voice, and a few lessons certainly wouldn't hurt.

"Smile so I can see your teeth at the sides of the mouth," he instructed her at the first lesson. "Good. Now sing: *eee, eee, eew.*"

Not a very attractive facial posture, with a smile like a grimace on the singer's face and the nasal *eee* sounding out. But the chiseling of her features, the delicate blush on her cheeks, the childish clasp of her hands in effort at her waist, were all very appealing. He found himself thinking traitorously that in some branches of music it was the presence that counted almost as much as the talent.

Each lesson a new vowel. *A* on the upper lips, *o* at the nostrils, *ooo* (as in long *u* sounds) just below the nose — the system Jonah taught to all his beginners. Twice a week, while his dissertation waited, he instructed Elaine, thinking he'd never seen such loveliness as in this girl as she touched her lips and made the proper sounds. It was good distraction for him, a rest. There was such a tremulous air about her, as if she were innocent of her own charm.

"That's it," he would say almost protectively, "that's where to control your breathing. Not with your shoulders, breathe below the ribs. In, out, in, out, that's it. Now let's try it on a note."

"Tch," Aunt Ann would cluck when the lesson was over. "Is our Modern Beauty Rose gone for the day?"

"Now, Aunt Ann, I can't see that she's doing anybody any harm."

Aunt Ann would sigh. "No," she would say. "I don't suppose you can."

The talent of Maddy Dow, on the other hand, was a constant challenge. Her ability pressed into action all Jonah's resources. He found himself reading books he hadn't read in years in order to help her. For Maddy he recalled favorite passages of music from his own youth. Now he had in front of him Bach's preface to an autograph of his *Inventions and Sinfonias.* Bach had written:

Proper instruction wherein the lovers of the clavier, and especially those desirous of learning are shown a clear way not only (1) to learn to play clearly in two voices, but also, after further progress, (2) to deal correctly and well with three obligato parts; furthermore, not only to have good *inventiones* (ideas) but to develop the same well, and above all to arrive at a singing style (Cantable Art) in playing while acquiring a strong foretaste of composition.

"A strong foretaste of composition." Jonah found himself wondering again. Did Maddy write music?

He continued on, reading from Landowska's chapter on the interpretation of Bach's keyboard works.

To understand the esthetic of Bach, so different from that of the romantic period, and to revive this CANTABLE ART according to Bach's spirit, let us study closely, with reverence and passion, an invention or a two-part prelude. Let us interrogate the voices separately; . . . Let us watch their slightest motion, follow their fluctuations. And lo and behold, before the quest of our indefatigable love, a miracle takes place.

Maddy caught details that Jonah himself didn't, so eager was she to understand the pieces he brought for her to work on. Tiny things: the difference between the usual dotted quarter note, three short beats, and Bach's dotted quarter, which implied two dots followed by a sixteenth note. Sometimes it took him half a year to explain Bach's dotted quarter to prospective classical pianists.

The inspiration of Bach and the mystery of his melodic line reveal themselves. This melodic line has nothing polished, nothing uniform; it is perpetually alive — exuberant and fiery, penetrating and incisive, this melodic line digs such deep grooves that it becomes polyphonic all by itself.

I must give this to Maddy, he thought. But he knew he would keep it for a while longer. To help this girl he would need Landowska for inspiration. However, Maddy herself was an inspiration.

What she seemed to come to naturally was what many inexperienced pianists stumbled over: the realization of each line of Bach's music as a separate singing voice. Somehow Maddy knew without being told that the sounds of Bach must not be spread across the keys thickly and with much use of the pedal. When Maddy played Bach it was with wrists and fingers, with strength, precision, neatness.

Now she was learning some of the *Inventions;* her voicing was instinctive, spontaneous.

She was singlehearted about music. Sometimes to the exclusion of anything else.

"When the music goes on," Aunt Bea said once, gently, "Maddy goes away."

It was true. She seemed to lose contact with everyone else, to climb inside some world of her own.

She hid so. Jonah shared a growing musical understanding with her, but no other details of her life. He knew she was sixteen years old and about to begin her senior year of high school, but she seemed so much younger, undeveloped, even unaware of her age, that all three of them, he and Aunt Bea and Aunt Ann, too, thought of her as much younger, a child.

It was a week before Maddy had trusted herself to laugh at the Cottage, and even then the laugh was brought up short. She never spoke of herself, although often, in a general way, about her brothers and sisters. She had none of the inflated ego of most talented young musicians. She was a worker, without conversation but eager to be taught.

Jonah drew on his experience. No child could have such a musical understanding without some kind of lively musical world within. Hidden, perhaps, but nourishing. Polyphonic lines, the Bach — how could the girl understand the voicing of separate lines so well?

"A strong foretaste of composition." The words had an echo, Jonah thought, a resonance.

Of course, that was it. Maddy Dow not only ate, slept, and dreamed music, she must be writing it as well. She had to be. No harmony training. She must write, or at least imagine, polyphonically.

As the remaining weeks of July passed into August and the Freedom chorus rehearsals got themselves going smoothly, as Jonah continued with Elaine's lessons, he became more and more convinced that Maddy Dow must come out of hiding with the music she wrote. She had to share, it was vital.

One day he happened to be in the kitchen as Maddy came across the field and Aunt Ann, standing at the kitchen sink, muttered, "What do you s'pose that girl is up to?"

"What?"

"Every day I see her stop there, at the edge of the lawn."

As they watched, Jonah saw the girl settle a little notebook into a pocket of her dress. She had three summer dresses, they all knew by now, just alike except for the color, which she wore to Aunt Bea's in succession.

"Like a uniform," Aunt Ann had muttered once. "And her hair. Why doesn't her mother —"

"Maddy doesn't care," said Aunt Bea gently.

Jonah thought, It doesn't matter to her what the dresses look like. All that matters is that they have a pocket big enough for a small notebook to hide in.

There was a crowd of brash undergraduates out there in the musical world, all busy proving their competence, while this girl hid away. It made him angry.

"Maddy," he said firmly that day at the piano, "you are writing music, I know you are. Now it's up to you, of course, but I believe you have a future in music, and to have it you must learn to cope with the outside world. No, better, to like it. You have to. Over the past weeks I've been so impressed with your work —" He had to stop. Her eyes had darkened.

"Jonah," said Aunt Bea faintly from the sofa, "you mustn't frighten Maddy."

"I'm lecturing?" said Jonah helplessly.

"A little."

"Maddy, am I lecturing?"

"It's only if — it's only if I'm not doing something right —" The big brown eyes, the face too tense, full of pain. "If you want me to go home or something —"

"No!" Jonah was at a loss. He searched through all the proper reactions of an educator and found nothing good. "I want you to trust us. You have more talent in your little finger than any student — any student—" He stopped again. There were no rules for this that he could see. "I want to help you," he said at last, simply.

She glanced away, at the doors, windows, plotting an escape route.

"Maddy," he said gently, "I want you to write a composition for us. That shouldn't be so hard. But your assignment is, once it's finished, to share."

"I —" She looked at him, afraid.

Afraid of him?

"If," said Jonah still more gently, "you are afraid of me, then your assignment is to share with someone else. Aunt Bea, perhaps. Someone. You must get used to people, Maddy. Music needs composers, but you need listeners."

Afraid of him? The tenseness of her shoulders, the severity of her expression, cut through Jonah's well-used words. Suddenly he felt the harshness of the rules he'd made, long before, to protect himself. He felt inadequate.

He shook his head. "I'm sorry," he said. "If I've spoken out of turn, I apologize, Maddy."

She lifted a hand, put it down, said nothing.

At the sofa sat Aunt Bea, her face full of pity. Aunt Ann had paused at the door on her way to the kitchen. Now she, too, watched. They all wondered, Would the girl get up and run away?

In his frustration it seemed to Jonah that he hadn't done anything just right: first the damn work in his typewriter, then Audrey, and now this girl, maybe the one greatly talented pupil he would ever meet in his lifetime. If only he were able to crack the shell of his usual polite manner, his customary responses. He turned away, staring out the window.

But they all reckoned without Maddy. Her life long she had been hearing music with no idea why and no reason, thinking she was crazy, feeling alone. She wanted to trust these people. She saw Jonah's silhouette at the window and remembered all the times over the past weeks when something she had done had brought light to his face, had excited him, sent him for research, opened new doors for them both. More than anything, suddenly, she didn't want Jonah to feel bad, as he was feeling.

"I have written some things," she said in a low voice. "Nothing much. Some things to practice on, mostly. I have this." Slowly she drew the notebook from her pocket and laid it on the piano. It was her precious notebook, a gift to him, all she had.

"It's nothing," she said. "Things that occur to me. Nothing whole, just pieces."

Jonah turned. He looked at Aunt Bea, whose eyes were full of love, and at Aunt Ann, who nodded, her lips clamped tightly together. He saw Maddy's fingers touch that little notebook as if to protect it, then leave it for him and grip themselves tightly in her lap. He saw that grip; it went straight to his heart.

"Thank you, Maddy," he said.

He picked up the notebook and opened it. Each page was a crisp rattle of indented, tiny, tangled notes, lines of melodies written every which way on the page, some scrawled in a hurry, some written so deeply into the paper that they could never be erased. He was astounded and moved.

"This is amazing," he said quietly to the form huddled, suffering, on the piano bench. "This is remarkable. Do you hear all these things, Maddy?"

Without looking at him, she nodded.

"Would you let me keep this for a little while? I'd like to look through it, to see where we might go from here. Will you let me, for a little while?"

Again she nodded.

"Ah." He looked through the pages. Toward the back the writing became so entangled, so complicated and small, he had to ask: "Maddy, why is this so crowded?"

Now she did not look at him. The severe little face grew puzzled and then, suddenly, light. "I — I have to — save paper." She gulped, tried to smile. "I'm sorry. If you don't like it, I —"

"Good God," said Aunt Ann, "I got notebooks all over the house. They're just going to waste. Hell, if it's notebooks you want, Maddy —"

"Yes, indeed," said Aunt Bea at once. "We have plenty of paper. Why —" She broke off, remembering something.

"Maddy," said Jonah, "will you write us a new piece?"

"Wait, Jonah," said Aunt Bea. "Wait 'til I find it. Oh, Ann, what if I can't find it." In a moment the two old ladies were searching a far corner of shelves. Jonah closed the notebook and smiled at Maddy. She was his pupil, maybe more like his child.

"Write us a new piece," he said. "And then, please, bring it here. Perhaps you'll show it to me? Please. We'll play it. We'll criticize maybe. You won't be afraid of that, will you?"

Mutely she shook her head.

"No," he said. "I know you. You'll be glad of it. We all need this kind of criticism so we won't be so lonely. And what I say, or Aunt

Bea or even Aunt Ann, will probably be no worse than what you've told yourself already. I'm willing to bet it'll be much better. But it doesn't matter, and it doesn't stop you — it's how to learn. And that's music. That's love, Maddy."

Jonah nodded at the girl, at the brown eyes — misted now, he thought — that so much wanted to believe him. In unguarded moments with his best pupils he was not ashamed to share himself in this way. With the best of them, he knew, it always came down to love. As for him, he had a yearning for those first true leaves, to help them grow upright.

"You mean any kind of music?" she said now. "Anything?" He saw her taste this, try it.

"Cantable art, Maddy. You know what that means."

"Anything that sings."

"Yes. And I would like to be your teacher." He had never asked this of anyone before. "If you will let me."

Her voice was very low. "I can't pay you, Jonah."

"Pay? Other people pay me. Do I need your money? No. When I do, I'll tell you."

"You'd do it for free?"

"Yes. Free. Completely free. For me it would be a bargain." Jonah saw suddenly that it didn't matter where he was, at the university or in Freedom, Maine. I haven't escaped, he thought. But I haven't left anything behind, either. It was strangely comforting.

"Jonah," Aunt Bea broke in, "I want to give Maddy a present, for her assignment. Here, Maddy, this is for you. Ann helped me find it."

She put in the girl's hands a leatherbound notebook of musical notation paper, quite small. "August gave this to me years ago. I never used it, but I'm a great saver of things. The habits of an old woman."

Slowly Maddy opened the leather cover. The pages were blank except for the musical staffs.

Jonah glanced at Aunt Bea. "Thank you," he said.

"I would like to — to write you a song," Maddy whispered. "To tell you something fine, something really beautiful." She lifted her eyes, and Jonah and the aunts saw they were wet with tears. "Because you're so nice to me," she whispered.

They looked about them, at each other, all close to tears. They weren't, at that moment, young or old, schooled or uneducated, cultured, talented, practical, or kind. They were these things, but more. Together, the four of them, they were much more. To Maddy it seemed they existed — and somehow she with them, for this moment — in some light place where all were equal, of equal intention and spirit, four very good people, with love for the present and hope for the future.

I will write you a song to tell you that, she thought. To tell you how we are right now to each other.

Aunt Ann said, "You're a good girl, Maddy, that's all."

"Yes," said Aunt Bea.

Maddy tried to smile.

Jonah said, "About the composition, Maddy. You mustn't feel any pressure. The assignment is, when it's finished, to share. Will you think about it?"

"How can I help but think about it?" Maddy said softly.

Aunt Ann snuffled, hunted for a tissue, blew her nose soundly. "Well, good then," she said. "Good enough. It's settled. As for me, I think we could eat. Don't you, really? My God, I'm starved. No breakfast to speak of. Couldn't take much lunch, either, come to think of it." She bustled off. After a moment Maddy went with her, shyly, because it was a joy to her when she was allowed to help.

"And if she does make it," Jonah muttered, staring at the little notebook in his hand. "Of course, I could be wrong."

Aunt Bea said, "Jonah, that girl will wring our hearts before she's through."

The song Maddy heard began in the middle voice, a minor key, up, then down and up again. As time went on and the assignment to share lay upon her, she didn't know if she should write it down. In fact, she thought maybe she should forget what she heard and write something different, something happier, more thankful. As the month of August passed into hundreds of footsteps on the path between the Cottage and her own home, she tried to think deliberately of something appropriate for sharing. But when she did try, there was only silence. Experience had taught her long before what that meant: if she was to have music at all, it must be what she heard. Finally she decided that she would write down the middle voice first. Perhaps it would become happier somehow. Or perhaps, if it did not, she could fix it in some way.

She didn't know how. She was afraid of what she might hear, suddenly.

She remembered how she'd thought at the age of seven that writing music was easy: you moved the flashcards on the music rack. She remembered, too, the heat of the stove.

She knew she couldn't deny what she heard. There it was, as clear as if it had been played on a real instrument, a hollow, lost, middle voice, cantably hollow. She listened.

As days passed and she listened, a new voice also appeared, like the bass in one of the fugues she'd been playing for Jonah. A new voice, lower, that seemed as day followed day to drive the other in front of it. The new voice pushed at the upper notes, herded them, forced them to climb. The upper voice continued its theme, but in cracks of time. helplessly.

Would she have to write that? Maddy wondered, but she knew, of course, that she would. To have music, you had to accept it all.

Once Jonah had said, "Bach's musical climaxes are not a matter of loudness, and there are no accelerandos. He played the harpsichord, the clavier, the clavichord — instruments that do not give themselves to dynamics and that he nearly always played at a fever pitch. His climaxes are internal, Maddy, a matter of rising pitch, inner concentration, many notes and themes, of timing, of juxtaposition of voices." Now she knew that that, too, came from Landowska.

Two voices, then. She would have to write them down.

Up in her room, Maddy at last opened Aunt Bea's notebook, drew in a treble clef, a bass. Bar lines next, a time signature — did she have one? A key? There. Now the middle voice begins: up, middle, higher still, with an inflection like a question: What notes, what notes?

Maddy didn't know, wasn't sure. And as she wrote in a few notes, haltingly, how loud the bass sounded.

Jonah would never like this. No one could.

She closed the notebook deliberately and picked up one of the books Jonah had given her to read. But the pages were like tissue and made a sound when she turned them. "What notes?" they whispered. "What notes?"

She closed the book and went to bed, but soon she was dreaming. "Did you ever write any music?" someone was asking her. "What notes?" She would have to write what she heard, that was apparent, even in her sleep.

Slowly, then, the next morning at the piano, with a blank lined page in front of her, Maddy began again to write down what she heard. The middle voice: four notes, five, six hollow notes, even a little polite in themselves, even, perhaps, helpless notes. Not desperate, but with a twisting melody. Now the lower voice. Maddy wrote in three notes. How would they sound together?

She tried it. Yes. But the second line needed a slightly different rhythm — there. Ten notes, and now both voices sounded louder, more intense, searching.

That inevitable bass! Clearly sounding, it must be clearly written. She wrote in three more bass notes, three warning notes. Deeply, and more minor, and again. She wrote. There she was, at measure seven, and what was happening: there was the bass she heard, driving at the upper line, which becomes driven. Oh, it had to be written!

She gave herself up to it, then, and went ahead.

She worked for several hours. In the end she had eighteen measures in a minor key, with a pressing bass. Was it music? Was it anything to share? She didn't know. It was only what she heard, the only thing she could write, for her music to survive.

Day by day as the chorus rehearsed and Maddy practiced with them she worked at her composition. Once she had truly begun, she couldn't have left it alone if she'd wanted to. By the end of August, the piece in Aunt Bea's notebook had grown to some twenty-two measures, and Maddy was both excited and afraid. She felt the urge to fill every line in the book, but she worked slowly. To make music was for her somewhere between a game and a religion; her best effort was to mull over what she heard with internal listening until the notes were utterly true.

Over the weeks, she found that the walk to and from the Cottage was a time for such listening, and as the field flowers gradually changed from buttercups to daisies to black-eyed Susans, and as the wild asters began to grow on treelike stems all over the field, she would watch them and listen. When the big house had disappeared behind her and the Dows' plain white house had not yet appeared at the other end of the fields, she would stand still, looking at the grasses, at the clouds, listening. Often Jessica would wait on the doorstep, all of a flap, and Maddy, "off," would suddenly awake to longer shadows and realize she'd walked home without knowing it, to Jessie's urging.

A whole summer had passed on the strength of what she heard. Rehearsals, catechisms, even in a way the Cottage — all had become at times secondary to Maddy as the measures took shape in her notebook, as she followed sounds to find out where they led.

One day not too long before the first Freedom chorus competition, Maddy walked home dreaming, hearing a persistent measure, mulling it over and over. In the middle of the field she stopped entirely, and next realized she was staring at clouds, a high bank of them rolling up into the afternoon sun. As she watched, it seemed to her that the white parts of the upper clouds were actually faces, many faces. They rolled up and around toward the sun, and then more faces came into the light and more, numbers of them — she could see eye sockets and noses. White lips were open: cloud people. They were singing, she was sure of it, singing something she almost heard, something beautiful, some high music, as they rolled toward the sun. Beneath their upturned faces was a heavy bank of blue-gray cloud that endlessly provided more singers. If she could only hear that music, have it, in some way.

Maddy thought the faces were happy. They came from dark into white and golden, and they sang and they looked into the sun without harm, and they were happy. They rolled away to the sun in wisps and disappeared, replaced by other faces. They were ghosts, Maddy thought. They were real. And that sweet music — if only she could touch those notes.

After a long time she began to walk down the field, her eyes studying the sky, so that for some time she didn't see Jessica standing on a tiny doorstep far away. She didn't see her sister's frantic waving, or hear her cry. Maddy was stumbling down the field, her eyes on the clouds, and when she came to the road she realized too late that her father's car was in the driveway. His face was in the window. There was no time to hide the package in her hands, some cookies from Aunt Ann.

He opened the door for her and slammed it on her heels. There was no supper; the violence came from everywhere.

He tore open Aunt Ann's box. His face bulged.

"What do you do over there, Maddy? Feed them some sob story? Tell 'em we don't feed you? Tell 'em some bad story about Jack Dow? Get them to wipe your tears for you?" He was standing a little distance from her, his face purple-brown with sudden anger, his lips pulling too far back from his teeth. She saw him and didn't want to look too closely. She was afraid to see his eyes, they might be red.

She tried to say "It was just a little present." Her dismay stopped the words. How often had it been some little, unexpected thing that triggered an explosion? From Jack Dow's superhuman control of details, this destruction.

"I saw you! I saw you down the goddamn field taking your time, not a care in the world, leaving your chores!" Now he had come so close that she could see the untanned lines about the eyes in his tanned face, white cracks in old leather. His eyes were black, but the fury in them — instinctively she put up her hands for protection.

He didn't hit her at first. His hand was on the back of her neck, dragging her. Light, dark, a room that twisted, snapped away, fell with a thudding sound. She realized she had fallen against a doorjamb. The wood had made a cut across one eyebrow. It would show. He saw this in her eyes and roared, "Oh, you think you're so good! You think you have something to use against me. Do you?" Like the bar lines at the end of many measures, the thumpings came: the back of her head against wood again and again.

That would not show.

"Vinnie!" Releasing Maddy, who slumped to the floor, Jack Dow grabbed his wife and held her squarely so that she and Maddy stared at each other. Maddy clung to the door frame, trying to stand, not daring to stand.

"Vinnie! You see her? You see your daughter?"

"I see. Jack, please." When her mother fought her father, it was always with such little motions. Why was that? Maddy blinked to clear her head.

"Well," he said, "I'm going to teach her to take better care of you and the others. Yes. Things just got a little too comfortable around here, I can see that right now. She's got to feeling a little too free, maybe." He released his wife, all but one wrist, her crippled wrist. Over in a corner of the room the other children huddled, not daring to move. On their faces horror grew as they stared at the diabolical fingers on that weak spot, their mother's crippled wrist. As they watched, the two dark fingers began to twist it.

"This is Maddy's fault," Jack Dow told them.

"Dad." It was a word like the sound of horror. Somehow Maddy got up, somehow stumbled forward.

"Uh-uh." Jack Dow's free hand lifted. "Don't come too close, girlie." His voice was now confidential. "See, every step you come, you make me twist a little more."

Maddy thought wildly that this was her fault. If she had cared for them all as she was supposed to do, none of this would ever, ever have happened. If she had been more careful. How could she have put them in such danger? Suddenly little Stephen turned to the wall and began to retch. Jessica held him. Phillip and Allison, their faces gray, their eyes like holes in their faces, stood stock still.

"Maddy's fault." A groan as their father twisted their mother's wrist still farther. No one dared to move: you couldn't stop him. They'd learned that before. Vinnie Dow didn't try. Maddy saw in her mother's eyes a watching look, like an animal gauging pain. Maddy's knees began to buckle. It seemed to her that the wrist must break. Her mother was bent forward from the waist, her whole arm twisted forward. In a peculiar way mother and father were twisted together, one solid form, the woman bowing to her husband.

For a moment Jack Dow stared at Maddy, and there was no mistaking his look of triumph.

Then, with a loud crack to her rear end with his free hand, Jack Dow released his wife. "You deserved that, Vinnie," he said. "As for you, Maddy, just you remember, there's always someone left at home."

The children were locked upstairs; they went to bed in horrified silence. No one dared to speak or move, no one looked at Maddy.

"I slammed into a doorway," Maddy told the Packards. It was, she assured herself grimly, the truth.

Jonah said, "But did you trip?"

"Something like that." Maddy tried to shrug it off. But Aunt Ann examined the three-cornered cut and bruise on her white face and ran for an icebag.

In the aftermath of this beating no one in the Dow family cried — it had hurt too much.

Then, locked upstairs one night, they did cry. Allison's face crumpled like tissue and she and Stephen wept together. Phillip stood by Jessica, biting his lips for control. Jessica's face did not move, only her shoulders shook, and she stared out the window. Tears rolled down Maddy's cheeks. They couldn't embrace or console one another. Who would be the next guilty one, the next victim? In an instant the children pulled away from each other and hid to cry. They were all alone.

Once again Maddy's bruises healed. Amid the late summer days, the rehearsals and church activities, she felt she moved isolated; she hated herself for not being able to forgive, to transcend. She began for the first time to question God, the All-Powerful, the All-Forgiving. The Great Never-Angry, who did not care who was hurt enough to avenge it, the Great Ever-Angry, who punished his children with each other and then told them, endlessly, that they must forgive, take care of each other.

The contradictions enclosed Maddy like the pickets of a graveyard fence.

Days passed. Her father smiled once or twice and she smiled, too. She didn't dare not to. The other children smiled except maybe for Jessie, who hadn't smiled in a long time. But everyone seemed so eager to forget the punishments, get on with life.

Am I crazy? I must be crazy, Maddy thought. She concentrated more on her music.

"Your assignment is to share," Jonah had said.

Still, it was a small piece, now thirty measures of hitching, climbing sound, in close juxtaposition, two lines of notes weaving in on themselves, but ever more tightly, tightly together. Soprano and bass, she heard them clearly. The bass pushed upward, crowding the other, and the soprano seemed almost to taunt the bass, beg. When the bass sounded, then the soprano also did in a hollow way, wrapping itself around the bass. The bass pushed, pell-mell, threatening the scale itself. The scale was a rock by an ocean; they would both climb to the top, only to fall off the other side.

She heard it, and therefore it must be written. But she was afraid. "Your assignment is to share," Jonah said.

Very well; she wanted to. But what if all she heard was a run, a tangle of music that cut itself off, that contained in itself its own destruction: that pounding bass? When the bass had pushed the soprano off they would both fall, then there would be no more music. Was this something to share? How could it be? And if it were not, all her life, all these golden days of going over to the Packards', Jonah, music, hope — she felt these would have to be illusions. And if that were true, why bother to live? If she couldn't write good music after all this time, if there were no good music in her to share, then why live?

"You eat a little more, Maddy!" Aunt Ann urged now. "Are you coming down with something?"

Old Aunt Bea studied her face, then distracted her with pleasant talk until sometimes she could feel almost happy.

Jonah, never given to personal comments, looked at her and said at last, quietly, "Maddy, don't work so hard. You'll get there."

Then one morning, shortly after the cut on her forehead had become a small white scar, as she sat at the piano, Maddy began to hear something new, a new voice, very high, very slight, one note only. It was a single tiny note, like a distant cry. She found the note on the piano: the right pitch, not the right resonance. She didn't know what the right instrument might be for that note; the piano would have to do for now. But it was a high small sound. Yes, she heard it, she was sure she could hear it, a single note, as if from an approaching pipe.

CHAPTER EIGHT

T HE HISTORY of Baroque and Classical accomplishment is for the most part an untried field in rural education today. There are too few attempts made to acquaint our students with Bach or Mozart. Bach himself took time to teach children, but in our time, as in his, there are only pockets of culture, and all too often these are affluent, urban. Music in the homes of our children is not a pursuit of history, except the most recent.

It was an outpouring, not the beginning of a chapter. Jonah couldn't help himself.

In the rural areas of our country as well as in the ghettos of our cities, one is likely to find historical ignorance about music, even a dislike for anything that isn't modernly packaged and produced. This is like organizing democracy without a concept of freedom; what kind of republic would that be? So with music, it is important for teachers to realize their importance, to make the connection between history and popular modern form. Too often these are divorced and the packaging becomes in many cases as important, sometimes even more important, than the content, and history is lost.

Paragraphs, occurring out of nowhere.

Still, if our children are taught, we will have a common ground. If we were to trace our musical history, we would find a classical interest in rural towns up until the turn of the century. Increasingly, since then, classical culture has become elitest culture, until now the

disparity threatens to extinguish the classical and the historical altogether. With a few exceptions, most classicists scrape along.

In rural areas the ability is there, even the eagerness, but too often
classicists are not willing to go where they might not, at first, be
appreciated for the breadth of their knowledge. It is easier to dismiss
the "uneducated masses" without discovering the talent in them.
Unfortunately, in doing so, classicists dismiss themselves as well.

The petrification of the historical. Did this hold? He wondered.
Or was there something in the public interest innately dangerous to
classical form?

Aunt Ann appeared at the doorway. "Excuse me, Jonah, Eleanor
is here. She's with Bea in the front parlor." She bowed so that all
Jonah saw was wide round shoulders and a small round gray head.
"Your presence is requested."

"Oh, hell." Jonah pushed his papers away.

"That's what I thought," said Aunt Ann.

In the parlor, Aunt Bea sat in her accustomed place, her shoulders
covered with a soft white shawl. "Well, Jonah, you come right in,"
she said. "Eleanor's here. I'm afraid you've had no time to work
today. Lesson all over?"

Jonah's mind was still on his writing, and he mumbled abruptly,
"The lesson was over quite a while ago, Aunt Bea. Eleanor, how are
you?"

"Very well, thanks. Sorry to disturb you, Jonah. How are my
daughter's lessons coming along?" The woman's eyes fastened on
him. He saw her hair and felt vaguely uncomfortable: blond wings
securely fastened. Was it a child's midterm report he was required
to give?

"Well, she works hard," he said.

"Eleanor," said Aunt Bea with the faintest hint of remonstrance,
"Elaine is not a child."

Eleanor Hebert only laughed. "I agree. A child could not run up
such bills. How much are the lessons, Jonah?" She took out her
checkbook.

"But perhaps," Jonah suggested, surprised, "Elaine prefers to make
her own arrangements?"

Eleanor shrugged. "Has she paid you at all?"

"No."

"I thought not. Look, she expects me to do it, Jonah. I always have. Elaine sheds bills wherever she goes, and I pick them up." Now Eleanor was writing in her checkbook. He found himself staring at the woman's hands: old-looking, hard-knuckled, tough. There was a lot of hard work in Eleanor Hebert. "How much do I owe you?" she said.

Aunt Bea said, "Eleanor, Elaine should really be responsible for this."

Her faint voice did not register. Eleanor Hebert was figuring aloud. "Ten dollars a lesson, two lessons a week, four weeks — eighty dollars. And I should pay you some in advance, then I needn't think of it again for a while."

"Oh, no," said Jonah. "Not in advance, please. Too many things can happen. I might get sick, or Elaine might change her mind."

"Elaine will not change her mind."

"Please. I must insist."

Eleanor Hebert inclined her perfectly dressed blond head, finished writing, tore off the check. "There. And there is something else, Jonah."

"Oh?"

"Yes. The chorus is doing very well. I thought when we started you might have chosen some music that was too —"

"Difficult?"

"Perhaps. I was a bit worried. I thought it was a gamble, if you'll excuse me. But now I think it's going to pay off, thanks largely to your direction."

"Well, you're kind to say so, Eleanor. They're a good group."

"Yes." She snapped her pocketbook shut. "Jonah, I have been considering what to do about costumes for the chorus."

"Costumes?" Jonah blinked. "Oh, surely, Eleanor —"

"No, I mean it. Some of the women have mentioned it already, and costumes," she said, smoothing her own blue knit dress, "would give us a unified appearance. We've been thinking it would be nice if the women had skirts and the men ties and vests — all matching, you know. Something appropriate, in a polished cotton, perhaps, Aunt Bea? Someone said red, white, and blue would be nice, since it will be for the Fourth of July."

"Oh, Eleanor," Aunt Bea said in gentle reproof. Aunt Ann, standing in the doorway, merely shook her head.

With some dismay, Jonah found himself looking into Eleanor

Hebert's eyes at last: blue ice, practically without pupils. Down corridors of ice he went, full of ice mirrors in which one saw, endlessly, only the surfaces of things. It was cold there. With an effort, he pulled his glance away.

"Well, Jonah? What do you think?" Eleanor asked.

"Eleanor." Jonah searched for the words. "It's what you and the chorus think, of course. But privately, I suppose, I couldn't be more opposed, especially at this stage. The singing itself is crucial. I want the chorus to believe the singing is what will win the competition."

"Red, white, and blue?" Aunt Ann hollered suddenly from the door. "Good God, give Maddy a hand organ, and Jonah, hell, he can carry a tin cup!" She snorted, shaking all over with her own joke. Barely, she managed to set down a tray of iced tea. "There, Bea, I've slopped it. Don't you get any on you, now. You're much too pretty today."

Jonah laughed. Aunt Bea was smiling, too.

But one tiny wrinkle had appeared dead center on Eleanor Hebert's perfect brow. "I find this hard to believe, Jonah," she said. "You don't care what our group looks like?"

"Of course I care, very much." Jonah tried to make a straight face. "And I know it won't be up to me. But a dark skirt or trousers, a white shirt — really, that's all that's necessary." He was still smiling a little.

Eleanor stood, regarding him levelly. As they faced each other, he suddenly saw how very experienced she was in handling opposition. She eyed him, sizing him up like a veteran, he thought. But she said only, "You must have foresight, Jonah. When we're on television next summer, we will have to be dressed properly."

"Surely, Eleanor, that's a bit premature now?"

She nodded — not a nod of acquiescence, he could see that. "Well," she said, "we have to think ahead, but it's too late for this first competition, anyway. We haven't time enough for that, of course."

"But I should have it in mind?" He tried not to sigh.

"Yes, I think so. You'll get used to the idea. It's what a lot of us want."

"Well, we'll have to work something out. I trust we will. By the way, so far, Eleanor, the Freedom chorus has been a model of good organization."

The compliment of an opponent; she accepted it as such. "Well, thank you, Jonah." She moved to the door. "No, no tea for me, Aunt Ann. I haven't got the time. Good-bye, Aunt Bea. Have a good day."

"Try to relax a little, Eleanor." Aunt Bea's voice trembled in the air.

"Oh, I know, you're right." With a grimace she was gone.

"Costumes!" Aunt Ann exploded when the front screen had shut. "Costumes!"

Jonah shook his head. "Packaging. I should have expected it." He sighed, so did Aunt Bea.

Aunt Ann said, "You look kind of tired, Bea."

"I am, Ann." The old lady's lips quivered. "Suddenly I am quite tired. If you will give me your arm, my dear."

"We'll go right upstairs." Aunt Ann helped Aunt Bea to her feet. "You'll rest, you'll feel fine. You're tough."

"Tough?" Aunt Bea's face turned up. Jonah saw her stare at Aunt Ann. Then the two of them began to smile. They giggled like children, Jonah thought as he watched them go: two old women, leaning together, making their way slowly up the stairs.

At first Judy Russell put up with baby Elana good-naturedly. She ended up carrying her around most of every morning, but at least that made the baby happy. Quietly nuzzled into Judy's shoulder or breathing into her neck, Elana seemed quite comfortable, and Judy didn't really mind learning to do her morning chores with one hand. Elana was a small-boned baby, weighing only about ten pounds, so she wasn't too heavy. Colicky, Judy thought. At three months, Elana should soon be over her colic. Judy sincerely hoped so.

Elaine left the baby almost every morning, but in the afternoons Judy relaxed. She had some quiet while little Russ napped. Sometimes she would take him for a walk outside. It was amazing, the amount of territory one two-year-old could cover in an afternoon.

They would go out into the dark shade of the old maple trees beside the house, then down the little knoll and into the field. Sometimes they went for the express purpose of berrying, and then little Russ would quietly give in and sleep in the pine grove while Judy hummed over her berry buckets: two quarts of blueberries for a good pie, with a cup of them, small and wild, left over for muffins.

Or sometimes while little Russ slept Judy would sit on a rock ledge in the middle of the field and hum to herself, thankful that she and big Russ had bought this rambling farm, half of which, as yet uncultivated, grew to berries that colored successively down the warm weeks of summer: strawberries, raspberries, blueberries, blackberries.

"Russ," she would sometimes tell him, "we mustn't disturb that north field, or at least not out by the woods."

He would grin, his teeth making a white slash in the face smudged with car grease from his job at the garage. "Pie for supper?"

"Yes. But promise."

"Okay, okay."

After a while, little Russ would wake up and sit and stare at Judy solemnly, a flush of pink on his young cheeks. Then he would sit on her lap, a sleepy solid bundle that drew Judy's cheek down to his hair and brought forth a softer humming as she sat and rocked him. Then he would stand up and be back in business again, holding on to one of her fingers with his fist and pulling her along, sometimes running ahead and falling, then setting himself sturdily on his feet again. His hair, once blond, was now growing more thickly, a faint orange wave like his father's. Sometimes Judy felt rich: she had a son who looked like his father. Sometimes she would stand and send her voice into the air in some high exercise out of pure enjoyment. Usually by the end of a calm afternoon she would have forgotten her struggles of the morning and baby Elana's unhappiness. After all, she had nothing to worry over in particular and much to enjoy.

But today, standing at the kitchen sink doing the lunch dishes at suppertime, Judy thought of her afternoons and wondered if she'd ever have another quite like them. She barely responded when her husband Russ chucked her under the chin and turned her face up so she could look into his greasy one with its extravagant cap of orange curls.

"Hey," he said gently. "Hard day? What's the matter?"

Usually the summer look of him, tan under his car grease, tired and a little hungry, and in his eyes the fire of being home from work and about to begin his real occupation — at this point pulling stumps out of some acreage — made her smile. Now she didn't. She pulled her chin away and went back to scrubbing.

"Money," she said.

Russ's shoulders drooped a little. "You had the baby today?"

Judy scrubbed on for a moment, then paused. "What is it about babies?" she asked. "Some babies you just can't make happy, no matter what you do. There are times when I —" Flushed and upset, she clanged the last of the dishes into the drainer. Her dark hair swung at chin level; abstractedly, she tucked it behind her ears.

Big Russ sat down. "So what happened?"

"I'll tell you what happened," Judy said. "First Elaine came in, all dressed up in her Peck's sundress, you know, and she left the baby. Then off she went to take care of her career, so she said." Judy struck an attitude, the helpless Elaine to the life.

"Oh," said Russ. He rubbed his greasy hands over his blackened face and dared to chuckle. "So did you tell her to take her career and stuff it?"

"No, I didn't! But I feel like it now, believe me!" Judy blew a hair out of her eyes and tucked it back, too. "So, off Elaine goes, supposedly to the big city, in her cute little — little red —"

"Roadster?" Russ supplied.

"Don't laugh at me!" Now there were tears in Judy's eyes. "Off she goes and that — that poor baby begins to fuss. I juggled that child all morning long, Russ. What ails a baby, to cry like that all the time?"

He shrugged. "I guess I didn't realize it was bothering you so much."

"Well, neither did I." Judy sat down at the table. "I thought I was happy enough."

Russ reached over and touched her damp fist. "I'm sorry," he said. "Look, it's no fun tending a shrieking baby half the day. You know, you don't have to do it."

"But you don't know all of it yet." Judy tried to laugh, but it ended in a hiccup. "Elaine went off, and from nine o'clock this morning until one this afternoon I juggled her baby. Russ, if Elaine didn't have such a good pediatrician, I'd say that baby needed a doctor. It's not right, it's not normal. I tried to tell Elaine, but she doesn't listen. Anyway, at one o'clock Aunt Eleanor came for a visit."

"Machine lady?"

"Right. Russ, let's not be cruel! It was just, here I had this screaming child on my hands, not a dish done, not a bed made, because she cried so, and little Russ had dragged out all his cars and trucks and every other last toy he owns all over the floor."

"Was he good today?"

"Of course he was good, damnit! He didn't have any other choice!" Judy pounded the table. "So in she comes — and you know Aunt Eleanor, not a hair out of place — and she says, 'Judy, dear, I came to pay Elaine's baby-sitting bill.' And she whipped out her checkbook."

Russ shook his head. "Must be nice," he said.

"So then she writes me this check, pays me all up and a month in advance, and hands it to me."

"In advance?" He frowned. "You took it?"

"I didn't want to. I told Elaine we'd talk about money and she never — Russ, I was so flustered. The baby, the mess." Scarlet-cheeked, Judy stared at him and he was touched.

"Look here," she went on. "Five weeks I've waited for Elaine to say something about paying me, and she didn't. Why? Because Mamma was going to do it for her. Here it is, two hundred and fifty dollars." Judy plunked the check down in front of him.

Russ whistled. "Let's buy a bathtub. Did you thank her?"

"When I'd shut my mouth, I did. I said, 'It's a pleasure doing business with you, Aunt Eleanor, but Elaine and I could work this out.' "

"You didn't."

"I don't think she even heard me. I don't think she's really looked at me or heard me talk in years, and I don't think she cares how we think about her. But then! Then, Russ, before I could give the check back, she said — she said —" Judy was close to tears again. "She said, 'It's so kind of you to take the baby so often, especially now that Elaine has her singing lessons.' "

"What?" Russ stared at her.

"Yes," said Judy. "All this time! Singing lessons!" It was a cry. Judy would have loved to have singing lessons if they could have afforded it. Now tears of pure anger were running down her cheeks.

"Oh," said Russ heavily. "I see."

"You know what makes me maddest? It's that here I was, thinking I was happy, and then Elaine does some little thing and my whole outlook swings around."

"Well, she always has had just a little more."

"Yes, since we were children!"

"And she always was just a little mean to you."

"She doesn't even know that, Russ."

"Oh? Don't stick up for her," he said grimly. "I think she does. So what do you want to do? Give the check back? You earned it. You will earn it. Elaine will never pay you, will she?"

"I guess not."

"Oh, hell, Judy, you're the best singer in town. Everybody knows that. So take this money, get yourself some lessons."

"Their money? Lessons because Elaine does? I wouldn't stoop to it!"

He said stubbornly, "You should do what you want. You earned it."

"I did, didn't I?" Judy blew her nose. "We'll get a bathtub," she said.

"Forget the tub, do what you want."

There was Russ, black with grease from head to toe. In the midst of her upset Judy began to smile. "Are you sure?" she said. "Have you looked in the mirror lately?"

"I mean it, Judy."

She glanced from his earnest look to his grease-black hands and smirked. He caught her expression and reached toward her, a broad, horrific leer on his face.

"Too dirty for you? Yeah? Well, pour me some water, woman, and get me some soap before I touch you and scar you for life."

"Oh, for heaven's sake," she said, and went to the stove, where she picked up a steaming kettle and poured water into a basin. He added cold to it, and while he washed, she went about putting supper on the table. It was comforting to move from stove to refrigerator to counter with him just there, to touch a little as she moved. When he was clean, he took her in his arms.

"If I have music lessons, Russ," she said fiercely into his shoulder, "it won't be because I'm jealous of Elaine."

"I know," he said.

"And I'll take care of Elana because I want to."

"I know."

"It's just . . . Damn Elaine anyway."

"Right."

Little Russ had been having a late nap before rehearsal that evening. Now he came thumping into the room. With a whoop and a holler, he was lifted high up in his father's arms. Watching them, Judy began to feel better.

"You know what I'm going to do about Elaine?" she told them. "I'm going to pretend everything is just fine." She avoided Russ's look and went back to her work.

By the time of the rehearsal that night, Judy was feeling much better. She really liked these rehearsals. She hadn't had such a good opportunity to sing in a group since high school. And singing with Jonah was more fun and more of a challenge. He was a fine director; his taste was impeccable. It was a joy to sing for him. Did the tenors miss their notes? He didn't urge them on as an amateur might have, to try harder, strain more. "Easy, tenors," he would say. "This is high, I know. Just come down onto the notes and relax. Don't reach, let it float." Were the altos floundering? "Listen to that alto line," he would tell the chorus. "It's a tricky one, I know, but it's very important here, a wonderful cello sound." He would stand in front of the altos and direct only them, crooning the sounds along with them with no loss to his dignity, only showing them his devotion to the proper notes. When they got it, he would be very pleased. "That's just fine," he would rave. "Just what we need! Good work, altos."

Sometimes he joked with the basses. "Come on now, move it along down there." And to the sopranos: "Try to get it out of your throats, ladies. More head tone, and not legato, we're not making corn syrup here." They all worked hard for Jonah, waiting for his cry: "Good! Good! Oh, that's very good."

Tonight Judy took her place in the soprano section and did not look toward Elaine. When the singing began, she concentrated as hard as she could on the musical line, watching Jonah, listening to Maddy. Maddy was even more intense than usual, paler, large-eyed, her hands so very precise. Her concentration touched Judy. They didn't share much conversation, yet Judy felt the undercurrent of liking that ran between them.

By the mid-evening break Judy had been singing hard and had pretty effectively forgotten about Elaine, but then she happened to glance into the alto section and saw Elaine, talking and laughing as if she wished to be noticed and was surprised to find herself noticed, all at once. Judy saw that Elaine had another new dress. Money was no problem, but how did she have time to shop for all those clothes? The dress was pink, and Elaine's lipstick and nail polish matched it. Her hair had been drawn back to show tiny pink earrings, and even her makeup bore that same touch of pink. It was fascinating — Judy acknowledged this grudgingly — but it grated. Why couldn't Elaine have told her about the singing lessons? Unless she had something up her sleeve.

Now even Jonah paused, Judy saw, to speak to Elaine, who flushed and batted her artificially — and probably individually, Judy thought meanly — curled eyelashes. Judy was relieved to see Jonah move away almost at once, but then he approached her.

"Judy, I've been going through my music and I've found a piece for the November competition that I'd like you to try if you would."

He smiled, and Judy detected a glow in the deep-socketed eyes.

"Of course," Judy said promptly, "I'd love to. What's the piece?"

"Well, it's a wonderful arrangement of 'America the Beautiful,' with a lovely solo and an obligato at the end, quite long, quite high. I think you will be perfect for it."

"Well, thank you." Judy smiled. "I'd be happy to look at it. By the way, Jonah, Russ and I have been wanting to tell you, we think you're doing just a great job."

He held up a hand. "Please. We'll see how the first competition goes. You'll do the solo, then?"

"Oh, yes, by all means, if I can. And if we get to it, of course. Do you think we will?"

"I don't know. But it doesn't hurt to think ahead a little. These pieces are shaping up. Okay if I announce to the group that you may sing?"

"Of course."

He moved to the front. "Okay, all right," he announced. "Party's over, back to work."

There were loud fake groans while the chorus resumed their seats. He held up his hands and, well trained by now, the group fell silent. "I've been picking out tentative programs for all three competitions," he told them, "because I think there's a chance we might win all three."

There was applause, laughter.

"The first one, as you know, will be held in Auburn, the Saturday after Labor Day. For that we will do the Vespugi, the Alton-Mayer, and the Greystock 'Hallelujah.' Now, for November, as you know, we have to do some new pieces. By that time, of course, we'll be so good, we won't even notice it." More laughter, applause. "One of the most wonderful pieces is an arrangement I have of 'America the Beautiful.' It's also a superb opportunity for a good soprano soloist."

"That's Judy," somebody called out.

"Yes," said Jonah. "Judy Russell, stand up, will you?"

She did, and there was a long moment of affectionate applause. She made a mock bow and sat down again.

"Now the spring competition," Jonah said, "is still pretty far away, but I'm thinking what we might do and how we might do it. As far as soloists go, I'm considering a number of pieces, one with an excellent soprano solo in it. Someone else in this chorus, one of our altos, has begun taking voice lessons with me and has expressed some interest in auditioning for a solo. I suspect there are others just as talented, so please, if you want to try, don't hang back. There are a lot of good pieces out there, and I want to tell you I think you're capable of doing them. We've made great progress so far, and I'm very pleased. Now, if you'll all stand, we can begin."

He motioned them up, and they began to practice again by singing a series of harmonies.

Usually Judy loved this, but now something scorching and noisy was happening inside her, something she didn't like. An alto? It must be Elaine. Nobody else would be having voice lessons. Wasn't there anything that girl wouldn't take?

Jonah signaled and with the other sopranos Judy sang, not as she should, she knew, for the sake of the harmony, but good and loud, so she could be heard. And that upset her so, just the thought of it, that she caught herself back and choked the sound, not singing at all.

Jonah stopped them immediately. "Let's all get organized" — he laughed — "so we can begin together. Ready? One, two, three, four, one, two . . ."

With an effort, Judy dragged her eyes away from Elaine. I took care of your baby, Elaine, she couldn't help thinking, all morning long.

But surely there was room in Freedom for more than one singer? Surely it didn't matter what Elaine did or didn't do? Judy made her voice blend, and as she did, she happened to look past Jonah's directing hands to Maddy Dow, the white face, the chiseled nose, straight mouth, eyes large and bright and intense. That face stirred her on somehow, and once again she forgot everything but the singing.

The next day Elaine Cummings went to her mother.

Eleanor Hebert was cutting flowers. She stood up, brushed off her fitted blue pants, removed her garden gloves, and stared at her daughter. "What is it?"

"I went down to see Judy this morning, to pay her and find someone else for the baby, and —"

"Someone else? But why?" Eleanor frowned. "I paid her in advance."

"Because, Mother, we are competing against each other. And there she is, watching my baby while I take singing lessons."

"Oh, for heaven's sake, dear," said Eleanor. "Judy is not as small as that."

"You don't know Judy," said Elaine, tossing back her blond curls. "Anyway, next time you pay her, could you at least tell me? It was embarrassing. I started to give her some money and she wouldn't take it, and I thought she was really mad. Then she told me you'd paid for me."

"You didn't want me to?" Eleanor looked at her daughter humorously.

"It's not that," Elaine said. "But you paid in advance. This morning Judy got that look, and said she guessed she'd been paid, she would deliver, and that it was a pleasure doing business with me."

"So?"

"So I wish I could find someone else to take Elana." Elaine looked at her mother.

Eleanor Hebert sidestepped. "My goodness, I don't know," she said. "We shall have to keep our eyes open, shan't we? Oh, and by the way, Elaine, I think I should tell you I also paid Jonah for your lessons yesterday. I wanted to pay him in advance, too, to have it off my mind, but he wouldn't hear of it. How are the lessons going?"

"I'm working like a dog," said Elaine. The often innocent blue eyes sharpened. "You'll be happy to know, Mother, that if anyone in this town makes it onto that television show with a solo next summer, it will be me."

"You have great determination, my dear."

"My mother's daughter." Her smile was satirical.

Eleanor sighed. "There is that."

"I'm off to town, now."

"Oh, a speaking part?" Eleanor's picture of a successful daughter was one who had many pieces to speak, preferably on television.

"No, just some modeling at Arturo's," Elaine admitted.

Eleanor tried to hide her disappointment. "Well, it's a start."

"Yes. See you." The girl moved away from the flower beds and down the lawn to her car.

Eleanor watched her daughter go. She was so beautiful, Eleanor thought. And you had to hand it to Elaine, she did have ambition. Sometimes, though, Eleanor wished her daughter had a little clearer idea of how other people were feeling.

There was that hint about taking care of little Elana. Eleanor could do most things for Elaine, but not that. Not on a regular basis, at any rate. There was just too much else that had to be done, especially this year. She sighed.

In her hands were blossoms Eleanor had gone to great lengths to encourage in beds around the foundation of her house. She could remember when she had first moved into this house with Arthur. So much to be managed, inside and out, but she did want flowers. She had done a lot of it herself: they might be well off, but they had to keep a tight rein on money. That first spring she had had Arthur dig the flower beds for her.

"Wide and deep," she'd told him. "Trenched with manure. I want them perfect."

Arthur got disgusted. "I have a whole farm to run, Eleanor, for chrissakes. I've already got men working all over the house." He was tough, bright, well educated, voted Farmer of the Year soon after that.

"All right, I'll do it myself," Eleanor said grimly. She had. She'd gotten up early, before anyone in town could see her, and worked like a slave with spade and pitchfork and wheelbarrow. That first year it had been cosmos and nasturtium and zinnia, all she could manage, the easy annuals. But she had designed them in clumps, arranging their colors carefully. They had made a brave display.

One day Arthur said shamefacedly, "Look, you need some help out here. I'll get a man to work with you. It looks damn good."

"You could have done that to start with," said Eleanor.

He shrugged stocky shoulders, his face well meaning enough. "I didn't know what it would look like."

From then on he'd left decisions about the house and grounds to her, his role that of provider.

Eleanor stepped back a bit to look at the total effect. Her flowers were the envy of the town. She had had a picket fence set on two sides of the house, and to the left, hollyhocks nodded. As a child, Eleanor had read a story about hollyhocks. They were little girls in fancy dresses; they couldn't move or run away, but learned to dance prettily in their places when the wind blew. On the other side, carefully pruned, sprayed, and staked, were her tea roses, set to catch the morning sun to dry leaves and stems, the afternoon shade for protection. She allowed a single rose to a plant, so that each was as big as a man's hand when fully opened. Between the two picket fences, all across the front of the foundation, were flowers in careful clumps, well laid out, perfectly bedded.

She gazed at it all, her eye pleased at the set of color by color, her mind on civic details. Strawberry festival, she was thinking. Barbecue pit. Bicycle parade? Crepe-paper buntings? Fireworks.

"A real down-home country affair," Jack Dow had said. "Shake money out of people's pockets before they miss it." He'd smiled to show he was joking. "Put Freedom on the map," he'd said. "Course, I don't know just how to do it. Need you for that, Eleanor."

"A lot of work, Jack."

"I'll owe you one, then. Who else can handle it?" He was a good man.

Eleanor stared at her house. It satisfied her. Almost. There were some pansies she would like to move. She was the only one who would ever know why, but it had to be done.

"Bread and pies," she'd told groups of women, and they'd agreed. "Give them away to advertise. Relays of baked goods at all the shopping centers — Portland, Grey, Lewiston-Auburn."

"Public service advertising," she'd told other groups. "Radio and television. We want to lure people in. Someday this church should have a minister of its own and not share him with two other churches."

Lately their young minister, Blaine Howarth, had said to Eleanor, "There seems to be a pretty homogeneous bunch of people in this church. What about the poor people in town? Where do they go?" The implied criticism troubled her.

"If the church were a little richer," Eleanor had replied, "we could cope with poor people. As it is, it's hard." She'd been busy, arranging flowers for the church service in big baskets. He had seemed very young. "These flowers," she'd said, "come right out of my garden. We can't even afford bouquets for the service."

"Ah," he had said, giving her arrangements a long look. Then he looked at Eleanor herself. He was so abstracted and gentle that Eleanor's heart softened. "Perhaps," he said, touching one of her prizes — she'd hated to cut it, but they'd had to have something — a white-throated Emperor lily, "we must simply consider these." His face was at once humorous and other-worldly. Eleanor couldn't be angry with him.

She was aware that not everyone shared her enthusiasms: the buntings, costumes, food. There were a thousand details to be planned, even this far in advance. But only the week before Eleanor's sister, June, had said, "Did it ever occur to you, Eleanor, that maybe we're doing the right things for all the wrong reasons?"

Now what kind of a thing to say was that?

June didn't have the big vision, that was all. She was just like Arthur. Couldn't see the garden unless it was in front of her, all arranged.

It would all work. Now that Eleanor was this far into it, it would have to. She stared at the flowers in her hands. Snapdragons and painted daisies, bachelor's-buttons reminding her of Elaine's eyes, that lovely, cool blue. Eleanor had courted blue flowers among all the other colors in the beds. Blue stars, just here, just there, where they were meant to be, always reminding her of Elaine.

She thought, If Elaine sang a solo on television, why, she would be a symbol of this town, of my whole effort. That would make it all worthwhile.

On the lawn of her house Eleanor Hebert stood thinking, trimming the stems of the flowers she'd cut until all the ends matched, diagonal points of stems, as sharp as a dozen even little knitting needles.

*

At the last rehearsal before the competition Jonah said, "I usually suggest that for concerts the men wear white shirts and dark slacks and the women, white blouses and dark skirts."

"No ties for the men?" Russ asked from the back. "Not that I'm objecting, you understand." There was a laugh from the group.

"A lot of choruses wear them," Jonah said. "But I think there's nothing more frustrating than trying to sing with your throat all bound up in an uncomfortable collar."

"Full-length or street-length skirts for the women?" somebody asked.

Jonah smiled. "I understand that there are endless permutations to a question like that," he said to laughter. "Will you women figure it out for yourselves and make sure everyone knows?"

"Jonah? May I please say something about dress?" Eleanor Hebert was on her feet.

"I've been expecting you to, Eleanor. Go ahead."

"Thank you." She turned to the group. "Of course, it's too late for the first competition, but some of the women and I have been talking, and we think we've come up with a way to provide some kind of costume for our group that will give it a unified appearance."

"Costume? You mean, dress up?" someone said.

"A monkey suit," somebody else muttered. There was some snickering.

Eleanor paused. "Many of us think that appearance will be very important, especially if we do make it as far as television coverage. We think that the way to get on television is to look as if we belonged there. Now, we won't get too specific yet except to say that if you have any ideas, call me, or my sister, June, or talk to us after the meeting, please, so that we can discuss it."

"No costumes for the first competition?" someone asked.

"No."

There was an audible sigh of relief somewhere in the crowd, then some more laughter.

"All we want you to do is think about it." Eleanor smiled at them all. Jonah found himself admiring her steely grace under opposition. She nodded at him and sat down, adding, "Thank you, Jonah."

"Thank you, Eleanor." He turned to the group. "Now, I should like to suggest that we table all further discussion about clothing for the moment and get down to the central issue here, which is, as I'm sure you will all agree, that rubato on the bottom of page eight in the 'Hallelujah.' "

The first competition for town choruses was held at Edward Little High School in Auburn, with six groups of four choruses competing. The winners of each of these competitions would meet in November in two separate divisions, with new music, and the final competition would be in March, after which the winner could begin practicing for the Fourth of July.

There were television cameras taping at the audition, which made it doubly exciting. Maddy found herself fascinated by them and by the judges' table, a long one set up at a distance from the bleachers, covered with papers and microphones. Four men and three women were introduced to the singers, two from the music department of the University of Maine at Orono, up north, one from a local milk marketing firm, two symphony members from Portland, the leader of the Portland Community Chorus, and a television executive from WGME.

After the introductions, the first group of singers filed onstage. There were about thirty of them, looking nervous as they moved onto the risers. The audience became quiet. The group began to sing in excellent three-part harmony. Their tone was good, diction and direction well rehearsed. Maddy began to wonder: Would it make a difference that Freedom's music was more complicated than this? Only, she decided, if they sang it beautifully.

After several selections the first group finished to enthusiastic applause. Then there was a long break for the judges and for organizing the next chorus. At last they filed onto the stage: twenty-five women. All the men's parts had been arranged for women, but up an octave, the audience soon discovered. Down the row Maddy met Jonah's eyes and saw his lips tighten. By now she was used to watching his face and knew, as everyone else in their chorus did, what he thought of this kind of music. The voices were true enough, but the melody was lost in all those high accompanying parts, and the sound was shrill. Someone beside Maddy muttered, "Women's work."

Maybe we've got a chance, Maddy thought for the first time. She had never dared to think she would be lucky enough to have the chorus continue on into the fall, or to have her association with it continue.

Applause again.

Jonah stood up, nodded at them. "Our turn," he whispered. By twos and threes, the Freedom chorus filed into a room backstage for their last-minute instructions. Maddy went to the piano in the back of the room.

"Line up, please. Music in your right hand, that's it. Now, we've heard some good things today, but I believe that if we want to we can do as well or even better," Jonah told them. "It's a matter of concentration. Think about the music, as I know you will." In a white shirt and dark trousers he seemed thin as a pencil, bowed and anxious. His face was pale, but his expression was calm. "It's going to seem strange on the stage," he told them, "but I'm an old hand at this, and I'm telling you, just keep your eyes on me, listen to each other, sing together, and we're going to do fine. Watch, watch me now. Get the sound going in your head before you open your mouth. Concentrate. Good luck. One chord, Maddy."

She gave them pitches, they hummed, he lifted his hands to them, and a chord blossomed. He gave them a quick nod. "Good. All right, we're ready. Maddy, you're in first."

The piano was set at an angle to the risers where the chorus would stand. It was an effort to go first, but Maddy gripped her music and walked across the floor of the stage. She saw the flooring in great detail: long, thin shining strips, black paint, the joints like funnels of light. A piano bench. She sat, reading the sharp etching above the keys with great attention. This was a Baldwin grand: her brain worked; her insides seemed to fall away. Still, she managed to adjust the bench a little. She was conscious of lights on the stage, of faces beyond the lights. Her hands were damp. She opened her music and laid it out, then unobtrusively she pulled from her sleeve a small white handkerchief.

"For luck," Jessie had whispered. "I didn't know I had this, but I did."

It was a small white cambric square. "Otherwise," Jessie said, "you might be tempted to wipe your hands on your skirt. I know you, Maddy." Jessie's expression did not change, but a light came to it that made Maddy smile.

The chorus was filing in: white above, dark beneath. They lined up on the risers. As she watched from the piano, Maddy's hands dampened again and she wiped them. The lights on the stage went up blindingly and her vision blurred, her heart pounded. She wondered what she was doing there, whether she would know how to play the instrument in front of her. In dismay she stared up at the unsmiling faces of the chorus and saw that they were wondering if, when they opened their mouths, any sound would come out. She caught Judy Russell's eye, and Judy gave her a slight nod, a veteran nod that said, "Oh, yes, we're scared silly, but there's no help for it now."

Jonah came in last. Tall and distinguished, he adjusted the music rack, which was much too low for his frame, then laid his music out with what seemed to be exaggerated slowness. Maddy felt he was too thin and too remote in the light and, as he faced her, like a stranger. Wildly it occurred to her that this competition was an impossible situation, that she couldn't play this piano, that no one would follow Jonah when he raised his hands and signaled. Probably, she thought, they should all just give up and go home.

Jonah turned slightly, his expression both severe and collected. He made sure every eye was on him and then raised his hands. At once the chorus raised their music, open to the page — a little thing, perhaps, but something. They could do that at least; that they had been trained to do. Jonah nodded at them, glanced at Maddy, raised one hand. Somehow she prepared to lay her fingers on the keys. He will set tempo, she thought.

Yes, there, he did: two, three, four, and *now*. Her fingers descended — there. Why, she was playing his tempo! Two, three-four — and yes, this piano was a Baldwin and different from what she was used to, but she could play it and it would be fine and here was the music — she glanced up: Jonah's hands. Two, three, four, one, two — chorus, begin.

Begun.

At Jonah's signal they inhaled together and a little sound came out, too little — they knew it, Maddy knew it — but something. All they could manage. Instantly Maddy supplemented her playing to support them, give them a chance to catch the music. A breath. Yes. Breathe together: that's right, she told them with her playing. And this is all right. Jonah beckoned to them. No, now, more sound, he signaled, more. The singers caught themselves and responded; there. There it was; good. The stage such a big place, more sound, more — they knew it. Suddenly they began to give it.

"Now, watch," Jonah's fingers said, holding the next instant of music up in the air to test their concentration. "Watch, watch."

They sang, they watched.

Oh, no! Ragged? Had it been ragged there?

Maddy, covering it, gave them no time to wonder.

"Watch!" Jonah's hands told them. "We are in it now. Now we'll see what we are made of. Think. Listen."

Sometimes in rehearsal the Freedom chorus had sung as if they heard each other thinking — these were always the best times, to Maddy. Now she heard them sing that way again, the words of the song aloud, and underneath them each other's thought: "Watch, watch, rest, rest. And, why, Maddy, there, see, Maddy. Yes, ready, two, three, four — now.

"Together. We're together. Oh, we're rolling. Sound, more sound, no strain now, are we straining? No. Two, three, four. Why, we're singing! We're concentrating and this isn't bad. This isn't bad at all. Watch. Watch the words now: 'When I am strong, Lord, leave me not alone / My refuge be.' Two, three, four — off — cut, together, yes."

As even as dancers they stopped singing, together. There was a silence, a place to breathe, but not an eye stirred, watching Jonah, not daring to do anything else for fear they'd miss each other.

Jonah was nodding, they knew his face. "Concentrate," it said. "Watch." Once again his hands were setting tempo, and Maddy began the slow piece, Alton-Mayer. The chorus thought, "Will we hear each other? Will the singing come? Oh, concentrate! There is Jonah, calling us. Will we all begin together? Will we all sing?"

"Yes. We will. Now more sound and more, and more — watch! This once, at least, we'll get it right! This once in a lifetime! This is the only time! This middle piece is the trickiest — can we do it?"

"Yes!" Jonah told them with his hands.

"Yes!" Maddy cried by bending to the piano keys. The sopranos were to sing triplets, one-two-three, imposed on a count of one-two in the other parts. They all knew how it should be: the high sounds should run down the rooks of the other parts like water on rocks, with a speed of its own. Would they do it? Could they? With every muscle Maddy signaled: "Careful, now."

Yes. There they were. There she was, and Jonah. "Don't falter, altos," Maddy called with Jonah. "Not now." It was a hard part for them. Her fingers found, softly, the alto notes. "There, there they are," Maddy thought. "And the tenor — here tenors, you have it, you hear it, yes? And the bass? But you never even faltered."

"Once." The chorus sang together as if speaking only to each other. "Once to get it right." Their eyes never moved from Jonah.

Maddy struck the final notes of this middle piece with a flourish and at once, cleanly, all singing and her playing stopped.

"Play the pauses, Maddy," Jonah had told her once. "The quiet between the notes is as important as the notes, the rest is as important as the sound."

Now they all knew he was playing the pause, that this particular silence had a heartbeat and he had found it, his music. "Oh," they all thought, "he is a good conductor. We didn't know how good this man was, how lucky we are."

Jonah's arms were up — there, ready. Intense, precise, his hands called to them all: "Tempo. Watch. Begin, Maddy."

Forgetting everything else, Maddy began. She forgot the written sheets in front of her, for whole moments of time they all did. It was necessary to have this by heart.

One person with many voices, the chorus sang: "If we could, we would be, just this once, one heart, each person doing what he could, each of us singing in his own way, with his eyes on Jonah, his ear to the group, for the sake of this music, to send it up as far as the song can go, up there, somewhere, up and out, where we wish in our best selves to belong, right now, always."

They sang. Jonah was a man possessed by sharing, open in all his musical feeling to them: now he was leading them with passion, restraint. "This is what I'm here for," he seemed to say, and they echoed it back to him: "This is what we're here for."

"You see me for what I am," his gestures told them. "I am the music, no more and no less than you are, and we share this good thing together."

Maddy bent over the keys: "Oh, let me belong, let me come with you."

"You were the first one there, Maddy," they sang. "We love you. We're right here."

All eyes were on Jonah's face, on his lips as he mouthed the words of the Greystock with them, on his hands while his fingers marked time and set consonants.

They sang their words exactly on his signal, out of pure love for the detail of it. At a motion of his head they knew: "All right, let go, let it ring out now!" They knew they were a small-town chorus, maybe, but this once, at least, they were taking a fling at something far outside themselves, beyond them, of great price, worth the price.

"This is the time, the one and only time in the universe," they sang to each other. "It may never come again. We may never be so able or so lucky or so touched this way again. Hallelujah! Hallelujah! Sing! Hallelujah! Hallelujah! Hold! Now watch, please, watch — his signal is coming, it is here! See that? Sing! Sing! Watch. Hold. Ready to stop! End — now!"

At the precise moment Maddy lifted her hands from the keys, she felt a joy and a loss so sharp that she wanted to run away and weep. Once, she felt, that once, there had been a greatness, a freedom, something so wonderful, that once.

The applause surprised them all except for Jonah, who looked up at them with a boyish smile. Then he turned and bowed and held out his hand to the chorus, who stood still, looking a bit sheepish, and then, astonishingly, he motioned to Maddy to stand and bow. At last the chorus filed out, the applause subsided, it was quiet.

Maddy, the last to make her way through the wings, was surprised to find Jonah, Aunt Ann and Aunt Bea waiting for her. "There she is," Jonah cried, "our good soldier." Before she knew what was happening, all three of them hugged her at once.

"You did fine," said Aunt Bea. "You were beautiful, Maddy. Jonah, you're sure to win, it was just lovely. At the end I couldn't help but cry."

"We'll go out for ice cream when it's over," said Aunt Ann. She held out her wide arms to hug everyone in sight. Beaming, her hands wide, she seemed to Maddy like a big shining circle.

It wasn't fair, of course. You had yourself trained not to want hugs, not to need affection, and when they came you knew how much you wanted and needed them. Maddy's eyelids scraped at her eyes and she blinked hard.

"It went all right, didn't it?" she managed to say.

Jonah put his head back and laughed.

He hugged Aunt Ann and put his arm on Maddy's shoulder, and Maddy wondered why she had ever been afraid of him. "Come on," he said. "Let's listen to the others and see how we did."

The chorus walked together back toward the door. They were touching each other's arms and nodding and smiling. The winning didn't seem to make so much difference. Still, they wanted to hear who had won.

Maddy's family waited by the door. Her father was first.

"It looks good," he told Jonah. "It looks real good."

And then, unbelievably, Jack Dow turned to Maddy and they looked at each other. "I was proud of you today," he said slowly. "I was proud of my daughter today."

Maddy's voice trembled. "Thank you, Daddy." She would go through any amount of pain if only, once in a while, he would love her.

"Jack?" Eleanor and Arthur Hebert were behind them. "It went well, didn't it?" He moved on.

Jessica drew near Maddy the minute her father's back was turned. "It was good," she whispered. "You're sure to win, Maddy." Vinnie Dow was quiet. "I had forgotten," she said slowly. "I had no idea."

They all sat on bleachers at the back of the auditorium, the young Mr. Howarth on the other side of Vinnie Dow. "Vinnie," Maddy heard him say, "you must be proud."

Vinnie Dow nodded, not looking at the minister.

The fourth chorus was filing onto the stage, a small group dominated, as it turned out, by the large stage and by one or two voices that recovered from the shock of it sooner than the others: one quite beautiful but altogether too powerful tenor voice, another a soprano, very strong, especially in the upper registers. She, desperately trying to help the others along, had her own ideas about tempo.

"I think there's hope for us," Jonah whispered down the row. There was loyal applause as the last chorus in their division left the stage.

The judges conferred. At last a short, stout man holding a microphone turned to the crowd.

"We've had a good competition in this division today," he said, "and your choral directors may come and pick up your ratings as soon as I finish here. I am happy to announce that the winners in our division are the singers of the Freedom church chorus, led by Jonah Sears."

"We did it," Jonah was heard to mutter. He stood and bowed to applause. In the bleachers around him, his chorus went wild. They hugged each other, slapped each other's backs, clapped, and whistled, and when Jonah returned to them, they wrung his hand again and again, and Jonah hugged as many as he could.

Aunt Ann, Aunt Bea, Jonah, Jack Dow, the children, Maddy, her mother — all on the bleachers, as if they were a family. You could almost think you were a family.

Then the word came down the aisle from her father: "Maddy must come home now, no ice cream today, perhaps some other time."

The polite lie filtered down: chores to do, busy day. The polite dividing edge between the Dows and the rest of life. Maddy wondered: Would there always be that edge? Some glimpses of love and beauty and then, this division. What, then, were those glimpses for?

CHAPTER NINE

AUNT BEA SAT at the table in her room. She didn't eat her breakfast, and when Aunt Ann brought up lunch she left it to cool while she stared at the mirror over the dressing table.

"I believe I'm getting old," Aunt Bea said. "Look how old I am, Ann. I'm not good for much anymore." Her voice trailed away.

"Now see here," said Aunt Ann. She drew herself up severely. "You just see here." She, who had eaten Aunt Bea's breakfast as well as her own, began to nibble reflectively on Aunt Bea's lunch, and there was a silence in the room. When all Aunt Bea's plates were clean, Aunt Ann sighed. Aunt Bea, hearing it, kicked off her slippers and with the tiniest little sad movements went to her bed, opened the covers, and, fully clothed, climbed in.

"I think I just don't feel very well today, Ann," she said sadly.

Aunt Ann looked sharply at Aunt Bea. The older woman had no color in her face and her features were drawn.

"Probably," Aunt Bea went on faintly, "if Jonah isn't here, our Maddy won't want to come either. Ann, did you think of that?"

"Oh, Lord." Aunt Ann sat down heavily at Aunt Bea's frail little table, rattling it. Feeling hungry, she looked over all the empty plates.

"She's our little girl, almost." Aunt Bea fretted. "It doesn't seem fair." Her lost voice trailed off again.

Aunt Ann stared into space. "Bea," she said, "something's got to be done. Or I'm going to blow up like a balloon, and you're just going to fade off into your pillowcase."

Aunt Bea didn't say anything.

"Something," said Aunt Ann. "Damned if I know what."

The two old women were still. There was another long silence in a morning of them.

First one woman sighed, then the other. Silence.

Suddenly Aunt Ann said, "Boiled dinner."

Aunt Bea raised up a little on her lace pillow.

Aunt Ann switched herself carefully in the lightweight wicker chair and twisted around to look Aunt Bea in the eye.

"Course," said Aunt Ann, "we'd have to have the right corned beef. There's a meat mart over to Westbrook where they make their own — no chemicals, you know. Just spices, *very* good." She began to calculate.

Aunt Bea sat up a little more.

"It just might work," said Aunt Ann after a moment, "if he really liked it."

Aunt Bea said, "He would stay here, do you think, Ann? Should we ask him? If he wants to. Whenever he wants to." Her lips trembled. "He might not want to, Ann."

"He will. He will when I get through with him. You wait and see what I can do, Bea. New beets, oh, and new potatoes. Kelly'll cut me a cabbage."

"Could — could Maddy come to dinner, too? Why, I could call her father, we could arrange it." Aunt Bea sat up completely. There was a light flush on her cheeks. "Do you think so, Ann?"

"Maddy? Hell, yes. You know, on rehearsal nights, why couldn't she eat right here and then go on to rehearsal with Jonah? You know, Bea," Aunt Ann said, "it's going to get dark earlier."

"She could get off the school bus here and stay right with us, couldn't she, Ann?" Aunt Bea laid her coverlet back. "I'll call Jack Dow right away. No, I'll call David, he'll fix it for me. Oh, do you think so, Ann?"

"Yeast rolls," Aunt Ann said, "oatmeal, just out of the oven. Jonah can't resist, Bea, you watch. Now it's just a little cooler out, funny how your mouth gets set for something like oatmeal yeast rolls and butter."

"Do you think he'll want to stay way out here, Ann? It's a half-hour to Portland from here."

"Yes, that's true. He does have a busy schedule." Both women were sitting forward, staring at each other, plotting strategy. Aunt Ann frowned.

"Cabbage makes gas," she said. "We wouldn't want that."

"Oh, no," said Aunt Bea. "Oh, no, not that." For an instant she looked as if she might want to go back to bed.

"Not this cabbage, though!" Aunt Ann slapped a fist into a plump palm. "I'll make Kelly cut me the nicest, freshest little cabbage, and I'll cook it 'til it melts in his mouth."

"Do you have time, Ann?"

"For tonight? I think so. Let me see, corned beef, three hours, potatoes, turnip, one hour, carrots, onions, cabbage. We have time if I hustle." Already she was collecting the empty plates.

"I'll call David," Aunt Bea said happily. "Maddy should have supper here tonight, for such a feast. Does Kelly have zinnias? Cosmos? Everlasting?"

"I'll send him in and go after the corned beef — we'll have to scoot." Aunt Ann heaved herself up.

Aunt Bea sighed. "There's only one thing, Ann."

"Oh, dear the Lord, what?" Midflight, Aunt Ann paused, frowning.

"I'm — I find myself, suddenly, just a little hungry."

"Oh, my goodness! Oh, my poor Bea! I've eaten every last skrit of your lunch. Now when did I do that? Lord love a duck, you just stay there one second, Bea." She rushed toward the door.

Then, from the doorway: "Damn. Look at this." The big old woman reached inside her collar and pulled out a string of white. "I got so excited my foolish slip strap broke."

"Ann." Aunt Bea began to laugh.

"Well, I ain't changing, Bea, I'll tell you that." Aunt Ann's plump hand reached into the other side of the collar and there was a shredding sound. Her wide form began to wriggle all over.

"Ann! What in the world?"

The wriggling stopped. Daintily Aunt Ann stepped forward, then back, and picked up something white. "Who needs the damn thing anyway?" she said, swinging it. "Lunch in just a minute, Bea."

As she thudded down the stairs, there came the cheering sound of Bea's startled laughter.

*

"Scotts contract? Got to get the lawyers back from vacation! I told the boys to go ahead and start filling the order anyways. Shouldn't be too much longer. Yes, Dave. Yes."

He was smiling. He'd thought it all out: two contracts, one for the Scotts people, and one with lower figures on it, for the Heberts. Signatures? He could fix them.

"You can take the computer over to the town office if you want. Yep, book's right there." Robbing Peter to pay Paul. Just get the Scotts money, all would be well.

"Yes, Dave. What? Maddy? Two nights a week. Well, I don't know, Dave. Aunt Bea Packard, I know. I can't deny her anything, no. Yes, I'll tell her. Oh, she'll be overjoyed. Really. Thanks, Dave. Talk to you tomorrow."

Everything was fine.

He looked around his office, stared into a blank space thinking he should turn on a light. It occurred to him that some things you could see better in the dark.

Maddy. She would have to be watched like a hawk. One secret, one little thing overlooked... He stared into the dark, seeing the myriad details of his life. They danced before his eyes like a thousand fireflies.

After the first competition Jonah Sears went to Portland. Audrey had left him a note at the university. "If you've finished the project, call me," she'd written. "If not, I want to continue to sublet." Since they'd both moved out, they'd sublet the apartment.

It was a bit of a shock to Jonah. He'd thought surely by the end of the summer she would be ready to try again, as he was. He thought, considering the agony he felt away from her, that she must be feeling some, too. He went to see her.

He was unprepared for the pain in her face when she opened the door to him.

"Jonah," she said, and tried to smile. He thought her tongue on his name was the only sound he wanted to hear.

"Well," she said, "did you write it?"

The question hurt. "Could I at least come in?"

"Yes." Two small rooms, comfortable. They smelled like Audrey, clean and sweet.

"Sit down," she said.

They faced each other from opposite ends of the sofa.

"I have written some things," said Jonah. "Beginnings of chapters, that's all. But Audrey, I think we should . . ."

Looking at him she saw the truth. He wished there weren't so many diamonds of light in her eyes.

"So you haven't done it," she said. Her auburn hair swung forward to hide her face for a moment.

"It's just a dissertation, you know," he said defensively. "It's not as if I have to go into analysis or something."

"You bet you don't," Audrey mumbled, her face still hidden. "It would never work with you."

"A lovely thing to say."

"I can't help it, I feel bad." She faced him. "The dissertation is a symptom, you're right," she said. "It's you. You drift around. Even into affairs, it seems."

"I was just overworking."

"So full of damn little compartments, with circumstances responsible for everything."

"In this case, it was just one of those things that happened."

"Why? Can't we ask that?" Her lower lip trembled. "Are we too polite to ask?" Her head bowed. "Go away," she told him from the depths of her hair. "I don't want to talk to you, Jonah."

He fought at the flat blank space he saw opening out in front of him. "But we have to talk, Audrey. A compromise, something." He wanted to touch her; he wouldn't.

"About this?"

Will of steel, he found himself thinking. Dedication of a nun. "Now, Audrey."

"No. Either you do this thing, or you'll kick around for the rest of your life. You know it and I know it. And that affects me. Jonah, as long as we're married, it affects every minute of my breathing life. You must know that."

"Well, I could work along on the dissertation." He hated his own lameness.

"The way you did before?" He saw her eyes, how he looked to her, a man old enough, educated enough, at the threshold of possibility or failure. He wished she wouldn't look so hard and knew at the same time that she looked because she loved him.

"Go away, why don't you?" she said now, her eyes full of tears. She blinked them back and motioned him away. "Just don't talk to me anymore."

He was angry. He stood. "Well," he said, "I don't know what in hell I have to do."

"No?" She stood, too, her mouth pinched, even crabbed-looking. "Jonah, so you write it down, what are you doing? Writing the truth, the best you can. Same with life. What's the matter with you, Jonah? Why can't you settle for the goddamn awkward truth?"

"Well, it's Christ-awful," he shouted suddenly, knowing she was right, "when you don't get any support from the woman you —"

"Love? Jonah." She held up her hand, but her whole body was tense, a band of steel. "How do I know if that's the truth, either?"

They stared at each other sorrowfully for a moment. The world's emptiest spaces lay between them. Jonah left.

He was a man with bowed shoulders and intelligent eyes in dark sockets. He was attractive. He had on a nice suit and polished shoes, and his blond-gray hair curled around his ears. But on the way back to Freedom, he pulled his car over and wept, in big ugly heaves.

That night Aunt Ann put on a dinner he would never forget.

"It's a long way for commuting," said old Aunt Bea tremulously. "But you would make us happy if you would think about staying a little while longer, think about it, only."

Jonah looked from one old lady to the other. Before him lay caverns of time, the interior passages of some submarine beast. Old jokes haunted him: "Jonah, how is it inside that big fish?" childhood friends used to holler. "Dark," he would yell back at them in fun. "And very big!"

"Aunt Bea, you've been so kind," he said now. "I would be grateful if you would allow me to stay. At least for a little while longer. At least" — he shrugged — "until I can arrange my affairs."

Maddy, there for the meal, permitted herself to smile. Both old women were ecstatic.

"Jonah, tell the truth," said Aunt Ann. "Did that cabbage melt in your mouth or what?"

"It melted," said Jonah. "Oh, yes." He laughed.

That night, like a man in prison, because he had nothing better to do, he sat down at his typewriter and for once did not bother to try to start at the beginning.

The interrogation went on until almost midnight. Jack Dow didn't hurt Maddy with blows, but she accepted his unremitting questions for the sake of her mother. Vinnie Dow sat within her husband's reach. From time to time she remonstrated weakly: "Jack, let's go to bed now."

Each time she said it, his questions renewed themselves.

"So you went into the dining room and sat down. What happened then?" Or, "How come all of a sudden they invite you to supper, too? Are you planning to live over there, Maddy?" Or, "Do they ever give you things, like money?"

On and on. By midnight Maddy began to answer like a zombie: "Yes." "No." She was thinking it would be better and quicker if he'd only hit her and be done with it. At last he sent her up the stairs. There was the click of the lock, then the soundless way her parents went to bed. She got into bed herself, surprised to find Jessie still awake. "Cheer up" came the ghostly whisper, with the clasp of Jessie's hand on hers. "It was all they could do, tonight."

"They?" Maddy, in her weariness, decided that Jessie had meant to say "he." She fell asleep.

But a voice called in the night: a tiny sound as if from a pipe, a very high note, a calling. A limit, Maddy thought, that's what it was, to tell the other voices that pushed as they were by the bass, this was as high as they could go. A tiny voice as high as a ceiling: that note said to her, "If you push me too far, I'll break."

The next morning, haunted, she went back to work on her composition. She didn't know where the voices were leading her, but she continued to sketch in notes, erase, fill them in more firmly. Now in the bass there were modulations that forced others in the soprano voice. Again and again those two taunted each other, chasing from key to key. Feeling for simpler notes, the signature she'd started with, Maddy held them back when she could, but now she had forty bars of music and still the bass crowded and the hollow upper voice called to it, mocked it, and played on.

She worked at the measures at home on the piano, in those moments between her time at the Packards' — still every afternoon, but now after school — and her father's coming home from work. After that, unless he had a meeting, all piano work had to stop. She ate her supper and went to her bedroom to study; when the schoolwork was done, she lay on her bed in the dark and heard those notes again and again.

At last, frantically, Maddy set her composition in front of Jonah. "It's not very good, I'm afraid," she said. "It's not ready to share. If you wouldn't mind, I don't know, just looking at this . . . it's scaring me."

"Something's wrong, Maddy?"

"I'm afraid this is so bad it may not be worth —" She couldn't look at him.

He took up the notebook and began to play. Forty measures, twisting voices, that tiny sound up high, the pushing bass reaching toward it. He stopped at the end and paused for a moment. Maddy looked ready to run away.

"What do you think will happen next, Maddy?" he said.

"I don't know." She forgot to be careful. "I'm afraid to listen. Every day something more is added to it, and I —"

"You're afraid?"

"Yes. I'm afraid that when those lower voices hit that upper note, the whole thing will break. That's what I will have done, this ugly thing. But Jonah, that's not the worst."

Carefully he said, "What is the worst, Maddy?"

"The worst part is, I hear it. It hurts me and I'm scared of it and I hear it. How can I? There must be something wrong with me. I'm no good at this, I can't do it."

Utterly distraught, she stared at him. He realized she was speaking to him directly at great cost to herself because she was desperate.

"You think the music will break?" he said slowly.

"Look at it. What else could happen? And when I've done that, maybe it'll all be over, I'll be through. There won't be anything worth sharing, and all this time I —" Pale and intense, she looked away from him.

"Maddy, what do you think I see here?"

"I don't know. Something bad."

"No." He said it sternly. "What I see is something unfinished. It's not bad at all. There is good work here." The next words he said had a personal echo, and he knew them, suddenly, for part of his own truth. "Maddy, you can't shut it off. You have to keep listening and get this finished, and when it is, you'll go on to something else. Why, Maddy, I think this is going to be good."

"You do?" The brown eyes were trying to see more of him than was there.

"I do. It is good. Nobody else could have done it. I know you're scared." When he said "scared" his lip curled a little, as if to tell her they both knew "scared" and maybe it wasn't worth very much.

He smiled. She looked up at him and tried to smile back. It was her courage that impressed Jonah, who thought, The girl teaches me.

He turned to Aunt Bea, who had been sitting quietly on the sofa all this time. "Aunt Bea," he said, a lift in his voice, "it's time we were helping Maddy decide where she should go to school. Musical training."

"Of course," said Aunt Bea at once. "You're absolutely right, Jonah. We haven't a moment to lose."

Maddy could hardly believe them, but she wanted to believe them. She took the notebook home again and listened, continuing to work. She tried to treat "scared" as Jonah had said, something beneath her, and she continued to listen, to write what she heard.

"School of music," Jonah began to say. "Piano auditions." Sometimes even "scholarships."

"School of music?" Jessica said in the dark, wondering. "Of music?" The whisper faded as she puzzled it out.

"Scholarship," Jessie whispered at last. "That's it, of course."

All through the fall Maddy went home across the field. The colors were bright at first and then, increasingly, muted. Bouquets of wild asters, some nearly ten feet across, dropped their petals and raised tiny seed pods like little fists at the edge of each stem. The grass lay flat now in a tangle of old green and dried yellow-white. She kicked along leaves. Night after night she felt dragged between two poles — the one, the composition she was writing, which still seemed to prove that she was no good musician, and that whisper, Jonah's talk: "school of music," "scholarship."

Jack Dow watched her. He seemed to Maddy like an animal making ready to leap, a giant cat gathering himself for one huge, horrible pounce. He seemed to be waiting for the moment when he had reached his limit with her.

Maddy's mother watched her, too, listened as she composed. In Vinnie Dow's eyes was a murky place. Was it misunderstanding? A few times Maddy tried to explain what she thought her mother must already see, that Vinnie Dow's music was not necessarily her daughter's. Was that the problem? Maddy thought it was. After all, now she played Bach, not Chopin.

But her mother didn't respond to explanations, said little, seemed, in fact, to encourage Maddy, giving her chores to Allison and Phillip, insisting she have whatever time she needed at the piano as long as their father wasn't around. There was a dullness in Vinnie Dow's eyes, a watching, a measuring of pain.

"No, no, you have your music," Vinnie would say. "Let the others do the work, they don't mind." There were a lot of chores Vinnie Dow couldn't do because of her twisted hand. Jack Dow assigned them, in order, to the children.

But Maddy knew how Allison hated her chores; she already had too many for a ten-year-old.

"Some people have all the luck," Phillip said grudgingly. He was a little boy who needed time to play, too.

Maddy was helpless.

As the weeks passed and her mother pushed harder and her father examined everything she did, it grew more difficult to maintain a balance. It was a tightrope. The younger children stared at her, distantly. She was the privileged one, she could hear them think as they did her work. She hoped they wouldn't begin to hate her.

What was really happening here? She couldn't tell. She only knew she was caught in some kind of a tangle she didn't understand and that only Jessie stood by her, sturdily watching over her.

Rehearsals came and went. Sometimes Jack Dow smiled, at least at the younger children. "You're good kids," he would tell them. "Not like your hoity-toity sister."

It was a joke, everybody laughed; they didn't dare not to. But Maddy thought she heard the younger children thinking: Our father, he just has his ways. He expects more than other fathers, that's all. He's not bad, not at all. Maddy is making trouble for him.

Maddy knew that for them it was like proving that good existed in the universe and God loved them if their father was not really that bad.

She couldn't talk about it to them. She felt they were too little to live without illusions. They had to have something to hang on to, and she felt she was to blame for their troubles.

Maddy, their eyes told her, how could you put us in this danger with your music?

She wanted to tell them, For our mother. Vinnie Dow deserved that much. Maddy, who had shared music with her, felt she owed something to her mother, some kind of obedience. If her mother wished her to skip chores to practice, why, then, Maddy would brave a little resentment, as well as the ever-present possibility of punishment, to do it. Vinnie Dow put herself on the line. How could Maddy do less than what her mother asked?

Also, Maddy knew guiltily, there was Jonah, Aunt Bea, Aunt Ann, the beautiful Cottage.

Meanwhile their father watched all of them. Vinnie Dow saw this, too. A smile an instant too long from Maddy, or any attempt to speak to the younger children, and her father's eyes hardened into two black spots like stones. Looking at him squarely was like staring into the open shutters of double camera lenses: everything you did recorded both for what it was and what it might be. No. She wouldn't jeopardize the younger ones by trying to explain herself to them.

"Maddy comes by it honestly," Aunt Bea told them one Thursday night at supper. "The Packards have always been musical, and in my family you can trace our musical history all the way back to the Reverend Mr. Seth Noble."

"Who was he?" Aunt Ann asked from the doorway.

Aunt Bea said, "It's all in a book August bought for me a long time ago. Seth Noble was famous in Maine in the late seventeen hundreds as a singer of hymn tunes. In fact, the town of Bangor, Maine, was named after one of Seth Noble's favorite hymns."

"Oh, for heaven's sake," said Aunt Ann.

"Yes. August and I used to laugh over it. You know, in those days people took some satisfaction in hymns with melancholy words. The words to 'Bangor' August and I used to recite together. It goes, 'Stoop down my thoughts that used to rise, / Converse a while with death. / Think how a gasping mortal lies / And pants away his breath.' " Silver-haired Aunt Bea pursed her lips and shook her head with mock sadness.

"Good God," said Aunt Ann.

"Catchy," said Jonah — this made Maddy smile. At these dinnertimes it was Maddy the glance of the adults turned to most often. It was a joy to see a soft glow in her eyes. In unguarded moments her pale face would relax and she would look beautiful to them.

Now Aunt Bea returned the smile delightedly. "How August and I would laugh, Maddy! August's family was all musical, you know. They came from Hallowell, Maine, one of a cultured circle of families who lived in the town then. Singers and musicians, all of them, and the first family, long after of course, to find an organ for the Hallowell church. August used to say that one of his ancestors studied at the feet of Carl Philipp Emanuel."

Maddy's eyes widened.

"Bach." Jonah spoke up. "Maddy?"

"Son of Johann Sebastian."

"Yes, good."

"For heaven's sake," said Aunt Ann again.

"Yes, Maddy, our family has a long and interesting musical history," Aunt Bea said proudly. "Maybe I shouldn't brag, but on my side of the family, we have Abraham Maxim."

"Abraham?" Aunt Ann settled herself by the roast. She picked at it a little with a fork while the talk continued.

"Oh, a very famous young man. Talented. He had composed a number of well-known songs when the girl he wanted to marry went off with someone else. Discouraged, Abraham went into the woods to commit suicide, poor chap." Aunt Bea sparkled. Jonah was reminded that fine conversation could be an art.

"Not much staying power," Aunt Ann commented. She had cut a piece of meat into tiny strips and was swallowing them absently, one at a time.

"Oh, but you haven't heard the whole story yet. He was in the woods, trying to decide which tree to hang himself on, when suddenly he heard a lonely sparrow singing."

"Figures," said Aunt Ann and shrugged in a funny way, rewarded by Maddy's smile.

"Anyway," Aunt Bea continued, "when Abraham Maxim heard

this sparrow's song, he started to write, on the bark of a big birch tree, some words to his lost beloved — before he died, you know. But he found that the words fit themselves into a verse, and then the verse to music, quite like the song of the sparrow he'd heard. He got so interested in making a song of it that he forgot to kill himself, and went home with a whole arrangement in his head, to have his choir sing. After that he became one of Maine's most popular hymn writers. So!"

Aunt Ann shook her head. "Hard to believe," she said.

"Oh, it's all recorded," said Jonah. "I had no idea you knew so much musical history, Aunt Bea."

"The province of old women, Jonah." Aunt Bea laughed and bowed. "I'll be quiet, now."

"No." This came, surprisingly enough, from Maddy. "I like to hear it, Aunt Bea. Is there — was there anything else?"

"Yes," said Jonah at once. "Please."

Aunt Bea stared at them for a moment, then began again, a trembling in her voice. "Well, there's — there's another story. August used to like to tell it. It's a story his grandfather wrote in a journal about the music in the church at Gorham, Maine. One of his forebears led the choir there, in about 1820. There was no organ, but people played instruments. But it seems the choir loft was too full, there weren't enough seats for everyone who wanted to sing."

"Unusual," said Jonah.

"The history says that the church choir was the only public place for 'masculine or feminine display,' " said Aunt Bea demurely.

Jonah burst into delighted laughter. "Showing off their Sunday clothes!"

Aunt Ann and Maddy grinned at each other.

"Anyway," continued Aunt Bea, "there was such a problem about seats that the choir eventually split into two groups: the Haydns, who were successful at getting the singers' seats, and the Handels, who were unsuccessful but who included some of the best singers in town."

Aunt Ann nodded at Maddy. "Human nature for you," she said.

Maddy nodded back, happy to be included.

"It split the church up," said Aunt Bea. "The Handels left altogether, and since they were the more musical group, they started up a new meetinghouse of their own. But it was an unusual place for

that time. It was what was called a Free Meetinghouse, where Metho-
dist, Baptist — any religious group who wanted to — could hold a
meeting. The Handel Society sang for them all."

"An early ecumenical movement?" Jonah suggested.

"Why, yes. You know, I often think that's what August had en-
visioned this church in Freedom to be — not any particular denomi-
nation but welcoming to everyone, and with good music, you know.
For a while it seemed that's what would happen, and then —" Aunt
Bea broke off. "I find it difficult to go to our church sometimes."

"Just people," said Aunt Ann comfortably. "Nothing to be scared
of, Bea."

"I know. But when I think back. When August was young he
and his sister — she died later, of diabetes, at that time there was
no cure — would practice their music in the evening, together. They
lived in Portland. People would stop on the street outside their house
just to listen. It was classical music, of course, but then people
seemed to like it."

It was the first time Maddy had heard about the history of her
family. She was excited; all this time she had needed a home and
suddenly she realized there was one. She spoke up, as she had begun
to learn to do in this house where there was no punishing, only
encouragement.

"Were there other singers in the family, Aunt Bea?" she asked
timidly. "And other pianists besides my mother and me?"

Aunt Bea nodded. "Many, many singers, Maddy. Many musical
people who married musical people. My mother used to say it was a
family tradition: any child could be taught to carry a tune if caught
early enough. She taught me and any number of children in town.
She gave voice lessons to adults, too, and had a wonderful singing
voice herself. I often think that's where young Judy gets it from —
she sings as my mother used to. Both Eleanor and June have very
nice singing voices, too. Oh, we had some times!"

Aunt Bea stared off into the distance. "The girls — Eleanor and
June — would sing together in public, they were very much in de-
mand. Their uncle August pushed them, perhaps a little too much, I
used to think. Their own parents died during the Depression. August
kept them busy, to keep their minds off it, he used to say. Later I
began to think that perhaps that wasn't the way to handle it. August
was determined: go here, go there, sing. Sing. Until, I suppose, they

got sick of it, always having to be together and sing together, dress just alike, and all the rest of it. They never said so, of course.

"Oh, yes, Maddy, there were singers, pianists. I could play, of course, and I had a violin I liked, and an oboe, and, oh, yes, a recorder. August had a flute. He and I would play concerts. We'd go off by ourselves and play. Sometimes I can still hear that music so strongly. I think August is just in the next room, and if I could only find my violin and get to him . . ." The rims around the fine blue eyes reddened. Aunt Bea shook her head.

Jonah cleared his throat. "Perhaps those times will come again," he said.

"I'm sorry to talk on so long," said Aunt Bea. "I got going on a subject I don't often have an audience for. But there's something about music, Maddy, don't you find? Once you've heard it in your heart you know it, even when it isn't there anymore."

Maddy, excited still, nodded. So I haven't just sprung out of the earth, she thought. One part of me, at least, has a history.

Tuesdays and Thursdays were the high points of Maddy's week; they were rehearsal nights, and she ate at the Cottage on those nights. The three grownups were always kind, always glad to see her. She thought it was like a party.

"Come right in, now." Aunt Ann would usher them into the dining room. "You sit down there, Jonah. Here, Bea, let me help you. Maddy. Oh, excuse me, all of you. I get so excited I feel I have to direct traffic."

Jonah would laugh. "You're not directing, Aunt Ann. You're orchestrating."

"You see?" Aunt Ann nodded. "I knew I had some music in me."

She never sat at the table for long, but bustled in and out of the kitchen. She was as wide as the doorway and it seemed her hands were always full — heavy dishes, empty ones. Chicken gleaming and golden in a cream sauce one night, pot roast and vegetables another. The pot roast she brought in triumphantly on a platter, surrounded by tiny carrots, onions, and potatoes flecked with parsley. "Now you three," she said, "you can eat anything, you luckies, so you get right to it."

Steaming hot. Mouths awater, Maddy and Jonah, who never gained weight anyway, didn't hesitate. Aunt Bea, always so frail, enjoyed food much more in the company of people who did. "Left to herself, she never eats as much," Aunt Ann fussed.

Back and forth from dining room to kitchen; finally Aunt Ann would alight for a moment or two, delicately hoisting her weight into a thin-legged dining room chair. "Well, there," she would say, big breasts in their shiny flowered dress heaving, "now see if that doesn't suit you."

Portland was a great place for shopping, and Jonah often brought Aunt Ann delicacies: imported cheese, pine nuts, spices, once even a bottle of wine, which she gave right back to him.

"I'm sorry, Jonah," she said. "But you understand, I couldn't allow a drop of stuff in my kitchen, not after my Roger." She stared straight ahead. Jonah hastily took the bottle away.

Aunt Ann ate, not with them, perhaps, but alongside them. She would have "a taste" of this, or "a touch" of that. No one knew exactly how much she did eat since she never seemed to help herself to a generous serving of anything. But somehow quantities of food vanished.

Maddy loved both the aunts, almost before she knew it. There was something in the walls of their rooms, in their shining glasses, the abundance of good food, that made her relax, smile, sometimes talk, sometimes, even, forget.

But not quite. She always knew that in her father's house, her mother sat tensely at a silent table by silent children. The light over that table was harsh, and the food was a necessity, not a joy. The memory would come to her as she touched a napkin or laid down a silver fork, or saw, suddenly, the light of a candlestick. It was like being there and not being there, like being two people. Helping herself to good food in shining dishes, lingering at the table to hear Jonah's stories of the university or Aunt Bea's reminiscences, Aunt Ann's laughter, her own comments about the music she was learning or that the chorus practiced — during that time, while she was one kind of person, she was also present at that other table, where the children ate what they were given quickly, so as to be away from the table as soon as they could, and were never quite satisfied.

From this safe place it came to Maddy to examine her home.

Scenes occurred to her in the midst of a pleasant conversation, and she could not ignore them in the way she had always done.

She saw herself washing dishes at the kitchen sink at home, as she had been the night before. Her parents were sitting at the table, which held a loaf of bread. Each child had had to have one slice — no more, no less — of that bread for supper. Those who were not hungry for bread choked it down dryly, so it lay in a lump in their gullets. Those ravenous for bread ate quickly and kept their eyes down, so as not to look for more. Then only Maddy and Jessie were left in the kitchen, cleaning up.

"Ought to be enough of that loaf for breakfast," said Jack Dow, counting the slices carefully. All Maddy could see was the back of his head, the swirl around his part, the black hairs firmly slicked down. Maddy's mother said nothing. Jack Dow's planning aloud made the laws in the house. He leaned back, ignoring them all.

Vinnie Dow did not look at her husband. After a moment, however, she reached out and took a slice of bread and ate it. Maddy stopped all work, to see this. Then, giving Jack a sideways glance, Vinnie took another slice. She ate half of it slowly, then crumbled the rest into a little pile in front of her.

A move toward freedom, Maddy thought. It had to be that, not a deliberate encitement. Jack Dow's face bulged.

Jessie happened to be walking by with a broom. "Give me that," he rapped out, and when Jessie didn't respond quickly enough, he scraped back his chair and tore the broom from her hands, sending her against the wall. "Get to bed!" he thundered.

Jessie turned and stumbled toward the stairs.

"Maddy! Finish those dishes and get going!"

Vinnie Dow didn't move, her eyes on the crumbled bread. Maddy rinsed the pot and followed Jessie. There was silence from below all the long dark night.

One thing Maddy kept remembering: her mother's sidelong glance before she took that second slice. What Maddy allowed herself to think was, If she wanted another slice, she had a right to take it, didn't she?

One night Aunt Bea laid her fork down and said gently, "Maddy is thinking of home, I can tell."

"A — a little," Maddy answered before she thought.

Aunt Bea asked, "How are they at home?"

Maddy hated her own response, born of long training: "They're very well."

She saw her brothers and sisters in her mind's eye, huddled quietly over their plates at home while she sat there, safe. She wondered, How young had they been when they learned not to laugh with each other?

"Are they?" Aunt Bea, glancing first at Jonah over Maddy's head, spoke more gently still. "You know, I often think of your mother. How quiet she's become. Why, as a child she used to be talkative, with a big sense of humor. Does she still have her sense of humor, Maddy?"

A question like a razor cut. The polite response failed. Maddy stared at her plate.

Into the silence Aunt Bea spoke again: "I often want to talk to her, but she seems remote to me. Sometimes I feel bad about it. You know, she stayed with me after her accident."

Maddy couldn't help herself. "Was her wrist crooked then?"

If Aunt Bea was surprised, she didn't show it. "After the accident, yes," she said. "How else could it have happened?"

I knew that, but I still thought he'd done it, Maddy wanted to say. She was silent.

Jonah found himself staring at Maddy. This child has been hurt, he thought. It hadn't even occurred to him before. Why did the term "battered" come to mind? He found himself studying her face, her arms. No, no bruises. He was dismayed with himself. In the midst of this pleasant meal, surely he was imagining things.

If so, suddenly he was not the only one. Aunt Ann spoke up. "You know, I was over to Westbrook today," she said, looking searchingly at Maddy. "There was a young woman over there, two kids. The meat was just lovely. Well cut, you know. The poultry is strictly fresh, no stuff injected into it. Anyways, I was just standing there, and it occurred to me to think how lucky I was, how comfortable — all this good meat I would buy, all the good meals to come, for good company, a nice place to live." Aunt Ann's lips tightened. "There I was feeling like — like the world was a damned garden, for God's sake, when this woman turned to her kids, who were just little, two or three, and racketing around the way young ones will do, and she said, 'You kids stand still or I'll kill you!' Yes, that's what she said. She glared at those kids and I thought she meant it. I was scared. So were the kids. They got this queer look and quieted right down."

Still Aunt Ann looked at Maddy, searchingly. But Maddy stared at her plate and said nothing.

"Awful," said Aunt Bea softly.

Yes, Maddy was thinking. You are on the right track now. But you must come and find me; I can't do anything to find you.

"Well, it was awful," Aunt Ann continued more slowly, waiting for something from Maddy. "The butcher saw it, too. He and I understand each other — over meat!" She blushed. "You were about to tease me, Jonah! I saw it coming."

Jonah was relieved. "Well, meat's a start," he said seriously.

"Oh, you!" Aunt Ann blushed a little more, mopped her forehead with her napkin, and fell silent. In all this time, she saw, Maddy had not moved or looked up from her plate.

"Anyway," Aunt Ann said, now very softly, "what the butcher said was, it was amazing how we lived, one lifestyle on one street, one on another. He said that two streets down from him a kid was killed last week. The police suspect it was a family problem. The parents had been called up on child abuse before, but it's awful hard to prove . . ."

Aunt Ann's voice trailed off as she looked at Maddy. One tear had rolled down the child's cheek, making a wet path.

Come and get me, Maddy wanted to cry. Here I am, down this well. Come and get me.

"We are upsetting Maddy," Jonah murmured. All three grownups suddenly seemed to pull together in the light. "Maddy, is there something wrong?"

Maddy knocked away the tear, staring at her plate, fighting for control. She wanted to tell them everything, but for the sake of the children still at home she could not. Her father would be too strong; there was nowhere they could all hide from him. "If I take the wings of the morning and fly to the uttermost parts of the earth, behold thou are there." He'd read those words in church last Sunday, and she'd known that he had all the rights and all the power, and she must protect the others. He wouldn't give them up, she suddenly knew, without a horrible fight.

"No," she whispered. "There's nothing."

"But if we could — I don't know — help in some way? If we knew what we were talking about here..." Upset, Jonah looked across the table at Aunt Bea.

Suddenly horrified, Aunt Bea looked back.

"No," said Maddy. "There is nothing wrong. Please."

"It's my fault!" Aunt Ann cried. "Gossiping! Upsetting everybody! Of course we're all right here! There's nothing wrong! This child just has a soft heart, that's all." She rushed to Maddy and patted her shoulder.

Maddy would have liked nothing better than to turn and weep in her arms.

Aunt Ann must have felt it. "Maddy knows if she needs us, we're here," she said, feeling the wiry strength in those thin young shoulders. Then, as the girl's suffering seemed to go on so that no one could bear to look at her set white face, Aunt Ann added, not knowing what else to say, "Well, young one, did you get enough to eat?"

The face eased a little. "Yes, thank you."

Unwillingly, Jonah glanced at his watch. "Oh, my gosh, it's six-thirty. Maddy, we've got to hop. Delicious supper, Aunt Ann, as usual. Thank you, Aunt Bea. Maddy, are you —"

It was the escape she'd been looking for. "Excuse me." She went off into the next room to get her music.

"Something's wrong, isn't it?" Jonah said after a moment.

"Quite wrong, perhaps," said Aunt Bea tremulously. She stood up.

"We can't drag it out of her, that isn't fair," said Aunt Ann. "Maybe one of these days it'll just come."

Maddy slipped back into the room. "Ah, here she is," said Jonah.

Maddy's eyes seemed larger and darker than ever. "Thank you for the dinner," she said. "Coming here is like coming to someplace I don't — I don't deserve or — know how to hope for." Out of words, she shook her head. "I'll see you tomorrow."

"At four." Aunt Bea smiled. Maddy, staring at her, saw how fine and silvery white her hair was, and that her eyes were full of love. "I wouldn't miss it," Aunt Bea said and smiled again.

Maddy thought she had never seen such beautiful eyes, such a lovely face. "Thank you," she whispered, and dropping her music, she went straight into Aunt Bea's arms. They held each other. Aunt Ann, watching, fought into her dress pocket and dragged out a hand-

kerchief. She blew her nose with feeling, then stepped up beside
Aunt Bea. "If there are hugs around," she said, "I hope I'm next
in line."

"You are! You are!" And then Maddy was hugging her, too,
finding herself enveloped in Aunt Ann's strong, steady embrace.
"You're a good girl," Aunt Ann said. "I don't know what we'd do
without you."

Jonah knelt to pick up the music. His face was red; tears were
rising behind his eyes, and he was glad to scrabble on the floor for
the music books. "She's a good girl," he said. "She has a lot of
friends, waiting to help her. She's going to go far."

At last, one arm still around Maddy, Aunt Ann bustled into the
hall. "Now, Maddy, here's your coat. Are you going to be warm
enough? Are you sure? Jonah, cover up those ears! There now, there
now, there! See you both soon. You be careful driving, Jonah."

They left.

Aunt Ann stood for a moment in the crisp October night. "Be a
frost by morning," she muttered. Jonah's headlights flashed on, the
car turned. She waved.

"These young people, they don't know how to take care of themselves. Cold by morning, I shouldn't doubt."

She shut the door and hurried back into the dining room to find
Aunt Bea still standing there.

"Cold by morning," Aunt Ann repeated, going to survey the left-
overs.

She felt Aunt Bea's light, small hand on her arm and turned.

"The child loves me," Aunt Bea said. "She loves us both."

"Yes, I believe she does," said Aunt Ann.

"I'd forgotten how that feels," said Aunt Bea.

"I know what you mean," said Aunt Ann.

CHAPTER TEN

THE SECOND COMPETITION would be on November 14, a Thursday. Jonah had worked out the time between the first and second competitions: twenty rehearsals and a dress rehearsal. More than enough time, he had thought in September. With considerable care he had mapped out strategies and objectives to accomplish at each meeting of the chorus. They would do three new pieces: the Hovhaness "God Is Our Refuge," Grieg's "O Blessed Country," and of course the Maser arrangement of "America the Beautiful," with Judy's solo and her obligato at the end.

When many in a chorus cannot read music, learning it becomes a matter of drill, and the director's task, of making drill attractive. Every page becomes a challenge. Jonah depended on his strong readers and singers because they paved the way for the others. In each meeting he devoted some time to voice exercises. There would also be a moment or two of musical theory for those who didn't know any. His chorus would sight-read, then drill. After a while they would take a break, then review and drill again, each night adding a new page or two. Jonah liked to end each rehearsal successfully, so in the beginning of the second round of rehearsals they finished by singing harmonies, and in later weeks, as the music became more familiar, he would end with a section they did particularly well.

In the month of September — such a beautiful month in Freedom — things had seemed to go pretty much on schedule. The rehearsals went as planned, perhaps even better than Jonah had expected, considering it was new music. He had spent a lot of time at his type-writer in September, alternating these spells with long walks in the fields of Aunt Bea's property. It was a fine autumn: scarlet maples, crimson and orange, the yellow leaves of ash and beech, the oak's green-brown. It did him good to look closely at trees he hadn't examined since childhood. He collected leaves, as he'd done then, tossed them away, filled glasses with them, went back to work.

Jonah hadn't worried too much about the chorus. Of course, at that point, he knew, they had not really begun "America the Beautiful," the piece with Judy's solo. They'd only done some preparatory sight-reading. But during October his singers began to concentrate on this piece more exclusively.

Then he didn't know where it started: he thought it was in the alto section. The altos would sing too loud and the men would open up, to balance. The sopranos, without Judy's support, would push too hard and turn shrill and breathy, and Judy, in all this commotion, would have to sing for all she was worth in order to be heard.

At first it had seemed an easy matter to quiet the supporting parts and soothe the sopranos. But Jonah began to be a little concerned. Judy Russell, with the strain of the part competition upon her, would lose control and her vibrato would go sharp. She could hear it, too, which upset her.

"I'm sorry, Jonah," she apologized that night after the rehearsal. "I don't know what's wrong. Maybe I'm just not good enough to —"

"Now, Judy, you're going to be fine," he told her. "Practice the pronunciations as I gave them to you, and I don't need to tell you, concentrate. You're going to have to carry a part and blend with the chorus, and the chorus itself isn't blending too well at the moment. But they will. First they have to learn the music."

"Only three weeks left." She stared at him, stricken.

Jonah laughed. "Now, you watch what will happen, Judy. We've drilled about every page. The chorus doesn't realize it yet, but they know this piece. In a few days they'll be doing it in their sleep. And doing it right, too."

Judy smiled; so did her husband Russ, sitting in a middle row with Russ Junior on his lap. The little boy whimpered tiredly and then went back to sleep.

"Well, thank you," said Judy. "I will practice."

"Please don't worry, it'll be the best so far," said Jonah as she went to join her husband.

She turned and said, "Good. I want it to be."

Her determination worried Jonah. "Remember that the greatest danger to a voice is to push it," he murmured gently.

Judy didn't hear. She was gazing down at her son. "Poor little boy," she said. "You know, one of our family dictums, handed down through Uncle August Packard himself, is that every child has a right to know he will have three meals a day, served on time, and that every child has the right to his own bed, on time, at night."

She stared at her son. "We know kids are tough. But when I see him like this —"

Little Russ's head moved far back on his daddy's arm, his face falling into the unremitting light from the fluorescent fixtures overhead. The light woke him and he stared and blinked.

"Well, son," big Russ said, "you ready to go home?" The boy frowned, looked about him dazedly.

"See?" said Judy gently. "He doesn't even know where he is. Come on, baby, let's take you home and put you to bed. Thank you, Jonah, for helping me."

"Oh, you're welcome, Judy," Jonah said. "Just don't work too hard on it now."

"No danger of that," she said. "I won't have time." They left.

Most people had gone home, but then David Hebert and Jack Dow came out of the sanctuary. They were deep in conversation and did not see Jonah.

"Well, I know he hasn't had it before," David was saying slowly. "But that thousand dollars always used to be in the parson's purse, Jack."

"I know, Dave, I know. I just question whether young Blaine is ready yet. We got to be careful, we got to be sure. Same with check signing. He should be here a little longer before he uses the church checkbooks."

"You really think so?" David scratched his head. "He seems reliable to me, Jack. But maybe you're right. We'll give it another month, maybe. But the thousand dollars for the parson's purse — he's got to have it well before Christmas, you can see that."

"People needing things then."

"At the parson's discretion, without answering to any of us, Jack. That's the way it's supposed to work."

"I know, Dave. Another month, though, okay?"

The men stood at the back. Jonah saw that Jack Dow faced David Hebert as a wrestler might: shoulders bent, hands cupped down near his knees. David Hebert stood a bit away, facing the sanctuary, his hands in his back pockets. Satisfied, even content, he made the contrast between his attitude and Jack's the more striking. Looking up, he caught sight of Jonah.

"Well." He nodded. "Another night's work, eh?"

"Yes." Jonah shrugged. "Getting close now."

"Doin' good, I think," David said. He beamed.

"Well, thank you," said Jonah.

David moved toward the door. "I'll go along. See you in the morning, Jack. We'll fix it up."

"Oh, sure."

Nodding affably to Jonah, he went out.

"Kids in the car," said Jack, turning smoothly to Jonah. "Time to call it a night."

Had the balls of his feet been oiled? Jonah wondered. For the first time he allowed himself to examine Jack Dow full front. The face was handsome, and dark. Jonah thought of Maddy and found himself glancing at Jack Dow's cupped fists.

"You going along, Jonah?" Jack asked. "I can lock up if you are."

"Think I'll stay," Jonah said, more to test him than anything. "I'll throw the lock when I go. No need for you to wait."

"Checked the faucets, have to. Otherwise it's a fire hazard." Along the sides of Jack's dark face muscles flickered, set. He smiled deliberately. "I always do lock up," he said.

His voice buzzed. Jonah wanted to reach out and wham something, as one might hit at a dangerous insect, or stamp on a scorpion.

A violent reaction in a peaceable man; he fought it. "Don't worry about a thing," he said in a friendly way. Then, again, a kind of test:

"Jack, is Maddy all right?"

The man didn't move a muscle. "Why do you ask?" he said.

"She seems quiet sometimes."

Jack Dow looked relieved. "Gets it from me," he said. "Don't worry about Maddy, everything's fine." He and Jonah stared at each other for a moment in which one searched for secrets and the other hid them. Jonah felt out of his depth, but still he looked. Jack's eyes dropped first. "You'll lock up?" he said.

"Yes."

"All right then." Now Jack seemed pleased to leave. The door banged behind him.

A fast retreat? Jonah thought, You can't call a man bad because you don't like his looks.

He stared around the empty church vestry, shut off some of the lights, then found himself wandering into the sanctuary, which was open. He was tired.

It had been a rough rehearsal. So often this chorus had pulled together; he wasn't sure why these October rehearsals were so difficult. Maybe early success hadn't been good for the Freedom chorus. They weren't watching him as they had before. Of course, the music was harder, but not so much harder that they needed all their concentration just to watch the notes. Seesawing in the parts. They jostled for place.

"Watch me," he'd told them. "Everybody, heads up now."

Some listened, some didn't.

Part of it, too, was a damned controversy over what the chorus would wear: a simple, stupid little issue, but beginning, in Jonah's opinion, to be blown up out of all proportion. Some of the women and a few of the men under the leadership of Eleanor Hebert were pushing hard for costumes, and that evening Eleanor had interrupted the second half of their rehearsal to show the chorus swatches of colorful fabric: red, white, and blue, stars and stripes.

Some people protested. Judy Russell had risen to her feet immediately with questions: "Perhaps this fabric is too expensive for some of us, Aunt Eleanor?"

"The cost," Eleanor Hebert announced proudly, "will be taken care of by the Women's Association of the church."

"But why assume that every woman can, or wants, to sew?" Judy said. "Besides, don't costumes make us look as if we're, I don't know, trying too hard, or something?" There were nods of agreement.

In spite of himself, Jonah had seen in this issue a family split as well as one in his chorus. Over something so small.

He intervened. "This will have to be put to a vote," he'd said.

"Perhaps we should just table it for now, think about it a little longer, Eleanor?" The last thing he wanted was any kind of issue that would split the group, and on the issue of dress they seemed to be about evenly divided.

Eleanor Hebert, politician that she was, saw this, too. She inclined her head. "Jonah, I must remind you that there are only three weeks until the next competition."

"I understand," Jonah had said. "We will all be thinking."

Once again Eleanor inclined her head. A queenly gesture, Jonah thought. She sat down.

A minor skirmish, maybe, but anything that interfered with concentration was, at this point, critical. His singers were getting tense. "Watch me. Watch me!" Some did not. All it took was one inattentive eye.

"Listen to each other," he insisted, but he knew if he had to insist too often they'd shut him off. "Don't break the melodic line — that's it, stagger your breathing." Finally the group had begun to understand, to polish up some lines. But it had been hard work.

The sanctuary of the empty church had a comforting smell about it, old plush and sweet-smelling books rarely opened. He sat down in the dark for a moment, the door behind him ajar and letting in a little light. In the front he could see the dim outlines of the painted woodwork: "God Is Love," "God Our Father."

He was tired. He exhaled wearily and let his jaw go slack, allowed himself to stretch, setting his feet far in front of him on their heels. He was drained and he was troubled about Maddy.

Tonight had he had a glimpse of the girl's real life? Was it dark and as full of threatening shapes as it seemed to be? All unspecific? He felt helpless. Abuse? Battering? Why did he keep thinking of these words? Jack Dow — his wrestler's stance, the dark fists — surely people who had known him for years could not be mistaken about a man's character? It would be a mean trick, God the Father, Jonah said to himself. Oh, he was tired.

Audrey. He missed her daily. Nothing lonelier, he suddenly felt, than what he had to look forward to: an empty bed in the cold dark.

There was something about Maddy that reminded him of himself. Her suffering made him remember how his own heart had split, a piece of it going south, a piece west. Small towns. He was angry. A joke from God the Father to bring him here. You weren't allowed to run away from history, but forced to confront the same issues again and again, repeating the old mistakes and hurting yourself until you learned. The rat trap set up by God Is Love.

He hated the trap. He loved it. He was distraught, challenged. It wasn't, he knew, just this little chorus. It wasn't just some childhood anger here. It was that he thought things should be better, and for the life of him he couldn't see how to do it. There was nothing he, Jonah, could do to make anything better.

After a moment he stood up to leave. Too bad, he thought.

Then he paused, staring into the dark. There was something so still in this church, something soft as velvet in the air, something clear as the shapes of pews, white in the darkness. "God Is Love." "God Our Father." He shrugged.

As he turned to go, however, a door at the front of the church opened. Blaine Howarth came out of his office, spotted Jonah, hesitated, walked toward him. "I'm sorry," he said. "Am I disturbing you?"

"Oh, no." Jonah felt just uncomfortable enough at being discovered there in the dark to make a joke. "To tell you the truth, I was thinking that in any case I won't be able to wear a red, white, and blue tie." Blaine, Jonah's best tenor, had been in on this discussion.

"Oh?" he said.

"No, I can't," said Jonah. "It would bring out the color of my eyes." Then, "Sorry, that's beneath me."

Blaine laughed. Both he and Jonah faced front. "Eleanor's heart is set on a big celebration." The young minister's voice was calm. "Well, they're planning for a big one next year, and all excited about it, too. Barbecues and booths, a big fair, earn some money." He spoke almost absently, sat down in a pew.

After a second Jonah joined him, asking, "For the church?"

"Just so."

That absent quality, Jonah liked it. "It sounds all right," he said.

"It does, doesn't it." Blaine Howarth sighed. "I suppose it is. I must admit, sometimes I get a little worried. I know they're trying to be generous and I know you have to be practical." He looked toward the front of the church; Jonah looked with him. The pulpit, empty on its platform, was like a block of dark in the shadow.

"You know," Blaine said, "last year they had a chicken barbecue."

"Oh?"

"Yes, Jack Dow told me about it. More people in this church than they saw all the rest of this year, he said. This year the idea is to do what seems best for the town and the church again."

"Yes," said Jonah, "I understand the idea." He would say no more. "I'm just here for the music, of course."

Blaine didn't seem to hear this. "You know, in July they had a church supper. All the food was donated. The charge for the meal was three-fifty a plate. Not much in some areas, but quite a lot for here. That three-fifty was almost free and clear income for us. Of course, and I told them this, some of the poorer people in town couldn't afford to come, just as they couldn't take their families out to a restaurant for a meal at that price. But that didn't matter, they said. These people of my new church thought they'd put a fair price on the supper. It was what all the other churches were charging — the going rate, they said, to make money for the church."

The young man paused, shook his head, spoke to the dark ceiling. "So we had this collection of suppergoers with money to spend, buying a good homemade dinner cheap. They saved money, and the poor stayed away."

He sighed. "But still, we were making money. That was all right, wasn't it? Money for the church. For missions, I tried to think at the time. If not for the poor here in town, then the poor somewhere. So I let it go. They earned three hundred dollars. But the money — Jonah, half of it went into the Women's Association treasury and has not been spent to this day." He sighed again. "A piece of it went for buying flannel to make layettes for babies in Appalachia, that is true. But you know where the rest went?"

Jonah shook his head.

"To buy plastic silverware."

"What?"

"Yes. You know, plastic silverware — you use it once, you throw it away."

"You do? But —"

"Oh, they have drawers of stainless steel. But, they informed me, these good and well-meaning people of the church, until the church can afford an industrial dishwashing setup, they can't handle regular dishwashing anymore, there are just too few people willing to do it. So now we will use and throw away plastic cups and dishes and silverware, too. So nice and so modern, Eleanor Hebert says, and it saves so much time. Jonah! You are in the belly of the whale!" Blaine Howarth stood up and began to pace back and forth, but his voice was calm, as if he was only trying to make sense of it.

"People without water in the deserts of the world, and we here in Freedom plan costumes. Oh, some churches do so much better than this. Some churches give what they can, everything they can. But here in Freedom, they pass the poor between the town fathers and the church and whoever has the most practical reasons refuses — as if the government and the church were one and the same, or as if they fed each other. What's for the poor? A little money now and then, like a payoff. People in town think they will never, never have to look a dead child in the face. Sometimes I don't know what to do. I mean, I pray, I try." He shrugged.

Once again both men stared front.

Jonah was embarrassed. "Not my field," he began.

The minister wouldn't let him off the hook. "I know, but what do you make of it?"

Jonah shook his head. He didn't look at Blaine. "Truth is, I don't even know why I'm here, Pastor," he said. "I haven't given money to a church in years, and I grew up in a church like this."

"Oh?"

"Yes. I guess my parents were pretty much like the Heberts." He tried to laugh, but it was a bitter sound. "Small-town desperation, if you'll pardon me. I'll never forget how my mother would count up the number of Sundays she'd played the organ at that little church, some astonishing, self-righteous number, Blaine."

Neither man looked at the other. After a moment Jonah continued. "You remember when *Time* came out with 'God Is Dead' on its cover?"

"Oh, yes, I was a little boy then."

"You *are* young. My father only said, 'So what else is new?' And the next Sunday they went off to church as usual. I can hear them now. My dad would say, 'Forty-five in church today,' and my mother would come back with, 'Only thirty-three fifty in the offering.' "

Blaine Howarth bowed his head.

"The worst was, they were doing everything in the church." Jonah went on in spite of himself. "Every damned job. And still the church was failing and they knew it. Hell, everything was failing. They were."

He found himself grateful for the dark. "They were failing," he said again, softly. "That was it. No matter what they did, they had to fail. It was no use." He struggled to keep his voice level. "That's me, too, I guess. I look ahead and all I can see is failure. I wonder what use anything is, what hope anything is." A short unhappy laugh came out. "That's the university for you, maybe. Happens in my dissertation, too. I don't know. I make rules, I keep to them. What else is there?"

"You are mourning, perhaps, Jonah," Blaine said.

"Me?"

"That's what the rules are for. They keep you from grieving. And, unfortunately, joy. I imagine music is one place you can have both safely."

"Rules in music, Pastor."

"Unless we step to the place where there are none. The church is like that, at its best. Some marriages, too. If you can step to the place where you don't need rules."

Jonah swallowed. Facing front he saw his wife, then suddenly his parents. "It split them up," he said with tears behind his eyes. "My mother went south when I left for college. My father went west. They seem happier now, they do what they want."

"Ah, I'm sorry. Jonah, what about you?"

It was a question Jonah didn't want to answer. Instead he spoke up, with more feeling than he meant to: "No, Pastor, what about you? I mean, if you'll excuse me for saying so, what is a young man like you, with his whole life ahead of him, doing struggling in a place like this?" Blaine laughed, a surprising, glad sound. "Fair question. You know, I suspect it's the same thing you're doing, Jonah, in a way. I'm here because I think the future is here. This is a town where the rich have to see the poor, and the powerful the powerless. This is a place with a potential."

"But it might swallow you."

"I don't think so. There are wonderful people in these towns, Jonah. There are children worth saving."

"Save?" said Jonah, disappointed. "Let's all be 'saved.' "

"I mean it in the truest sense," Blaine insisted quietly. "That is, that they find out what they're here for, what they're meant for. How many really know that?"

"One here, one there," said Jonah. He shrugged. "Is it —"

"Worth it? Of course. But all that really matters is that I answer for myself, what I was sent for."

"Ah." Jonah sighed. "You sound like somebody I know."

"What I was sent for. I'll know I've tried."

"Pastor, if you could prove that even one person, even one." Jonah stopped, tried to laugh. "It would be like a —"

"A sign. I know. Meanwhile, Jonah, that we're here, that we feel that — I think that's a sign."

"If you could see what I'm writing."

"I can see your pain," the minister said. "I'm sorry." They didn't look at each other. It wasn't something you could talk about facing one another.

"Maybe," said Blaine Howarth, "that's a sign, too."

There was a silence. Jonah said, "I've got to go, I've got a chapter to finish. I have to tell you this, though: you're the first minister I've talked to in twenty years."

The two men stood up. Blaine Howarth chuckled in the dark. "You're the first chorusmaster I ever talked to," he said.

"The Freedom chorus is not getting dressed up like a bunch of monkeys at a circus. Not with that money."

"Ah."

"I'll see that it won't. We're here to make music." Jonah stopped. "Sorry. I don't sound much like a disinterested educator, do I?"

"Maybe you've been waiting. We're both waiting. For what?"

The lights were all out, and they were shrugging on overcoats at the threshold of the church.

Jonah couldn't help it. "God only knows," he said.

There was a whoop of surprised laughter from Blaine. They both bent into the wind, got into their cars, and were gone.

CHAPTER ELEVEN

YOU COULDN'T HATE a little baby, but sometimes in the last two weeks Judy thought she almost did. Those two weeks — Elaine knew Judy would need them for practicing her solo — had been one long round of taking care of Elana, sometimes from eight o'clock in the morning until five o'clock in the afternoon. It wasn't fair. It meant Judy had no time for herself and no time for little Russ. She thought Elaine must somehow understand this and that she did it for one reason only: to ensure that Judy had no leisure in which to be ready for the second competition and her solo.

The baby fussed constantly. Judy had tried to tell Elaine that perhaps it was Elana's stomach that bothered her, but Elaine simply laughed. "Good heavens, Judy, we've got the best pediatrician in the state, and he says she's fine. He's got her on cereal now, with her special formula."

"But," Judy tried to insist, "when she cries she gets bright red all over, and draws her little legs up."

"Oh, she always does that."

Could a baby be unpleasant? Deep down, Judy doubted it. Certainly someone else's baby could seem strange, a different-sized bundle than you were used to. The baby blankets smelled of Elaine's perfume and Elaine's house, so that not only was the bundle strange in your arms, but the baby's smell, however clean, was not of your house. The fingers were not those of your child, nor the little head with its soft fringe of blond hair. For all that, little Elana tugged at Judy's heartstrings and made her feel protective.

It was the constant fussing, now for whole days at a time, that got Judy down.

When he dared, big Russ joked about it. "Well," he'd say, "did Elaine give that baby her crying pills today?"

Little Russ would speak up. "Twyin' pills?"

"Yep. Just like vitamins make you strong, crying pills make you cry."

"Yup," little Russ would say. "De baby has twyin' pills today, awight."

They'd both laugh. Judy didn't think it was so funny.

"If it weren't all day," she would say. "Every day."

"Elaine must be a real advertising personality," Russ said.

"Either that or she's got somebody on the side." At Russ's startled glance, Judy only sighed.

The baby was an incredibly light sleeper. The slightest noise would awaken her and the fussing would begin. Sometimes, after hours of it, it was hard to decide whether it was a stomach problem or whether it was just some kind of spoiled crying that made the stomach problems, the spitting up, the constant necessary diaper changes.

Now it was less than three weeks before the November competition and her solo. The music wasn't going well, and Judy had not had time to practice.

Jonah had chosen a real showpiece of a solo: the obligato at the end went to a high B, at the top of Judy's range. She wanted to work on it, she wanted to perfect it. The piece was beautiful music, it should have been a joy to sing.

But by the end of a long day with Elana, Judy was usually so tired it was all she could do to get supper. Her throat felt like sandpaper, and she just wanted to sleep.

"Remember now, Judy," Jonah had said at the latest rehearsal, "don't try too hard. Sing it from the heart. The obligato at the end must be treated very delicately. That part isn't a solo, it's a piece of the harmony, and should lift not only itself but the whole chorus, and all the harmony with it."

That was what Judy wanted, too. But she needed the leisure to discover the perfect placement for this work.

Damn Elaine anyway!

Judy sat in a corner of her kitchen, humming notes under her breath. By some fluke, both little Russ and Elana were asleep at the same moment, and Judy had crept to the corner of the house farthest away from the upstairs bedrooms. There she sat with her music across her knees. She began to go over the words to herself using the pronunciations Jonah had suggested.

Judy hummed, loving as always the feel of the singing, the sound as it rose inside her, filled her head, and bloomed into a tone that was rich. She was in good voice, she could feel it. She hummed the solo through from start to finish and then came to the obligato, sung on a long *ah* sound. It rose beautifully. There, with remarkable control, was a fine, high B.

Behind it was a wail, a long, familiar cry. Elana.

How could she be awake? Judy thought. She just dropped off. For once, out of sheer orneriness, Judy didn't get up immediately. Since Elana was awake anyway, she might as well just go ahead and sing it out. Just once. Judy began again with the obligato. Here came the final line, beginning with middle G and flying up to the B.

Judy sang, determined for once to drown out the crying in the upstairs bedroom. She sang so loudly that she didn't hear little Russ pump across the floor of his room and down the stairs.

Up . . . up . . . was all she was thinking. She knew she might be a little angry at Elana, but she didn't care about that. She tried to listen to the notes she was singing. Sharp? Oh, was it sharp?

"Mommy," said little Russ, touching her hand. "Mommy, baby am twyin' again."

Judy ignored it. She stood up and moved away from him, still singing. Was it sharp? Oh, Lord.

"Mommy," insisted little Russ, now pulling at her skirt. " 'Lana am twyin', Mommy."

Judy was on that last climb of sound. Upstairs the baby wailed; downstairs little Russ tugged at her skirt. With pure, stubborn determination she reached, held the high B, tried to analyze it. She was afraid of sharping the vibrato.

Little Russ wasn't used to being ignored. "Mom-my," he roared up at her, hitting at her hands. "Don't sing anymore! Don't sing anymore!"

Before she knew what she was doing, Judy had reached out — she, who didn't believe. in spanking a child without a darn good reason — and slapped little Russ so hard that he whirled and tottered, then fell to the floor.

Horrified, Judy watched him fall. He gasped once and then began to cry. Instantly Judy was filled with remorse. Wretched and helpless, she went to her son and he lifted his arms to her. She scooped him up and carried him to a chair where they sat together and he clung to her for dear life, still crying, hanging on as if he would never let go.

She cradled his head against her shoulder. "There, Russie, there," she whispered. "You're all right. Mommy's sorry. Hug me. There, there."

When at last his sobs subsided, little Elana's howls still remained.

Judy settled him in the chair, washed his hands and face, gave him a guilty kiss and a smile. He smiled back. Did he forgive her? She couldn't ask. She thought she could still see the print of her hand on his cheek. She left him munching a cookie and with another clean wet washcloth headed up the stairs. Elana cried her accustomed, evenly spaced, high-pitched howl. Sighing, Judy went into the bedroom.

"Oh, now Elana," she said softly. "What seems to be the trouble? Shh, now, shh."

It seemed to ease the baby to be held upright. She wasn't strong-limbed at all. At this age, almost six months, little Russ had been pushing his feet into Judy's stomach to stand, he'd been beginning to hitch himself around on the floor, sit up on his own, roll over in his bed. He'd been sunny and sociable, an agreeable handful. By contrast Elana only hung on, riding upright like a little monkey.

Sometimes Judy sputtered to Russ: "If Elaine would just take some time with that baby, rock her, cuddle her, give her some security."

"Change her?" Russ laughed.

Elana needed to be changed often. The special formula passed through her rapidly, filling her diapers with sour curds. Back when she'd first taken care of the baby, Judy had been dismayed to find that both little buttocks were covered with the round hot burns of diaper rash. "Why, little Russ never had more than one tiny spot! No baby in our family has ever —" As if it were, as it was, a personal insult, this rash.

Russ had patted her shoulder. "Don't worry," he said. "I know your family has always had the most comfortable butts in town."

Then he'd ducked, as well he might have.

But now that she had had Elana almost constantly for two weeks, the rash had cleared up. "If you were my baby," Judy whispered, lifting the clean, snuffling Elana from the changing table, "I'd have you down to the doctor's, right down to Dr. Bailey, so fast you couldn't see straight, and we'd find out what's wrong with you."

Because you couldn't help but love a baby, could you? Even a strange baby who belonged to Elaine, even a baby who did nothing but cry. You wanted to step right in, do everything that the child needed, and you couldn't because, of course, the baby wasn't yours. So instead you had to put up with what the parents wanted, even when they were incompetent, or uninvolved. The frustrations were too much. All the money in the world was not enough to make Judy stand by helplessly and watch someone else's child suffer. Time and time again she'd said to Elaine, "You know, the baby fussed a lot today and I think —" But Elaine always interrupted impatiently.

"Yes, she's a scrappy baby, that's what Dr. Renberg says. She fusses at night, too, Cyril says. I never hear her anymore, but he gets up and walks her around until she goes back to sleep."

Fulfilled motherhood. Thank God for Cyril, Judy thought.

It was hurting Judy too much. The baby needed help, and she was Elaine's responsibility. It was tearing Judy apart, and what had it done to little Russ today?

For the last time Judy gathered little Russ and Elana into her lap in the living room. She studied the clock: three in the afternoon. Elaine would be back by four-thirty.

Very well, then, Judy thought. An hour and a half. For one hour and a half, little Elana, I will do the best I can for you, and that is the end.

She laid the baby up over her shoulder in the way that eased Elana the most and tucked little Russ against the hollow of her arm. He had his book, Mother Goose rhymes set to music. Judy began to sing where his stubby finger pointed. "Little Jenny Wren fell sick upon a time . . ." They rocked and Judy sang the little rhymes, the simple tunes. Only an hour left, only a half-hour. Little Russ was happy. The baby dozed against her shoulder. In spite of herself, Judy knew helplessly, she loved this baby.

If you were mine, she thought, we'd soon have you right.

Only ten minutes left, five.

Judy shivered, feeling the breathing bundle stir sweetly against her neck. She was full of regret. Little Russ closed the book at last and, giving his mother a beatific smile, went to take out his trucks. Judy argued with herself.

Let Elaine give up her singing. Let her take care of her baby. Elana will forget her troubles with a proper mother. Just as little Russ had forgotten that awful slap Judy had given him earlier in the afternoon.

He had forgotten, hadn't he?

Full of self-doubt and determination and regret, Judy waited for Elaine.

No one needed to know, Elaine was thinking as she drove to Judy's, that she had spent the day in bed. These days she was so tired, and she needed time to herself, to put herself together. Helene, down at the agency, called her for work now and then. Just the week before Elaine had modeled for a fashion show at the Eastland; very often there were things for her to do — tiring things. Also, she saw Jonah Sears twice a week, and it was hard work practicing for him. She needed her peace and quiet, time to relax.

More and more time, these days; sometimes life rose in a roar about Elaine's ears. Quiet, relaxation of the body — these were what eased her. Once a week lately she had been going to André's Salon for several hours: in the whirlpool, the sauna, a cold shower, getting an upper back massage, shampoo, facial, manicure, makeup session. It was a wonderful experience, the high point of her week, to which she clung. But from there the days seemed to go slowly downhill so that by the Wednesday before the Friday at André's, it was all she could do to drag herself around. Tuesdays and Thursdays, of course, were her lessons with Jonah, so she had to be up for them, but Wednesday was quite often a nothing, a big, tired, empty zero. Elaine would get herself a stack of magazines, lock the doors, turn off the lights, and go back to bed.

She'd done that today. Then, at three-thirty she'd awakened, done a few exercises, showered, slipped into the clothes she'd been wearing when she left the baby off at nine o'clock in the morning, done her hair, gone through her makeup routine, and hurried to her car.

She supposed she was depressed. Maybe about the fashion show? It had been a glamorous affair, put on by the more expensive down-town shops, by invitation only. The rumor was that there was even a modeling agent from New York City there. Helene worked tire-lessly with the stores to put on a production the likes of which had never been seen in Portland before. There were ramps, seating arrange-ments, floral decorations, refreshments.

Elaine had auditioned for the announcer's job.

It had been hard for her. Every time she stood in front of a group of people she felt the same way, that somewhere there were eyes watching her, to make sure that what she did was good, which meant perfect; that she looked nice, which meant, of course, flawless; that when she spoke, her elocution would be clear, which meant that it would carry the weight of Moses, coming down from the mountain.

It was a terrible burden to carry, but Elaine hardly realized it. The weight of somebody else's expectations, someone else's summary glances — whose? Elaine couldn't have said. She simply knew she must obey, she must measure up.

The audition had been on a Tuesday. Several women had been at the Eastland to try out, walking across wires for the lighting and microphones, standing in a shadowy place with Helene and some other listeners maybe fifty feet away. No chairs, no podium to stand behind, just you, just the papers you were reading from. Who was watching her, who, testing every aspect of her appearance?

Elaine began to read well enough, but in the middle she'd had some trouble: her voice had fogged, her tongue had slurred. She'd had to ask for a glass of water — the kiss of death. She'd been al-lowed to finish the reading, but her lips had felt like two pieces of putty, making strange shapes through which sounds somehow came.

"We'll be in touch, dear," Helene had said when Elaine finished. There was pity in the older woman's eyes. Helene was a friend of Elaine's mother's and, like her, had hoped for great things from Elaine.

In the end she was hired only for a bit modeling part. She'd ap-peared three hours before the show, dressed, put on makeup in a tiny cubicle marked off by hung sheets. She'd stood in line behind the scenes for an hour, then walked briefly down the ramp, postured, smiled for one hardly endurable moment in the bright lights. Ten minutes later, she was out on the street again, exhausted.

Harder and harder! Her whole life was spent this way: hours in the wings and mute moments of agony in the light.

But after time in bed and time to dress in peace Elaine felt better, ready to go to war again. A quick ride in her little red car woke her up entirely. By the time she stepped up to Judy's house and stood in the doorway, she looked as she knew she should look, all blue eyes and shining blond curls.

"Hello, you folks!" she cried gaily, looking fresh and rested.

How does she do it? Judy wondered. After a whole day of work.

"Hello, Elana," Elaine cooed to the baby she hadn't yet taken out of Judy's arms. "Here's Mommy, darling, come to Mommy. How's she been, Judy?"

Judy made a little face. "Kind of fussy, Elaine." She handed the child over, trying not to feel the emptiness in her arms when Elana was gone. "I really think —"

"Has oo been fussying?" Elaine said to the baby. "But oo is such a dood baby, never dives oo Mommy twouble." She giggled a little, shaking the baby back and forth. Elana gave a kind of brainless smile and Elaine hugged her, too hard.

"See," she said to Judy, "such a good baby."

"Yeah," said Judy thickly. "I see. I'm not going to be able to take care of Elana for you anymore, Elaine."

"Oh?" Elaine felt the roar of the world, rising. All Judy saw was that Elaine had forgotten, suddenly, to look beautiful.

"I mean," Judy went on stubbornly, "she's very fussy and I don't think she's digesting properly. I think she needs medical attention, Elaine. Meanwhile, I seem to be neglecting little Russ."

On Elaine's face was the narrow-eyed predatory look Judy recognized from childhood, the look of Elaine thwarted. It didn't occur to Judy that Elaine was also desperate.

"You know, Judy," Elaine said smoothly, "all you have to do is give this baby a little attention."

For Judy, that did it.

"Attention! Elaine, you don't know the half of it! Why, I've spent more time with Elana in a day than I spend with little Russ in a week! Elaine, that baby has something wrong with her. I know you don't think much of Dr. Bailey, all right. But I'd take her somewhere else. I'd have her looked at, I mean it. She's not digesting. Her diapers—"

Below her words Judy still questioned herself. Was it that she couldn't cope with the baby? Or was she jealous of the mother? Still, she stuck to her guns.

Elaine's eyes began to snap. "Judy, are you lecturing me? About my own baby? Judy, dear, how would you know? When little Russ was a baby, all you could afford was Dr. Bailey. It went all around the family how the public health nurse had to give little Russ his shots because you were too proud to take money from your parents, even for your baby's sake."

"Well, at least he's healthy," Judy said. "He's not always whimpering and fussing, Elaine, he never did."

Elaine's world was roaring. She fought back. "Okay, so you were lucky he has a strong constitution. Lucky, because some kids couldn't survive in the kind of home you brought him to — drafty, dusty, with broken floors. You couldn't even afford the right foods. I know. It was all over the family! Sometimes, Judy, pride amounts to neglect."

This hit home. "You witch!" Judy whispered. "Just take your baby and get out of here!"

"If you will give me Elana's bottles and the rest of her things, I will! We won't be back, Judy!"

"That was the general idea!" Judy cried. Feeling a loss that she couldn't possibly admit under the circumstances, she went past her cousin into the kitchen, where she packed formula, bottles, and all the other paraphernalia, helter-skelter, into a bag.

"There you go." She caught sight of the baby's innocent head as little Elana fussed against Elaine's shoulder. "Elaine, please, take her to the doctor."

Elaine ignored her. "Oh, by the way, Judy," she said, putting Elana's new little bunting on quickly, "Jonah Sears said to say hello to you. He and I have been working hard. I'm learning quite a lot. In fact, I may be doing solo work before we know it." She turned to leave; she'd always been good at exit lines.

Judy saw red. "You tell your mother not to come paying your bills for you!" she yelled at Elaine's back. "Tell her she owes me for two weeks, and it's on the house!"

With a crash, she slammed the door shut.

She was still upset when Russ came home from work that night. She told him what had happened, everything, including the baby crying and how she'd slapped little Russ and the argument with Elaine. "What is it, Russ, what did I do wrong?" She burst into tears.

"You?" he said. "Come on now, honey, be fair. It's only a little bit you, isn't it?"

"I can't bear it, Russ! I can't!"

"What, that you couldn't stand Elaine's bad little baby?" All he could see was smooth brown hair. Judy's face was in her hands to hide her crying. He tried to take her in his arms, but she wasn't having any.

"Only fussy, that's all!" she fumed. "She needs a doctor, Russ, and Elaine won't —"

"Not your baby, Judy, damnit," he said gently. He smiled, trying to cheer her up.

She only shook her head. "That little head, lying against Elaine's shoulder ..."

Russ tried to reason. "Does Elaine care about you, Judy? Does she give a damn about little Russ, would you say?"

"No."

"No. Here she is, doing her best to keep you out of the singing, and she was using her baby to do it."

Slowly Judy raised her head and said, "See, we don't know that, Russ. We only think so. Maybe she wasn't using Elana at all. Maybe that's only part of the problem. Oh, Russ, the look of that baby's head! Aren't we meant to do more?"

"Hell, Judy." His eyes clouded. "I know how you feel. But what in the world can we do? Not one damn thing. I'm sorry." They stared at each other.

That night Judy was awakened by a baby's crying. The cry was so real that she got out of bed and went in to check little Russ, although she knew it was not him she heard.

CHAPTER TWELVE

A ND NOW," Eleanor Hebert said with a sigh the next day, "I haven't a peaceful minute to call my own."

She stared at her sister.

June Hebert was sympathetic, but she also bit the inside of her lip a little as her sister talked, and she tried hard not to look too knowing.

"Poor baby," she murmured. "Isn't she getting enough vitamins?"

"This baby," Eleanor announced, "has the best pediatrician you can get, and more vitamins than you can shake a stick at — vitamin drops, vitamin formula." Eleanor tried to shift the child from one damp shoulder to the other, cleaner one. Baby Elana began to howl. As one driven, Eleanor Hebert paced the floor.

"What does Elaine say?" June asked.

"Elaine says the doctor says there's nothing wrong, it's only colic."

"But how old is she?"

"Seven months last Saturday."

The sisters stared at each other. Between them, back when Judy and Elaine were babies, there had been quite a competition to see which baby would sleep through the night first, which baby would cut the first tooth, crawl, stand alone, walk. Both babies had had colic, and both colics had gone away when they were supposed to, when the baby books said: at the end of three months.

It had been, June remembered now, a matter of honor.

But she admitted to herself that it was just a tiny bit nice to have

Eleanor, the mother of the perfect Elaine, in this kind of predicament.

Over the years it had grated on June a little. While Judy seemed to be moving farther and farther away from her family, to the point of not accepting money even when she needed it, Elaine had stayed right under her mother's wing, done what was expected of her, and, of course, reaped all the benefits — the house, the car, all of it. June crossed her stockinged legs and glanced around Eleanor's kitchen.

Eleanor went in for long spaces of counter and small bouquets of perfectly arranged flowers, often so perfect you had to touch them to make sure they were real. Today, however, there were diapers and bottles and receiving blankets lying about, and the only bouquet in sight had to June's eyes a wilted look.

"Well, dear," she said, offering what comfort she could, "don't worry about a thing. I'm free, and I'll go down to the town hall today, and we'll get some things done. Don't worry, we'll handle as much as we can without you."

"A grandstand," Eleanor murmured helplessly. "Be sure to tell them I said we'll need one if we have the state senators and all, and the parade. Tell them I said to —"

Baby Elana began to howl. One wing of Eleanor's hair drooped.

Once more June bit her lip. "Don't worry, dear," she said. "You just relax and take care of that poor baby. I'll see to everything else. Good-bye, little Elana. I hope you feel better soon."

Off June Hebert went. At this moment, at least, she was able to banish the thought that it was a rare occasion when Judy left little Russ with his maternal grandparents.

It was perfectly simple, June Hebert thought. All that ailed baby Elana was that niece Elaine thought life was one long beauty contest with a great big prize at the end.

For two weeks Eleanor Hebert was trapped into taking care of Elana. It was frustrating. Nothing else got done. Whenever she tried to pin down Elaine about finding someone else for the child, she flitted out. Elaine was working hard, she kept odd hours; Eleanor found herself baby-sitting steadily, some days from morning until night.

She felt she hadn't been this uncomfortable since Elaine was born twenty-five years before. Then she'd managed to hire a nanny for Elaine, a nice woman who'd kept the child in ruffles until she was school age. It had been a convenient arrangement, leaving Eleanor free for church work and politics. Of course, they'd had the money. Arthur, as the oldest of the Hebert family, had inherited first interest in the many Hebert holdings. David, a younger son, hadn't had quite the same prospects. Eleanor suspected that that was when the race between her and June had begun in earnest: when June realized suddenly that she wouldn't have everything Eleanor had. Or was that it? It was impossible, after all these years, to understand. She and June did almost everything together, yet between them there was a rift like a razor cut, barely perceptible at first, but deep.

Eleanor carried the baby into the living room and laid her on her side in the car bed. When Elana set up a squall, Eleanor reached in and more abruptly than necessary switched the baby onto her stomach.

"Now, you shush, you," said Eleanor. "You just shut up a minute and let me think!" It was the tone that counted. Babies couldn't really understand what you were saying.

Elana didn't shush. Her face grew bright red with effort and she drew her little legs up and wailed. Eleanor picked her up and, like a trapped animal, began to walk around the room, pausing occasionally to stare out a window. All her windows, she realized suddenly, were barred with grids: six panes over six, a Colonial house with an Early American flavor. She was, quaintly, caged.

She stared through the bars. Where had the summer gone? Where was fall?

She realized she'd had no real experience of either. Too busy. She stared out at the skeletal trees, the gray-yellow landscape of November. If she could only find time to understand something simple, like what today's weather was really like.

Today, as every day of the last two weeks, she spent her time walking with Elana, passing from one window to the next, trying to think how she could get out of her cage, whom they could hire, how they would do it, to take care of this baby, so Eleanor could get her work done.

She paced, frustrated, wondering.

By rehearsal time that night Eleanor was exhausted. She couldn't remember when she'd felt more relief than at the moment she handed

Elana over to Vinnie Dow at the church nursery. This had been arranged in advance with Elaine. Eleanor's duty was over for the day.

"Here," she said to Vinnie. "Do what you can with her, she's fussed all day."

At that moment Elana, too, was tired. Her transparent eyelids fluttered over her eyes; her face was relaxed, her cheeks flushed, her mouth open. Small and perfect she slept, the picture of innocence.

"Fussed out," said Eleanor abruptly. She tried to smile. "I've had a day, couple of weeks! Thank you, Vinnie." She walked away rapidly, before Elana could awaken and cry again.

"This, as you all know, is the last rehearsal before our second competition," Jonah was saying as Eleanor took her seat. "Perhaps we should get the wearing apparel issue out of the way first. I know it's been brewing behind the scenes. In general, I must tell you I am opposed to any kind of costume-making. I think it's expensive and time-consuming, and it diverts energy, divides our interest, and is, maybe, even a bit presumptuous under the circumstances. I fear that costumes may only make us look as if we're trying too hard. Perhaps we should wait until we're sure of a television performance before we do any more about this issue." Expecting opposition, he faced them calmly, but there was some applause.

Tired to her bones, still Eleanor couldn't let this go without a fight. Costumes were only one of the issues she'd had to table in the previous two weeks, but something had to be done. There were people counting on her, the whole town was counting on her. She was on her feet in a moment. "Jonah, may I?"

"Of course."

"Jonah, the Women's Association will fund and make the costumes," she said. Tiredly she remembered she hadn't put this before the Women's Association yet, but of course they would follow her lead.

Then she became aware of a restlessness in the group: someone whispered, someone snickered. She was so tired. Had she gone too far? Was she losing her grip? Did they care more about Jonah, whom she had hired, than about her?

Raised to be politically sensitive by August Packard himself, Eleanor looked around at the faces of the chorus. They seemed polite but distant. She saw in the back of the room a movement — the Reverend Mr. Howarth, peeking into the nursery.

That baby, Eleanor thought suddenly. Is she all right?

Eleanor knew with her skin that the people of the chorus weren't with her, although she was too tired and too confused to know why. She felt for August Packard's wisdom: if you can't win, defer.

"Just a suggestion," she said. "Perhaps we should wait and see, at this point, if we win the next competition. But then, surely, we should give this issue some real consideration." She sat down. For once she was grateful to sit down.

Three rows back in the soprano section, Judy Russell sighed with relief. She thought, Now, let's sing.

Jonah nodded at them. "Thank you, Eleanor. We will discuss this again, I'm sure. Now, ladies and gentlemen, if we could begin, please. Everyone stand."

They stood.

"Good. Let's warm up a little. Basses, this note." He hummed, glancing at Maddy, who found the note. The basses picked it up, a low hum. He listened, nodded.

"Altos, tenors, sopranos." He gave them each a note. "That's good. Hum, lips closed. Watch my hands now, be ready. Altos, change; sopranos, all up a half step."

At a twist of his fingers the chord moved up the scale, modulating.

"Oh, oh, soft!" he cried at them in a whisper. "Softly! That's it. Now, sing *ah*."

The humming chord blossomed. "Good! Now *oh*." Harmonically the tone changed.

"Good," he said softly, pleased. "Watch. Watch. Now, everybody up, a half step more." A twist of those fingers; again. Again.

The chord climbed, major, minor, major. Accurate? Yes. Every eye was on him to make sure he would be, still, pleased with them.

He nodded. "Watch. Watch. Up altos, basses, now." The voices stepped up, still in harmony. "Breathe when you have to — no one should know," Jonah said in that same whisper. The whisper one used with children around a lighted candle, Judy thought, so as not to blow it out.

"Now, Judy," said Jonah, "pick an upper note, obligato, please."

Maddy found her a high note and Judy took it. The choral voices rose up another step and Judy placed her voice perfectly, softly, above them. Now the chord hung in the air, a lovely thing, with her note at the top. Dew on a petal, she thought, holding the sound without a tremor. One tiny drop.

Jonah's hands cut them off suddenly: it was silent. His hands flourished again, and as one voice, all five parts sang. His hands spread, lifted, lifting the sound out of them, louder, louder, with Judy's voice always like a sparkle at the top of a wave.

They were cut off, they sang, they stopped, all together, on signal. Then they were hushed, all eyes on him to see what he would do next.

He watched them, felt them waiting for a sign. In fact, their expectation was so palpable that at last he broke down and clapped for them, and everybody began to laugh.

"Waiting for me!" he cried, pleased, even carried away. "That's good. That's excellent. That's the kind of response I need for every phrase of this music. Now let's try it. Turn to page fifteen of the Maser. You see at once Judy's obligato. This is not solo work, her solo comes earlier. What an obligato means is that your voice, Judy, must do just what it did a minute ago. It must be a final wonderful touch with an obligation to the other parts. It means that the chorus, too, must hold their own, and not feature Judy's part as a solo. Nor — and this is even more important — nor must the chorus compete with Judy, to drown her out. It's a delicate middle stance we want, and if we can get to it, I promise you, we'll know, and we'll never want anything else after that. Voicing. That's what we're trying to do here — so important, so subtle." His eyes glowed, his cheeks were flushed with hope. His excitement was infectious. "Now, let's start at measure thirty-six."

Judy stood comfortably, holding her music up at the required angle, although she hardly needed it. She understood what Jonah meant. The last few weeks without Elana she had had a chance to practice, to analyze.

Jonah set tempo, his arms moving with flashing specificity. Maddy came in: *the* beat, *the* note.

This is a wonderful piece, Judy thought suddenly.

"O beautiful," the chorus sang in well-balanced harmony, first the women, then the men. "O beautiful," they sang, each part beginning in its turn a run of notes, then coming at last all together, a chord. It was the first time in all their practicing that the running parts balanced with the holding parts. Judy could hear the harmony, almost see it change from note to note, in a wave of colors, at the motion of Jonah's hands. Now it was her turn with the obligato — two, three, four — at the precise moment, the precise sound.

But just at the instant of beginning she caught sight of Elaine.

Immediately Judy shifted her eyes to Jonah's hands and began to sing, off stride, however, floating in the sound that issued from her throat, then climbing on top of it in a way she had not intended.

Not that it was bad. It was too good, a solo beneath which the chorus fought, suddenly, for footing.

Jonah caught on immediately, and not accustomed, in his courteous way, to interrupt a soloist, he tried to signal her with his hands.

Judy saw his widened flourish on her behalf, but once started, it was too hard to change in midstream. This is mine, she was thinking. Something that is mine.

She knew it was not good. She heard the piano speaking to her, felt Maddy speaking with the set of her body, the attitude of her head, the care with which she played reminders of the notes softly, as they should be played. "Judy, share this with us," Maddy was telling her.

Widely, so as not to embarrass her by stopping everybody cold, Jonah moved his hands in Judy's range of sight. Judy couldn't help herself. She thought, I can look right through him and not see him at all.

She sang, unforgettably, then ended. They all ended. Not together but raggedly, a bunch of individual voices again.

Judy knew: her voice had soared with power while below her thirty other voices had embarked on thirty suicide missions. "Judy," they'd sung — now she knew this, too — "come back, help us." And what had she sung? "Can't you see, I can't help you now, I can't help myself. Who will help me?"

There was some applause for Judy by singers with humorous eyes. She smiled, but she hated it. Close to tears, she stared at Jonah.

"Sorry, I guess that's just what you were trying to avoid." She gulped, unable to look about her. Somewhere in the group someone laughed shortly. There was a hardness about the sound, like sympathy.

"Yes," said Jonah, as sunk as any of them. He pulled himself together. "Look, we almost had it," he said. "Did you hear that first part? It was exquisite, the best ever. Let's try. Start at the beginning."

Once more, as in the weeks of other rehearsals on this piece, with courtesy and dedication he pressed them into action, beginning once again with work on the basic chords, then adding Judy's voice to them. At last he nodded, satisfied.

"Now, Judy, let's give the Maser another try."

This time it was better, almost right, maybe as good as they'd ever get it. Jonah continued to work. To humor him the singers cooperated, but it never did achieve just the right balance. Finally he let them go: "That's all for tonight. But I want to tell you, it takes a special kind of soloist, one with a lot of heart, to do this work properly, as Judy is trying to do it, and a special kind of chorus to keep slogging away at it. You're going to be surprised at how beautiful it is."

Judy felt very low, and this graciousness touched her, as it did everyone. As people rose to go, many came to her and told her not to worry, they'd all get it right. She nodded gratefully and tried to smile, hanging on to Russ's arm.

So much fuss, Eleanor Hebert was thinking tiredly. The girl is obviously a showoff, out to outsing everybody else. She shouldn't have had the solo to start with.

Eleanor was a little upset, perhaps, over her own problems with costumes. She slipped out of the church, leaving the baby for Elaine to pick up.

During quiet moments, when the chorus had not been singing, Eleanor had listened tonight, thinking that Vinnie Dow must have a magic touch to keep baby Elana so quiet.

She and Arthur got into their car and pulled out of the church driveway. From habit they drove home hardly speaking to each other.

Vinnie, Eleanor thought. Of course. The very thing. Why, all she would have to do was call David in the morning, and he would call Jack Dow, and it could all be arranged.

Relief washed over her. "You know, there's a solution to every problem," she said to Arthur in the dark car, "if you can just get the peace and quiet to think about it."

Arthur only squinted at the road ahead, as if to say: "We both know how impossible that is."

Back at the church, the rest of the chorus was leaving. Jonah watched them go. Judy paused a moment on her way out to speak to him. "Jonah, I still don't know if I should be doing this at all. I don't feel as if I've got it. It's a matter of attention."

"Don't worry," said Jonah. "We'll do it, you'll see."

"I want it to be right. Tonight I got away from myself. Somehow I have to watch."

"Don't worry," Jonah said. "When the time comes you will, everybody will."

He didn't know just how, yet, but he would have to manage that, at least.

"I don't know what the hell happened, Dave. Wish I could tell you. They just pulled out. No contract, no nothing. How could I know?"

But he had known something was wrong as October gave way to November. "It hurts. The lumber? Put it under cover, I guess, sell it piecemeal. I take complete responsibility. Well, just so's you don't fire me. Not yet, anyways. That's good of you, Dave."

Orange and yellow, flashing behind his eyelids. "The computer? All set, are you? Tomorrow? Well, give me a couple of days. Sure, check up on the whole operation. Oh, all right. I don't blame you. Just bring it right on in.

"She does. She does. Well, you know how I feel about Eleanor. No, no trouble. Sure, Vinnie'll take her, Vinnie loves babies. Call Eleanor and tell her to sit tight, I'm on my way. Sure, no trouble. Okay, then. Bye."

Jack Dow hung up the phone and stared into space.

Words he'd read that morning came to him; he practiced from the Bible every day, to keep himself in good reading voice. "Take thyself no wife, nor beget sons and daughters, for in this evil time they shall die of diseases and no one shall mourn their passing, they shall be buried in the dung."

You couldn't take every word in the Bible that seriously, he thought. Nothing was as bad as it looked.

He stared down at his fingernails, all even, all clean. He looked at his desk, its cleared blotter, its neat stacks of papers. The Cummings baby?

For one more minute he would not move, he would remind himself: he was Jack Dow, the nice guy. He was good to everyone. People kept piling things on him, but he could take it. Another baby, that was all. He could handle another crying baby.

"Oh, Jack," somebody whispered now. "What you doin', friend? We been lookin' for you. Come back to work with us, old boy. You don't belong here." Only a whisper, as from dusty throats. There was no one in the room.

Jack Dow sighed, put his head in his hands. After a moment he began to mutter: " 'They shall die of diseases, and no one shall mourn their passing.' Oh Lord," he said, "I have no brothers and sisters. They're dead."

"Did you cry for them, Jack?" This was a new whisper; he hadn't heard it before. Still there was no one in the room.

"No!" The knuckles on his clenched hands whitened; he'd spoken aloud.

"You will cry," this new voice whispered. It was high and sweet.

"Those who do not serve me will not mourn," the new voice said. "Nor will they be comforted."

Whose voice was it? Jack closed his eyes.

The old familiar calling, the other voices, came to him again hoarsely: "Jack, buddy, we wait for you this long day."

He saw darkness. He saw fields, endless rows of green and the shuffling, bending forms of his brothers and sisters, leaning, forever leaning to the stems of plants, their dusty clothing, dirty shoes or bare feet. All the children who never made it in school, never had a chance, at the age of sixteen doomed.

"No," he mumbled. "I am the prophet. I don't cry for them. I only ring in the judgments, I read from the Book."

"You do not mourn?" The new, high voice.

"No. Hell, no." He laughed sharply, aloud. He listened. No one outside his office had heard. "Who are you?" he muttered.

Sweet as welcome tears the answer came: "I cry for you, Jack."

"No." Again, aloud. He looked: no one.

Now he saw a woman staring at him with horror on her face. She was nowhere in the room, she was right beside him. He closed his eyes; he knew this was imagination. "Ugly," he muttered.

"Jack?" A little question, little voice.

"No," he mumbled, "I don't cry for her."

"Then, is she alive?"

"No."

In a second he was on his feet and out of his office, shutting the door carefully upon that empty room.

Down the road from the sawmill: stacks of wood once yellow, now gray. The gray grass. Here at the corner, an odd trick of the eye; as one dreaming he saw only black and white, shades of gray. Turning the corner, he looked down the long slope of the road toward the church and the landscape stood before him in a strange negative: all that was light blackened, but shadows on fire, a nice white flame.

His car moved by itself. Down the hill, black houses to the right and left, tarred drives wildly white. Black tombstones, dead grass in gray, outlined by cold pencil marks of flame. A black church with a black steeple, the Heberts' farmhouse black, black barns. White tree trunks, dead flower beds white with fire. All the windows were aflame with white.

He pulled up at Eleanor Hebert's, closed his eyes, waited for the world to turn right side out, or his eyes to.

He thought nothing would be fine anymore.

He opened his eyes slowly. Here it was. A fine-looking white house, its wide flower beds mulched with peat. He mopped at his wet hairline. For a moment he stared down across fields. There was the Mettagawasett, a ribbon of shimmering white. There were the woods, blue and gray, waiting for snow. Snow would be black, the river black, all those tree trunks, branches, twigs, would glow at the edges with tiny hairs of flame, like a head on fire — no. He pulled himself together. In his stomach was a prefainting sickness, in his ears a buzz. He had never fainted in his life. He did not dare.

He got out of his car and walked to Eleanor Hebert's house, where he scraped his shoes on the mat inside the door, although the walk was dry and clean.

"Jack, I'm so glad you're here," Eleanor said. "I spoke to Elaine this morning, and she said it was all right with her if it was all right with Vinnie." Eleanor looked tired, eager.

"Well, Vinnie won't mind," he said.

"You don't know how much I appreciate this, Jack. You'll have to make two trips, one with the car bed and the playpen and all, one for the baby." Directing him, her hands shook; he saw it.

His own arms and legs felt like stovepipes. His body was hollow, his mind gone for the moment. He was a fetch-and-carry, now back up the walk. Once again he scraped his feet.

"This is so nice of you, Jack. I have so much to do today." Eleanor handed him a bundle of baby, almost lost in snowsuit and quilted bunting. It was lighter than he'd expected.

"Is there a baby in there?" he said.

Soft pink bunting in those dark hands. For a moment Eleanor felt guilty, but Elana was quiet.

"Oh, you'll hear her," said Eleanor. "You'll know. Wait 'til you put her in her car seat. She hates that." She laughed.

Jack saw the relief on Eleanor's face. He stared at her dark wool dress, her clean hands, her careful hair.

"Jack!" his mother screamed at him suddenly. "Come and get that baby!"

Eleanor Hebert was saying, "Tell Vinnie she's a saint to do this. We won't forget it, Jack."

The bundle was so light in his hands, but now it wiggled a little. He had rarely held his own babies. At first they were accidents, and then, darkly satisfying.

"Come on, baby," he said awkwardly. "Time to put you in the car seat."

Little Elana began to fuss as he set her into it and, as he struggled with all the belts and buckles, to cry aloud. It was an awful sound, a seesaw sound that teetered off into silence as the baby caught a breath. He finished all the belts, straightened, turned to wave at Eleanor Hebert — he'd known she was watching him through the storm door of the house — and then climbed into the car, into the noise of the crying itself.

"Jack," a sweet voice whispered, "do you mourn?"

There was no one in the car but him and the crying baby.

He stole glances at the red-faced, screaming infant as he drove her to his home.

He saw that when the baby screamed he bore down on the gas pedal a little, when the screaming stopped, he let up. It was not enough to be noticeable, only enough to make him feel sick. His hands gripped the wheel. He thought, over and over, When I was little my mother told me to watch the baby, it was all I was good for.

The car was chilled; it was a cold November morning. The sweat on his face dried cold. Past the good houses, around a corner, up into the woods. Nothing wrong with his eyes now. It was all distinct, each outline separate, colors clear. Or too clear. You looked into a world where light hurt the eyes and each object was too real.

The squashes had been picked, he saw this now. The little space where the plants had been was now a snakepit of cold-softened vines. Dying fingers. Had his brothers and sisters been there and he not seen them?

"Jack, friend, we're here in this cold room." It was them. *"Pour in the gas, light a match, turn it on! Come closer, Jack, we'll get warm."*

"Jack, the baby, for Christ's sake!" His mother.

"Jack, do you mourn?" Now, who was that?

Rutted, frozen dirt, brakes, fresh air. Into Vinnie's surprised arms he thrust the child, who screamed, then stilled, as Vinnie automatically held her up against one shoulder.

"But Jack, what —"

He could not answer. He pushed past his wife's little form and into his house. He stood looking around. Yes, this was his nice house, his nice world. There was only this clean place, where everyone had plenty and did what they were supposed to do, and everything was fine.

Without a word he turned, brought in the car bed and the other equipment. "I told the Heberts you'd take care of Elana," he said abruptly.

"For — for today?" She watched him. She always watched him. Sometimes he thought she woke up in the night when he was asleep and hypnotized him into thinking strange things. He would have to be sure to keep Vinnie right where he wanted her. Or she would do the same to him. Or maybe she was doing it?

"I don't know how long. Elaine is busy and Eleanor can't!"

His wife stared at him. Elana was quiet.

"It's the least we can do, Vinnie!"

"Take — take care of their baby?" She blinked, grasping the situation before she admitted it. She stared at him and he felt afraid of her, of what she might do next. He covered this with his power.

"Yes, damnit," he snapped. "I told them we would. Don't give me any trouble, Vinnie, or you know what I'll do."

He could see she wanted a threat, needed one, and so he gave it to her. Just a pleasant little threat, not out of place in this nice home. Now and then you had to open a trap door and let in a little shadow. He balled his fist. The baby muttered against his wife's neck.

"Mother and child," he said sarcastically. He knew what she waited for.

"Open your blouse." He lifted the fist back, as if for a blow. "Vinnie, open it!"

"No. Oh, no, Jack, I couldn't." Wide-eyed, pale-faced, she blinked at him, but it was all an act. Her fingers fumbled at the buttons, she opened them.

For a second he waited, testing her subjugation. Something in her still fought, still begged.He had to answer that. He put his clean hand inside her clothing, caught something soft, scooped something hard into his palm, squeezed.

It was not enough, What did she want?

"Let the baby suck here," he ordered. "Let me see that."

"Oh, no, Jack, I couldn't." He saw in her eyes that she would.

Jack reached a hand between his wife's legs, cupped a furrow, squeezed. "Let the baby suck," he told her gently after a moment. The blouse fell, and the underwear beneath it.

Elana's mouth rubbed along the unfamiliar breast, fussing. Her little lips opened, took in the nipple whole; too much of it pressed too hard between her lips; she spat it out, mouthed it like a new pacifier, began to chew and suck.

Vinnie Dow's eyes closed. She stood straddle-legged against Jack's hand. When at last he took the hand away, he could feel her missing the point of his fingers.

She opened her eyes and stared at him, shifting the baby from one stiff nipple to the other. Jack watched the moisture on the one nipple disappear. His wife's pelvis jutted toward him.

He was throbbing, he knew what she wanted. But this once he would not let her win.

"Now, Vinnie," he said gently, "you just take good care of that baby. You better. You wouldn't want your relatives to see you now."

Deliberately eyeing away from her bosom, the baby sucking, he went to the door, slammed it, climbed into his car. There, he thought. I've won. For now.

Behind him Vinnie Dow's parts swallowed air. They both knew this.

The upper winding voice moved in spirals, urging at the bass. To-gether the two voices modulated, up and up. Maddy struggled with the music, trying to control it. She even wrote what she didn't hear, but no, that was no good. She would put the notebook down and go away, but never too far away. Now there were fifty measures ap-proaching the edge.

Jonah said, "Maddy, in the spring you'll have some auditions, and next year you'll be in a music program, where you belong."

"The — the money?" The only objection she could give voice to.

He waved that aside. "We'll find the money. The point is, to find the right school." He was looking. He brought college and music school catalogues to Aunt Bea's, gave them to Maddy. "Read that. Read this."

"You could study with Bruckner," he would say. "Harmony, yes. Solfège, piano. You could compose with him, perhaps . . . no. Well, let me take a look." A small collection of catalogues. He made her take them home, but she hid them in the maple cabinet behind all the music. Her father never opened the cabinet. Her mother knew the catalogues were there, but so far she hadn't mentioned them.

It was all improbable to Maddy. How could she leave? Wherever she went, there would be the others, left behind; she felt this every time she went to the Cottage. Still, she didn't tell Jonah or the aunts how or why she suffered. She could not, it was too dangerous. Maybe after she'd talked to her mother more.

Meanwhile, it was enough to go to the Cottage. The day of the second competition was also, blessedly, a Thursday, so she could get off the school bus there, practice, have an early supper, and then drive to Portland City Hall Auditorium with Jonah and Aunt Bea and Aunt Ann. Maddy would take her competition clothes to school with her, and the whole day would be charmed and safe: a day at school, an afternoon at the Cottage, and an evening with the chorus. All of that, with no one to be frightened of.

But that day, when she walked up the steps to the Cottage, a satchel of clothes in one hand, a bunch of music and books in a bag in the other, she was met at the door, not by Aunt Ann, but by old Aunt Bea, who ushered her in with a mischievous look.

"Maddy," she whispered, "don't go to the piano just yet. Come into the kitchen. You have to see this." Aunt Bea's face was a study of concealed merriment, her eyes twinkled. Mystified, Maddy put down her bags and followed the old lady to the kitchen. Usually even the approach to that room smelled good, but today there were chemicals in the air.

Aunt Bea opened the door and turned to Maddy, her fingers over her mouth to keep from laughing. Maddy looked in. Straight ahead sat Aunt Ann in a mountainous plastic apron that fell from her neck to her ankles. Her head was tipped backward over the kitchen sink, her hair all wound up in little pink and blue plastic curlers. She was yowling.

"It's down my neck! It's in my eyes! Oh, the nasty, stinking stuff!"

Beside her stood Mary Mower, a hairdresser in the town. "Now, Aunt Ann, don't fuss so," she was saying. Her feet were planted firmly apart and her sturdy form was not to be disputed with. She dried her hands on her hip-length flowered apron. "You wanted me to do this, remember? You asked me to."

"Left eye! Left eye!" Aunt Ann quivered all over, her hands groping along the sink for a towel.

"Why, I've got a towel right here, Aunt Ann." Mary Mower handed it to her. "I never saw such a fuss."

"It stinks to high heaven, Mary! I'm telling you. I never smelled such a stink in all my life." The huge plastic apron shook. Aunt Ann's eyes were squeezed shut.

"Oh, don't be so silly. A perm nowadays is nothing, nothing. Now, you hold still." Mary Mower looked up, saw Aunt Bea and Maddy, and winked. She turned on the sink's spray arrangement. "Here's the water, Aunt Ann, to rinse, and we're done."

"Too hot! Too cold! Oh, God." Aunt Ann jiggled in her chair and it groaned in a way that worried them all.

"Oh, what a lovely fuss," Aunt Bea cried. "I haven't had such a fuss in this house in years. Oh, isn't it fun." The frail old woman clapped her hands and pulled Maddy into the kitchen.

Aunt Ann heaved a huge sigh.

"Okay, okay, Aunt Ann, that's that." Mary Mower wrapped the

woman's head in a big white towel. "Now, go sit under the dryer for a while and stay out of trouble. Go on, I've had enough of you!" Her eyes were laughing. "Aunt Bea, I'm loaded for bear. You next?"

"Yes, please, Mary. Just a wash and a set, I think?"

Mary gauged Aunt Bea's silver hair at a glance and nodded. "I think. Hello, Maddy. I know you by sight, at least. How are you?" Mary had a flat, kind face. Her own hair was a disheveled gray, and now she ran a hand through it distractedly, snarling it up even more. She was the wife of a farmer, and did her hairdressing for friendship and a little pocket money.

"Fine," said Maddy.

"You gonna have your hair done, too?"

"Oh, no, I —"

"But why not?" Aunt Bea caught the idea at once, excitedly. "It would be lovely. Unless, Mary, it would take too long."

"Oh, wouldn't take long," said Mary. "With all her curl, all we'd have to do is cut it a little." She stared at Maddy, then nodded. "Be kinda fun," she said. " 'Specially after —" She nodded in Aunt Ann's direction.

"Oh, no," said Maddy. "That is, I don't think I could."

"Oh, please," said Aunt Bea. "Please, Maddy, my treat. Oh, it'll be fun, the three of us. When Jonah gets here, he'll see three glamour girls. Please, Maddy."

Maddy was tempted. She didn't care about the haircut so much, but to be allowed to sit in these chairs and to smile and talk and be at home with these women . . .

"I — I need to practice," she said.

Aunt Ann put up the dryer hood. "God's sake, Maddy, sit yourself down! Think how easy it'll be. Not like me. You got the curl already." She sniffed and patted her own bristling head.

"Time to practice later?" suggested Aunt Bea. "Her hair won't take that long, will it, Mary?"

Mary considered. She tapped one sneakered foot on the floor and fingered the piping on her apron. Then she shrugged. "Half-hour," she said. "Start to finish."

"Lucky." There was a low moan from Aunt Ann as she pulled the dryer cap back over her rollers.

"Sit down, Maddy, do, oh, please do." Aunt Bea begged again.

"Have a cupcake while you wait," Aunt Ann hollered over the noise of the dryer. "On the counter there."

Maddy made a conscious effort to lift herself away from suffering, far away into the middle of this golden time. She felt frivolous and delicate, and she wanted to be persuaded. Just once, she thought. This once. She sat down on a kitchen chair and helped herself to a cupcake.

"Well, good," hollered Aunt Ann.

Satisfied, Mary Mower turned to Aunt Bea and began to wash her hair, then set it on large rollers. "Going to look beautiful tonight, Aunt Bea," she remarked. "In my family we're all going to eat early, to get down there and watch."

"No singers among your children, Mary?" said Aunt Bea.

"Gosh, no. Tone deaf, the whole bunch of us." Mary's fingers flashed. Her lower lip stuck out a little as she concentrated. "But you know," she said after a moment, "somebody has to sit and listen. My kids are good at that. They've had to listen to me all these years. I don't think they mind, somehow." She grinned at Maddy, and Maddy knew that none of this woman's children had to protect themselves, or her. "Well, there, Aunt Bea. We'll get Miss Fuss out from under the dryer, and you can go right in."

"Damnit, Mary," Aunt Ann expostulated coming out, her head a forest of curlers. "I don't see that it was necessary to wrap each individual hair."

"With you it was," said Mary imperturbably, motioning Maddy to the kitchen sink. An apron was found, and Maddy relaxed in a chair while water coursed over her scalp. Mary began a gentle massaging scrub. "Aunt Ann, I never saw such straight, uncooperative hair as yours."

"Well, I know," said Aunt Ann, "but still . . ."

"You should have hair like this," said Mary. "Look." She brought Maddy up from the washing and toweled her hair. Maddy's thick curls lay damp and every which way all over her head.

"I can't stand it." Aunt Ann groaned. "Maddy, if you knew what the rest of the world goes through . . ."

Maddy blinked. It was pleasant to have someone wash your hair for you.

Mary wrapped a towel around Maddy's head and went back to

Aunt Ann, took out a curl, shook her head, wrapped it back up again.

"What're you doing?" Aunt Ann cried.

"Not quite dry. You sit there a couple more minutes."

"Oh, for God's sake." Wearily Aunt Ann subsided against a table. Then she winked at Maddy. "Always something to keep me humble."

"Don't you listen to her," said Mary. "Now let's part it here, don't you think, Maddy? This side?"

"I don't know," Maddy admitted. "It's always so curly, I never think to part it at all. I had it long most of my life, and then I always just tied it back. Now I just run a brush through it and let it fall where it wants."

"I could cry," muttered Aunt Ann.

"Lovely, lovely hair," said Mary, "with the proper cut. Will you let me try?"

"If you think it's worth it." Maddy shrugged.

"Now, I think it is." Mary set to work, combing, lining hair up along her comb, clipping, until it lay in a short, curly wet cap. "There," she said. "I think you're going to like this, Maddy. You sit tight. Air drying's the best, keep the dryer away from this, and in a little while we'll see if you need anything more."

Mary bustled a little, obviously in her element. "Three to a blow," she said. "Aunt Ann, you fussy? Let's get you back under the dryer for a little while and Aunt Bea out."

"Oh, hell, I'm going to be last." Aunt Ann lumbered mournfully back to the dryer, amid giggles from Maddy. She liked the giggles so much that she hammed it up, for Maddy's sake. "Wouldn't you know. Start on me first, finish me last. Let me help you out, Bea. All the tormentors of hell aren't done with me yet."

"That's not a nice way to talk at all." Mary Mower snickered. "Now, Aunt Bea, let's do you." The clips were taken out of Aunt Bea's hair. Snowy white, softly curling, it was brushed high off her forehead and into lovely waves on either side of her face. "Yes, Mary." She nodded at last, satisfied. "That's just how I like it."

"Thought you did," Mary said.

Suddenly Maddy was feeling quite giddy. She reached a hand up to touch her own curls. They were very short and now almost dry. She wondered what she would look like. Would she look like a real person? Could she?

"Almost ready." Mary smiled at her. "Just let me take care of this one. You have perfect hair, Maddy."

"I have perfect hair," Maddy repeated. Everyone laughed.

"Yes," said Aunt Bea, still looking in the mirror. "*Very* nice, Mary."

"Thank you, Aunt Bea. All right, now you," she said to Aunt Ann.

"You mean, I'm not last after all?"

"Why, I couldn't stand to listen to those groans another minute."

"Well, I've never been so uncomfortable in my life, Mary Mower," said Aunt Ann.

"Oh, squawk, squawk," said Mary. "Hold still, you." She attacked Aunt Ann's bristling rollers.

At the least touch Aunt Ann quivered. "Now, Mary, you know I have a delicate scalp."

"Mmm. Delicate horsehide," said Mary. By the time she had the rollers out everyone was laughing.

"An Afro," said Aunt Ann, reaching up to touch her head. "A cannibal hairdo! Just as I thought. Mary, I've never trusted those perms."

"Aunt Ann," said Mary, "please. Give it a chance."

"Look at that! Sticking right up into the air!" Mary began to comb, and Aunt Ann said, "Now, don't forget that back piece, Mary, I never saw anything so curly." And then, "Now, oh, my God, it's so short, I just don't know."

She spoke it all in a funny way and the kitchen was full of laughter. With the touch of an artist Mary Mower transformed Aunt Ann's hair, and it lay in a neat round halo of curls about her head.

"There now," Mary said. "Let's just make a wave across the forehead."

"Got to," said Aunt Ann. "Hide the worry wrinkles."

"Oh, for God's sake." At last Mary mopped her forehead with her apron. By now her own hair fairly stood on end. "There, Aunt Ann. You look good."

"Is this a cannibal hairdo?" Aunt Ann demanded. "Bea, the mirror, please, quick!"

Aunt Bea, who had been watching the whole thing delightedly, spoke up. "Why, yes, it is a cannibal hairdo, don't you think, Maddy?"

Maddy nodded, looking serious. "It just might be."

"What?" Aunt Ann bounced. "Mary, if you've done something weird . . ."

"There." Mary handed Aunt Ann the mirror, laughing. "Now see if that suits you."

Aunt Ann's face was a study. The frown between her eyes went first, then the lines at her mouth. Her round eyes began to shine like buttons, and suddenly she blushed a brilliant pink. "Why, I'm gorgeous," she whispered. "I really am. Mary, I didn't know you had it in you."

"You say that every time," said Mary, sighing. But she was pleased, too. "Now, Maddy."

"No," muttered Aunt Ann. Still bright pink, she was talking to the mirror. "I don't look half bad."

Mary began to run a comb through Maddy's hair. "Considering what I had to work with . . ."

"Don't insult the customers," said Aunt Ann.

"Well, you give me more trouble, Aunt Ann Packard, than any other two people I know."

"Oh, for heaven's sake." Aunt Ann heaved herself up from her chair. "You want a piece of pie, Mary? Cup of coffee?"

"You bet I do. Soon's I finish with this child here. Who is, I might add, being very nice and quiet. Now, Maddy, you hold the mirror."

Suddenly in focus, Maddy's own face, dark eyes, pale skin.

"Is that me?" She gawked. Everybody laughed.

They think I'm funny, she thought. They like me.

"Yep, short and curly," said Mary. "Now this is what you do: take your comb, see, curls on the forehead, like this, a few wisps at the sides." With magic movements, her hands created little curling tendrils at Maddy's ears and neck. Maddy stared. Usually she didn't look in the mirror much, what was the point? Now she was thinking: I might grow into something someday. I might be someone.

"Then you won't have to do another thing," said Mary. "Just, when you wash it, comb it like this, and this. When it's almost dry, then use your comb to make some wispy curls around the eyes, there. Now look at that."

In silence everybody looked.

Aunt Bea said, "Maddy, it's perfectly beautiful. You're just lovely."

Aunt Ann said, "Why, Maddy, look at you."

Mary said, "What do you think, Maddy?"

Maddy was still looking in the mirror. "I think I look good," she said wonderingly. "I think" — she looked up at Mary Mower — "you are a magician."

Mary was pleased. "Well, you just remember how I told you to comb it, you can't go wrong then."

"It brings out the lovely shape of your head, Maddy," said Aunt Bea gently. "Take the mirror and go into the hall and look at the back. It's really an excellent cut, Mary, just beautiful. Go on, Maddy, go and see."

When she left, the three women smiled at each other conspiratorially and didn't say a word.

Maddy couldn't see the smile.

"The things I go through," Maddy heard Aunt Ann mutter as she left. "But this time, Mary, it was worth it."

The back of my head? Is this me? Maddy stared through one mirror into another and saw the curve of head into neck, the neat curls clinging to that neck. She turned her face a little and saw that somehow Mary had managed to compensate for the thin nose with extra height at the top of her head and little curls at the sides of her face. She studied herself. Her head was well shaped. As good as anyone else's, maybe. She saw what she might be: as good as normal, as good as ordinary. It seemed very rich.

One more second and she was running into the kitchen.

"It's a wonderful haircut! Thank you very much. I should pay you for it. I haven't any money, but I want to."

"Oh, no, my treat," said Aunt Bea.

"On the house," said Aunt Ann.

"It's all paid for," said Mary. The three women looked at each other sheepishly.

Maddy didn't notice. "I could earn a little money. Or I have some in a savings account." She thought suddenly of the two hundred dollars Jonah had put away for her.

"No, Maddy," said Aunt Bea gently. "Let me pay for this, please. It's the least I can do. Why, you've paid us already, in the company you give us every day and the music. The music you're helping the chorus to give. Why, if we were to start counting up payments, we would end up owing you, I'm sure."

"But —"

"I mean it. Please, Maddy. Please?"

Who could resist Aunt Bea? Swallowing, Maddy nodded.

"Oh, good. Now you can go along to the piano, if you want. To-night's a big night."

"Well, I have to be on my way," said Mary, finishing her pie. "I got some folks at home to feed, not that I'm going to be able to eat, now. Oh, that's good pie, Aunt Ann. Good luck tonight, Maddy, we'll be rooting for you."

"Thank you! And thanks, I —"

"Now, don't say another word. Gosh, Aunt Ann, that pie was good."

"Another piece, Mary?"

"Well, you know, I don't mind if I do!"

"You old limb of Satan, you. Maddy, supper's in forty-five minutes."

"I'll come to the piano room," said Aunt Bea. "It'll be nice to listen and rest a little." She took Maddy's arm.

Why, I could be as good as anyone else, Maddy was thinking. She ushered Aunt Bea into the piano room, where she plumped the pillows to give her the most comfortable seat.

Then Maddy went to the piano. Why, she was thinking giddily, I could almost belong here, in this room. She touched the keys of the piano as if, even after all this time, she could hardly believe they existed. Aunt Bea, watching her, said, "You know, Aunt Ann polishes those keys every day, just for you. We're so glad to have you here, Maddy."

Maddy laughed gaily, shakily. Suddenly music whirled her away, a dance from somewhere, she didn't know where. Oh, yes, the music Jonah had given her, was that it? She had learned it, not knowing she was learning it, and, suddenly, it made sense to her to dance. Her hands touched the keys; she began to play. Around her head was a light feeling, almost a borrowed feeling. She played a sad-happy bumbling dance, somehow graceful. She felt it was she, learning to dance in this room, about the tables, the books, the stuffed chairs Aunt Ann had moved in when this room became such a social place. Faster and faster, not feeling anything but lightness, not seeing anything but shine, whirling in the music.

When the piece was over she sat still for a moment, happy. Aunt Bea was smiling.

And then Maddy heard it: that high piped note, like a cry.

What is it? she wondered. What should I do? Too late, it was all upon her: the pushing bass, the hollow soprano, those crowding, dark notes. "Maddy! Maddy!" the piped voice called. She found the note on the keys and played it, then suddenly lifted her hands and buried her face in them. How could I have forgotten? she thought.

"Maddy," said Aunt Bea, "what is it?"

Now Jonah was standing in the room. "Hello, Aunt Bea." He went to kiss the old lady's cheek.

"Jonah, we didn't hear you come in."

"Didn't want to interrupt the music. How are you, Maddy?" As she lifted her head to look at him, he gasped. "Good heavens. This is our Maddy, isn't it?"

The piped note called, but Maddy ignored it, trying to reply as if she were a real person in a real room, as indeed she might be. "It's my haircut," she said. "This afternoon, we all had them. It made me feel like —" Sometimes, still, she ran out of words. But not so often.

"Like celebrating," said Aunt Bea.

"Silly," said Maddy.

"Not at all," said Jonah. "I never heard that Kabalevsky played better."

"I didn't work today," said Maddy suddenly. "I'm sorry."

"Didn't work?" Jonah chuckled. "But what were you doing when I came in?"

"Having fun, I guess."

"Maddy," he said, "you are impossible."

"No, she's not," said Aunt Bea. "She's a good girl. And doesn't she look nice?"

"Terrific! You both do. And so do you, Aunt Ann."

She had come to the door. "So do I what?"

"Why, look nice. You all look beautiful."

"Then maybe it was worth the effort." Aunt Ann shook her head. "Maybe. Better come and eat. Biscuits about out."

"You'll join us?" Jonah offered Aunt Bea his arm.

"What? Eat?" said Aunt Ann. "After the reek of that permanent?"

"Oh, Ann." Aunt Bea was laughing.

Aunt Ann sighed hugely, delicately. "I couldn't touch a bite," she said. Then, "Well, maybe a bite."

CHAPTER THIRTEEN

So," SAID Jack Dow. "She's trying to escape."

It unhinged him. He saw his wife's expectant look. "Vinnie, she is your daughter. You must both be punished."

There were children sitting around the table, all but Maddy. In the sharp light from the overhead fixture their faces were white as fire. It was the night of the second competition of the Freedom chorus, he had to remember that. He looked into the living room and saw, again, the evidence.

A moment ago Vinnie Dow had not been making dinner. She had been playing the piano. A cabinet Jack had not thought about in years was open.

Had that girl thought to hide it away from him? New England Conservatory, Eastman, Boston University. She will leave us, escape, he thought. Leave these children with their faces on fire?

"No," he muttered. "But she will try.

"You! Vinnie! You put her up to this." He saw in his wife's eyes that this was true, and that she'd done it for him, only for him. He thought she liked the little war between husband and wife. A little, comfortably violent war, that was what Vinnie Dow liked. He remembered how he'd left her, with an empty jutting pelvis and a baby at a breast.

Did that girl think she would escape? She thought she could run away and leave them all to burn.

Jack saw his wife, the glint in her eye. Foolish woman, she couldn't see how serious this was? Either that or she did see, and she was laughing at him.

It was the night of the second competition of the Freedom chorus, he had to remember that.

"Get to the table!" he rapped out. His wife sidled past him, a familiar gesture with familiar overtones. She sat to eat.

"Bow your heads," he told them. He said grace.

He served the food. He smiled at his children. He had to be careful.

"Maddy," he said. "She doesn't give a good goddamn about the rest of you, does she?"

He appeared to consider his words. He looked at his children, one by one, to be sure they were listening. "Look at her, never at home, she never does what I tell her. Getting your mother into trouble. Why, that girl makes the rest of you suffer for all her shenanigans."

There was a silence. He could see them thinking. He smiled at them again; he knew just how hungry they were for smiles.

"Yes," he said regretfully, "if it weren't for damned old Maddy." This was an old refrain. He'd used it again and again in her absence, every rehearsal night for the last six weeks, at every meal Maddy had missed. "If it weren't for Maddy, we could be a happy family," he said now. "I'd like to be a happy family, wouldn't you?"

He smiled his infallible charming public smile. Hungry for smiles, his children smiled back. All except Allison, who now, with the strain, began to sob. "I hate Maddy!" the child cried. "I hate her! I hate her!"

"Oh, now, you mustn't hate your sister," said Jack Dow. "Oh, no. But she'll have to be punished. We'll all have to punish Maddy, won't we?"

He stared into the eyes of his little boys, and saw them begin, at once, to understand just where the real threat lay. Phillip nodded, then Stephen.

"Good," said Jack Dow.

They got into the car. It was the night of the Freedom chorus competition and they had to, before they punished Maddy.

There she was, up on the stage, far away from them.

She had a brand-new hairdo.

"Wait," said Jack Dow to his family. "We'll see if she'll make us all miserable." He looked at his sons. It was just as well if a man's sons were on his side. He stared at their faces all dark, and the hair on fire.

Jonah had begun his last chapter and pushed it aside several times on the day of the competition.

"Paean" it began. He meant to make an ironic comment of it, but when he tried, it didn't wash.

He wanted to have a rough draft done by Thanksgiving so he could take it to Audrey to read. She'd give him an honest opinion, anyway.

The last chapter should be about forty pages long, a summary and conclusion. What he needed was a unifying thread, a focus. An ironic treatment of "paean" would work, but it did not satisfy him.

At last he gave up on writing and went to a book he was skimming about the lives and works of famous conductors. He was worried about this second competition, about whether he had taught his chorus properly, or led them properly. It was really the last piece he puzzled over, the Maser. Sometimes they'd almost gotten it, those wonderful choral effects, when the sound washed and flowed from one part to another. But too often they didn't remember, and the piece became a thick, unremarkable chunk in which every well-meaning soul sang his darned head off, without knowing when to increase, when to decrease. It was a qualitative difference, what the judges would be looking for, what the music called for.

He guessed he was looking for a unifying thread for the chorus, too. What was he doing wrong? What would work?

Just before it was time to leave, he came across an anecdote about a conductor named Reinert. It was a wonderful story; Jonah read it several times.

He and the aunts and Maddy arrived early at the Portland City Hall Auditorium. Jonah loved this stage and auditorium. It had quite a history, having been built in the Victorian era. The place had recently been restored, the walls painted a dove color and white, with gold on the fine filigree at the top of the stage. The city owned one of the three municipal organs to be found anywhere in the nation. Only two of these organs now worked, Portland's and one other. The Kotzschmar organ, here in Portland, was a fine instrument now being restored; it contained more than six thousand pipes.

It had pleased Jonah and Audrey to become members of the group of patrons who were finding the money to restore this organ. Many of the pipes for the wonderful instrument had fallen into disuse and had collected inside layers of dust that changed the tone. The pipes were being cleaned and repaired at great expense, a really heroic job undertaken with donated money and volunteer help supporting the experts, who knew they worked on a public landmark as well as a truly great instrument.

The console was quite small and had been rolled out of sight. It contained four keyboards and three panels full of stops as well as foot pedals, and swells. One stop even created the sound of a snare drum. The organ was a serious instrument, and the sound it could produce was a mighty one, even an orchestral one.

As they entered the auditorium, Maddy gasped to see the organ pipes, which rose above the back of the stage thirty or more feet, to the ceiling. In the center was a bay of twelve thirty-foot pipes, flanked on either side by an enormous array of smaller ones.

"From thirty feet to one inch, that's the range," Jonah whispered. "It's astounding, really. Once the instrument is restored, there'll be only one other like it in the country."

"The music of the city," murmured Aunt Bea. "They used to have organ concerts, and the whole city came to hear. Do you think they ever will again?"

More people were gathering. Seats had been marked off for the Freedom chorus, and Jonah stood by them, beckoning. Soon they were filled. It made a lovely contrast: the gray and white walls, the bright red seats, and the white and black of the group's clothes.

The auditorium was filling; the balconies, too, were becoming crowded. Between choruses and spectators, there would be few seats to spare. As always, Jonah's insides crawled away from him a little: stage fright.

Tonight they would be last on the program, a good spot. When the hall could hold no more, a man walked onstage to introduce the judges and make some announcements, then the first chorus stood up and went backstage. In a few moments they filed out.

They were very good. In fact, each of the choruses had wonderful points in their favor. By the time the third group of singers had filed onto the stage, Jonah felt his insides trying to get up and leave him altogether. The last chorus, too, seemed especially fine, their attacks crisp, their consonants clipped, closed for them by a tiny motion from their director's hands. Jonah studied this man. He was short and plump with a long mane of white hair. He had the attention of his group, all right. It was either that they loved to look at him, Jonah thought, or that they didn't dare not to.

Judy Russell was sitting in back of him. "No solos," she whispered, nodding at the group on the stage. "No pain." Her smile was tremulous.

"It's going to be all right," Jonah said. "Just watch me."

"Watch me, watch me." He heard his whisper ripple through the group. Applause. At last it was their turn.

They lined up backstage, warmed up. Jonah gave Maddy the nod and out she went first and seated herself at the piano. From the wings, Jonah watched his group line up on the risers. He knew how nervous they were, their faces visibly pale under the lights. This music was difficult, and they hadn't once done it justice in rehearsal. Jonah thought as he walked out on the stage that music was like self-examination: each singer had to wrestle with his own private devil. There were two ways singers might jump in this kind of struggle: they could be scared enough to do it right, or so scared they ran away with it. Which would it be?

He took his place and adjusted his music rack — too short, as usual. He looked up and smiled at the group. Some of his singers managed to smile back, some seemed to be studying a diminishing point in space. He raised his hands so they would raise their music. They did, but not evenly.

Oh, God, Jonah thought. You better help me, now.

Reinert. Remember.

Jonah raised his arms, but not as high as usual. He turned to Maddy and set tempo, but not in a flashing way: begin! Maddy played her introduction, as ever hardly glancing at the music she already had by heart. He could feel her attention, at least. He depended on it now.

Chorus? His hands were up, the gestures the same as usual, but smaller in scale. The singers came in, mercifully, together. "Whom shall we send?" they sang. "And who will go for us?" From the anthem of dedication. "Here am I, Lord. Send me."

"Easy," Jonah told them with his hands. "Watch, watch." Reinert. Every time he restrained his gestures, he felt their concentration grow.

Perfect gestures, but very small: Jonah worked to make the quiver of a finger as eloquent as a whole hand flashing through the air. His hands raised themselves slightly, the chorus sang louder; hands down, they softened. He cupped his hands a little, they softened as they should, and sang with a hush, the proper hush. Fingers up, they were off.

Was that it, then?

The second piece. The chorus now looked half-awake; they realized something was different. They were watching, at least. Jonah worked to control every action, make it essential and telling on a radically reduced scale.

"I can't do any more," he was trying to tell them. "This is how it should go; you know it and I know it. Look, I leave it to you."

But they were watching him, he realized. They were remembering he existed, and on each page, what he had said about it.

Jonah's hands moved as if they rocked the world, gently, in the tiniest soft body.

Set tempo, he was thinking. Would Maddy begin? Of course she did, watching him and playing as always with precision and feeling. She had always watched him, down to his least expression.

Good, he thought. Now, you others.

He lifted his hands only a very little and cupped his fingers to remind them: "This should begin softly, like a prayer."

They understood. Softly, softly, they began to sing. They were listening to each other.

Jonah began not to be frightened. "We are all technicians now," he told them with the smallest motions. "It's up to you. All right, now build, build, tenors up, yes, sopranos, up. Good. Softly, now, softly."

He raised his hands a very little. "Watch, watch," he told them.

They did watch, they were all watching. They sang with a lovely swell of sound, a beautiful swell that rose from the beginnings of the piece and then diminished toward the end. "Now, off, off," his fingers cautioned them. Together, they were still. Maddy continued quiet chords to the end of the piece. Not a head moved among the singers, not an eye flickered. "Watch, Maddy," his hands said.

She did watch, to the final chord. Off!

Not a sound, not a sound.

Now the last piece, the Maser.

Jonah lifted his hands a little. "When you don't see me," he meant to tell them, "you are not remembering to watch."

Judy's eyes never moved from him. "Yes," she was saying. "I am watching you. I will watch, Jonah."

Elaine had stopped her on her way to line up with the chorus. "Good luck, dear," she'd murmured in a way that meant she wished Judy no luck. Judy had wanted to reach out and smack her then, as she had never been allowed to do when they were children. She wanted to shake her, maybe, or reason with her, or really talk.

"Make me watch, Jonah," Judy asked silently. "Make me forget."

Concentrating on the tiniest motions of those hands, she did forget. Voices surged up like an ocean, her own among them. Softly, Judy, she thought. Make it blend.

Tiny motions: "Hear the basses, hear the tenors, now the altos."

There was Maddy, unerring, concentrating, a lesson in concentration. I shall match Maddy in concentration, Judy thought. Maddy is teaching me. And then, God help me! It was Judy's turn, for the solo early in the piece.

Jonah's hands scarcely moved, but exactly to tempo. His nod at her was barely perceptible. Because she had to watch him closely, she began to sing without fuss, without strain. Watching him only, she allowed the sound to flow, relaxing with it. Then there was no more solo, but only music; she was alone with it, part of it, Jonah was with her — see those tiny motions? There was Maddy, speaking to her in the softest chords: "Here we are, stay with us."

This is simple, this is easy, Judy thought as she sang. My Lord, I forgot how easy it is to sing.

"O beautiful, O beautiful . . ."

Only music, singing your own part, as simple as laughing. Judy held the final note of the solo section, staring with joy at Jonah's hands and face as they moved. At the instant he signaled, she was still.

Maddy continued to the end of the interlude. "Here is the music," she played. "It needs you."

Again every eye was on Jonah, studying the least movements of his shoulders, arms, fingers, the cords of his neck and the motions of his eyes. Picking up cues almost as he thought them, the singers began. They were breathing together, singing together, his hands moving very little.

"Now basses, now altos, now tenors." Washing over each other in waves of sound they sang. They knew they were getting it right at last, they felt each other get it right.

He made the suggestion of a motion in Judy's direction: "In harmony. Now." There was her voice, hardly hers, but something above her or around her, like a star by a sunrise, a tiny pinpoint of light, very faint, hardly perceptible, a perfection of light on top of color. Judy saw clouds moving, passing into the air.

"Cloud singers, beautiful faces, souls in the clouds," Maddy played. "Singing into the light." She loved the singers in this chorus, every one of them. She hoped, wanted, everything for them, her beloved singers. The sound of them floated, touched at the top with Judy's delicate ringing voice, like a jewel, like the first blessing at morning, a morning star, simple and hopeful.

Jonah's hands scarcely moved; his face was severe with concentration.

"O beautiful!" they sang. "O beautiful!"

"Ah . . . ah . . ." sang Judy. "How beautiful!"

Jonah's face shone. "Will you hear each other?" he asked them. "Will you be able to stop together? Watch me, I shall make one tiny motion. Hold, hold, now — off."

The singers stopped on a single breath. Together.

There was applause, a lot of it. Jonah didn't turn around for a second. Wrung out, he only lifted his head back and stared at the lights. Then he was bowing, then Maddy stood to bow. To the chorus the applause was nothing beside what they carried inside them. In the wings they stared into each other's faces. "We didn't know we had it in us," they said. "We'll celebrate tonight."

"I think we might have done it this time," they said.

Then, an afterthought: "Do you think we won, Jonah?"

"I don't know," he said. "I was too busy listening."

There were cries of outraged appreciation before they mobbed him and Judy and Maddy. Here and there, surreptitiously, hankies were passed, noses blown. They took their seats in the beautiful auditorium. The results came quickly.

Once again, the Freedom chorus had won.

Blaine Howarth questioned Jonah afterward. "It was different," he said. "I can't quite put my finger on it."

"I'll tell you," said Jonah, "but nobody else. I was reading about a famous conductor named Reinert, very precise, an excellent musician but a bit of a dictator. One day his orchestra got tired of it and plotted that at the concert they were giving that evening, they wouldn't follow his direction at all. Just to teach him a lesson."

"Oh boy, disaster."

"You'd think so, but it wasn't. Within seconds during the performance Reinert realized something was up, but instead of waving his arms wildly, trying to get their attention, which was what they wanted him to do, he controlled his gestures to the point where the orchestra had to watch him or flounder, and for that reason they did watch. The performance was wonderfully successful, one of the best Reinert ever conducted."

"He was lucky?"

Jonah shrugged. "I guess. But it seemed to work for us, too."

"The tiniest evidence of a motion, that was what we were watching for, Jonah."

"I know."

The tiniest evidence, Jonah thought later, as he sat down at his typewriter.

"Paean." He typed it again, then tore it out.

The cold car, the house, the too-sharp light of the living room: the Dows came home from the competition.

"You children get to bed! Except you! You stay here!" None of the children glanced in her direction. In Maddy there was a deadened feeling: too much dread, numbing.

"Now, Jack, let's go to bed," Vinnie Dow pleaded. "We're tired."

This excited him all the more. "I'm tired! Tired of you both! Look at her!" His long arm reached out and his hand held the back of Maddy's head, held her neck in his grip. "Fancy new hairdo. You gave her money for this, Vinnie. Without my knowing."

Vinnie Dow shivered, a small obviously powerless form.

"No!" Maddy cried. "It was only Aunt Bea. They were having theirs done, so I did, but it's not important at all. Just a little thing.

"I should think you'd be glad," she cried, still under his hand. "We won the competition, and everybody is happy with me." It was a mistake to say so, she knew it immediately. She had learned to talk a little, it did her no good now.

Her neck was at the snapping point. "I know all about that!" he roared.

"Jack, please, leave her be." Vinnie Dow's voice was so soft.

Maddy's head twisted to one side at a mad angle. Her whole body bent to that twisting.

"Jack." Vinnie shivered, approached.

"Don't come another step, Vinnie."

Maddy caught a glimpse of her mother, standing in front of them. Small and pale, her face expressionless, Vinnie Dow stared at her husband. Maddy thought suddenly, Is something else going on here?

Like two hypnotists, her mother and father looked at each other. Suddenly her father let Maddy go in a way that made her skitter across the room, half falling.

"Get up the stairs, for now," he said, still staring at her mother. "But I'm not done with you yet, young lady."

Maddy scrambled for the door, but he caught her first. She spun, landed in the hall, crept to the stairs. There was the click of his key in the lock of the hall door.

"Vinnie!" she heard her father cry. "You get to bed!"

A shredding sound, as of clothing. Silence again.

Maddy stumbled up the stairs. Her music catalogues, her notebooks, sheet music, had been scattered all over the sofa in the living room — she realized it only now.

Hadn't her mother been able to hide them?

Dark. The juices in her mouth choked her. She moved up the stairs. Her side ached, her person ached. She paused outside the boys' room. Were they asleep? They couldn't be, not yet.

"Phillip? Stephen?" The open-mouthed whisper so that no one could hear but them. "Are you awake?"

There was no answer.

Were they angry at her? If so, it was more than she could bear.

"I'm sorry about tonight," she whispered. "It was my fault. Please don't be mad at me."

No sound. The silence was like a blow, like hate.

"Oh, please . . ."

"Maddy, just go to bed." In the doorway stood ten-year-old Allison, thin as a wisp, her nightgown ghostly white. "Why don't you just leave us all alone? Don't you see how you hurt our mother?" Her whisper was like a cry in the wind. "We're a family," she whispered. "Maddy, why don't you just go away?"

"A family?" Maddy whispered. Didn't she have a family, then? Weren't they her family, too?

"He's hurting our mother right now because of you."

It was a hateful whisper. Maddy looked into the child's face: white skin, dark holes for eyes. "I'm sorry," she said. "I just need — I just wanted — someone to — please."

Allison melted away from her. "He'll punish you, Maddy." Her whisper floated back. "Then we'll all feel better."

The doorway was empty. The boys in their beds had not moved.

Maddy whispered, "Phillip? Stephen?"

No answer.

"I've taken care of you." This came on a sharp intake of breath. She wanted to reason with them, ask them to love her. They must hear her .

No answer.

Her fault.

She stumbled away, into Jessie's and her room, undressed, crawled into bed. She didn't dare to cry aloud, but tears fell. Tonight Jessie was far over on her own side of the bed. Maddy didn't dare speak to her.

"Maddy," Jessie whispered after a moment, "are you all right?"

"Oh, Jessie, do you hate me, too?"

"They'd like me to." The quiet girl sighed. "I mean, it sounds reasonable, Maddy, you must be to blame. It would be reasonable, maybe, if this were a reasonable world."

"I am to blame. He hurts you all because of me. Right now, he's hurting her."

"Maddy, stop it." Jessie's face rose up in the bed, a dim white stone, rising. "What I want to know is, why does our mother put up with it?"

"Put up — what do you mean? Why, Jessie, any fool can see —"

"Any fool is meant to see. It's all the children see, of course. You go 'off.' Maddy, she left that maple cabinet open tonight. Okay, so it was a mistake! But I've been watching a long time. I don't want to say this, but I think there's something in our mother that —"

"Jessie, how can you?" Incredulous, Maddy searched for an explanation. "Are you feeling all right? Are you sick, Jessie?"

"Okay, don't believe me. Maybe I'm wrong. But I think it's more complicated than just protecting us, Maddy."

"No," Maddy said. "No."

Downstairs the hall door was unlocked. Both girls heard it and were, instantly, quiet. There were heavy footsteps on the stairs.

That is it, Maddy thought wildly. That is just how the bass approaches.

"Maddy, get up." Jack banged open the door. The noise made both girls quiver. Light from the hall — he was the only one who dared to turn it on — flickered across her face. That is just it, she thought. That is the bass. The soprano? Whose voice was that? No, she thought again.

"Get out of bed!" he yelled. "Now, damnit!"

Before Maddy knew what was happening, she had been lifted bodily and thrown toward the stairs. She lay still, on the edge of the top riser.

"You!" she heard her father holler at Jessica. "Are you in this, too?"

Jessica said steadily, "I don't know what you're talking about, Dad. I don't like her any better than you do. She just shouldn't hurt the rest of us, that's all."

Jessie, too?

Maddy felt the stairs spin away from her. She felt she was falling, falling, and there was no one to catch her. There was the utter dark, and no one to help, to catch —

Caught by the head. "Maybe next time," her father said, wrenching her upright and speaking into her ear, "you'll take a little better care of your mother and brothers and sisters." He spoke loudly enough so that Maddy knew all the children would hear.

The stairs spun again. She thought, If I could learn to fly, I wouldn't be so afraid to fall. Endless space, no one there, nowhere to land.

She picked herself up off the hall floor at the foot of the stairs only to whirl again into the living room. She spun against the piano, grabbed hold. She realized she wasn't falling, she'd been thrown, twice, three times.

She held on to the piano. The room was brightly lit. Her mother sat hunched in a bathrobe in a chair opposite.

"I'm sorry," Maddy tried to say. "This is my fault." Her lips twitched; the sounds came out weirdly. Over her father's shoulder she could see her mother sitting and didn't it seem to Maddy, suddenly, that a real, loving mother would do more than just sit there?

"This must be my fault," she tried to say, to make sense. No one hit her, but the room spun away again.

"Well, she's just a little bit scared, Vinnie," Jack Dow said. "Look at her, hanging on there."

"Now, Jack," said Maddy's mother. "She didn't really want to —" The voice trailed off.

Maddy looked at her mother: pale white face, dark circles around the washed-out eyes, circles of suffering. A look from that face was enough to put your heart in chains forever.

Maddy thought, Did I do this? Could I have done this to you? How could she have, since she loved the contours of her mother's face better, even, than she loved her own?

Deeply Maddy was sorry. She caught sight of her father, his dark square head, the hair short and somehow still neatly combed back, the heavy jowled muscles on either side of his face, the white lines about his eyes, and then the eyes, all pupil, all black. A face on fire — the eyes were red coals.

"This is my fault," she wanted to tell him. "Punish me." Instead she cowered against the piano, unable to make a sound.

"Look at her." He laughed. Then, "You see these? Where did you get them?" He gestured. She saw that he had laid out the music catalogues, admission forms, everything from the maple cabinet. All in a stack on the sofa.

Maddy felt this must be what it was like to face death.

"Answer me!" he cried, but she couldn't answer.

"You think you're going to get out of here?" he cried. "Leave your mother, your brothers and sisters? Escape? Tell them secrets about me?" The question itself enraged him. "Pick them up! Pick them up, damnit!"

Maddy went to the sofa; the books were heavy. She looked at him. "Take them to the stove!"

She did as she was told, moving toward the kitchen wood stove. He was behind her, dragging Vinnie Dow by one bent wrist. "Vinnie, I want you to see this. Maddy is going to build a good fire."

Maddy stared at him. Vinnie groaned.

"Oh, it'll be easy," he said. "I had some gasoline in the garage." On the kitchen floor was a big gasoline can.

"All you need, Maddy, is a little touch of that."

Had he gone crazy?

Maddy couldn't move. She stood gaping while he took the papers, notebooks, music, out of her hands and stuffed them all into the stove. The gas can was heavy. He slopped out a cupful and splashed it on top of the papers. "All right," he said to Maddy. "Light it!"

"Jack, no." That faint voice. Why was her mother's voice always so soft? This was dangerous, didn't they know that?

"I — I can't," Maddy managed, staring at all the rumpled papers. Beethoven — his two-inch lettering damp. The *English Suites.*

"Light it!" he cried. "Vinnie, tell her to light it!"

There was a sound in Maddy's throat, of panting, strangulation. Her parents stared at each other.

"Maddy," Vinnie Dow whispered, her eyes on her husband, "better light the fire."

With shaking hands Maddy reached for the matchbox, scraped a match. She was afraid of the gasoline and lit a piece of paper that had not been soaked with it. Even so, the stove began to roar, the fire, to explode. Maddy clanged the dark cast-iron tops down into the openings. As she did, she saw handwritten music from one of her own notebooks begin to curl into flame. It was covered by dark. The stove hummed; no one seemed to hear it but her.

"Vinnie," Jack Dow said, "tell Maddy: tomorrow after school she will go to the Cottage and tell the old women she won't be going up there anymore. Tell her!"

Maddy couldn't see her mother's face. She stared at the hot black iron of the stove, at the frantic white flames she could see through the grate at the side.

"Maddy, do as your father says."

A hollow voice. Familiar; where had she heard that voice before? Numbed, Maddy could not answer.

"She doesn't hear you, Vinnie." She saw her father reach out and dig his fingers deep into the shoulder of her mother's robe.

"Maddy!" cried Vinnie Dow. "Do as your father says, do you hear?"

"I — yes!" Maddy said. "Yes."

Jack Dow laughed. "Tell your daughter, Vinnie, that tomorrow when she sees Mr. Jonah Sears, she will tell him she will only play for the chorus from now on. She's not interested in any more college talk. Tell her, Vinnie."

"Maddy, go to Jonah Sears tomorrow —"

"Mamma, I —"

"Will she do it, Vinnie?" Jack Dow screamed suddenly; his jowls purpled. "Will she?" His two hands shook his wife's shoulders, then crept to her neck.

"Maddy," gasped her mother.

"I'll do it," Maddy cried. "Just, please, let her go."

He did let her go. He turned to Maddy, laughing. The show of teeth broke open his face.

"You don't know the half of it," he told her. He picked up the gasoline can. "How'd you like a little bath, Maddy?"

Maddy didn't answer. She felt her ashes already rising, up the stovepipe, in the smoke.

"Get to bed," he shrieked. Little dribbles came from the spout of the can as he motioned. Little splashes. Maddy retreated, ran through the living room, up the stairs — was he behind her?

She heard the hall door banged shut, locked.

We're in danger, she thought. What if he hurts her, burns her? I have to get help. She knew there was no way out of the locked upstairs: the least little noise could hurt their mother, or one of the children.

"Jessie?" she whispered, once in the bedroom. There was no answer. Did Jessie hate her, too?

Shaking, Maddy sat on their bed. She sat for a long time, listening. Nothing. At last she lay her head against the pillow. When she did, she found Aunt Bea's notebook, carefully concealed in the case.

Jessie was beside her. "It was all I could save, Maddy. I'm sorry, I tried." Hands grasped Maddy's in the dark.

"Jessie, did you hear him?"

"I heard. Will the house burn?"

"I don't know."

"What are we going to do?"

"I don't know."

For a long time they were very still, listening for the crackling of fire. If the house burnt, they would be trapped on the second floor, no one nearby to help, no way to get to a phone, no way out.

Jessie said, "Maddy, about tomorrow. What are you going to do?"

"What he says, Jess. I have to! There's Mamma, there's you, the children . . ."

"Yes, I see." A whisper. A long, listening silence.

"Jessie?"

"Yes."

"What if there's never any way out?"

"Oh, we'll do it, Maddy. Somehow."

The house didn't burn. They waited. After a while they slept a little, restlessly, listening.

Maddy heard music and woke up again and again.

At first light, before she knew what she was doing, she was opening Aunt Bea's notebook. There it was, the driving bass, the accomplice soprano. How they climbed, how they reached; like an ocean breaker reaching for a pinnacle, high up, of intact land, they pushed upward, and there was that tiny piped sound, up high. When the water reached that point the land would be gone, there would be a swirling, an ocean storm, a shriek, and nothing. No more music. Music would be dead. Somehow, without knowing how or why, without — oh, certainly without wanting to! — she was the guilty one, she had made this music die, as surely as, last night, she had lit the match.

In Maddy's veins abruptly the music ran, this awful music, the thudding bass, the driving hollow soprano, that tiny piped note, calling, and she knew she couldn't hold back any longer, it had to be written in.

She found a stub of a pencil — it came to her hand before she wanted it — and wrote in a chord, no. But there it was, to be played again — no. It was no chord. It was chaos! It was a cry! She threw down her pencil and gripped the pages of the notebook and sobbed, spotting the notes with tears. Gasoline spots, she thought. Her shoulders shook. She heard the awful chord again: bass, soprano, tiny cry, together. She forced herself to write it one last time. Now she was weeping, from the deep strings of her soul, all that hurt, all that she had done, and the dead tiny voice. The music was dead. She wept, rocking back and forth.

Jessie found her there, the notebook wet and rumpled in her hands.

"It's all right," Maddy whispered.

There was a gray place, she saw, that not even Jessie could come to, a place where tears made no difference. You could cry forever and no answer would come.

"Maddy?" Jessie's usually white, still face turned slowly pink, and her eyes filled. "Please," she said. "Please, Maddy, we mustn't cry. Please."

From the gray plain Maddy heard her. "It's all right," she said. "Just finished, that's all."

Their father was awake.

"Maddy." He screamed up the stairs: "Maddy!"

She rose and went and found him in the living room, pacing.

"No, the children will stay home, Vinnie. Where I can see them. All except this one, who has some unfinished business. Maddy, you will go to the Cottage on the way home from school, and tell them, all three of them. You will come home. Ordinary day, everything fine, right? Anything else, and your mother will begin to cry, Maddy, I promise you. You wouldn't want that to happen, would you? You wouldn't want your mother to cry?"

"No! No, I —"

"Vinnie, your daughter wouldn't want you to do that."

"No, Jack," said Vinnie Dow through pale lips. She looked nowhere.

Maddy stared at her mother's face. All she allowed herself to think was: Look what he's done to her. How could he do this? How could I?

"Get dressed, Maddy. Get dressed, damn you."

She did as she was told.

Jack Dow was lit with energy. "Hello, Dave? Yeah, Jack." He talked into the phone. "I'm not coming in today, Dave. Oh, a little virus, maybe. Hot, yeah. Been so long since I stayed home from work, I don't know how to act. Take the computer guy in? Tomorrow, I hope. Oh, sure, we'll fix it all up. You know me."

He hung up.

One of the children tried the hall door. "Keep it quiet!" he screamed. "Get back up those stairs! Can't you tell I'm sick?" This appeared to be funny. His lips pulled back over his teeth in a snicker.

"Jack, let me give them something to eat." A neat, abject little request from Vinnie Dow, it waved itself, like a flag. Maddy wondered: Didn't her mother sense that?

"No," he cried.

Midcry, there was a knock on the front door. Vinnie Dow, still in her bathrobe, scuttled into the bedroom. A peculiar, free little action. Maddy was startled.

At the door was Elaine Cummings, and on one arm, her baby.

"Well, Elaine," Jack Dow said in his other, public voice. "You are an early bird."

Elaine stepped into the house and blushed prettily. Her hair curled in soft waves all around cheeks flushed scarlet and blue eyes brightened by the cold. "Why, Jack, I didn't think you'd still be home. Sorry I can't stop, an early call, tell Vinnie. Tell her Elana hasn't had her breakfast yet, but I've put everything she'll need in the bag. Hello, Maddy, how are you?"

"Fine." Deliberately, Maddy looked away.

Elaine hesitated for a fraction of a second. The house was silent.

"Vinnie is around?" she said, the tiniest star of doubt in the center of each blue eye.

"Oh, yes. She's just dressing." Jack Dow grinned his public grin. "I'll be sure to give her all the messages, Elaine. Don't you worry about a thing."

Maddy saw Elaine's eyes go blank. "All right, then." She smiled. "Here, Elana, here's Jack Dow." Placing the baby in Jack's arms, she turned to leave.

At once Elana squirmed and began to cry, but Maddy didn't dare to rescue her.

"Oh, Lord," said Elaine, laughing. "Well, tell Vinnie I said good luck."

"I'll tell her," said Jack. He smiled as the baby wailed. "I'll be sure to, Elaine, don't you worry. Vinnie can handle anything."

At last Elaine went running out the door, through light and frost to her car. She was gone.

"Vinnie!" Jack Dow's voice rose above Elana's wail, his own cry going higher and higher as Elaine drove away. "Vinnie! Come and get this goddamn baby!"

Now the front door step, and there was Aunt Ann, and Maddy was in.

"Well, slippery! I smell snow," Aunt Ann said. "You come right in, young one, tea water's on."

Pretty rooms, the familiar old-fashioned spice smells, the dark shining hall. Aunt Ann stood there laughing, happy to see her, her plump arms out for a hug. Aunt Ann, one button of her bodice hanging by a thread and a big hole in her left carpet slipper, had never looked better to Maddy than now, when she had to say good-bye. She did not hug Aunt Ann or say a word — it would have made her cry. She had spent the day wrapping herself in layers of toughness for these few moments.

A look of astonishment came onto Aunt Ann's face. Her arms dropped.

"What's the matter, Maddy?" she said. "Don't you feel so good?"

I don't feel anything, Maddy thought. "Oh, yes," she said aloud, surprised at her own self-sufficient voice. "I'm fine."

"You are? Well, Aunt Bea's in the piano room. Give me your things." Maddy did not. Aunt Ann blinked and stared.

"No," said Maddy politely. "No, thank you. Today I can't stay."

"You can't?"

She couldn't explain. She left Aunt Ann standing there and made for the piano room, where Aunt Bea sat in her usual place. "Maddy, Maddy, hello! Try the piano. The tuner was just here, we talked about the celestial choir, I want to know what you think," she called, laughing, before Maddy was even in the door, and then blew her a kiss from the sofa. Jonah, standing by the piano, nodded. "Maddy, haven't you got your coat off yet?"

The piano. Maddy's skin suddenly felt very thick, the sockets of her eyes like the boles of a telescope. She moved her husk of a body toward the beautiful instrument, she kept her coat on, she didn't answer Jonah.

Share? She would share. She set Aunt Bea's notebook before her on the stand, laid her hands on the keys, and played. Immediately the bass began, then the soprano. They pushed pell-mell upward, held back but not held enough, and then that tiny piped voice played like a cry, not even a note, not even a piano note. The bass pushed, the soprano wound around it; they modulated, clung together, climbed, reached. There was the chord! And there, and there!

Silence. She touched the piano a last time.

"Maddy," said Jonah, "are you all right?"

Maddy didn't answer. It was no good, she thought. Even on a piano like this, it was never any good.

"Maddy," said Aunt Bea anxiously, "is something wrong?"

"Aunt Bea." Maddy stood away from the piano. "I want to thank you and Aunt Ann, and you, Jonah, for all you've done for me. But I've decided that the time has come for me to practice at home."

"Why, Maddy ..." It was clear Aunt Bea did not understand. Her white hair glistened like silver, the last glint of November sunlight.

"Yes," said Maddy. "I've enjoyed all of this very much. But now I have to go home. Jonah, I've been thinking that I don't want to go to music school after all. I'm sorry if I caused you trouble."

"But, Maddy, it was no —"

"I'll see you at the next rehearsal." She backed toward the door.

The look of alarm on Jonah's face was genuine. "Maddy, let's talk about this, please!"

Aunt Bea lifted her arms, half a smile on her face, as if to say "This isn't real. Maddy, come hug me."

Maddy backed through the doorway. Everything about her felt thick and cumbersome. "I'm sorry," she said in that same clear voice. Was this what she had learned to talk for? "I've thought it over, and I have no composition good enough to share. Goodnight, Aunt Bea."

She turned and walked deliberately out of the house.

Aunt Ann, huffing into the piano room with a box of cookies, found Aunt Bea sitting very still, her hands folded in her lap, and Jonah, staring out the window.

"Can we do that?" Aunt Bea whispered. "I mean, let her go like that?"

Jonah was hearing again what Maddy had just played for them. He went to the music she'd written, picked up the notebook, looked at the notes.

"Will she be back, Jonah?" Aunt Bea clung to Aunt Ann's arm on her way toward the stairs.

"I don't know, Aunt Bea," he said. "It depends on what she can hear."

What Jonah heard was that last series of chords, like a death.

CHAPTER FOURTEEN

FROM THE OUTSIDE, Jack Dow was thinking, his house looked neater than most. In the early afternoon he had picked out all the dead petunias and carried them by the roots to the garage, where he stowed them in a trash can. He swept up the dirt in his tracks on the garage floor. It was impeccably clean, unassailable. Nothing, no evidence.

He was supposed to be sick, but it was afternoon and the baby was crying. If he stood very still and listened, he could hear it even out there.

"Vinnie had better shut that baby up," he mumbled.

The house was full of children, they'd been locked upstairs most of the day. That was all right. Vinnie was probably neglecting that baby right now, to feed the children. He had unlocked the hall door himself, and as they filed down the stairs so quietly, he'd told them, "You have your sister Maddy to blame for this."

Vinnie had made the children a good meal, no doubt. The spotless Vinnie Dow.

It made him grin. It made him laugh, standing out there all alone in his cold, swept garage. The spotless Vinnie Dow. The helpful Jack Dow. They could do anything, thanks to that wicked girl, Maddy.

But who would have thought a baby could cry like that, off and on all day?

His own had cried sometimes. When they did, it was Vinnie's

fault. She would look at him. Sometimes he thought she hurt her babies to make them cry. So that he could fix it for her. "Vinnie, put the damn baby to breast and roll over." He liked the flesh of her back and buttocks. You could hold and twist and mutter, "Is he sucking, Vinnie?"

"Yes," she would whisper, and then it would be Jack's turn to speak, in a dry, dry voice, rattling.

One thing was sure, Elaine Cummings mustn't come and find her baby crying. She would think there was something wrong.

Jack turned and went back to the house, opened the door. In his mind was white, black, the impression of flame. There was the dining table, beyond it the kitchen; to the left was the living room. There were children at the table. His. Quiet.

"Well," he said, "I guess it's about time you ate, isn't it?"

He smiled. They all smiled back.

"Well," he said, "damn that Maddy anyway, right?" He smiled at the two little boys and they nodded. "Yessir," he said, "that damned old Maddy puts us through a lot."

Allison stared at him worshipfully, he liked to see that. Jessica said nothing at all, but she never did.

Beyond in the kitchen he could see Vinnie, pacing with the howling baby. The baby was stiff with crying, making a sound like a saw. When you got close, it cut into your brain.

"Vinnie," he said suddenly, "give that baby to me."

His wife turned to him. One eye was rimmed with black and purple. Now, when had that happened? He had no memory of it. He approached her, examined that eye.

"One of a thing," he told her at last, "is no good. There ought to be two. To match, Vinnie. That will make everything all right."

She reeled away. When she looked at him again there was red skin turning blue on the other eye. Both her eyes glinted at him fondly.

He took the baby from her: little head, little red face, little kicking feet. One foot swung and nudged at his hand. The first thing, he thought, is to stop all this kicking. That will neaten things up.

Little legs were easily straightened.

"There," he said. "There." The noise went on.

"Jack," said Vinnie, "now this baby is going to need a doctor."

"Jack," his mother said, "take the baby, goddamnit!"

"Jack," Vinnie said, "where are you taking her?"

Of course Vinnie made no effort to stop him. He went outside. He looked at the baby. The legs dangled — no more kicking. The face was blue, the mouth open, screaming, screaming.

"Better close the mouth," he said. It made sense, easy. A hand like his could cover the whole face of a baby.

"Don't you struggle so," he whispered, his lips close to one small scarlet ear. "Jack has got you now."

"Jack," said an ugly woman, his mother, "where are you taking her?"

"Poor little crying baby," he mumbled. "See? I will take care of you, baby. I will make you safe."

Carefully, so he wouldn't stumble, he made his way across the road, into the field. Carefully he paced through the dead grass in the field, back and forth.

"Don't worry, baby, I will take care of you," he said.

On his arm the little body seemed to stretch and stretch, then, suddenly, relax.

"See there?" he whispered, taking his hand from the still little face. "I'll take care of you, baby."

"Jack, the baby is dead, you killed her!" His mother's voice again.

"No." Oh, how he hated his mother! He looked down. Elana was askew, half out of her pink blanket. With great care he wrapped her up again. Her eyes were closed, with eyelids on which tiny veins were etched. The lips were a little open, as if to breathe.

As if to breathe. As if?

"Jack, friend,"

He heard an old raspy whispering, his buddies: "Jack, did you think you could ignore us so long?"

"I don't know what you mean," he said.

"Oh, yes, you do," they whispered. "You killed that baby, Jack."

"I didn't. I couldn't. I am a good citizen. I pay taxes, I go to church."

"Sure. Come on back to the fields, Jack. You can work it off." They called cunningly, his brothers and sisters. "Everything you owe us."

"I won't come back. Don't you know I read from the Book? Why, I lead the prayers. Sometimes I do."

In order to reason with them better, he thought he should lay the baby down, so he did, covering her a little with soft, dead grass. He stared at her.

Then he heard another voice, higher, tiny, a child's voice: "Jack," it called, "do you mourn?"

"No." Sobs were coming as he stared at that baby. Sobs from the roots of him.

"Jack," the little voice called, "take the baby, go home. Tell everything. Ask them to help you, Jack. They'll help you."

"They don't know me."

"Jack, please."

"If I tell them, they'll hate me. I'm not like them. I'm worse than them."

"Jack, listen: I tell you there are no choices beyond your power to make." So high, so close.

He looked off toward his house. Dead as charcoal, its windows aflame. "My home is burning," he muttered. No, there it was, a nice white house.

His old friends began to talk. "Jack, we been waiting for you this long day. Pick the fields with us."

Then it came to him: he, Jack Dow, would rather work the fields of hell than go back to a nice home, nice town, nice church, and horrify them with a dead baby, with himself.

That was it, then. What he would rather do. He nodded to his friends. "A little while," he told them. "A little while longer."

He left the baby in the grass and walked back to his house. It would have to burn.

"You should see what Maddy has done," he told the children in his house. "What that damn Maddy did is too horrible to tell."

All the little heads nodded. Vinnie, with her two matching eyes, nodded, too.

Gray fields, matted grass. Maddy's arms felt heavy, her legs made of wood. She faced her house, a field away now. Nothing about her outer self moved; inside was nothing.

One more field, gray and brown, and the quiet lighter color of grasses on the path she had trodden down on her daily trips. The path would grow back in on itself, she guessed. All those trips. The evidence of them would soon be gone. A tiny path, wide enough for one. She stared the length of it, searching for the old self who had lingered on that path and dreamed. I have to get on, she thought. If I don't, someone will get hurt.

She began to walk. Halfway across the field she saw, not far from her, a little pink bundle, so out of place in the dead grass.

A doll blanket? she thought. Has some child been playing out here?

She moved toward the bundle. It wasn't until she got quite close that she saw the tiny, faintly blue hand of a baby, reaching out.

The hand did not move.

Maddy knew at once: this was the Cummings baby, and it was dead. Her father had left it here, a warning.

I must not be afraid, she thought.

Dropping her books, she knelt and touched the bundle, picked it up. Little Elana's limbs moved under Maddy's cold hands. Was she sleeping? Unconscious? Maddy listened, her ear near the little, bluish lips. There was no breath.

She, Maddy, held a dead baby. Her hands and arms felt uncomfortable, stiff and shaky. She trembled. She had never been near a dead thing before. She stared at the baby's face, not wanting to look, making herself. A still little face, like a doll's, but with skin so soft no human dollmaker could match it.

Maddy waited for the little eyes to open, something to move. Nothing. What she held and trembled over was a finely made, intricate shell.

From head to foot Maddy was trembling. Somebody has to make this right, she thought. She would have to go home, and make this right somehow. Holding the bundle, Maddy headed for the house.

Once inside the door she paused.

She saw the children huddled in a corner of the dining room. They were staring at her with horror.

She spoke through numbed lips. "I brought you the baby," she said. "She's dead." Nobody moved. "Did you hear me? Somebody has to make this right."

She stopped. Were they all deaf? The children hadn't moved. Vinnie Dow sat in a dining room chair. She didn't look at Maddy.

Her father was on the phone.

"Sure, Elaine," he was saying in his public voice. "Another couple

of hours, then? Oh, no, no problem. Glad you called. Oh, well, she
was a little fussy earlier, but . . . All right then, yes." He hung up
the phone, turned, saw Maddy with the pink bundle in her arms.
His eyes glowed at the huddled children in the corner.

"See?" he said slowly. "Oh, the poor baby. I told you what Maddy
had done."

His face was square. He could look right at her and lie and make
it seem true.

"No," she whispered. "I wouldn't hurt anyone. It was you." Her
eyes grew large. "Daddy."

"Me?" Jack Dow shook his head. "Hell, no. Why, I tried to save
her. Oh, look what Maddy has done."

"Mamma!" Torn out of Maddy, a cry that had waited years to
come. "You tell him! You have to tell him I didn't do this. You tell
them. They have to know I couldn't — I wouldn't hurt a baby." She
laid the little corpse down on the dining room table carefully, protecting its head from the wood with a piece of its blanket.

She went to Vinnie Dow.

"Mamma?"

Her mother wouldn't look up, her face shadowed by her hand.
Maddy threw herself to her knees. "Mamma, please, tell him."

She looked into her mother's face and saw the bruises, swollen,
heavy, purple, through which her mother could barely see.

"What has he done to you?" Maddy whispered. "Oh, you must
hate him. Tell him the truth. Tell them, you have to. Then we'll get
them out of here, we'll get you out of here."

Jack Dow cried, "Vinnie!"

Vinnie Dow's head snapped up at once, as a dog's might at a
master's call.

Maddy stumbled to her feet and tried to back away. "No," she
muttered. Her father caught her, held her by the shoulders.

"Tell her, Vinnie," he ordered.

Vinnie Dow's bruised eyes searched the room. She saw the huddled
children, saw Maddy struggling in her father's arms. There were
tears on Vinnie's cut cheeks, the tears ran past swollen lips. She
looked at Maddy.

In that glance Maddy saw all she'd known of a mother's hope and
love. Crippled.

"Vinnie," said Jack Dow, "if you're not careful, I'll tell them all about you."

Once again the squinted eyes raised themselves to her husband's face, and Maddy saw in their depths a tiny light that grew and flickered. Was it anger? Hate? If so, they might all be free.

"Mamma," Maddy whispered, "remember the music...."

The light grew, and now Maddy saw what it was: the depth of her mother's unhappy, unholy attachment to Jack Dow. Guilt.

What had she been guilty of? Surely, only of hiding the beatings. Surely, only that.

"You couldn't help it," Maddy cried.

"Oh, yes," said Jack Dow. "Oh, yes, she could."

"Mamma," whispered Maddy. "Please. I burned my music for you."

Now someone else spoke, Jessie, her words guttural. "Maddy, listen," she said. "I saw a man and a woman sitting like toads at a table." Jessie spoke deliberately, rocking with feeling. "They had made a food called bitterness and they were forcing their children to eat it."

Unexpected, unrelated. True.

The room twisted; Maddy landed at the far wall. Without a word, Jack Dow went to Jessie and slapped her face to one side and then the other, back and forth, until she, too, spun to the floor.

"This here," he told his other children confidentially, "is another bad girl. We'll fix her, we'll fix them both. Where is my gas can? Where are my matches?"

"No," Maddy cried.

Like lightning Jack Dow hauled Stephen forward, twisting the little boy's arm. "Don't you move, Maddy," he said. "Look what you do to these children when you move."

"Bad Maddy! Bad!" shrieked Allison, overwrought, her blond hair flying about her head like fire.

"Here," Jack Dow said, releasing Stephen after a moment. "Take care of your brother." He flung him to Phillip and Allison. The three children clung together blindly, taking care of each other.

Elaine Hebert Cummings had forgotten her five-thirty appointment with Jonah, but now she dressed for it carefully. What was it he wanted to tell her? She hoped for good news, not knowing how she could bear to have bad. She hoped it was about singing a solo for the third competition, that he had picked a song just for her. She tried not to dwell on those times when he had seemed to hint that perhaps the singing lessons were not for her. Of course they were for her, she was the best. She would prove that to everyone.

Jonah had also forgotten about the five-thirty appointment with Elaine in his worry for Maddy, but when she appeared, he didn't waste time.

"Elaine, thank you for coming by," he said, courteous as always as he bent over her and shook her hand. "I'm afraid I have bad news for you, but at this point I don't think it will surprise you too much. I have to tell you that after our win last night, it was obvious to me that Judy Russell will have to be the soloist of choice for our next competition. I'm sorry."

The world was in a buzz, but Elaine tried to ignore it. "Oh?"

"Yes. Judy has a great talent, and she takes direction."

"Judy?" said Elaine.

"Yes." Jonah, however worried about Maddy, felt a little sorry for Elaine at that moment. As he watched, he saw her eyes fill with tears. She was delicate, so unable to defend herself, he felt. But musically she was far too inexperienced to do a solo for the competition coming up. He thought back over their last few lessons; he had tried to tell her this in every possible way and she hadn't heard him until now.

"Oh, no, Jonah," she said softly. "I thought, after all this time . . ."

"I've tried to caution you, Elaine. Surely you must have suspected."

"But we . . ." She searched for a defense. "We paid you money, Jonah."

That only touched steel in Jonah. "You may have the money back, if you feel it will help."

Tears fell.

"Please," said Jonah, patting her shoulder awkwardly. "I know it's a blow. But you're still young, Elaine, and you are beautiful, and you have your whole life ahead of you."

She stepped into the circle of his arms. He held her and knew, without a shadow of a doubt, that Elaine had charmed him, had planned this, an emergency plan, from the beginning. She was weeping prettily against his shoulder. She was beautiful.

But he had other things to do. His dissertation was nearly finished. There was Audrey. And Maddy.

He stepped back. "I'm very sorry," he said, a shade firmly.

There was a roar in Elaine's ears as she realized her mistake. She took a deep breath. "Judy will sing on television, too?"

"Yes," said Jonah, "if we get that far."

"I'm sorry," said Elaine, looking directly at him. "I guess I'm feeling a little lost."

Jonah thought her lips were too red, startling. He was silent.

"I guess," she said after a moment, "I'll just go get my baby. Yes. I think I'll just go get my baby and take her home and hug her for a while."

Jonah felt some sympathy. He nodded. Elaine left.

By the time her headlights had played along the windows and gone he was back at the piano, looking again at Maddy's composition. He fingered the final chords.

"Stay out of it," he told himself. "That's a good rule. She's all right."

When he took his hands off those chords, it was so very quiet.

"Too damned quiet," Aunt Ann said. She took a tray up to Aunt Bea's room. "Here, now, Bea, let's eat."

The form against the pillows was too frail. One heavy breath might blow it away. The old lady's eyes were red.

"You been crying, Bea?"

"Yes, Ann."

"Damn. I'm sorry, Bea. You're not planning to get up?"

A hand moved shakily in the air, dropped. "Ann, I'm so tired."

Aunt Ann looked with misgiving at all the food on her tray. She thought of Maddy.

"Bea," she said the next moment, "we've had enough of this."

She set the tray down, went to the bed, and lifted Bea gently but firmly upright.

"Ann, what in the world —" But in the red old eyes was relief mirroring Aunt Ann's own.

"It's time to get up," said Aunt Ann. "I'm not having the world go off and get sick on me."

"Ann, now really, I —"

"No, we got work to do, Bea." Aunt Ann left the old woman sitting and turned to her bureau, opened it, rummaged through.

"Here's stockings, a slip," she said. "You need a dress, you got to have a dress." She began to throw clothes about in Bea's carefully ordered closet. At last she emerged, a dress over one shoulder and one big fist full of underwear.

"What are we?" she demanded. "Two old ladies dying in their beds?"

Aunt Bea was close to tears. "All right," she said. "I'll get dressed, Ann."

"Well, good," Aunt Ann said. "We'll go right over there now and get a few things understood. Because if that child doesn't come here to practice, Bea, I won't be able to stand it."

When the two old ladies made their way to the front door a few minutes later, they were both muffled in heavy clothing against the cold.

At the door they met Jonah, also dressed to go out. For a moment they studied each other's faces.

Jonah said, "I think perhaps we should all go together."

Elaine Hebert Cummings's little red car flashed down the road.

I will say, "Mother, it was offered to me and I turned it down, because now that Elana is older I want to spend more time with her," Elaine thought. But no, that's not anything Mother would understand.

I can say, "Mother, it turned out I was just not good enough. Not as good as Judy, anyway."

She'd never had to say that before in her life. All her little problems, all life long, had never amounted to that sort of failure before. Elaine had always been better than Judy.

Too much thinking. She would figure it out, there would be a way out. Right now, all she had was her child, her little Elana. Torn up inside, all Elaine wanted to do was sit somewhere and hold the baby. Her baby loved her, her baby didn't care about anything else, only her, and comforting her. Elaine would pick up her baby and go home and she might not ever come out again. If only she had that warm little body in her arms.

*

In the Dows' dining room the light was weird and sharp. Maddy's father came toward them. It was quiet. Maddy's inner ears were dead: no music for escape, nothing. She thought she must be dead already. She gripped Jessica's hand.

"Maddy," Jack Dow said, "get me the goddamn gas can, get me the matches."

She clutched Jessie's hand. "No," she said, "I won't."

"Look out!" Jessie cried.

Maddy saw the fist coming. It swung her half around.

"I said, get me the matches," her father roared.

"No." It was enough, suddenly, to learn to speak. If only to say that. Maddy waited, small and shaking, one side of her face puffing strangely as she spoke. Another fist, a cracking sound, a reeling room. She fell to the floor face down, but at once he was on top of her, he was pounding her back. She couldn't breathe, couldn't take a breath.

"Mamma," she gasped, "take the children. Run."

"Get off her!" Jessie was screaming. "Daddy, you'll kill her. Get off."

A thud, a grunt. Jessie fell on her knees beside Maddy, blood coming from her nose and mouth. Jessie was limp; his fists slammed her this way, that way. Maddy struggled, crept over to set her body as a shield in front of her sister.

Somewhere in the room she could hear a murmur from their mother. "It'll all be over soon, it'll all be over. If we can just hold out."

There was a blow to the back of Maddy's head. She felt the pain in her teeth, neck, shoulders. The floor began to slip. She was falling.

"Have to get the gasoline myself," someone said. She saw big feet swirling across the floor toward the back door.

"Mamma," Maddy choked out. "This is enough. Look at me." Somehow she managed to drag herself up and face her mother, but Vinnie Dow looked away. Maddy swayed. Something sticky ran down the side of her head and malingered at her collar: blood. She made it across the insubstantial floor and put her hands on either side of her mother's head, forcing Vinnie Dow's gaze upward.

"Mamma. Look at me."

She did look. A strangeness came into the bruised eyes. She was looking into a mangled mirror of herself in this swaying daughter.

"Oh, God," she whispered.

"Please," said Maddy. "We have to leave now."

Her mother didn't move. In a far corner, the three younger children huddled together. Someone was crying.

"Mamma, we have to go. Come on now."

Tears streamed from Vinnie's eyes. "Maddy, he'll be sorry," she said. "When he's sorry, he cries. We have to take care of him."

"Get the baby," Jessica said suddenly, groggily. She stood and picked up the tiny body of Elana. She held it from her, swaying, shaking. From her lips blood spilled down the front of her clothing, spotting the pink blanket.

The knob on the back door rattled and began to turn. "The baby," Jessie muttered. "Oh, the poor baby." Maddy took the little corpse from her and grabbed Jessie before she could fall.

"Mamma, we have to go!"

Her mother was no longer at the table. She was huddling the other children into their corner. "Don't look," she was saying. "It's all right. Don't even bother to question."

Stephen pulled loose. "Maddy! I want Maddy!" he sobbed and ran to her, lending his little strength to help the swaying Jessie. Together they pulled her, bleeding and unsteady, from the house.

"Maddy!" Phillip cried from somewhere behind them. "Help me! She's holding me! He's coming!"

"Yes!" Maddy called back. "Just as soon as I —"

Toward the light. Headlights. Elaine? Maddy could barely see. The form in front of her was willowy and insubstantial. Did she see they were bleeding? She didn't say so.

"Oh, Maddy, you have the baby?" Elaine said brightly, calling out into the cold, her hair swinging, curling at her shoulders.

"All ready?" she cried. "Just for me?"

Maddy forced herself to walk toward Elaine. "I'm sorry," she managed to whisper through stiffened lips. She was crying, tears stinging in the bruises. "I'm sorry, I'm sorry."

She put the bundle into Elaine's arms. The world swayed; Maddy caught at it.

Elaine looked down at the baby's body, one long look. She said, "Don't worry about a thing, I'll just go and call my mother."

She started up the walk to the house.

Then suddenly Elaine began to scream, fell to her knees, screaming and screaming. Maddy knew at once: this was the final chord she'd heard. It played again, again and again.

She must stop it somehow.

She started up the walk to the house.

The walk was a snake's body. Its stones were like scales, loosely connected, swinging in coils.

Maddy tried to speak, but she couldn't make a sound. Elaine walked on the snake, up ahead of her. The tail lashed back and forth. Elaine reached the door, opened it. Smoke rolled onto her, over her; the snake was a dragon. Elaine fell. The dragon's mouth flamed, the dragon roared. Everywhere there was light, leaping flame.

Inside the house someone was crying.

Someone else — Allison? — screamed, "Maddy!"

"No, Maddy, don't — it's on fire." Jessie rose in front of her, sank; dark swallowed her. Stephen was crying in the dark.

Maddy took a step toward the house, another.

The path moved, the dragon roared. She fought to stay upright on its tail, to step forward into the open mouth, onto that tongue of flame. Everything was alight, behind her, in front of her.

Someone called, "Maddy! Maddy!"

Aunt Ann's voice? Could it be? Maddy held out a hand, one, and turned to look, reaching into the dark, safe night toward that cry.

One hand, hers. A hand was not heavy, but this one made her fall. Headlong she went, falling and falling.

CHAPTER FIFTEEN

I T WAS ELEANOR HEBERT who visited the family vault. Elaine had left her husband, Cyril, and was now at home with Eleanor, but she did not get out of bed. Eleanor made all the arrangements for the funeral, including this one. Someone had to.

Eleanor had been inside the vault before and now she went alone with the key, finding little comfort in the swept white granite steps, stained-glass window, carefully dustless interior. Not a speck of dust, she thought. Not a cobweb.

The vault had been constructed in 1891 by a Packard predecessor, and the walls of the small granite building were made of rows of compartments. Some stone plates had names carved on them: Lily Ann Packard, 1897–1923, Rest in Peace; Glenn Everett Packard, 1922–1924. Eleanor remembered Glenn Everett dimly, a small cousin unfortunately smothered in a silo of grain. August Emory Packard, 1895–1952 — her uncle August. He had died of a heart attack, but no words explained this on the stone. There were only his dates and his name, anonymous details.

Eleanor thought, I wish they would put down the cause of death. It would help. I wish they would say, right on the stone, whether it was a struggle or not, or something about the person's last hours. So if you didn't know him, or you weren't there, you would understand something about him. Lily Ann, she thought, staring at another stone, how did you die?

The remains were all in brass compartments, locked with smooth stone, so clean. There wasn't so much as a fly in this place. Eleanor studied the floor. Looking for what? she wondered. Not a bug crawled.

Light came from the one window: "I am the Way, the Truth, and the Light." Scrollwork in stained glass — she saw first its construction, the red panes, blue ones. In the center of the room, among all the stone faces both blank and carved, was a little altar made of granite. It was far too cold here for a person to kneel.

The baby? In here?

Eleanor Hebert, dressed neatly in a lined trenchcoat and sensible shoes, shivered and thought, Oh, won't our baby be cold?

"I am the Way, the Truth, and the Light." Cold comfort. A nineteenth-century sentiment in this nineteenth-century building with its roof ornament, a draped urn of stone, and outside its statue of a weeping woman, lilies dropping from her fingers.

Eleanor stood in the center of the vault and stared at the empty faces of stone.

"Here, Elana," she whispered. "We'll put you here, near your uncle August." She touched a blank stone face, unmarred, salt-and-pepper white, smooth. "After all this time, Elana, he will know how to take care of you."

Eleanor clenched her teeth together; she was too cold to cry. There was a cold place inside her where the baby lay, ready to be put away. She wouldn't think of that.

She had planned to visit quickly, but it was slowly that she came out of the little building, locked it, walked down its immaculate stone steps. She said, for courage, "Now I will be able to tell them where . . ."

She found herself staring up at the statue of the kneeling woman, with her flowers. "You had better take care of that baby," Eleanor told her. The woman didn't move.

There were tears at the corners of Eleanor's eyes; she would not see them. Instead she looked down the cemetery at the rows of stones.

Across the road from the church, the burial grounds of Freedom extended for quite a few acres. There were gravestones from as early as the 1700s, some cracked, some of limestone fallen and propped up. Here and there was a pot of dead flowers, old vines. The Packards were the only ones with a large vault, but there were some smaller ones. To one side was a jumble of more modern stones, unmatched, set in rows two feet apart. Eleanor's eyes swept past this ugliness quickly. She preferred the older section: sometimes a small piece of statuary, whole families resting around a center stone, "Mother, Father, Sister, Brother." Now the dead leaves had been raked away. The ground was bare and hard, waiting for snow.

She wandered through the cemetery, pausing to read engravings, sometimes remembering those who had been buried, more often not. There were many babies. Oh, how could you leave a baby in this place?

At last she stood still, half lost beneath one of the many trees, knowing she must go back and carry on with the rest of her plans for the day. She thought, I am to blame for this, Elana. If you must hate someone, hate me. I am so sorry to put you in this cold place. It's my fault.

Then Eleanor Hebert, a careful woman in a practical coat, standing all alone in acres of stones, allowed herself one hard noise, caught in her throat.

Her hands in fists in her pockets, she stumbled back toward her car, still somehow reading the stones as she went. She came upon an old one with the remnants of some now-undistinguished summer plant wrapped around it lovingly, as if to hold it up. Martha Freedman Hannigan, she saw. Another unfamiliar name. 1841–1883.

Not a long life for Martha, Eleanor thought. Under the date, in barely legible words, was written: "She Did What She Could."

Eleanor caught back another sob, then put her face in her hands.

Oh, had Elana been ill, their baby? Their poor little baby, Elana? Oh, had she been in pain, and no one to help?

Oh, Elana, Eleanor Hebert thought again, trembling all over as the hard tears came, won't you be cold?

She broke down and wept.

Maddy was wandering in a field. It was full of dead grass. She was carrying a pink bundle.

"Maddy." A little whisper. She looked up.

Standing there were her father and her mother. Their faces were white. Around their eyes the skin was black.

Maddy cleared her throat. "You killed this baby," she said.

"No. No, Maddy," her father said. "I saved her. Didn't I, Vinnie?"

"Yes, Jack, you did." The look on Vinnie's face was adoring. She stared at her husband. Together they took a step toward Maddy.

If only she could make them understand. She held the baby up, looking into its small, perfect face. "You see," she said, "it's like a little blue doll."

Her parents came closer. Maddy thought if they could see the dead baby, that might help. She held it up to them.

But suddenly Jack Dow cried out, "Can you hear them, Vinnie? Can you?"

"Yes," Maddy's mother said at once. "We'd better go, Jack. We'll be late." Their pale faces nodded simultaneously, their blacked eyes stared.

"And leave me here?" Maddy said. "Oh, no, don't leave me. You know, this baby is not breathing." It was only part of what she wanted to tell them. She stared at their white faces.

Were they in pain? Were they sorry? She thought if they were sorry, that might help. The baby was dead; nothing could change that. But if there were in Maddy's mother and father something like the sorrow she felt, a sadness that went through the bone, down deep. "Are you sorry?" Maddy whispered.

Jack Dow called over his shoulder to someone Maddy couldn't see. "I'm coming," he cried. "I'm bringing Vinnie. Wait, friends."

"Please." Maddy spoke again, louder. "Are you sorry? Please, can you hear me?"

They were moving away from her, back into the woods. They floated out of sight. Maddy watched. Maybe they're not sorry, she thought. Maybe they don't care.

Then all the shells, the tough, silencing husks, fell away from her. "Mamma!" she cried. "Daddy?"

They were out of sight.

Still holding the baby, Maddy ran a little way. "This baby is me," she called to them frantically. "Mamma? Daddy?"

They were gone.

"I'm lost," said Maddy. "I'm falling."

"No, you aren't," said Aunt Ann. "You're right here, Maddy Dow. We're not going anywhere, and you're here, with us."

"Mamma?" cried Maddy, struggling upright painfully. "Daddy? I'm falling."

"It's all right, Maddy." Jonah stared into the girl's frantic bruised face, into the eyes that were still seeing nightmares. "You're here. Jessie's here, and Stephen. You're all right. You're going to be all right."

Aunt Ann held Maddy's shoulders. She felt the child relax. At last she laid her gently back down on the pillows.

"Asleep," she said after a moment, and the two others in the room nodded and tried to smile.

CHAPTER SIXTEEN

PILLS. In the morning Elaine would awaken, in her parents' house now, and time would sit upon her, as a cat might sit on a bed. The light coming through the carefully curtained bedroom windows was strange and diffuse, and she woke up with a feeling of loss. Sometimes, although every muscle seemed weighted down, she managed to get up. Sometimes she even managed to get dressed. She could not manage to care.

This was her childhood room. It was, as it always had been, in perfect order. Her father had built shelves in her closet so she could put her dolls away when she wasn't playing with them. She never did play with them. When you walked out of your room, she had been taught, you should leave it neat. It should look as if no one had ever been in it.

Schedule; there was always a schedule, too. Lessons, practicing for lessons. School functions, church work, church functions. One had to have a schedule, her mother had always said. It's the only way to get things done.

How Elaine had worshiped her mother. Eleanor always knew what to do, what her husband should do, what Elaine should do. In the morning, even at breakfast, Eleanor's hair would be carefully combed and she would have managed to put on lipstick. Of course, her robe and slippers always looked new. Elaine had shared her father's feeling of awe: so this is what a good woman was, and this was what she did.

Her father the facilitator. Anything they wanted, they could get from him. He never spoke much. He was in the home to bring in the money, and he worked long hours to make sure he did. He liked to spend money, too, and always had a new car, or a new boat, or a new kind of garage door opener, snow thrower, lawn tractor. The house was full of special lighting effects, her father's hobby: floodlights, recessed lights, dimmer switches, hidden fans. Mostly, Elaine thought, her father was a man who stood in hallways, jingling the change in his pockets.

Now she would go to the kitchen, late, because of the pills she had taken the night before, and she would get herself breakfast, by herself, and eat it, and it wouldn't matter what she did or didn't do. There wasn't anybody around. Elaine walked through the house. She did no work; there was none to do. She watched television, allowing one show to lapse into another, throughout the day: white noise, to keep her from caring.

But a whole day of being careful not to care amounted again to caring too much. By the time her mother and father had come home at night, Elaine had in general gone to a place where people with large eyes and nasty tongues looked at her and thought, Look at the wreck of Elaine. Look at what a failure she is. And she comes from such a good home, too.

By the time her mother was in the door, Elaine would be weeping.

Eleanor would come in and find that the shades in all the rooms had already been pulled down, that there were water glasses and dishes with nibbles of food left on them here and there in the house, just left around. Elaine might be dressed, but she never bothered to brush her hair anymore, never bothered with lipstick. She didn't make her bed. All of that wasn't so bad. It was the endless crying that frightened Eleanor.

"Oh, Elaine," she would say in the sympathetic but faintly disapproving voice one used for erring children, "don't cry anymore. Come on, now, let's brush your hair, you'll feel better." But the only way to stop the crying, she knew, was to reach for that little plastic bottle of white pills the doctor had prescribed the night of the baby's death. Little round white pills, instant magic. Before supper, in order to get Elaine to stop crying and eat, Eleanor would give her half a pill. Then she would eat. At bedtime, a little more, and if she didn't go right to sleep, a little more. It was all Eleanor knew to do, to comfort her daughter.

Part of her knew that pills were not enough, would never do the trick by themselves. As she watched herself give Elaine the little white half before supper and the rest of it at bedtime, she searched her mind and her heart, trying to think, trying to find the knowledge to help Elaine become "normal" again. It began to occur to her, the prime mover and organizer in the town of Freedom, that this was a job she was not capable of doing.

It was several days before Maddy Dow was awake enough to talk. When she did wake up she was in a bedroom at the Cottage.

"Oh, good," said Aunt Ann, as if she'd been waiting. "Drink this, Maddy, it'll set you right up."

So quiet.

Maddy drank. She had been taking liquids for days, she knew dimly, but this was the first she had really felt on her tongue and tasted. Frothy and smooth and cool and filling. "That's good," she whispered.

"Well, there," said Aunt Ann.

It was so quiet. A window, broad daylight. "White?" Maddy said. "It's been snowing."

Maddy lay back. So quiet. Peace, the cool white of soft snow, like a blanket.

Much later she was awake again. Jonah looked in.

"I don't hear anything," Maddy told him.

"Music, you mean?" he said. "You're alive. Don't worry about it, Maddy."

She couldn't worry, she was too tired. She lay back in the snow — that was how this bed felt. Its mattress was solid, the ground. How wonderful it was, after so much falling, to lie back on the ground and be covered with snow.

So quiet.

Morning again. Aunt Bea was in the room. "I'm sorry," she whispered. "Did I wake you? I was trying to shut this curtain." She came to the bed, a wise old woman, a vision in white clothing, silver-white hair, and blue eyes, so kind.

"Are you real?" Maddy whispered.

Aunt Bea laughed. "Oh, yes." She came to the bed and touched Maddy's hand with dry old fingers. "You've been asleep a long time."

"And you all have been taking care of me?"

"Yes."

"But —"

"We wanted to." Aunt Bea touched her cheek.

"Is Jessie here?"

"Yes, and Stephen."

"Are they all right? He —"

"I know. They're all right, you mustn't worry."

She had to ask, she couldn't help it, although she knew the dreadful answer already. "The others?"

"Maddy —"

"They called to me. Are they gone?"

"Yes, Maddy."

"Burnt?" It was necessary to specify, to be completely specific.

"Yes," said Aunt Bea.

"Oh, God." Rocking in her bed, Maddy began to weep, from a gray place, a pool of grief so deep it seemed it would never empty. Aunt Bea wept right along with her.

"I know," the old woman whispered after a while. "You loved them. I know."

Elaine did come to the door, but she gave Judy a vacant stare. "Judy?"

"May I come in? I thought I — I'd just come over and see how you're doing." She saw Elaine's uncombed hair, her food-stained bathrobe.

Elaine stared at her cousin. What she saw was someone from another space and time, someone whose arms and legs moved properly, who lived life as she herself had lived it. Or had she, ever?

"Come in," Elaine said. "There's no one here but me, though."

On Aunt Eleanor's shining coffee table were three crumbling cookies. Judy stared at the powder of sugar on that impeccable surface and then she knew that there was a drastic rearrangement going on in this household.

"I'm sorry," Elaine apologized, following Judy's glance.

"Oh, don't worry on my account," Judy said. She tucked her own neat hair behind her ears.

"How is little Russ?" Elaine asked.

"Just fine. Everything's fine."

A silence. Elaine smiled, a strange little movement of the lips.

Judy cleared her throat. "I came to see if there's anything I can do, Elaine. I feel bad. I . . . feel to blame, and I miss the baby. If there were anything. . . ." Her eyes filled. There was a long silence.

"You can get me out of here," Elaine said after a moment.

"Out of —" Judy looked around.

"Yes," said Elaine slowly, running a hand through her tangled hair. "I hate it in here."

"In this house?" Judy asked.

"No. In here, in here." Elaine's hands touched her chest, throat, head. "I hate it in here, Judy. I can see you out there, and I can't get to you."

Judy was frightened. "I know what . . . you mean," she said. "Please, Elaine, don't worry."

That night she and Aunt Eleanor and Uncle Arthur had a long talk.

A residential brick building was what the Heberts came to at last. There were windows in the door and cars in the garage. It looked like any normal family house. Eleanor, on one side of Elaine, stared up at the square edifice with its large old-fashioned windowpanes and caught her breath. Through Elaine's body Arthur Hebert, who had his daughter's other arm, felt hesitation and paused. Usually he wasn't a man of feeling, he couldn't afford to be. Short, stocky and balding, he felt old today. His dark neck was very red. He swallowed. Over Elaine's head he and Eleanor glanced at each other once, like strangers. This was the hardest thing they had ever done.

"Dr. Marie Elias," Eleanor whispered, like a good luck charm. Arthur nodded. They went up the steps.

They were met at the front door by the doctor, who took them into the living room of the house. It was a comfortable room, the furniture and carpets a bit run down to Eleanor's meticulous eyes, but nicely arranged. There were books and plants. Dr. Elias had told them, "A chance for Elaine to get away, put herself to rights."

A young girl came into the room. "Elaine, would you like to come with me?"

Elaine did not smile, but her expression broke Eleanor's heart: she looked grateful. She followed the girl without a word. At the last moment she turned and went back to her parents. Eleanor kissed her, Arthur kissed her.

"Let me know if you need anything," Eleanor said, but by that time Elaine had left the room.

Gently Dr. Elias led them to the door; now they walked down the steps, and back across the walk, and now they were at the car.

"We'll come." Arthur Hebert's usually authoritative voice was shaky. "We'll do everything we can."

Dr. Elias nodded.

He started the car; they were driving away.

Gradually Maddy realized there was a large painful bandage on her head, and parts of her face were tender to the touch. Her hands, when she held them in front of her face, were fine, but there were painful spots on her arms, shoulders, and neck. She realized there were no mirrors in the room and wished she had one. There had been days of sickness and tears, day after day. It was so quiet. Jonah came in, standing tall and thin by the door.

"Maddy, how are you?"

"Better." She nodded. "Not crying. At least not right now. I'm sorry about all the tears, Jonah."

"Think nothing of it, Maddy." It was amazing to her: he had sat through all that, and still he liked her.

"Jonah, I can't hear anything."

"Music? I know. You keep saying that." He sat down, bending away from her, thinking, his eyes quiet.

Maddy felt close to him, felt he had something to say, something for them both.

"Landowska," said Jonah.

"What?"

"What we both need, Maddy." He lifted his head back and stared into space, then began to quote: " 'Silence is at the origin of the rest signs in musical notation,' " he said. " 'One must give the rests the same care that is given to notes. A performer must make the rests resound; he must "play" the pauses.' " He broke off.

He was gone, back in a few minutes. "You must have this," he said, his head on one side, his face full of feeling. "A gift. Read it if you wish." They exchanged a long, nurturing look. "Please, Maddy, if you're alive, that's enough. We love you," he said, and cleared his throat. "You rest. You deserve a rest."

He left before she could speak.

Landowska on Music. Maddy touched the book. She was tired again, she would sleep. But sometime she would read.

The next day: "Jessie? Stephen?"

Aunt Ann brought in a mirror. "I want you to be warned, it looks pretty bad," she said. "But the doctor says it will all heal. They want to see you, too. Stephen's fine, but you might as well know, Jessie looks about as you do, except she has no upper front teeth, Maddy."

It was bad. Her hair was covered with a bandage. A yellow bruise extended the length of one cheek. Her forehead was purple and swollen. Her lips were bruised. "You took care of me," she said, "when I looked like this?"

"Course we did," said Aunt Ann.

Jessie's face was badly bruised. Her arm was in a cast and sling. "Maddy, I had to see you. Are you all right?"

"Oh, yes. Oh, Jessie."

"I am so tired," Jessie said, "I can barely move." Movement in that bruised face was excruciating to see.

"Are you all right, Jessie?" As best she could, Maddy hid her shock. Somehow she sensed Jessie was doing the same.

"Oh, yes. They're taking good care of us." Her face was swollen and puffy. She moved with great difficulty across the room to Maddy's bed. Her upper lip was sunken; when she talked, the bruised gums showed blood.

"Maddy," she whispered, "I have to tell you something."

"Jessie, you should rest."

"You have to know this, you have to know." Jessie's bruised face came close. "Look at me. Look at you. Maddy, you were not to blame." Her voice sank low; the words came out slurred. "I was not to blame, but no one ever blamed me. It was you, they put it all on you, Maddy. From the start. But I'm saying this: you were not to blame." Jessie's glance held hers. "Someday, maybe, I will write a poem, Maddy. It will begin, 'I saw a woman and a man, like toads

at a table.' You were not to blame, Maddy. That means that you are
free. You are. Free." Their glances held.

A tiny knock, a door opening cautiously, a little boy with dark
curly hair, wide eyes, a pale face.

"Maddy?" he whispered. "Jessie?"

Maddy caught back a sob.

Stephen flung himself across the floor and onto the bed. Like the
lost link between the two sisters, he hugged them both, touching their
hands, holding on to them wherever he could touch without hurting.

"Maddy, Jessie." His pale face was wet.

"There," said Jessie. "There, there." They were all crying.

Days of quiet, of rest. The big bandage on Maddy's head came off,
then a smaller one. The bruises began to heal. She got out of bed and
began to walk around the house, a little at first, more and more. By
this time Stephen and Jessie were familiar with the Cottage, and,
Stephen especially, with Aunt Ann's kitchen.

One day Maddy heard banging noises vibrating all through the
house and went to see. Stephen was having some kind of a race. He
thundered around the dining room table, through the pantry, then
burst through the kitchen door, banging it loudly behind him. There
was a cheer from Aunt Ann, some laughing, silence.

The coast seemed clear. Maddy slipped into the kitchen. "What's
going on here?" she asked, a little dazed by the commotion.

"Door-slamming lessons," said Aunt Ann. "The quiet around
here is driving me out of my tree. Now you just listen to this." She
nodded at Stephen, who was huffing against the sink. He stuffed the
rest of a cookie into his mouth and took off, pausing only long
enough to give the door a good one on the way out.

"Hooray!" yelled Aunt Ann. "Come on, now, do what Aunt Ann
tells you, baby!" There was a thunder of little-boy footsteps, and
the door crashed open and then swung to with such force that it
rattled the dishes in the pantry.

"Yay! Hooray!" yelled Aunt Ann, beaming. "Give that boy a
cookie!"

Stephen approached, his face flushed with his daring, looking about
him as if he expected punishment. When none came, he managed a
little smile at Aunt Ann and held one bashful hand out for a cookie.

By this time Jessie had come to the kitchen. She slammed the door behind her. "May I have a cookie, too?"

"You bet," said Aunt Ann.

"I can slam better than that!" Stephen said suddenly to Jessie, dimpling a little, half frightened at his own mischief.

Jessie looked shocked, but for once replied without having to think: "You can not!"

"Can too!"

"Are they fighting?" Maddy asked. Fighting had never been allowed. The three children looked at each other, remembering that.

"You bet they are," said Aunt Ann. "Doing a darn good job, too. Got to raise the roof a little. Here, here's one more cookie. Now no more 'til supper, so don't ask me again. Out, and try to make a little more noise, you kids, and get under foot now and then, so's I have something to complain about."

The three Dows left the kitchen together. The door banged, twice.

Aunt Ann waited for the third bang, and when it didn't come she shook her head, not satisfied. "Maddy," she muttered. "Something's got to be done, stop 'em looking over their shoulders."

When she explained what she wanted to Aunt Bea, the old woman nodded. "Of course. It'll help Maddy."

Maddy had not been near the piano room.

Maddy was thinking, I'm not meant to hear any more music. I'm only meant to hear the rests. The great gray rest. It's out of my hands, she thought.

The Reverend Mr. Howarth came to her and Jessie and said, "The aunts have asked me to ask you. We should have some kind of service for your parents, and Phillip, and Allison." He tried to speak as gently as he could.

"Service?"

This was too much pain. Phillip, Allison — their last cries came to Maddy now. A service? This must be another church craziness, she thought. Like "Honor thy father and thy mother," when your mother was too guilty to run and your father laid a dead baby in a field and set his own house afire. Part of a pretense, a bunch of lace on a dark arm.

"Why?" was all she could say.

She stared into Mr. Howarth's eyes, then her own dropped, seeing his goodness.

"Funerals are for the living, Maddy," he said softly. "So they don't need to be angry anymore."

"Angry?" said Maddy. "I'm not."

"We have to say good-bye to them, Maddy," Jessica said. "I'd like to say good-bye." Her lips trembled.

"Of course," said Mr. Howarth. "Just a small service, Maddy. The aunts would like it, too. At the church. Some music, a few words, some prayers."

"No music," Maddy said.

"Oh, yes," said Jessica. "There has to be music. For our mother. She might need it."

A small, quiet service, no more than half an hour. Maddy sat with the aunts and Jessie and Stephen, but even when Mrs. Chamberlain played the old-fashioned hymns on the organ Maddy was alone, in a land of utter gray silence.

Mr. Howarth said, "We must remember all the good things, the church work, their contribution to town life. We must remember that we all, at one time or another, have been children trying to rescue ourselves, and we will have faith that, at last, Jack and Vinnie and all of their children have been rescued."

The music began again, but this time Maddy couldn't hear it because she was crying. Many people were crying together, damp arms and crumpled faces, touching each other with the best they knew of loving mercy. Eleanor and Arthur Hebert, with tears in their eyes, embraced the Dow children. Everyone wept. As they left the church, many arms reached and turned to reach, to help each other down the steps.

"Food," said Aunt Ann. "Come to the Cottage." Throughout the afternoon people came and went, bringing food, eating.

In each face Maddy saw her own pain and an attempt to understand, or at least to offer help. It was not a time to hide tears; that time was over, she saw. Now tears could be shared, like food. She hadn't realized how many good people there were in the world, how many people were willing to share.

It made it easier to say good-bye if you knew that there were, around you, people willing to help. There was no need to fly, she saw suddenly. The falling was over.

"Good-bye," she whispered. Not a hard word, suddenly. A word before turning. Now, she would have to turn.

Now, she would have to do nothing at all. Around her were all the loving people in the town of Freedom, her singers. She didn't have to turn; they were near her and Jessica and Stephen, on every side.

A few afternoons later Mary Mower came in. Aunt Ann, Aunt Bea, Jessie and Maddy were all in Aunt Ann's kitchen. Stephen had gone out to play, and Jonah, to see his wife. "About time, too," Aunt Ann said.

It was Maddy's turn to lie against the sink. Mary Mower's hands were soothing in her hair. Aunt Ann was looking through a hairdo magazine with Jessie. Aunt Bea and Mary gossiped sociably while Mary's hands moved carefully around the place that was still sore on Maddy's head.

Maddy's eyes were closed. Water ran on her scalp. She felt it spray, heard it run. It made a sound like the wind, only wet, she thought.

Idly she listened: maybe there was a note like that sound? It was, could be, a note. Something high and small, a sound like a number of those notes. What could they be? Maddy listened. What note would sound like that? A high, tiny sound, and then all those others, like running water, water that danced. Those notes, that tiny note — what would they do? How would they flow?

"Maddy," said Mary, tapping one foot playfully, "did you hear me? I said, do you want curls in front, do you think?"

Maddy blinked. She was sitting upright now, with a towel on her head.

"Maddy?" said Aunt Bea gently. "Are you all right?"

"Oh, yes." Jessie spoke up automatically, without looking. "She was just 'off.' " Then she lowered her magazine and stared.

"Was I?" Maddy stared back. "Why, I was. I think I was, Jessie." Jessie's lips curved.

Maddy looked up at Mary Mower and smiled.

"I think I'll have curls, please," she said.

Jonah was reading aloud, but he had one eye on Audrey. "So we find that in the field of musical education, the less there is, the greater the potential. In the minds and hearts of many of our children is a silence that waits. We can give them more if we will."

He looked up. Audrey's auburn hair swung back over her shoulders. She gazed into the distance speculatively, then looked at him. "It's not bad," she said. "It's almost finished."

"What?" Jonah stared. "It is finished."

She shrugged. "Maybe."

CHAPTER SEVENTEEN

JUDY SAID, "No, Jonah, not this time, it's not for me. Next time."

"Why, Judy? You're perfect for it, and last time what you did was good."

"I wouldn't have without you, Jonah. I feel I have some things to understand, first. Competitions, for one." She laughed. "Listen, I have an idea. Why not ask Maddy?"

"A piano solo?"

"Why not?"

"You are going to sing with the chorus, Judy?"

"You couldn't keep me away."

Who was that girl, pink-cheeked and strong, dark curls against her face, who played the piano with fingers that moved like lightning?

"You watch her," said Jonah proudly. "You just watch her go."

Jonah's old professor from Eastman had to see the television tape only once. "Bring her in, Jonah," he said. "It's late in the season, of course, but we'll arrange an audition. It looks very good."

"That's all right," Aunt Ann told Aunt Bea consolingly. "She'll be home for vacations, and we'll still have Jessie and Stephen."

Blaine Howarth said, "From now on I promise you that I will speak out, loud and clear, and that will not be a failure of love on my part, but a measure of love overflowing, to figure out who we are together, to figure out what it is we love. Let us pray."

Judy hummed a little, quietly, as she left church that day and moved out into the sunshine. Blaine Howarth, she thought, was just what this church needed.

She looked around for her son. Under the ash tree in front of the church was a half-circle of people who were standing very still. Big Russ was among them. As Judy approached, he smiled at her and raised a hand to his lips. Together they moved closer, and then she heard it. High and pure, a beautiful child's voice, somehow familiar. Judy peeped between shoulders. Seeing her and Russ, people smilingly made way.

There was little Russ, his back to them all. "Once in Royal David's city," he sang with a child's pronunciation. He was pushing some blocks along the grass, oblivious to the grownups behind him, the sun caught in his hair. Not a soul moved until the last note finished. He'd sung, Judy realized, right on the tune, right on the note.

"That's just about the nicest thing you ever want to see," someone said to Judy. "That's a gift."

"I had no idea," said Judy. "Why, I had no idea."

Alone, Maddy faced the notebook, the piano. She played what she had written. Then she played it over and over, even the last three chords, especially those, until she wasn't afraid, and it didn't hurt so much. She knew there was more, she'd heard it. The sound of water dancing.

At the end of the summer she took Aunt Bea's notebook to Jonah and pressed it into his hand.

"This is for you," she said shyly.

He opened it. After the winding bass, the driving soprano, the high notes, the chords, he saw, there were new notes. He laid his hands to the piano keys while she stood there. "Maddy's Song," she'd written at the top.

He played the three chords. Then there were three full measures of rest, he gave them their full count. Then the high note came back, the one that had called so in the first part of the composition. The one, he thought suddenly, that could wring your heart. It played once, again. Pianissimo. Staccato. The catching of a breath. Then again, again.

"Why, Maddy," Jonah said, as the notes began to ripple, to sing, "this is a dance."

He stopped, played the composition from start to finish. "This is what you hear?" he asked.

"Yes."

He played the whole composition again, quite carried away. "Maddy," he said, "we have some things to do."

"What? Isn't it good?"

"Oh, yes. It's very good. But you need —" Abruptly he was off the piano bench.

"Get Jessie," he said. "Get Stephen. Get Aunt Bea and Aunt Ann. I have to make a phone call."

They all drove to Portland. "Maddy." He was laughing now, almost crowing. "Wait 'til you hear."

They were all mystified. Down Congress Street he ushered them, and in a side door. "Wait," he crowed. "Wait."

The stops, keyboards, the huge pipes, the small ones: Maddy sat at the bench and stared. "Jonah, are you sure?"

"Oh, yes," he said. "It's all arranged."

Four keyboards, the pedals. She had so much to learn.

The sound eventually came out as it was supposed to, deep and powerful. The perfect instrument for a little pipe that called out, then danced. This was the Kotzschmar organ in City Hall Auditorium, a room with a million voices that rose and sang. There were no walls. There was only singing and light and safety. She played for all she was worth, a slight figure at the console, her face like the sun.

"Only a few minutes," Jonah said on the way home. "All I could talk them into. But someday, Maddy." He nodded, a promise.

At the Cottage he tried to hand back the notebook. "Oh, no," she said. "This is yours, to say thank you for all you've done."

Later, after the girls had gone to their rooms and Jonah sat alone in the west wing, he found the inscription. It was in the back, not the front of the music. A quotation from Landowska:

"What is of capital importance for a future musician is to be acquainted as early as possible with the ideal sonority that someday he will be able to produce himself. The teacher must emphasize this sonorous vision."

Maddy had written: "Thank you, Jonah."

"Paean," Jonah typed. "The word comes to us from the ancient Greek god of healing. It is a word we must use today."

When he was finished he nodded at Audrey, and, satisfied at last, she nodded back.

"Good," in Eleanor Hebert's vocabulary had always meant "perfect and unassailable." "Elaine," she would say before a school program or church play, "you want to do a good job, don't you?" She meant "the best job among all possible jobs."

"Pretty" meant "perfectly presentable, unmarred," and "fine" meant, simply, "the best."

"Do you see what I mean?" Dr. Elias said.

"Oh, yes," said Eleanor. "I see."

Another time Dr. Elias said, "Why don't you give yourself a break, Eleanor?"

"So hard, too hard."

"No. It's simply this, you were doing the best you could in one direction. Now you will turn, maybe, and try another?"

"Yes. But if Elaine never —"

"Well, we don't know about Elaine. We can't predict about her. There is only you. What do you think? What will you do?"

Eleanor went home and sat still. For a whole day she practiced sitting still. It wasn't easy.

"What will I do? What do I want to do?"

I want to have time to live in, she thought. I want to see things, not touch them or change them, only see them. I want to enjoy something.

One by one she gave duties up, delegated responsibilities she'd taken over through the years because somebody had to do them. She gave up the flower committee and the Women's Association presidency and the music committee and all the Fourth of July committees. Amazingly, to her, there were people to do most of these things without her, and what didn't get done maybe didn't need to get done. Why had she been so busy? She hardly knew. Perhaps she'd felt guilty, and it had all gotten out of hand until she was responsible for everything, everybody, every minute. Elaine, her daughter, had been only one of the perfectibles.

Something was happening to Arthur, too. He was still a selectman, but no longer with the old fervor. He was far less apt to bury himself in work or meetings. One day Eleanor came upon their old wedding picture, and Arthur said, "Put it on the mantel, I like it."

"I'm doing my sitting-still exercises," said Eleanor when Arthur found her sitting in the grass one day. She was wearing old clothes, her hair mussed, her feet bare.

"Oh?" he said. "Maybe that's what I need, too." For a long time they sat together in the field, just sitting, watching the curve of the grass.

When they visited Elaine, she was distant with them. Dr. Elias said, "I must warn you, she may not come home to you again for a very long time."

On the way back to Freedom that meant nothing. It meant nothing at all until Eleanor, coming in from the kitchen, found Arthur in the living room weeping, his shoulders moving in great heaves. "There," Eleanor whispered as he clung to her. "My dear."

Sometimes she went to Aunt Bea's for the afternoon, just to sit.

Late in the summer there was a party for Maddy, and Eleanor went. For a long while she visited on the porch, then stood.

"So soon?" said Aunt Bea.

"Yes," Eleanor said. "I have a date for a walk with Arthur. But I'll be back. It's so pleasant here."

She walked slowly across the lawn, carrying her shoes, and went to speak to Maddy, out under a tree with Jessie.

Jonah had been watching her. "Is that all?" he said to Blaine Howarth, who stood nearby. Blaine smiled. " 'And should I not pity Ninevah, that great city, in which there are more than a hundred and twenty thousand persons who do not know their right hand from their left, and also much cattle?' "

"The Book of Jonah," Jonah said. "Oh, yes. I recognize it." He chuckled. "I didn't grow up in a small country church for nothing, Pastor."

Maddy and Jessica were out under the trees.

"Sometime," said Maddy, "we'll have to think about it. We'll have to talk about it when it comes back to us."

"I know," said Jessie. "When it does, Maddy, they'll be here." She gestured up at the porch, where Aunt Bea and Aunt Ann sat with Jonah's wife, Audrey. "Such good people," she said.

There was no answer. Jessie looked back at Maddy, whose face was up, eyes suddenly distant, staring at the clouds.

Jessica recognized that look. With characteristic patience she settled back in the grass, hugged her knees, and waited. At last Maddy moved, looked at her.

Jessie said, "Were you 'off'?"

"Yes," said Maddy. "I was — listening."